A Daring Venture

ELIZABETH
CAMDEN

BETHANYHOUSE
a division of Baker Publishing Group
Minneapolis, Minnesota

Published by Bethany House Publishers
11400 Hampshire Avenue South
Bloomington, Minnesota 55438
www.bethanyhouse.com

Bethany House Publishers is a division of
Baker Publishing Group, Grand Rapids, Michigan

Printed in the United States of America

ISBN 978-0-7642-1882-8 (trade paper)
ISBN 978-0-7642-3196-4 (cloth)

Library of Congress Control Number: 2017963585

Scripture quotations are from the King James Version of the Bible.

This is a work of historical reconstruction; the appearances of certain historical figures are therefore inevitable. All other characters, however, are products of the author's imagination, and any resemblance to actual persons, living or dead, is coincidental.

Cover design by Jennifer Parker
Cover photography by Mike Habermann Photography, LLC

Author is represented by the Steve Laube Agency.

18 19 20 21 22 23 24 7 6 5 4 3 2 1

Prologue

Connecticut, 1890

"You and your brother are to go to the music room, close the door, and don't come out until I say you can."

It was strange for the maid to be ordering Rosalind around, but nothing had been normal since Mama and Papa got sick.

"But I'm thirsty, Flora."

The maid grabbed Rosalind's arm and tugged her up from the floor where she'd been working on a puzzle with her brother, Gus.

"We're all thirsty," Flora said brusquely. "Come along and behave yourselves. After Dr. Morris leaves, I'll try to find something for you to drink."

All it took was the words *Dr. Morris* to make Rosalind's ten-year-old heart beat a little faster. Dr. Morris was so handsome that she secretly liked looking at him whenever he paid a visit.

She obediently went to the music room with Gus and closed the door just like Flora had ordered, but when Dr. Morris arrived, she cracked it open to peek at him. The doctor looked tired as he shuffled toward the sickroom. To her disappointment, he wasn't carrying his medical bag. That bag always fascinated Rosalind. It was plain leather, but when Dr. Morris opened the flap, it was a portal into a huge and magnificent world brimming with possibility. The mysterious tonics and instruments fired her imagination with dreams of someday understanding the world of science.

Maybe Dr. Morris had run out of medicine, because it seemed the whole town was sick. At first it was just two families, and Dr. Morris made them go live in the pest house because cholera was a "stinking awful mess," and he didn't want it to spread. Then other people started getting sick, and now the pest house was full and anyone who got sick had to stay at home and promise not to go out.

Rosalind heard him leaving the sickroom after only a few minutes, and she went to sneak another peek through the cracked door. What she saw was so strange that it didn't make any sense. Dr. Morris and Flora were lugging Papa down the hallway, his body stretched between them. He wore only a nightshirt, and Flora carried him by his bare ankles.

"What's wrong with Papa?" Rosalind asked, opening the door a little wider.

Flora startled and dropped Papa's feet, but Dr. Morris held on. Papa's head lolled to the side, revealing a face all purple and shriveled in like a raisin. His eyes were open and his lips were black. Rosalind gasped and looked at Dr. Morris.

"Your Papa didn't make it," he said, pity radiating from his kind eyes. "We need to take him to the carriage house so your Mama can get better. It's going to be a while before a proper burial can be arranged. I'm sorry, Rosalind."

Did this mean Papa was dead? It didn't seem possible, but she'd never seen anything as awful as that darkened face.

Gus bumped into her from behind, trying to nudge through so he could see. She shoved him backward and slammed the door.

"But I want to see," Gus said, his eight-year-old voice full of curiosity.

"No." Rosalind wished she hadn't seen. Papa's terrible face was burned in her brain, and she had to protect Gus from seeing it. She'd do anything if she could wash it out of her mind.

For the next two days, they stayed mainly in the music room. After Rosalind broke the rules and accidentally saw Papa, she had been following Flora's orders to the letter, which meant staying away from the sickroom and keeping Gus out of trouble. But they were so thirsty.

There was nothing left in the house to drink. Dr. Morris said that cholera spread through the water, and Flora had them put bowls outside to collect rain, but they'd already drunk what little they had. They'd opened the vegetables that had been put up for the winter and drunk the water from the jars of peas and asparagus. They even drank the vinegar from the pickled onions and cucumbers. Now there was nothing left in the entire house to drink.

The last time Flora had checked on them, it looked like she might be getting sick too, and it had been forever since they'd heard any sounds from the sickroom. If Flora was sick, someone else needed to go take care of her and Mama.

"Rosalind . . . I'm thirsty," Gus said, curled on the sofa, his voice scratchy.

She was too, but complaining wasn't going to make things better. And someone had to check on Mama.

Rosalind opened the door of the music room and crept down the hallway toward the sickroom. She'd been warned repeatedly to stay away, but she didn't know what else to do. She and Gus would die of thirst if they kept waiting for Flora, and no one lived nearby to ask for help.

The paint on the sickroom door was cold against the side of her face as she pressed her ear against it to listen, but she heard nothing. Maybe they were sleeping? She didn't want to go inside. Everything warned her against it, because even from here, the smell was bad.

She twisted the knob, recoiling at the stench. "Mama?"

Flora and Mama both lay on the bed. Their skin looked just like Papa's had, dark and shriveled. Their lips were black. Rosalind's face crumpled up. She was pretty sure they were dead, but the only way to tell for certain was to touch them. She held her breath, stepped forward, and did what she had to do.

They were dead.

What was she supposed to do now? It seemed everyone in the village was sick, and there had been no sign of Dr. Morris in days. Maybe he was sick too.

She didn't want to see Gus yet, because she would have to tell him that Mama and Flora were both dead, and that she was scared and didn't know what to do. She ran to the parlor, curled up on the floor, and cried.

Her eyes didn't shed any tears. Was that normal? Maybe she was so thirsty there wasn't anything left in her body for tears.

They would have to go to Grandpa Werner's house. He lived two miles away, but maybe people there weren't sick and he would have something to drink.

Gus wasn't in the music room when she returned. He wasn't in the kitchen or dining room either.

"Gus?" Her voice echoed in the house, and there was no answer. A horrible thought struck her, and she ran for the back door. He was in the yard, kneeling in front of the pump and gulping from the jets of water.

She knocked him away from the pump. "You can't drink that!"

Gus started to cry, but he didn't have any tears left either. Every cell in her body longed to fall to her knees and catch the trickle of water still dribbling from the pump, but she didn't want to turn sick and shriveled like the others.

"We have to walk to Grandpa's house," she said. "Maybe there will be something to drink there."

"I'm too tired." His white-blond hair, so like her own, tumbled into his face, but she could still see the exhaustion in his eyes.

"It doesn't matter. Get up. We have to go." If Gus went back inside, he might see Mama and Flora, and that would be awful. They had to leave now.

Rosalind took his hand and started walking down the path toward the lane. The glaring sunlight shone in stark contrast to the fear inside her. It was two miles to Grandpa's house with nothing but pine trees on one side and cranberry bogs on the other. She always liked visiting Grandpa Werner, even though he could barely speak English and Rosalind's German wasn't so good.

After a half hour of walking, Gus wanted to sit down. "I don't feel good," he said.

"I don't either, but we can't sit down until we get to Grandpa's house."

"I think I have to use the privy."

They were still on the woodsy part of the road, and there wasn't a house in sight. "Wait until we get to Grandpa's."

"I have to use the privy *right now*."

She sighed. "Then go behind those trees."

Gus took a few steps but didn't make it. He sank to his knees, pulled his pants down, and fell as the diarrhea hit. Oh no—oh no, that was the first sign. But she mustn't panic. This was going to be okay. She wouldn't let herself think anything else.

"I'm sorry," Gus said, starting to blubber, because he probably knew what this meant too. "I shouldn't have drunk that water," he sobbed. "I'm so sorry, Rosalind."

There was nothing they could do about it now. Gus had a few more hours before things got really bad. That meant they had to keep moving, and they had to move fast.

"Stand up," she ordered, wishing she didn't have to sound so mean, but they didn't have much time. "Stand up and start walking."

"I don't think I can."

"Stand up and get moving. We're not giving up." She hauled him upright, even though it made her head ache to tug that hard. "Don't you dare sit back down!"

"But, Rosalind, I don't think I can keep—"

"Then don't think, just keep walking."

Because they didn't have any other choice.

Chapter ONE

Jersey City, New Jersey
June 1908

Dr. Rosalind Werner adjusted a dial on the microscope, and the tiny organisms beneath the glass slide zoomed into sharp clarity. *Salmonella enterica*, the bacteria that caused typhoid, was surprisingly pretty, its midnight-blue shade clustered into graceful, blooming colonies. Her mission in life was to figure out a way to kill it.

The door to the laboratory opened, but she didn't look up until she had finished counting the number of live cells on the slide. Most were already dead, which was good. It meant their solution was working.

"I have news," Dr. Leal said as the door clicked shut.

She looked up from the slide, alarmed at the despair in his voice. For a man as endlessly optimistic as Dr. John Leal to sound dejected was alarming, especially since there was only one thing they both feared. She stood, gazing at him across the laboratory tables and holding her breath.

"The judge has issued his ruling. We lost."

She didn't move a muscle. The monumental, two-year court case they'd been waging was a fight against backward and antiquated beliefs. Powerful forces and millions of dollars had been invested on both sides. She and Dr. Leal had been hired as consultants by the defense counsel, but they were more than hired experts. They were crusaders fighting for a cause. They knew how to eradicate disease from the public water supply so that everyone could have clean, pure water. They had dedicated their lives to the quest.

There was only one thing to do.

"I'm not giving up," she said quietly.

The corner of Dr. Leal's heavy mustache twitched as he smiled.

"Me neither," he said, strolling deeper into the lab where they'd been feverishly working to prove they had the ability to purify drinking water quickly and effectively.

Dr. Leal had begun his career as a medical doctor after earning his degree here in America, while her degree in biochemistry came from Germany. They were unlikely players in the lawsuit between Jersey City and a private company that had built a massive new water supply system. A fortune had been invested in twenty-five miles of pipeline to bring water from rural New Jersey into the city, but now the government refused to pay for it. They claimed the water wasn't pure and had sued the private company for breach of contract. The struggling company had hired Rosalind and Dr. Leal to present an inexpensive and effective technique to purify drinking water.

"What are we up against?" she asked.

Dr. Leal pulled up a lab stool and set a thick stack of papers on the counter. "The judge has ordered the water company to build an additional filtration plant, plus upgrades to the sewer systems throughout the rural and metropolitan region."

His voice was flat. The order would bankrupt the company,

which had already sunk millions of dollars into this project. Of more concern was the fact that the filtration plant wouldn't work. Rosalind knew exactly what they needed to do to ensure a clean drinking supply, but it was a new and frightening idea few people welcomed.

"Can we appeal?"

"Absolutely. The company is already gathering funds, but the judge gave us a single lifeline. He doesn't know enough about our research to dismiss us out of hand. He's given us a ninety-day deferment to make our case."

She plopped back down into her laboratory stool. "That's what we've been trying to do for the past two years!" They'd run dozens of clinical tests and delivered stacks of research papers proving that chlorine killed waterborne diseases.

But nobody wanted chlorine in their drinking water. It was an alien concept people instinctively rejected. Plenty of scientists believed it would work, but no city anywhere in the world had authorized it. She wanted Jersey City to be the first.

"I propose using a new tactic," Dr. Leal said. "Instead of focusing our efforts on the judge, perhaps we can start working on the opposition's consultants. If we can get a few of them on our side, it might deal a body blow to the city's case."

"Which consultants did you have in mind?"

"Nicholas Drake."

She repressed the urge to roll her eyes. Nick Drake was the epitome of the type of man they'd been battling for years. He was opinionated, brash, and unwilling to compromise. They had never met, but she'd been in the courtroom when he testified on the city's behalf. He'd been wearing a flawlessly tailored coat, vest, and starched collar, but he seemed too restless to be comfortable in a formal suit. Like a wild stallion dressed up in Sunday clothes.

"Why him? He doesn't seem like a natural ally."

"That's why I want him. Plus, rumor has it he's about to be appointed as the next commissioner of the State Water Board of New York."

She was aghast. "They would never do that! He's got no qualifications."

"He's got money, power, and influence. And he's been acting commissioner ever since the last one was fired six months ago. From what I hear, the governor wants to make it official." Dr. Leal began pacing, weaving in and out of the series of black slate laboratory tables. "All of our work will come to nothing if we can't convince the judge, but I don't think the proof is going to come from within this laboratory. We need to get out in the field and wage this battle person by person."

And apparently he thought Nicholas Drake was a logical place to start.

The mansion ballroom was crowded. It seemed every lawyer, engineer, and financier in Jersey City was here celebrating the court ruling that had been announced that morning. Knowing the judge's decision was imminent, Nick Drake had left his home in Manhattan to join the Jersey City officials and lawyers at the town hall for the announcement. After all, he was the plaintiff's lead witness and had fought hard on behalf of the city. He had staked his professional reputation on this case and hadn't accepted a single dollar in payment. He was no hired gun. Nick had chosen this fight for the principle, not for money.

No one rejoiced louder than he when the ruling was handed down. While the stuffy lawyers merely smiled in relief, Nick unleashed a war whoop of victory, pumping the air with both fists and giving bear hugs all around. The cost-cutters on the other side had lost, and the ordinary people of New Jersey were the winners.

While he would have rather returned to Manhattan to scoop his daughter into a hug and sleep in his own bed, it was important to attend the celebratory dinner. Plus, he had a favor to collect on his way out the door.

A waiter approached him with a tray of caviar on tiny crackers.

Nick eyed the tray skeptically. "Do people really enjoy this stuff?" he asked. "Raw fish eggs?"

"Some people do," the waiter said.

That meant Nick would choke it down, because that was what people at fancy black-tie gatherings were expected to do. In the past five years, he had learned to pick his battles carefully. He might be the most unwelcome person at this evening's celebration, but he had earned his place here. He wore a custom-made tuxedo, had sat for a shoeshine in the lobby of his hotel, and even submitted to a manicure. A manicure! He'd been appalled when he first learned that rich men actually paid to have someone trim and buff their nails, but he started doing it as soon as he left his old job. It had taken months for the final traces of plumber's grease to disappear from beneath his nails, then another year for the last of the calluses to be buffed away. Now he looked as polished and groomed as any of the other blue bloods here this evening.

That didn't mean he would ever be welcome in their ranks. But he didn't care about being welcomed, he cared about getting appointed to the State Water Board of New York. Only then could he ensure that poor people and immigrants got the same quality of water that rich people took for granted.

He made his way to Mayor Jenner's side.

"Mr. Drake!" the mayor said in a hearty tone, pumping Nick's hand with vigor. Obviously the hefty contribution Nick gave to the mayor's reelection campaign had not gone to waste. "Welcome to my home. You remember my wife, Adelaide?"

Mrs. Jenner wore a pearl choker that probably cost more than a typical plumber earned in a year, but she had a kind smile as she greeted Nick. "Congratulations on today's victory! My husband says your testimony was key in persuading the judge to see reason."

That was because Nick spoke in plain English, not like the witnesses on the other side, whose scientific blather and chemistry tomes could bore the paint off the walls.

"How's that charming daughter of yours?" the mayor asked in a booming voice. "She must be, what, eight? Ten?"

"She turned three years old last month."

"Oh yes, I remember now. Charming girl. Sally?"

"Sadie."

"That's right! Sadie! And her mother is doing well, I hope?"

This probably wasn't the time to explain that Nick's wife had died two days after giving birth to Sadie. Most politicians were masters at remembering the names and family details of their supporters, but it appeared Mayor Jenner had imbibed too much celebratory champagne, and Nick saw no point in embarrassing him. He swiftly changed the topic.

"I was hoping to discuss the meeting you've got scheduled next week, dealing with the new subway to Manhattan. I understand the governor of New York will be in attendance."

"Will he? I suppose so."

"I'd like to be invited to the meeting."

Mayor Jenner set down his glass. "I wasn't aware you had any interest in subways."

"I don't, but I'd like to meet the governor. I can make myself available if you can arrange the introductions."

It was the governor who would appoint the new commissioner to the State Water Board. As the acting commissioner, Nick was the logical choice, but he didn't have the personal connections of the other men vying for the job. If he could meet the governor, he'd be able to prove himself. He didn't have a fancy college degree like his competitors, but he had more real-world experience and a knack for relating to people. All he needed was to get his foot in the door with the governor, and he'd have a clear shot at the appointment.

Mayor Jenner laughed uncomfortably. "I can't imagine you'd be interested in a meeting like that. Just a lot of arguing about subway tunnels and tax money."

"I'm interested. Can you make it happen?"

A pause stretched between them, and Mrs. Jenner rushed to her husband's rescue. "Oh look, the harbor master of Port Elizabeth just arrived. Perhaps I should introduce you?"

"No offense, ma'am, but perhaps your husband can introduce me to the governor of New York. I think I've earned that."

The mayor shifted uneasily. "That's not how business is done, Mr. Drake. I'm sure everyone in this room understands why you've been invited to this event, but it wouldn't make sense for you to be at a high-stakes political meeting."

"How about because I just saved your city a million-dollar payoff to a water company that didn't deliver on their contract? I think you can spare me five minutes with the governor."

The city's lead attorney broke the tension. Herman Dressler was a thick-set man who had suggested the unconventional tactic of recruiting Nick as a plaintiff expert who could explain complicated water filtration systems to the judge.

Herman extended his hand. "You're a good man to have in a fight, Mr. Drake!"

"My pleasure, sir." And it had been. It was a privilege to be part of a team committed to ensuring the growing cities of the eastern seaboard continued to have plentiful supplies of clean water.

"With luck, we will no longer need your services," Herman said. "But should the deferment prove difficult, will you be available through October?"

"What deferment?" he asked.

Nick's temper heated as he learned that instead of a complete victory for the city, the judge had hedged his bets by allowing the defendants an additional ninety days to let their scientists make the case for a chemical alternative. Two of the defense experts had managed to persuade the judge to give their bizarre and unproven technique another bite at the apple. Their plan amounted to a newfangled method using chlorine to kill germs in the water. They claimed it wouldn't harm humans, but it had never been tested or proven anywhere in the world. Nick wouldn't stand aside and let them test it on his family or the people of Jersey City either.

"I'll be available," he promised. The opposition was grasping at straws, turning to a pair of meddlesome scientists to avoid building another pricey filtration plant. He looked pointedly at the mayor. "And I'll be available for next week's meeting with the governor. I trust you will make it happen."

It was a statement, not a question, and Nick succeeded in collecting his favor before leaving the gala celebration.

Chapter TWO

Rosalind awakened early for her meeting with Nicholas Drake, but everything was going wrong, and it was still an hour before sunrise.

"Have you seen the two beakers of water I had on the kitchen counter?" she asked her brother, Gus. "They were here last night, but now I can't find them."

Gus ducked beneath a line of baby diapers strung across the tiny kitchen, eyeing the counter. "Ingrid washed baby bottles last night. She probably washed the beakers as well."

That meant Ingrid had dumped out the water. Brilliant. Rosalind had intended to bring the chlorinated water samples to prove to Mr. Drake that it was impossible to smell or taste the difference. Ingrid probably hadn't done it on purpose, but Rosalind couldn't be sure. Ingrid's simmering hostility had been impossible to overlook ever since Gus returned from overseas with his German bride. Rosalind's house was too small for all of them, and Ingrid still resented her for what had happened in Heidelberg. On top of all this, the baby was cutting a tooth, and none of them had gotten much sleep last night.

In one hour, Rosalind and Dr. Leal were supposed to meet Mr.

Drake to begin the herculean task of persuading the opposition's lead expert witness that water filtration was inefficient, overly expensive, and not nearly as effective as chemical treatment. Dr. Leal thought a breakfast meeting would help set the right tone. People tended to be on their guard in a courtroom or in an office. It was much easier to establish a rapport over a meal, and a breakfast meeting at a restaurant had been arranged by Mr. Drake's secretary.

Rosalind navigated around the laundry line to stand before the tiny mirror on the back of her kitchen door, trying to tack the ivory button that secured her high stand collar to her blouse. Her fingers slipped, and the button pinged on the floor.

"Don't be so nervous," Gus said.

"What makes you think I'm nervous?"

"You can't fasten your collar, you won't sit down for a cup of tea, and you've checked your portfolio three times to be sure your papers are in order. And this is after you paid a messenger to carry copies of the same research reports to Mr. Drake's office yesterday. Over-preparation is a sure sign you're terrified."

She forced her fingers to be steady and successfully inserted the pin into her collar. "I should think Mr. Drake would want to read our papers in advance of the meeting. I was being considerate in providing the copies."

"Rosalind, you know I love you, but your research papers are so dull, they could actually be used as a weapon against unsuspecting readers, causing them to die of boredom."

She turned around to peer at him. "Our research caused quite a sensation when it was published. The American Chemical Society was so excited that they—"

"And is Nicholas Drake a chemist?"

No. He was a plumber who had somehow vaulted into a position of great power over the water systems of the entire state of New York. It was maddening that a man with no scientific qualifications had so much influence, but Dr. Leal was right. They needed to do a better job persuading ordinary people of the benefits of treated water.

She would let Dr. Leal take the lead in their meeting this morning, for one thing was certain: she had absolutely nothing in common with Nicholas Drake.

By the time Rosalind arrived at the crowded Manhattan restaurant to meet Mr. Drake, her nerves were wound as tight as a piano wire. Dr. Leal had abandoned her! A telegram arrived just as she was leaving to say that his son was ill and he would be unable to attend the breakfast meeting. *I have full confidence in you*, he had concluded the message.

Rosalind wished she had that level of confidence. What Gus had said was right. She wasn't good at communicating scientific information in plain English. It was going to be impossible to find common ground with a man so starkly different.

Sal's Diner was on a street corner, nestled between a laundry and a fishmonger. Mr. Drake had picked the location, for it certainly wasn't the sort of place she would normally eat.

"Oh my goodness," she murmured as she entered the diner, barely able to squeeze through the door for all the people lined up at the counter. Every table was occupied, and the clatter of utensils, the sizzle of meat, and boisterous voices filled the air. Some of the customers wore coveralls, others wore suits with ties. The only thing they had in common was that they were all men.

She scanned the crowd, looking for Mr. Drake's tall frame. A pair of policemen jostled her as they angled out the door. It certainly appeared to be a popular restaurant, but it would be hard to converse over the din of a hundred people being served in a place no larger than a matchbox.

"Let me find you a table, ma'am."

She looked up at the grinning man who had appeared alongside her. Thank heavens, Mr. Drake had rescued her! He looked so different than he had in the courtroom, where he'd worn a formal suit and a fighting expression. Here he had an open collar and dark eyes flashing with humor. Even though he was physically imposing, with a strong build that towered over her, he seemed so friendly that she was immediately at ease.

"Do you already have a table?" she asked.

"I do, but let's find a place for you to sit at the counter, or those barbarians lined up for the next batch of Sal's doughnuts will never let you through. Stand aside, yokels! Lady coming through." Mr. Drake shouldered his way through the crowd, tugging her along behind him.

"I'm not eating with you?"

He grinned down at her. "Nothing would please me more, but I'm here for a business meeting." He scanned the counter, but every seat was already filled. "Tell you what, since it looks like none of these guys are close to being finished, you can sit with me, provided you've got the constitution to last through a pointless lecture from a pair of do-gooders. It won't take long."

So he hadn't recognized her. She let him guide her to a booth tucked along the back wall and slid onto the bench opposite him.

"I've never seen you here before," he said. "First time at Sal's?"

"Yes. Is there a towel, perhaps? The table is a little sticky."

Before she finished the sentence, he stood, reached over the patrons at the counter, and grabbed a damp towel, then wiped up the splotches left by an earlier diner. He tossed the towel back to the waitress and handed Rosalind a two-sided card with the menu printed on it. The cardboard was a little shabby, with coffee stains and a few unsanitary grease marks. She didn't touch it.

"I'll just have whatever you're having," she said.

Mr. Drake stood and cupped his hands around his mouth. "Hey, Martha," he shouted. "Make that an order for two!"

Rosalind put her portfolio on the table and set out copies of her research articles, since it appeared he hadn't brought the ones she'd sent him. She opened her wire-framed spectacles and put them on, then scanned her paperwork quickly, making sure she had everything in order. When she looked back up, Mr. Drake was staring at her with a dazed expression.

"What?" she asked.

He swallowed. "No disrespect, ma'am, but I think those spectacles make you look like an A-class fetcher."

"A what?" Having spent most of her adult life in Germany, there was a lot of American slang she didn't quite grasp.

"A fetcher. As in 'really fetching.' Top shelf. Classy."

Heat gathered in her cheeks. The last thing she'd expected was to be paid such compliments. Mr. Drake would never rival the great poets for an elegant turn of phrase, but there was a sincere admiration in his eyes that made his compliments immensely flattering.

She adjusted her glasses. "Thank you. I think. I just need to be sure I've got all the paperwork in order, and then I can . . ." She was babbling. A strange attraction to him was growing by the instant, and she needed to rein it in. She took the glasses from her nose and set them aside. "Did you have a chance to read the articles we sent you?"

He lifted a brow. "What articles?"

"The articles on calcium hypochlorite distribution as an alternative to water filtration." She waited for recognition to dawn, but he just stared at her as though she were speaking Greek. Now that she could see him up close, she noticed he had the strong, even features of Michelangelo's *David*, complete with the curling dark hair, chiseled features, and strong line of his neck.

"Who are you?" he finally asked.

"I'm Dr. R. L. Werner, but I go by Rosalind in real life. Or Dr. Werner, if we are being formal. I'm afraid Dr. Leal won't be able to join us this morning."

He looked befuddled. "That seems like false advertising. Making everyone assume you're a man by writing those articles under your initials."

It was true that many people instinctively distrusted the work of female scientists, but she had plenty of other reasons to hide behind her initials. The last thing she wanted was to attract attention.

"Did you have a chance to review the articles?"

He scrutinized her over the rim of a coffee mug as he took a long drink. That dark gaze had the power to render her a speechless idiot, and it was disconcerting.

"Are you really a doctor?" he asked.

"My specialty is biochemistry. I study the effects of chemical compounds on microorganisms."

"So you don't treat patients?"

"No. I'm afraid of blood."

His laughter was warm and appreciative. "Well, Dr. R. L. Werner, that makes two of us. When I hear 'doctor,' I automatically assume someone who carries a little black bag and wears a stethoscope. I didn't know there was any other kind."

The tension between them eased. "I suppose that's understandable. I don't treat patients, but I hope that my research will help prevent disease before it starts."

He was gaping at her again with that dazed look in his eyes. He was so open and blatant in his admiration that it ought to be uncomfortable, but it seemed the most natural thing in the world to simply smile back. She never wanted it to end.

The waitress arrived and set two large platters of steaming food on the table before them. The spell was broken.

Oh dear. She wasn't going to be able to eat this. Generous slabs of bacon rested beside three eggs served sunny-side up, the uncooked yolks glistening brightly. Mr. Drake pierced all three of his yolks with a fork, stirring and dribbling the liquid across his bacon and toast.

He looked up and caught her appalled gaze. Immediately, he dropped his fork, folded his hands, and bowed his head.

"Dear Lord, thank you for this meal and the fine company. With your help, I'll do my best to make this rowdy and irreverent city a better place. In your name we pray. Amen."

"Amen," she echoed, even though her horror hadn't been because he was skipping a blessing, but entirely due to the unwholesome and downright dangerous meal before them.

He ripped his toast in half and sopped up some of the uncooked yolk, took a bite, and grinned at her across the table. "Nothing beats Sal's cooking," he said with good-natured appreciation.

She looked down at her plate. The toast might be okay to eat. "Were you aware that eating the uncooked yolk of an egg is dangerous and liable to give you a salmonella infection?"

"You don't like eggs sunny-side up?"

Hadn't she just implied they could cause crippling gastric illness? "No," she said gently. "They are a health hazard. I could not in good conscience let you or anyone else consume such a potentially dangerous meal."

Mr. Drake grabbed her plate and stood. "Hey, Martha! Can you ask Sal to put these eggs back on the griddle and scramble them up? My fault. I ordered wrong."

Rosalind winced as the harried waitress swung by their table, reached for the plate, and disappeared behind the counter. Rosalind hadn't meant to cause such a scene, and the toast would have been fine, but the waitress and her plate disappeared before she could protest.

At least Mr. Drake didn't seem offended. If anything, he seemed amused as he leaned forward to speak in a conspiratorial tone. "You might want to cover your eyes, ma'am. I'm about to take another bite of my dangerous breakfast, and I wouldn't want to frighten you."

Laughter bubbled up inside her and leaked out in an ungainly squeak, causing a healthy grin to break across Mr. Drake's face. She really shouldn't laugh, because health was a serious business, but his humor was contagious, and it felt good.

"I shall brace myself," she said. "I'll be the Duke of Wellington at Waterloo, facing down immeasurable odds."

"Did he win?"

"He did."

Mr. Drake grinned. "Then I'm good! Since my chosen meal is little better than a plate of infectious disease, what does a typical breakfast at Dr. R. L. Werner's home look like?" He scooped yolk onto his bacon and ate with relish.

"I live with my brother and his wife. We usually have a bowl of fruit and some muesli."

"What's muesli?"

"It's a combination of rolled oats, nuts, and seeds. I first ate it when I went to live with my German relatives in Bavaria. It's a very healthy food. It's hard to find in America, so I asked my brother to learn how to make it. It's almost as good as what my relatives in Germany make."

"So you've got your brother making muesli, Sal fixing your eggs, and the court of New Jersey in a tizzy over this blasted lawsuit. Anyone ever call you bossy?"

She cleared her throat. "I just have passionate beliefs about—"

He cut her off. "Don't get me wrong. I like bossy women. Especially if you put those spectacles back on. Something about a beautiful woman wearing spectacles makes her look really smart."

"Not to put too fine a point on it, Mr. Drake, but I *am* really smart."

He grinned, and a hint of challenge lit his face. "Smart enough to have been admitted to the American Water Association?"

"Naturally. It's the most important professional organization for the kind of work I do. Why?"

He took a long sip of coffee before setting the cup down, casually turning it in a circle with a single finger. "They've denied my membership."

"Oh." This was a little awkward. Membership in a community of scholars wasn't something that could be purchased; it could only be earned by formal qualifications. "Why is it so important for you to belong? You seem to have acquired a good deal of influence without it."

"There's a vacancy for a commissioner on the State Water Board. I want it. The governor makes the appointment, but I need to prove my qualifications to get it. The board is ruled by three commissioners. One man in charge of finance, one in charge of engineering, and one for labor. That's the opening I want. The last guy who had the job didn't even last six months because of the pressure. I'm good at leading men, but I need the backing of scientists for a position like this. Getting accepted to the American Water Association would be a big step."

"I'm not sure how I can help you." Which was true. She was a member of the organization but had no role in setting the rules for membership. She was fortunate that they accepted women at all.

"Next time you go to one of their fancy meetings, chat up the president of the organization. Tell him I know what I'm talking about. That I'd be a good member. I'd even toss in a few thousand dollars if they need to fund something."

She didn't know how to phrase this delicately, but it seemed Mr. Drake was a man who valued plain speaking. "I have a confession to make," she said, reaching for her mug to hide her discomfort.

"Something scandalous, I hope."

She nearly choked on her coffee. "Actually, it's about you. I have no idea who you are. All I know is that you used to be a plumber but managed to acquire extraordinary influence over the water systems throughout the entire state."

"Except with the American Water Association," he pointed out.

"Yes, except that . . . which I assure you is a rather dull group of stuffy academics. So who *are* you? And how did you come to be here?"

"I'm a plumber," he said. "My father was a plumber, and my grandfather too. Except my grandfather was also an inventor."

The harried waitress swung by their table again and returned Rosalind's plate. The steaming eggs had been scrambled and cooked so long that they were like little pieces of rubber, but she could hardly complain.

"Yes, go on," she said after the waitress left.

"You know all those tall buildings filling the skyline of Manhattan?" Mr. Drake said. "None of them could get running water pumped up past the fourth floor until my grandfather invented a valve that regulated water pressure. It earned a fortune. He never saw any of the money because his brother swindled him out of it, and the valve was the center of a court case for forty years. Five years ago it was settled, and the money came to me."

He said it so simply, but Rosalind was stunned. "That sort of invention must be worth a lot. Maybe even a couple of million."

He scoffed. "Try sixty million. It was split between me and some of the other heirs, but I got the mother lode. Why do you think Martha was so eager to scramble up your eggs? It's not because of my charm, Dr. Werner." Humor glinted in his eyes.

Oh my, he was attractive. And it wasn't because of his money or his looks, it was the bottomless well of humor and self-deprecating charm that made him so appealing. She started smiling like a besotted idiot again, and he continued talking.

"I took a class in chemistry at Columbia so I could make sense of the reports and charts people like you write up, but for the most part, my insight comes from real-world experience of how the water supply system works."

"Just one class?" she asked. Maybe that was why he was so intransigent when it came to new developments in water treatment. "It's hard to appreciate chemistry after a single class. With a little more work, you'll delve into the far more interesting aspects of chemical reactions and structure-activity relationships."

He shuddered. "All I need is to read the reports and make sense of them, not conduct the experiments. I guess that's your job. Better you than me!"

"Oh, but I love it. I've always considered it a privilege to do this sort of work."

He seemed to like her comment, because he was gaping at her with that beaming look of approval again. What an excellent idea this had been. Dr. Leal was right. By meeting Mr. Drake outside of his office or a courtroom, they were able to rub along quite well.

She looked at him with new respect. "Mr. Drake, it occurs to me that we are both outsiders. Me because I am a woman in a man's field, while you vaulted from the working classes into the highest echelons of society. We both have a constant weakness to overcome."

His smile was filled with roguish delight. "Ah, but I don't see it as a weakness. Everyone wants clean water, right? But getting it to them is a tricky business that mixes politics, money, and power. Everyone knows I'm filthy rich, so no one accuses me of doing this for the money. That gets me a lot of influence, and people listen to what I have to say. I just want to do what's right."

His voice nearly vibrated with passion. She always admired people passionate about a cause, and Nicholas Drake certainly fit the bill. Too bad he was wrong about the best way to keep the water clean. It was going to be a challenge to get him to reconsider the filtration plant, but it had to be done.

She pushed her plate to the side and slid her stack of research papers to the center of the table. "Did you have a chance to look through any of the work we sent you?"

For the first time, Mr. Drake looked unsettled. "I think both sides are pretty well entrenched in our positions. I don't expect that to change."

"Are you aware that the stockyards in Chicago have adopted chlorination for the animals' drinking water? They turned to chlorine after the filtration method failed. Chemical purification has been working beautifully."

"For cattle. I don't care if you test chlorine on animals, but we're talking about humans here." Laughter lit his eyes again. "At least we're human on *this* side of the river. I can't vouch for you folks on the Jersey side."

"I live directly across the river, and yes, we count as humans."

She was grinning again. He probably thought she had a loose screw in her head, the way she couldn't stop smiling, but at least he was smiling back. She'd been on this earth for twenty-eight years and never experienced this soaring feeling of bliss mingled with admiration for the man gawking at her across the breakfast table. They both gaped and smiled at each other like fools, and it seemed like the most natural thing in the world. It ought to be embarrassing, but it wasn't. It was wonderful.

But Dr. Leal had sent her here on a mission, and it was too important to set aside merely because a handsome man flattered her.

"I'll leave these research papers with you," she said. "You'll see that our experiments confirm what other scientists all over Europe and America have reported on the efficacy of chlorine."

"Really, you don't need to bother—"

"Because I am convinced the future lies with chlorine. It can sanitize immense amounts of water quickly, safely, and cheaply."

"It's not a tested method," he said flatly. "The judge ordered an additional filtration plant, and that's that."

This was just the sort of hardheaded ignorance he'd showed in court when he testified. He probably hadn't even read her research papers. He probably knew nothing about cholera or how fast it could kill a healthy person. All it took was a sip of tainted water, and an entire family could be destroyed.

She held on to her temper and tried to speak calmly. "You cannot filter cholera out of the water supply. Chemical treatment has the ability to kill cholera, typhoid, and every other waterborne bacteria we tested it on."

"It's not a proven method. Filtration has been working for the past eighty years."

"Except when rainstorms overwhelm the system with runoff from farms filled with animal waste. A few drops of chlorine can solve that. Most people are ignorant of its benefits, but it is an—"

He cut her off. "First of all, I'm not an ignorant person."

"I never said you were, but we both know what happens when rain overloads the filtration plants. Filtration is slow and expensive, especially when all it takes is a miniscule amount of chlorine to solve the problem."

He must have sensed the tension in her voice, for it seemed his patience was growing thin too. "I looked up *chlorine* in the dictionary. It's poison," he said flatly. "I won't let it be added to the water supply."

"That's what many uninformed people think when they first hear about chlorine."

Mr. Drake's face iced over. He leaned forward until his nose was only inches from her, his eyes snapping mad. "Outside that window are four million people who depend on the water that gets sent through the pipelines and into their homes. I want our cities to grow and prosper, while your side bellyaches because filtration is too expensive. Who will people blame if the taps run dry? It won't be you or Dr. Leal. I'm fighting for the future of American cities."

"So am I!"

His hands clenched, and his lip curled. "You want to put a toxic chemical in the water supply. An untested, unproven, dangerous chemical. You aren't going to test it on my daughter," he said fiercely. "You say your plan worked on cattle. Cattle! I don't care about cattle, I care about my daughter and Martha the waitress and every other hardworking person crowded into this city. And if building an expensive filtration plant is what it takes to protect them, I'm going to make it happen."

He stood, tossed his napkin on the table, and stormed away without a backward glance. The meeting was over.

Chapter THREE

After her complete failure with Nicholas Drake, Rosalind turned to the one hobby that always soothed her. Assembling the tiny gears, screws, and springs of a music box was a challenge that usually demanded her complete attention, and a task she had been performing since that first summer she and Gus arrived at her uncle's house in the remote Bavarian farmlands. Uncle Wilhelm had taught her the skill, and she seized upon it as a salvation after first losing her parents, then her grandfather less than a year later. After leaving America and her entire world behind, Uncle Wilhelm's farm had been a blessing.

Gus handed her the pieces as she steadily assembled the cogwheel. Ever since returning from that morning's disastrous breakfast meeting, Gus had been trying to calm her down and put things into perspective. She let him. All their lives, they had leaned on each other. Sometimes she was the leader, and other times she faltered and needed Gus to prop her up. Neither one of them were quitters.

There was no one she'd rather have at her side. Not only did she have complete trust in her brother, but Gus was a lawyer and could help strategize, now that she had failed with Nick Drake.

"Would it be illegal for me to approach the judge directly?" Rosalind asked. "After all, Judge McLaughlin lives just down the street, and I've met his wife."

"It's not illegal, but he would disclose the meeting to the plaintiffs," Gus replied. "At least, I think so. I'll need to look it up." He pushed away from the kitchen table to write a note to himself.

Gus's legal training all came from Germany. Since arriving in New Jersey earlier in the year, he had been studying to pass the necessary tests to begin practicing law in America. Until he passed those hurdles, he, Ingrid, and baby Jonah would share Rosalind's too-small house, but she couldn't complain. After all, it was her fault Gus and Ingrid had been forced out of Germany.

"Are you sure you aren't making too big a deal out of this?" Gus said as he rejoined her at the table and handed her a tiny screwdriver to align the music cylinder into its casing. "You're so tenderhearted that your feelings get hurt if you startle a bird into flying away."

Maybe, but Gus hadn't seen the anger smoldering in Mr. Drake's eyes. It was especially hurtful since they had been getting along so well and she hadn't expected him to turn on her like that. She still wasn't quite sure what set him off.

"In any event, don't take this so personally," Gus continued. "If you lose this lawsuit, there will be other cities in need of better water purification."

"But Jersey City could be the first. If we can make our case here, other cities will be clamoring to do the same. It just takes a single city to be brave enough to be first."

"Rosalind, how often have you told me to be patient over the years? You and Dr. Leal are doing good work. You had a setback this morning. There will be more. Just stay the course."

A smile curved her mouth as she continued working on the music box. These last few months crammed into a tiny house with a teething baby and resentful sister-in-law had been difficult, but she enjoyed these casual chats with Gus. It hadn't been his choice to return to America, but he didn't seem to hold it against her.

"Okay, let's set the cylinder in," she said. Gus handed her the song they had chosen, the Minuet in G Major by Bach. The brass cylinder was smaller than a spool of thread, and she lowered it into the casing and aligned it with the metal combs. Two minutes later, it was screwed into place, and she met Gus's eyes in anticipation. "Ready?"

"Ready!"

She held her breath as she twisted the dial to set the cylinder in motion. Instantly the tines began picking out the delicate, metallic sounds of Bach's minuet.

"Bravo!" Gus shouted, and she couldn't help laughing.

The spindly metallic notes stirred wonderful memories of her years in Germany, where she and Gus had been so happy. Bach's timeless melody illuminated her modest kitchen with a tiny glimpse into pure joy, and she laughed from sheer happiness. They were *so* lucky. Despite their struggles, despite the setbacks and disappointments, she and Gus were truly blessed. By the grace of God, her brother had survived a devastating battle with cholera. They had found a safe home on the other side of the world, where they fell into the arms of a large and loving family. Even though it hadn't ended well, she had been blessed with a magnificent education and had the opportunity to use her knowledge to make the world a better place.

If she couldn't succeed with Nick Drake, she would find another way.

Although building the music box with Gus had helped cheer Rosalind, Dr. Leal was unusually upset by her failure with Mr.

Drake when she told him the news at the laboratory the next morning.

Actually, upset was a mild word for Dr. Leal's reaction. He curled over in his desk chair, covering his face with both hands, his shoulders sagging in defeat. She stood opposite him, nervously clenching her hands and waiting for him to say something.

"Is there any hope he'll change his opinion?" Dr. Leal asked, his voice so faint she could barely hear it.

"I don't think so," she whispered. Never had she imagined Dr. Leal would be so bizarrely despondent over her failure, but he remained slumped at his desk, the sound of the ticking clock the only thing breaking the silence in the laboratory.

He finally drew a deep breath and dropped his hands from his face. "All right, then. We'll have to try something else."

It was only ten o'clock in the morning, but Dr. Leal left the laboratory without another word to her. She thought he might just be stepping out for a bit of fresh air, but the hours slipped past, and by the end of the workday, he had not returned. Rosalind worked alone to prepare a new round of tests to document chlorine's effect on contaminated water.

The next day Dr. Leal was back, but he was still preoccupied, tense, and moody. She hoped he would snap out of his melancholy soon, for their ninety-day clock was ticking. Dr. Leal was the lead researcher and she was merely his assistant, but he seemed disinterested in the new round of experiments. Time and again, Rosalind looked up to catch him staring into space, a hint of fear clouding his features.

"Shall I proceed with the chloride of lime tests on typhoid?" she asked. Normally Dr. Leal handled anything involving chloride of lime, but it had been two days, and he hadn't even begun to prepare the samples.

"No," he said weakly. "I don't see much point in it."

Still bewildered by Dr. Leal's mood when she returned home that evening, Rosalind was surprised to see a package among the afternoon mail. The parcel was wrapped in plain brown paper, and the return address was from Nicholas Drake. Her heart did an involuntary lurch at the sight of his name. She ripped through the wrapper, opened the lid of a fancy package, and lifted out mounds of tissue before she saw the tiny jeweled music box inside.

It was so small that it fit in the palm of her hand. The breath left her body in a rush. How did Mr. Drake know she loved music boxes? It was drastically different from the plain wooden boxes she had learned to make in Germany. This one was so ornate, she was almost afraid to wind the stem.

When she opened the lid, the mechanism played the haunting melody of the *Moonlight Sonata*. The tune matched the outside of the box, which was covered in rich cobalt blue enamel and offset by tiny crystals that looked like stars scattered across the night sky. The moon was a disk of shimmering opal circled by a diamond-dust halo. The label on the box said it was from the House of Fabergé.

A card was enclosed.

Dr. Werner,

When I saw this box, I thought it was as pretty as a moonbeam, and it made me think of you.

We both have strong feelings about how to make sure people have clean drinking water, but I shouldn't have let my temper fly the way I did. I can be a bull in a china shop when I get worked up over something I care about, but I don't usually go after nice ladies like you. Please accept my apology.

Nick Drake

She cradled the precious music box in her hand, strangely upset by its beauty. It was a thoughtful gesture, but it couldn't erase the disappointment she felt at her complete failure in making headway with him. It was easy for him to be magnanimous, as he was on the winning side of this battle.

She was still thinking about the music box as she headed toward the laboratory the next morning. Normally on Thursdays she went to the nearby college, where she worked with a team of students learning the chlorination technique, but she felt compelled to go to the laboratory this morning instead. Something was wrong with Dr. Leal, and she needed to get their research back on track. They had only eighty-one days left to prove their case.

She loved the tree-shaded walk to work, which took her past the candy factory a few blocks from the lab. This morning it smelled like they were making toffee, and she breathed deeply as she braced herself for another difficult day with Dr. Leal.

She entered the squat brick building that held the lab and headed down the hall toward their workspace. On the other side of the closed door, she heard laughter. Well, that was good! There weren't supposed to be any lab assistants today, but at least it sounded like Dr. Leal was emerging from his strange despondency.

She opened the door and walked inside. "Good morning, Dr. Leal."

The laughter abruptly ceased as two men whirled around at the back laboratory table, looking at her in surprise. One was Dr. Leal, but she'd never seen the plump businessman with round spectacles before. The stranger quickly rolled up some oversized papers and inserted them into a cardboard tube.

Dr. Leal cleared his throat. "Rosalind. I didn't expect to see you this morning. I thought you were at the college today."

She wished he would call her Dr. Werner, especially when

other people were in the room. Perhaps it was foolish, because they'd been working together for three years and were good friends, but such familiarity could give rise to rumors.

"I thought it would be best to press ahead on the research this morning," she said.

He didn't seem to be listening to her. With a flick of his hand, he shuffled a few papers into his top desk drawer. He locked the drawer before stepping forward.

"Well, allow me to introduce George Fuller. Mr. Fuller is a respected sanitary engineer, and he's agreed to help us with the ongoing water litigation."

Dr. Leal continued speaking, but she quit listening. She blanched the instant she heard Mr. Fuller's name, for she knew exactly who he was. George Fuller's reputation in water purification was extraordinary, and they couldn't ask for a better man on their team. The question was, did Mr. Fuller know who *she* was? He had been studying in Berlin during the worst of her scandal. If he made a connection between her and that notorious woman from Heidelberg, it could take a wrecking ball to her reputation all over again. Even worse was what it could do to Gus. . . .

She masked her anxiety from her voice. "Of course I'm familiar with your work," she said. "Welcome to Jersey City. We are honored to have you aboard." She studied the older man's face, searching for any hint of recognition or disdain. There was none.

"Dr. Werner," he said with a little bow. "You have a nice laboratory here."

It was Dr. Leal's lab, but she still managed a slight smile at the compliment. An awkward silence filled the room. She glanced at the table where the two men had been working before she walked in. All the papers had been hastily put away, and the surface of the black slate gleamed in emptiness. They made no move to tell her what had held them so engrossed before she walked in.

"A fine day we're having," Dr. Leal said. "Do you think it's going to rain?"

Now she knew something was wrong. In the three years they'd worked together, Dr. Leal had never once resorted to talking about the weather to fill a void.

"I don't think so," she murmured as she headed to the small icebox in the sitting area. Most of the lab was dominated by black slate tables, but a small kitchen and sitting area had been added, for she and Dr. Leal rarely had time to leave for lunch.

As she put her cheese sandwich inside the icebox, a terrible thought seized her.

Was Dr. Leal about to fire her? Was her failure with Nicholas Drake so bad that he had given up on her and was turning to George Fuller as a replacement? It would explain why he'd been so gloomy the past few days.

Her mouth went dry as she walked to the lunch table, fiddling with the vase of daisies she'd brought in a few days ago. As she pinched off a wilting blossom, her gaze tracked to a stray document on the table. It looked like some kind of architectural blueprint.

"What's this?" she asked.

Mr. Fuller closed the distance between them in three steps. "It's nothing," he said as he pulled the paper toward him, rolling it up and inserting it into the tube he carried. "Just plans for a shed I'd like to build someday."

He didn't meet her eyes, and silence took over again. Mr. Fuller looked uncomfortable as he scrambled for something to fill the awkward silence. "I gather you studied at Heidelberg University, yes?" he finally said.

Oh heavens, he did know who she was. She'd been naïve to

think her reputation would not eventually catch up with her. "Yes, yes, I did," she said, but the air in here was stifling, and she needed to get away. "If you'll excuse me."

She couldn't get out of there fast enough. She'd accepted what had happened in Heidelberg years ago, but hadn't expected to be slapped in the face with it this morning.

It was a cool morning for June, but she still felt overheated as she strode down the avenue, heading toward the candy factory a few blocks away. Maybe there would be a delivery. She liked watching wagons of cocoa, sugar, and fruit preserves arrive at the plant. Stupid, but it would give her something to watch as Dr. Leal and Mr. Fuller continued the conversation she had interrupted but was not welcome to join.

"Rosalind!" Dr. Leal scurried down the street, waving a hand to flag her down.

No matter how badly she wanted to avoid this awkward conversation, it would be foolish to run. She turned and waited for him to catch up with her.

"I'm sorry," Dr. Leal panted as he reached her. "George and I had some business to discuss, and it isn't something we're comfortable sharing with anyone else."

"I understand," she said, even though she didn't. She and Dr. Leal had been working nonstop on water purification for the past three years. How could he have been pursuing other research interests without her knowing about it?

"Does Mr. Fuller know who I am?" she asked.

"Of course."

She turned and began walking again, trying to release the tension coiled in her body. She and Gus had already paid such a price for her naïveté in Germany, but perhaps she'd never be able to escape her past completely. "And is he going to run to the press with news of the fallen woman you have employed in your laboratory?"

Dr. Leal's bark of laughter was genuine. "My dear, we have far bigger fish to fry."

It was hardly a comforting thought, but the enthusiasm in his voice caught her attention. "Is he going to help us with the case?"

"Oh yes." A world of confidence was packed into those two tiny words.

She stopped in the middle of the sidewalk to face him. "How?"

Dr. Leal was normally so placid and kind, but indecision warred on his face as he turned away and started walking again. They reached the end of the street, where a picket fence bordered the property of the candy factory. He appeared engrossed as he watched factory workers offload sacks of sugar onto a platform.

"We aren't sure it's a good idea to tell you, but I don't think there's any way to avoid it. You've already seen the blueprint for the treatment facility."

"That little building? It looked like a simple shed."

Dr. Leal looked up and down the street. There was no one within earshot, but still he lowered his voice. "That 'simple shed' is going to house a chlorine feed system. It will provide a dilution of chloride of lime calibrated for release into the water reservoir west of the city. We're going to proceed with chlorinating the water supply."

She tilted her head in confusion. "You mean, after you've got the judge's authorization. At the end of the ninety-day deferment, correct?"

"No. I'm starting now."

She was aghast. "Just like that? Don't you need to get permission?"

"There is no law against it."

"But . . . but . . ." Her mind was so scrambled that she couldn't even get her mouth to form the words. Maybe there was no law against it, but probably because no one imagined anyone would have the audacity to do such a thing! It didn't seem right. Or moral. Nick Drake's impassioned face rose in her mind. *You're not testing it on my daughter*, he had growled. At the time, she thought him paranoid, but wasn't this exactly what Dr. Leal proposed? Releasing chlorine into the water supply without anyone realizing it? She felt hot and light-headed, certain this was a wrong and reckless course of action.

"Rosalind, you know this is going to work. You know that it's safe. For pity's sake, it's safer to drink treated water than to rely on the inadequate filtration system currently in place. Once we activate the chlorine feed, Jersey City will have the safest drinking water anywhere in the world."

"I still don't think it's right. We need to check with the authorities and notify people. We need the city to sanction it. We need to go through the proper channels and—"

"We've got less than three months to make our case," Dr. Leal said as he gently cut her off. "We just went through two years of courtroom litigation, trying to persuade them with teams of experts, and we failed. It's time to *show* them."

Her mouth opened, but she was rendered completely mute as shock set in. She had to find a way to stop this. She admired Dr. Leal and had never met a man so dedicated to the cause of pure, clean water, but he was exposing himself to a terrible risk. She had to protect him.

"When are you planning to put this into action?"

"We break ground on the shed next Monday. It will take a week to build. Then we start the chlorination."

"Please," she whispered. "Please don't do this."

Dr. Leal's eyes crinkled at the corners as he gave her a fatherly smile of understanding. "I've already gone through all the emotions you're feeling. The doubt, the panic, and yes, the fear. I've wrestled with them, and I've won. I know it's the right thing to do, and I'm willing to take the risk. You don't need to participate, but let George and I proceed with this. All I ask is that you keep the secret."

He was about to set off a scientific bombshell. Gus always teased her about being a persnickety rule-follower, but this was beyond the pale. Even if she didn't participate, keeping Dr. Leal's secret seemed dishonest and immoral.

But he made a good point. They knew their solution was safe. Their chief opposition was not science but ill-informed paranoia from people who did not understand the lethal danger carried by tiny microorganisms.

She nodded. She would keep the secret for now, but she had just over a week to find a way to stop him.

Chapter FOUR

Rosalind had to be smart about this. The only way she could stop Dr. Leal from proceeding with a potentially catastrophic decision was by getting the judge to change his mind, and for that, she needed more allies.

She'd figured out her mistake with Nick Drake at their breakfast meeting. The moment she implied he was uneducated, he threw up his defenses and hunkered down behind the barricades. She could do better. Mr. Drake wasn't ignorant, he was merely ill-informed. She could take him to their laboratory and show him what lived beneath a slide and how quickly it died when exposed to a mild chlorine solution.

Rosalind didn't know where he lived or worked, but she knew exactly where he would be on Saturday. In last week's *New York Times*, she'd read a story about Manhattan's millionaire plumber. Apparently he was something of a celebrity on the Lower East Side of Manhattan, the working-class hero who hadn't forgotten his roots. He regularly showed up on Saturdays to install plumbing in poor tenement houses and public buildings that otherwise would do without. For the past two months, he'd been installing washrooms and kitchen plumbing in the Hester Street Orphanage.

Interrupting him while he performed charity work was not ideal, but she was running out of time.

On Saturday morning, Rosalind awakened early to make another journey across the river to see Mr. Drake. She had never been to the Lower East Side, but she'd heard plenty of rumors and read Jacob Riis's groundbreaking book about immigrants crammed into tenements that lacked fresh air and clean water. The pictures of the slums had been appalling, and only a fool wouldn't be a little frightened.

She clenched the strap on the crowded streetcar as it took her farther down Orchard Street, where the buildings were tightly packed and laundry lines stretched across alleys. And the noise! Peddlers hawked their wares, women on balconies hollered to their children playing below, and horses clopped down the street.

She got off at Hester Street but had no idea where the orphanage was located. She asked a man standing behind a table weighed down with handwoven rugs for directions. She had to ask him twice before he understood.

"Five blocks down that way," he answered in German.

"*Danke vielmals*," she thanked him in his native tongue. She had clearly just wandered into Little Germany, with pushcart vendors selling pastrami and pickled herring. Narrow storefronts faced the street, and the variety was astonishing. Tobacco shops, beer halls, pawn shops, and Jewish delicatessens. The air was filled with a pastiche of English, German, Yiddish, and plenty of other languages she could not identify.

She finally found the orphanage. At least she assumed she was in the right place, for a dozen children loitered on the front steps, most playing jacks or hopscotch, but some simply watching passersby on the street. The building was six stories high, with more children leaning out on the narrow balconies above.

She ducked as a boy on a balcony tossed a ball to a youngster a few steps away.

No one complained when she walked through the entrance doors. A woman sat behind the front counter, sorting a stack of freshly delivered laundry.

"I'm looking for Nicholas Drake," Rosalind said. "Do you know if he's here today?"

The woman peered at her skeptically. "Are you a reporter?"

Did he really attract that much attention? She wished scientific discoveries warranted as much coverage from the popular press. Maybe people wouldn't be so violently opposed to chlorination if they understood it better.

"No, I'm not a reporter. Just a friend." At least, it seemed like they were on the way to becoming friends during breakfast last week.

"Good. They were here earlier because they heard the washrooms are finally going to be finished today. They wanted a picture of him in the new washroom with the children, and Mr. Drake hates that sort of thing. He's up on the fourth floor."

Rosalind climbed three flights in the narrow stairwell, stepping out into the end of a long, dimly lit hallway. The hall ran in only one direction, and a cluster of children gathered near the other end, where an open doorway led to a white-tiled room. The tile wasn't complete, and a man with a trowel was spreading a thin layer of mortar on the wall while a young boy passed over tiles. Rosalind navigated around the children to get a better view and spotted the legs of a man lying flat on his back beneath a counter with three sinks.

"Now the socket wrench, Karl." It was Nick Drake's voice. The adolescent boy kneeling beside him rifled through a toolbox and handed over the wrench.

"And what am I *not* going to do with this wrench?" Mr. Drake asked.

"Strip the threads off the screw," Karl answered.

"That's right. And how might I accidentally strip the threads? Someone else answer besides Karl."

"If you twist it too tight," a girl with braids answered.

"Good girl," Mr. Drake said in a booming voice from beneath the sink.

Rosalind stood in the doorway and watched him work. All she could see of him was his plain canvas trousers and scuffed work boots sticking out from beneath the counter, but occasionally a hand reached out for a tool. A big, strong hand smudged with grease and dirt, but she liked that it was a capable hand. By the end of the day, those hands would give these children the priceless gift of a functioning washroom. There was something wildly attractive about a man who could do that.

She had learned plenty about plumbing during her research into water. She had helped install running water at the research station in Germany, and the first thing she did after purchasing her house was upgrade the kitchen plumbing with her own two hands.

At each step, Mr. Drake told the children what he was doing, and some of them even hunkered down to peer beneath the counter for a closer look. Although some of the children seemed bored, others hung on his every word. This might be the only attention they got from an adult male all week.

It was in that instant that Rosalind knew she could turn Mr. Drake into an ally. He cared. He believed in helping ordinary people. He was smart, and that meant he could be reasoned with. She would find common ground with him, hopefully in time to stop Dr. Leal from his reckless and daring venture. If she could convince Mr. Drake to come to her laboratory to see her research in action, she would return the favor by listening to whatever he had to say about filtration.

"Okay, now I've got the coupling nuts attached to the drain

trap," Mr. Drake said. "Who can tell me what the drain trap is for?"

There was a pause, and when none of the children spoke up, Rosalind decided to respond. "It holds water in the pipe to block sewer gases from coming up through the drain and into the room."

Two hands grasped the underside of the counter, and Mr. Drake pulled himself out into the center of the washroom, still flat on his back and staring up at her from the floor. He looked as surprised as if the queen of England had appeared at the orphanage.

Then a smile split his face wide. "Well, well . . . Dr. R. L. Werner in person," he said in a delightfully intrigued voice. He glanced over at the children gathered in the doorway. "How about that, kids? Did you know a woman could be a doctor?"

They hadn't. One of the girls backed up until she bumped into the sink. "Are you here to give us shots?"

"I'm not that kind of doctor," Rosalind said. She was about to explain, but as soon as the children learned they weren't about to be vaccinated, they lost interest in her.

Mr. Drake rolled into a sitting position, resting his forearms on his bent knees as he peered up at her. "I suppose you're here to carry on our tedious conversation from last week?" If he still carried a grudge, he gave no sign of it.

"The first thing I want to do is thank you for the music box."

"You're welcome. What's the second thing you've come for?"

"To carry on our tedious conversation from last week."

He scrutinized her with a half-curious, half-defensive gaze. "Do you think you have a prayer of changing my mind?"

"It's a long shot, but I'm here to give it my best."

"Well, then," he said. His voice was both curious and cautious. "Just so we're clear that we stand on opposite sides of this fence."

"I wish we didn't."

"Me too, Dr. Werner," he said slowly. "You can't imagine how much."

Her gaze locked with his, and she was trapped. The combination of heat and admiration on his face nearly drove the breath from her lungs. The others in the room faded into the background as she stared at the most attractive man she'd ever seen, sitting on a washroom floor and looking healthy, vibrant, and alive.

A bell rang, and a voice from downstairs summoned the children to lunch in three different languages. Never had she seen children scramble so quickly as they tore down the hallway toward the staircase.

She and Mr. Drake were now alone aside from the other man laying tile. She glanced around the square room, still midway through construction.

"Is this a brand-new washroom, or are you upgrading an existing one?" she asked.

"Last month it was a bedroom. We're adding a washroom on every floor. By the end of the day, this one should be ready to see action."

"What did the children use before?"

"City law says that as long as a building has a privy for every twenty people, it's legal. The privies are in the alley behind the building. They aren't anything I'd want a kid to use, but they're better than nothing."

She nodded. Privies were a public sanitation nightmare. Local regulations insisted they drain into the city sewer system, but illegal privies were often hastily thrown up and simply leaked into the groundwater, causing all manner of waterborne illnesses. It was probably what had killed her parents.

"Thank you for doing this," she said. "It's important work on so many levels."

"It's no bother," he said with a shrug, but she could tell by his flush that her words pleased him, even though everything she said was obviously true. The sooner cities were fitted with modern plumbing, the safer everyone would be.

"Look, I'm about finished here, but I need to go to the boiler room and get these lines hooked up to the hot water. Want to come with me?"

She did. Hopefully there would be privacy in the boiler room, for she needed to broach the topic of the lawsuit, and it would be easier if they were alone.

She followed him to the basement, where a nickel-plated boiler gleamed in the dim light. A number of pipes and flues were rigged to the system, and she couldn't begin to imagine how it all worked, but Mr. Drake walked confidently forward and began hooking up some tubing to the existing pipes. She took her glasses from her reticule for a better view.

Mr. Drake must have noticed, even though he never took his gaze off the boiler as he screwed a pipe into place. "Careful, Dr. Werner," he murmured. "You know what I think of those spectacles."

She hid a smile. "Would you please just hook up those sinks to the hot water? Dozens of orphaned children await the results with breathless anticipation."

It was hard to concentrate with Dr. Werner less than a yard away, watching his every move.

"How did you know I like music boxes?" she asked.

"You do?" Pleasure filled him, even though it was dumb luck that he'd picked something she liked. His sister said he should apologize in person, but he'd never been good with words and took the easy route by going to a department store to pick out something delicate and fancy.

"I love music boxes," she said. "I learned how to make them when I lived in Germany and still enjoy tinkering with them. It feels good to make something with my own two hands."

"You actually *make* them? From the ground up?"

"Everything except the music cylinder. That I buy."

His attraction to her tripled. Ladies of her class didn't normally work with their hands, and his fascination with her started spiraling out of control. Again.

"I bought it because it reminded me of you," he confessed. "When I first saw you, I thought you were as pretty as a moonbeam. The music box had a glowing moon in a night sky on it and I . . ." His voice stumbled to a clumsy halt as he remembered his first glimpse of her in the doorway of Sal's crowded restaurant. He'd never seen such silvery blond hair, and it reminded him of moonlight. She looked delicate and dainty and pretty. Without stopping to think, he'd vaulted from his booth to steer her through the crowd.

Then acted like a dolt when his temper got the better of him.

"Anyway, I'm glad you like the box," he said ineptly, wishing he knew how to talk to a college-educated woman. He didn't want to talk about water filtration or court cases. He wanted to know how a woman like her got to be interested in machinery. Maybe they had something in common after all. "Do you want to see how to hook up a hot water tank?"

"Do you mind? I've never seen anything like this up close before."

Mind? He was out of his head with delight when she adjusted those prim spectacles and moved in for a closer look. He wanted to laugh and hug her and kiss her all at the same time.

Instead he asked her to hand him the socket wrench. Rather than ask what a socket wrench was, she asked what size drive ratchet he needed to go with it. She wasn't putting one over on him either. Ever since he'd gotten rich, a lot of women pretended to like him, simpering and giggling at the dumbest things he said. He didn't trust any of them, but this lady was different. She knew what a drive ratchet was and how water got pumped in and out of a city.

He'd never had this sort of immediate attraction before, and he needed to know if she was a free woman.

"So, Dr. R. L. Werner, is there a Mr. Werner in your life?"

"I've got a brother who answers to that name, but no husband, if that is what you're asking."

He was grinning too widely to provide an immediate answer. "Yup. That was what I was asking. There's no Mrs. Drake either. Just in case you were wondering."

"I was, actually. You mentioned a daughter the last time we met."

"Sadie," he confirmed. "My wife died right after she was born."

He married Bridget because he liked and trusted her. They grew up only a few blocks away from each other, and it was time for him to settle down and start a family. He'd just inherited a fortune and had an instinctive mistrust of the well-bred ladies who suddenly showed such interest in him. Those ladies wouldn't have looked at him twice when he was a plumber, but he'd always gotten on well with Bridget O'Malley.

Marrying her might have been a mistake. He didn't mind when people looked down their noses at him or sneered behind his back, but Bridget wilted beneath that sort of scorn. He remembered when they'd gone to a ballet in Carnegie Hall because Bridget wanted to see the dancers in their costumes. She hadn't realized how formally people dressed, and wore a nice blue gown with lace at the collar. All the other ladies glittered in diamonds and shimmering silk. The next time they went, Bridget wore a brand-new silk dress she'd bought just for the occasion, and he thought she looked pretty as a peach. But during the intermission, Bridget overheard a couple of ladies from Gramercy Park giggling about making a silk purse out of a sow's ear. That was the last time Bridget had gone to the ballet. She died less than a year later, and to this day, it steamed him that Bridget only got to see two ballets in her entire life, and both times she felt out of place.

Hankering after a woman like Dr. Werner probably wasn't the brightest move he'd ever made, but he couldn't shake this feeling of delight that swamped him every time she came into his line of sight. Even knowing she was here for that court case and not for him. Even knowing she was out of his class. He still wanted her.

As he continued hooking up the valves, she asked intelligent questions every step of the way. Every now and then, some of the children crept down the narrow stairwell to spy on him, huddling on the stairs as he worked. They were hungry for attention, and usually he lavished it on them, but today he couldn't tear his mind away from Dr. Werner.

"I suppose even fancy doctors like you need to eat," he said. "Can I take you out to lunch when I've finished here?"

"Might we discuss the court case while we eat?"

He didn't want to. If she started trying to push those awful research papers in his face, all it would do was make him feel stupid and aggravated. He was no expert in chemistry or bacteria, and any conversation about it would be pointless.

"Perhaps someday you'd like to come to my laboratory, and I can show you the experiments we've been working on," she continued.

"If I agree to go, can I call you Rosalind instead of Dr. Werner?"

"If you'd like."

He was being an idiot by not letting her talk about what she'd clearly come all the way across town to do. It took guts for a woman like her to venture into this part of town, and he wasn't going to get anywhere with her until they cleared the air about this court case.

"What I'd really like, Rosalind, is to spend an hour with you when there are no little kids running around or court cases hanging between us. I'd like to grab you by the hand, run outside, and forget about installing washrooms or hot water heaters. I'd really just like to get to know you. Everything about you."

She sent him a teasing glance. "The children are hoping for a working bathroom this evening. You wouldn't want to disappoint them."

"Watch me. I'm a low, impulsive person when you get down to it, and right now I want nothing so much as to run away with you." He'd been a widower for three years and hadn't touched a woman in all that time. No one had set his heart or imagination on fire the way this woman did.

Rosalind's face softened. "Don't underestimate yourself. People like you make a huge difference in the world. Hardly anyone reads my research papers, but once these washrooms are in order, two hundred children will thank their lucky stars you came into their life. You're making their world a better place."

It was like the wind had suddenly filled his sails, and he was soaring. He had to look away so she wouldn't notice how much she got to him, but he managed to find his voice.

"You know how to make a man feel . . . really great." He wished he had better words, but she made him feel so terrific he didn't care.

His eye met hers, and every ounce of his own longing and excitement was mirrored in her face. She felt it too. This wild, unwieldy attraction that lit them both up like fireworks. She was looking at him like she was dying of thirst and he was a glass of water. Even the children huddling on the stairs noticed it and started giggling.

He threw down the wrench. "Come on. We're going outside."

"Yes." Even that single word sounded breathless.

He grabbed her hand and dashed up the stairwell, down the hall, and out into the alley beside the orphanage. He whirled her around so she was facing him. Never had he felt so electrified, but he had to clear the air first.

"You know I'm not going to change my mind about the court case."

"I know. I have to try."

"Fine, but try later. Okay?"

Her face looked radiant. "Okay."

He hauled her into his arms and kissed her as though his life depended on it. She was so tiny, she fit against the frame of his body perfectly. And she smelled pretty. Soft. Wonderful.

She withdrew, but her expression was dazed and delighted as she gazed up at him. "This is crazy."

"I know. Kiss me again."

She did, reaching up on her tiptoes to wrap her arms around his neck. Every nerve ending in his body was alive. Without breaking the kiss, he scooped her up in his arms, lifting her off the ground and above his head. She pulled back to gaze down at him, but he didn't feel like setting her back on the ground just yet.

A *pop* and a flash came from down the alley, and he dropped Rosalind onto her feet, whirling around to spot a photographer holding a flash lamp, ready to take another photograph.

"Don't try it," he hollered, then turned to Rosalind, whose face had gone stark white. "Don't worry about it," he said gruffly. "They're just a pair of reporters who like to write up stories about me working at the orphanage."

"Reporters?" she asked weakly. She turned away and started heading down the alley.

He reached out to grab her elbow before she got very far.

"Whoa . . . it's dangerous back there," he warned, but she looked a little sick, and he was worried about her. Standing close, he pulled her behind him and out of view of the photographer. "It's okay," he murmured. "They can't see you, and I'll smash that camera to pieces if he tries to get another picture of you."

She didn't answer him, and he gave her a little shake. "Okay? You okay down there, Dr. Werner?"

"I'm okay. I just don't like reporters."

He gave a snort of laughter. "You and me, both. They have their uses, though."

Craning his head to look backward, he recognized Frank McLean from the *New York World*, one of the better reporters he'd dealt with.

"Hey, Frank," he hollered. "How about you schedule an appointment with my secretary for next week, and I'll tell you everything you want to know about the orphanage. Plus an exclusive on what building we're going to overhaul next."

He felt the muscles in Rosalind's arm relax as the reporter agreed and backed away, the photographer following in Frank's wake. Maybe she was just shy. Bridget hadn't liked being the focus of any kind of attention, and maybe Rosalind was the same. Maybe that was why she went by her initials when she wrote those highfalutin articles.

It didn't matter why she was rattled. She was clearly upset, and it was his fault for putting her in this situation.

"Why don't you and I head inside and finish up? The reporters aren't allowed inside the orphanage, and they know that. You'll be safe with me."

Her only response was a heavy sigh.

"Come on, Rosalind," he softly urged. "You were mighty impressed by the way I hooked in those hot water pipes. I can't wait to see you light up when I solder the toilets into the main sewer line."

That got a laugh out of her, and he grinned like an idiot. He loved that he could make this smart and pretty woman giggle like a five-year-old.

Ten minutes later they were back in the dimly lit basement, Rosalind sitting on an overturned bucket while he acted the hero and sealed the joints to the outside hose bib. He was almost relieved when she went back to nagging him about the court case.

"Have you ever been inside a research laboratory?" she asked.

"Nope."

"Would you like to?"

"Nope," he said, not even breaking rhythm as he methodically twisted the wrench. He could practically hear her getting worked up over there, so he put her out of her misery. "Not unless you'll be there, of course. In that case, I'll show up with bells on."

"Of course I'll be there. I'll have live samples of typhoid and cholera specimens to demonstrate our technique."

He turned his head to see if she was joking.

She wasn't, but her eyes danced with humor, and once again he was bowled over by her. Just like that. The last thing he wanted was to bicker with her over waterborne diseases, but if it weren't for this court case, he never would have met her, so maybe this was the price he was going to have to pay.

"Will you be wearing those spectacles?" She'd taken them off when she sat on the bucket, and he kind of missed them.

"If it will persuade you to listen to me."

He would gladly listen to her read the telephone directory if she wore one of those prim dresses and those tiny spectacles. He hadn't been this irrationally attracted to a woman since . . . well, since never. Physical attraction wasn't the best foundation for any sort of relationship, but when he'd learned she was smart and funny and had a solid core of good-hearted principles . . . well, he didn't see any reason he shouldn't pursue her. He didn't want to be a widower the rest of his life. In less than ninety days, this court case would be officially over, and he could begin wooing her in earnest.

"I'm busy on Monday, but I can come over to your lab on Tuesday," he said.

She winced. "Tuesday is the start of the annual meeting of the American Water Association. I'll be at the conference."

Ah yes. The scientific organization he was not welcome to join. It didn't matter. It looked like he was going to succeed in getting appointed to the State Water Board without their help. After last week's meeting with the governor, it was almost certain.

The water conference would be over late on Wednesday, so he'd take the first opportunity to see her the following day.

"Then I'll be at your lab bright and early on Thursday morning," he said. "I'm happy to learn about new technology, but please understand . . . I'm not going to change my mind about this."

"All I'm asking for is a chance," she said earnestly.

"Me too, Dr. Werner."

But he had a feeling they were speaking about entirely different things.

Chapter FIVE

Rosalind felt honor bound to confess the incident in the alley to her brother. If the photographer hadn't snapped that picture, perhaps she could have ignored it. After all, those two men didn't know her name, and without that, her reputation was secure. But a photograph changed things because someone might recognize her. She had to warn Gus, and it wasn't going to be pretty.

She waited until Ingrid went upstairs to get little Jonah dressed for the day. Not that Gus wouldn't immediately tell his wife what had happened, but it would be easier to discuss it without Ingrid's judgmental presence. Rosalind had been trying for years to win her sister-in-law's forgiveness, and this incident was only going to harden Ingrid's heart even more.

"Were they close enough to get a photograph of your face?" Gus asked, his fists clenched as he sat at the kitchen table, his breakfast growing cold before him.

"I don't think so," she said. In all likelihood, the photo would only show the silhouette of two people in a provocative embrace. "They don't know my name, so I'm probably panicking over nothing. I only told you because I don't want to have any secrets between us."

"What about this Drake fellow? Can you trust him not to speak to the press?"

"He promised the reporter an exclusive interview to discuss the orphanage. Nothing else. He won't leak my name." She was certain of it. They barely knew each other, but she sensed a raw strength and honesty about Nick. He'd promised to protect her, and he would.

Gus pushed back from the table and took two steps to the kitchen window, where he glared out at the vegetable garden in her postage-stamp-sized yard. When she'd bought this cottage, it was fine for her needs. It had a kitchen, a parlor, and washroom on the first floor, and two modest bedrooms upstairs. It was clean, with freshly painted wainscoting, enameled hardware in the kitchen, and a covered front porch. It had been perfect for her, but she never expected Gus and Ingrid would be forced to leave Germany as well. Offering them a home was the very least she could do to make up for the scandal she'd brought into their lives.

"You work alone in a laboratory with Dr. Leal, opening yourself up to all sorts of rumors. Now you're kissing virtual strangers in public." Gus's voice simmered with tension, but Rosalind remained stone-faced. She had nothing to be ashamed of with Dr. Leal, and Gus knew that. It was another story with Nick Drake.

"It is disgraceful."

Rosalind turned to see Ingrid at the base of the steps. Splotches of anger marred Ingrid's pale cheeks, a stark contrast to the neatly woven blond braids coiled around her head. Ingrid crossed the parlor and stood in the arch leading to the kitchen. "Do you expect Gus to bail you out of this humiliation as well?"

Gus stepped in front of his wife. "There's no need to panic," he said in a placating tone.

"No need?" Ingrid screeched. "She ruined our lives. I can't

go home to Heidelberg. Now she behaves in the same disgraceful manner here?"

Rosalind raised her chin but said nothing. Ingrid had disapproved of her since the moment they met six years earlier. Germany was a traditional society where it was rare for a woman to go to college, and even odder for her to venture into a scientific field.

It had been difficult after their grandfather died and Rosalind and Gus moved to her uncle's farm in Germany. They clung together like two orphans in a storm. They weren't yet fluent in the language, and everything seemed a little different in Germany. Neither better nor worse, just different. People were very formal. Adults who had lived in the same village for generations referred to each other by their title rather than their first name. Women dressed modestly, and hierarchy was respected.

After a while, she and Gus learned to speak German like natives. They spent their summers tromping through rugged forests and fishing in mountain streams. Her cousins taught her how to milk a cow, and in the long winter evenings, she helped them assemble handcrafted music boxes that were sold in Heidelberg. Her uncle even took her into the city, where he taught chemistry at the university, and she got her first opportunity to see a real research laboratory.

Once she'd thought Heidelberg was heaven. Now all that word brought was memories of shame and fear. Gus had helped her through the worst of it as her lawyer, but ultimately she had fled the scandal like a coward.

In the end, Gus had to leave as well. And until he passed the necessary qualifications to begin practicing law in America, they would all be sharing this house.

"You will not see that man again," Ingrid declared. "I will not raise my child in a house with a woman who behaves in such a manner."

Rosalind tightened her mouth, waiting for Gus to remind his wife that they were guests in her home.

His face flushed, and he shifted uneasily. "Everything is going to be fine," he said in a placating tone. "I'm sure Rosalind won't see that man again."

"But I *will* see him again," she interrupted. Nick had agreed to come to her laboratory next week, giving her another chance to persuade him of the validity of their research. She would not squander that chance because Ingrid had eavesdropped on a conversation.

"You have a duty to your family," Ingrid sputtered.

"And I have a duty to scientific research that outweighs the people who live in this cottage." She turned to focus on Gus. "You of all people should understand that."

He flinched at her words. Anyone who had suffered through the horrors of cholera understood the importance of clean water. Gus cast a nervous glance at his wife, then nodded in acceptance. "Of course you're right, Rosalind. It shall be as you say."

He turned back to the stack of law books spread open on the kitchen table, pretending to study, but tension still sizzled in the air. Ingrid scowled as she banged the teakettle onto the stove, making as much noise as possible as she moved about the kitchen, preparing breakfast.

Rosalind went to the shelf for a teacup. At least she could prepare a nice cup of tea the way Gus liked it. A twinge of guilt pinched her for alluding to his bout with cholera. When push came to shove, Gus always deferred to her.

She reached for the tin to prepare the peppermint-steeped tea Gus liked so well, but Ingrid batted her hand away. "You're making a mess of my kitchen. Why don't you just let me cook and go do your own business?"

Rosalind clenched her teeth, but this wasn't a battle worth

fighting. Gus still had his nose buried in the law books, but both his fists were clenched. She owed it to him to make peace with his wife.

"Thank you, Ingrid. We all appreciate your housekeeping." But she was as tense as Gus as she headed outside for a walk, leaving the house she loved but no longer felt was her own.

Nick led a team of men through the underground tunnel toward the new vertical turbine pump. As always, there was a dank feel to these brick-lined tunnels that drove some people crazy, but Nick enjoyed it. He'd spent more than a dozen good years working in this vast underground network of tunnels that provided the city with water. He rarely got to go underground anymore. The past five years had been spent crawling up the chain of command at the State Water Board, working at a desk instead of twisting a wrench. As much as he loved the ability to oversee the entire water system, he sometimes missed the chance to go underground and get his hands dirty with the other guys.

He recognized Gino Vanelli standing beside the turbine pump that had been in operation for more than twenty years. The question to be decided today was if the new aqueduct would use a similar pump or switch to in-line booster pumps. Nick had brought a couple of men from finance with him, as they would be paying for the pumps.

A grin spilt across Gino's face as he recognized Nick. "What are you doing down here, stranger?"

Nick declined the handshake and tugged Gino into a quick, back-pounding hug. "Just coming down to visit the best work crew in the city."

"How's that baby girl of yours?" Gino asked.

"Smart as a whip. She's already figured out how to unfasten the kitchen cabinet latch and get into the cookie jar."

"She inherited her daddy's knack," one of the other plumbers said.

"Let's just hope she hasn't inherited her daddy's belching skills," another added.

Nick roared with laughter and promised a round of drinks after work. As much as he loved his new job, it wasn't possible to roughhouse and joke with government bureaucrats the way he could with a work crew.

He sobered and got down to the business at hand. "This here is Michael Robinson and Harwell Smith, both from the finance department. We're going to need at least fifty or sixty pumps on the new aqueduct, and I've already warned them it's going to be pricey."

Harwell Smith held a handkerchief over the lower half of his face, but he shifted it in order to send a quick greeting. It didn't smell too bad down here, but Nick always forgot how squeamish people could be the first time they went underground to tour sewer facilities.

"All right," Nick said, "tell us about the ongoing maintenance with this beast and what kind of men we need to keep it in operation."

He already knew the answers, but it was important for the finance men to understand too. Sometimes men who wore suits to work assumed that laborers were interchangeable and could be had cheaply. The kind of plumbers and mechanics needed to keep these room-sized pumps in operation were expensive, and the new aqueduct was going to require over a hundred skilled laborers.

Gino explained the system, and the finance men asked all the appropriate questions. While another mechanic took the two men to the opposite side of the pump to explain the maintenance procedures, Gino pulled Nick aside.

"What's this I hear about you in line to be the next commissioner of labor?"

Nick bit back a smile. It was too early to say anything publicly yet, but he'd been privately assured the appointment was his.

"Nothing is official yet," he said. "I expect the governor to make an announcement sometime this week."

Gino looked uneasy. "Yeah, well . . . there's something I want to talk about, then. Rumor has it that a bunch of Irish guys have been hired to work on the new aqueduct."

Nick met Gino's gaze. "And?"

"And I don't think it's going to go over well with the men down here. We risk our lives for each other every day. I don't trust those clodhoppers to know what they're doing."

This was exactly the reason Nick was being considered for the commissioner's job. The number one requirement was the ability to handle rowdy work crews, labor unions, and hot tempers. Nick had spent most of his life with this crowd, and no one understood them better.

"Those men have been hired to work above ground. I doubt the turbine crews will have any direct contact."

Gino shifted his weight, his expression hardening. "Yeah, but we still don't like the idea of those jobs going to Irishmen. There's a bunch of Italian guys who could use the work. I've already talked to—"

"The new aqueduct is going to employ thousands," Nick interrupted. "I've signed off on a crew of eighty Irishmen to begin work on the Ashokan leg. They start next month."

"I still don't like it."

"You don't have to like it, you just have to show up and do your job. Working in the best city in the world, the biggest underground water system, and in a job where you won't even see those men. Got it?" Nick flashed a tight smile, took a step forward, and offered a hand to shake.

Gino mumbled something and returned a halfhearted handshake.

Nick didn't let go. He just stepped closer and squeezed hard. And then a lot harder. "Have you got it, Gino?"

It was a staring contest. Gino tried to return the iron grip, but Nick had gotten the jump on him and was grinding hard. This was too important for Nick to lose. He hadn't even officially been appointed the new commissioner, and he wasn't about to back down already.

"I got it," Gino ground out between clenched teeth.

Nick released his hand and clapped Gino on the back. "Good! Nice seeing you again. Make sure I don't have to repeat this conversation with the rest of the crew."

The two men from finance looked relieved when they finally emerged above ground. They headed back to the office, where the State Water Board occupied two entire floors of the building. They would spend the rest of the day working out a plan to staff the new pumping stations and drafting pay scales and maintenance schedules.

Nick headed into his office to scoop up the paperwork for manning the pumping stations, but his secretary was waiting for him. Miss Gilligan was a godsend. A whippet-thin woman with eyes as sharp as a hawk, she kept his office running like clockwork.

"You had a telephone call from that snooty servant at Oakmonte. He wants you to return the call."

"Did he say what it's about?"

"No, just that it's urgent."

Nick asked Miss Gilligan to let the others know he would be delayed a few minutes. For the past four years, he had been paying the footman at his uncle's country estate to slip him information, and these conversations rarely took long.

He had to wait a while for the operator to patch the telephone call through a network of exchanges to get him to Oakmonte, but the footman's message was brief.

Nick's uncle was dying. He'd been suffering seizures, and the doctor expected him to succumb within a week.

Nick digested this information, his face as impassive as if he was hearing a weather report. He could not pretend to feel any grief. The demons that haunted Nick's childhood nightmares all had the face of Uncle Thomas.

He replaced the receiver in its cradle, rose, and prepared to join the meeting about the new pumps. Then he paused.

In the past few years, his circle of family and friends had grown increasingly smaller, and he didn't like it. His uncle's death could change things. It might prove to be a disaster, but if he could patch together the tattered remnants of his family, it was a risk worth taking.

Chapter SIX

Rosalind stood on the deck of the ferry as it pulled into the 42nd Street depot. Normally she enjoyed crossing the river as the towering buildings of Manhattan drew near, but the ferry had been delayed for almost an hour that morning, meaning she was running badly behind schedule. And she hated being late. Her German sense of punctuality had been drilled into her since childhood, which was why she always left well ahead of schedule. She was cutting it very close this morning.

After disembarking the ferry, Rosalind boarded a crowded streetcar to ride the final three miles to the campus of New York University, where the American Water Association was holding their annual conference. Scientists specializing in water came from all over the country to share insight into water research, hydrology, and contamination. She was excited to hear about the latest advances, which made her lateness all the more galling.

She tugged at the collar of her prim white blouse, wishing the lace didn't itch so much. Walking into the auditorium with the morning session already in progress was awkward, but at least the door didn't creak too badly as she stepped inside and slid into a seat in the back row.

A discussion on the effect of lead leaching from pipes into the water supply was the subject of vigorous debate. She wondered if chlorine would exacerbate the problem. She opened her notebook to scribble a reminder to look into it.

Someone was watching her. An inexplicable tingling caused her to raise her head, and she immediately spotted him. Nick Drake, sitting smack in the middle of the auditorium, craning his neck to see her. He flashed her a grin and a nod. She returned the nod, and mercifully he turned back around.

Heat flooded her cheeks, and she fanned herself with her notebook. He wasn't a member of the organization, but their meetings were open to anyone willing to pay the fee. He might not have the first understanding of science, but he was willing to educate himself, and that counted for something.

Throughout the morning, she found her gaze trailing to his dark head. It was a relief that he made no effort to seek her out during the few minutes between speakers when people stretched their legs. She wasn't sure what she'd say to him. Never in her life had she behaved so wantonly as when she literally ran outside for the chance to kiss a man she barely knew. It was mortifying and embarrassing . . . and a tiny bit thrilling.

Lunch was held in the campus cafeteria, where she ate with Dr. Leal and a professor from Iowa. Professor Gottschalk's research on arctic groundwater was fascinating, and he agreed to send her copies of his articles. She had plenty of questions, all of which he answered courteously, but never once did he ask a single question about her own research.

Which was fine with her. Questions about her research could stray into her work in Germany, a dangerous topic she'd prefer not to discuss. For the most part, she let Dr. Leal carry the conversation and any discussion about their work in chlorination.

There was still plenty of time before the afternoon sessions, and Washington Square Park was just across the street. She stepped outside for some fresh air, strolling toward the marble arch built to commemorate George Washington's inauguration.

That was where Nick found her.

"Thought I might see you here," he said, sweeping his hat off and giving a little bow. He wore a tailored suit of dark superfine wool and sported a gold watch chain. So different than the last time she saw him, in suspenders with a wrench in his hand.

"Mr. Drake," she said with a nod.

"Ouch. I thought we'd dropped the formality."

It had been dropped when she gave him permission to use her first name in the boiler room, then smashed to pieces when they'd kissed like there was no tomorrow in the alley. As though he could read her mind, his face settled into a warm tenderness.

"I thought you might like to know that there's no need to worry about those reporters in the alley," he said. "They published a story in the next day's newspaper, but most of it was just about my work at the orphanage."

She latched onto the one problematic word. "Most?"

He shrugged. "They mentioned that I was caught kissing a woman in the alley. No name, and no photograph. They still don't know who you are, so you are completely safe. It's over."

Relief flooded through her. The prospect of another scandal had been making it difficult to sleep, and now that the fear was lifted, she couldn't help but smile at him like an idiot. It seemed that all he had to do was come within ten feet of her to make her spirit come alive and the sun shine brighter. He was smart and funny and could work with his hands, installing all sorts of complicated plumbing.

"I've been anxious to hear about how the toilets at the orphanage are coming along," she said.

His laughter rang out through the park. "Only you could

talk about toilets while looking and sounding like the most attractive woman in the city."

"Don't prevaricate, or I'll think you weren't up to the task."

"Tell me what 'prevaricate' means, and I'll tell you about the toilets."

"It means a reluctance to answer a direct question. You know . . . the kind of thing plumbers always do when they don't want to admit they couldn't hook up a bunch of simple toilets for some poor orphans."

"I've got four floors in operation. One more to go. Want to come next weekend and watch?"

Heat gathered in her face as she glanced around the park. "Last time I did that I got into trouble."

"I know. That's what I'm hoping for again."

"And will there be photographers on hand?" She'd had a close call last weekend and couldn't be so careless again.

"Like I said, Frank is going to keep quiet about what he saw. That's the thing about newspapermen. They hunt for gossip like sharks sniffing blood in the water. I can't stand them."

Rosalind knew all about being the target of journalists swarming in for the kill, but she wasn't prepared to condemn the entire profession. "I don't believe there are any truly bad people," she said. "Only people who sometimes do bad things. There's a big difference."

"Ha!" Nick burst out. "You've never met members of my extended family. You could dissect my Uncle Thomas down to his core and not find a single redeeming quality."

She shook her head. "I've never met your uncle, but I believe God has given all of us qualities of great valor. Sometimes fate causes our lives to intersect in ways that mean we only see the worst of each other, but most people are good. My brother accuses me of being a hopeless optimist, but it's what I believe."

"I kind of like that about you," Nick said, tucking her hand into the crook of his arm as they strolled deeper into the park.

They continued teasing and prodding each other as they circled the small patch of green in the middle of the city. It would be nice to spend the entire day with him, except her sides would probably ache from so much laughter.

At five minutes before one o'clock, they headed back toward the auditorium. He held her elbow as they crossed 4th Street, keeping an eye on the rackety automobiles and lumbering horse-drawn carriages, holding his hand up to slow them down as they crossed. It was totally unnecessary, but it felt good to have a man be so protective of her.

As they entered the building and crossed the lobby, a man flagged them down. "Mr. Drake!" he shouted from the far side of the room. The portly man hurried across the floor, a young woman in an emerald-green walking dress in tow. "I'm glad I caught you before the presentations begin again. You remember my daughter Matilda?"

Nick gave a polite nod. "Of course. How are you, Miss O'Grady?"

Rosalind missed the girl's reply. She was too busy looking at the father, a man she recognized as a biology professor from Princeton. Proper decorum would have dictated that he introduce his daughter to her as well, but he seemed oblivious to her presence as he stepped back and propelled his daughter closer to Nick.

"I was hoping to catch you at lunch," Professor O'Grady said. "Matilda enjoys conferences such as these, and I'm sure she'd be very interested in your work with the New York aqueducts. Perhaps we can all go for a cup of tea and discuss it?"

Nick glanced at the clock hanging above the door to the auditorium. "Maybe some other time," he said. "I don't want to miss the next discussion, and I know Dr. Werner doesn't either. Have a good day, Professor. Miss O'Grady."

With a polite nod, Nick left the pair staring after them as they headed toward the auditorium. He leaned down to whisper in her ear. "They'll throw their daughters at me, but they won't let me join their club."

She opened her mouth to say something, but they both knew he was correct. She hurt a little on his behalf. He truly had no business being part of this scientific society, but it was painful to see him try so hard when they would never grant him membership.

When she headed toward her seat in the back aisle, he joined her. There were still a few minutes before the next speaker stepped up to the podium.

"Why do you come if you know they won't let you join?" she asked.

"Would you believe me if I told you that I've been waiting all my life to hear a speech on"—he flipped the schedule open and squinted at it in the dim light—"the use of deep freeze as a means of eliminating spurious contamination in water?"

She tried to block the laughter from her voice. "You've been waiting for that?"

"My whole life, Dr. Werner." He put the program on the seat beside him. "Especially since the speaker later this afternoon is General Mike O'Donnell, one of the three commissioners in charge of New York's water supply. And it seems good politics to attend his speech."

Suddenly she understood his reason for mingling with a group of people who would never open their ranks to him. All morning he had been working the room like a seasoned professional. The commissioner of a water board needed connections across a huge range of industries. He needed to understand engineering, labor unions, political networks, and scientific research. Now that she knew him better, she realized Nick Drake was actually uniquely qualified for such a position.

It was hard to concentrate on the presentation with him only inches away. She feared he might try to carry on their flirtation when the lights were lowered, but he didn't move a muscle and paid full attention to the speaker.

He respectfully took his leave at the next break and proceeded to mingle with others for the rest of the afternoon's sessions. But at the end of the day, he materialized at her side. She was heading toward 4th Street when he jogged up alongside her. With his jacket draped over an arm and a loosened collar, he looked more appealing than when he was all buttoned down with old-school formality.

"Can I walk you to the subway station?" he asked.

She shook her head. "I'm off to catch the 42nd Street Ferry. I'm afraid I couldn't impose on you to go such a distance."

He looked confused. "Why would you go that far out of your way? The subway station is just a few blocks over."

She didn't want to confess her fear. The first subway line to New Jersey had opened to great fanfare only six months earlier. It was faster, cheaper, and closer than the ferry, but it would mean taking one of those awful escalators deep beneath the city, and then riding a train that tunneled under the Hudson River. She didn't trust it. The notion of traveling beneath the river, with no fresh air, no natural light, no way to escape . . . no, absolutely not.

"I like the ferry," she said. "I like to look out over the river and feel the breeze on my face."

"It probably adds at least half an hour to your trip," Nick said.

More like an hour, given the additional travel she had on both sides of the river, but she wouldn't admit it. "I don't mind," she said. "The ferry is so much more pleasant."

"Have you ever ridden the subway?"

She sent him a pointed glare. If she admitted she'd never ridden it, he would know she was frightened. It made no sense to go so far out of her way for a ferry when the subway could slice an hour off her travel time.

"Come on. I'm riding it with you. Then you'll see there's nothing to be frightened of."

"Don't be ridiculous," she said, but he'd already taken her arm and set off toward the Christopher Street station. He was being very assertive in taking over, but in truth, it would be nice to learn how to ride the subway. Her mind told her that thousands of people rode it every day, but each time she tried to screw up the courage to attempt it herself, the thought of being trapped in a metal compartment beneath the river made it hard to breathe.

But she was going to ride it this time. Nick's brash confidence was bolstering her courage.

"All right," she said with conviction. "Let's do it."

Nick enjoyed every second of escorting Rosalind on her first subway ride. The moment they started descending the escalator into the Christopher Street station, she clung to his hand as though it were a lifeline, and he did his best to calm her. The station was new and featured gothic arches and electric lamps with shaded glass bulbs that made the place look like a church. It was a far cry from the water tunnels beneath Manhattan where he'd worked as a plumber for twelve years. The work had been tough, challenging, and dangerous, but he'd been good at it.

It also made him perfectly at home deep beneath the streets, which Rosalind clearly was not. A departing train left the station with a rumble that escalated to a mild roar as it hurdled into the tunnel, the suction pulling a gust of wind with it and causing a few tendrils of silvery-blond hair to tug free and float about Rosalind's face.

"I think I'll catch the ferry after all," she said as the noise died away, already heading back to the escalator. He slipped an arm around her waist and guided her toward the benches on the platform.

"I've already bought our tickets, and they're nonrefundable," he said reasonably.

"They cost five cents, and you're a millionaire."

He grinned. "But I grew up a plumber, and that sort of thriftiness isn't something you forget. I'll charge you the five cents if you back out on me." He couldn't resist smoothing a lock of hair behind her ear. "I wouldn't push if I didn't know it was entirely safe. I'll be right beside you the whole time."

And just like that, her eyes softened and she looked up at him with a combination of trust and admiration that practically knocked him flat. He locked gazes with her, trapped in the clear blue eyes that reminded him of a cloudless summer sky. By all that was holy, this woman could get to him.

Another oncoming train soon roared into the station, but still he gazed at her like a lovestruck fool. The hiss of the pneumatic doors sliding open roused him from his temporary trance, and he guided her aboard. They shared a bench, her slim hand entirely engulfed in his.

She startled as the train jerked and pulled away from the station. "How long is this going to take?" she asked.

"Eight or ten minutes. It will be over before you know it."

She sat rigidly on the bench and clung to his hand.

"Take a breath," he reminded her.

She did. "Are we under the river yet?"

"Probably. And the air is still fresh and plentiful, right?"

She agreed. And like magic, her muscles relaxed and her entire body eased.

"There's something you should know," he said hesitantly, uncertain where this sudden shyness came from. He didn't want to brag, but he wanted her to know that he was more than just an uneducated grunt who'd lucked into a fortune.

She looked up at him expectantly, and he was struck again by her delicate prettiness. She was so smart and well-bred, and maybe someday soon he would actually be worthy of her.

"Last night I got a telegram from the governor's office. I'm going to be appointed the next commissioner of labor for the State Water Board of New York. It's official."

He hoped he didn't sound like he was boasting, but he'd been the only man at that conference without a college degree or a fancy title. Tomorrow the announcement would be made at the conference and printed in the *New York Times*. He would be a person worthy of respect in his own right, and not just because of the fortune dumped in his lap.

Instead of looking impressed, a hint of disappointment flashed across Rosalind's face. "Congratulations," she said tepidly. "I know you've been working toward that appointment."

"Nonstop for the past five years, ever since I started at the water board," he said.

"Does this mean there's no hope of New York adopting chemical purification for its water?"

A stab of annoyance hit him, but he tamped it down. "Water quality is only a tiny piece of the job. I'll be overseeing labor unions and making sure the new tunnels and reservoirs get built on schedule. I'll make sure the crews have everything they need to get the work done."

There was a lot more to the job he didn't care to discuss. He was going to be charged with carrying out difficult decisions that already made him uneasy. It would have been nice to confide in Rosalind, but she seemed to have a one-track mind when it came to chlorine.

"New York and New Jersey share some of the same watershed," she said. "Dr. Leal and I would love the opportunity to meet with you to discuss techniques for—"

"I think you already know my position on chlorine," he said. "Besides, the judge in New Jersey has already ruled—"

"He gave us an extension. We've still got seventy-six days left to make our case."

Nick had liked her better when she was timid about riding the subway. Her fear gone, she was back on the quest to dump chemicals into the drinking water, and he'd gone and made himself a target by getting appointed to the water board.

But he couldn't help it. He found her bossiness insanely attractive. On the outside she looked as fragile as spun glass, but beneath it was the heart of a crusader.

"I'm installing the last of the toilets at the Hester Street Orphanage this weekend. You've got an open invitation to join me."

There! He caught the quick flicker of interest and a renewed spark of attraction crackling between them. If he could only clear away the aggravating court case and let this glorious and unwieldy magnetism have free rein. He was tired of being alone. He'd wanted Rosalind Werner from the instant she stepped into Sal's Diner looking for him.

"Tempting, but I've got a ticking clock keeping me in the laboratory, working to make our case. Of course, you might intervene on our behalf. . . ."

"Forget it, Dr. Werner. Either you want to come help me with the toilets, or you don't. On the other hand, we can wait out the next seventy-six days, and once the judge drives the final stake through your case, I can court you like a normal man who fancies a woman." He lowered his voice. "I'm hoping we can run out into an alley again and act like smitten idiots."

She sucked in a quick little breath. "Can we please forget that happened?"

"I can't. Can you?"

"It would be better if we could. Glass, china, and reputations are easily cracked and never well-mended." At his confused look, she clarified. "Benjamin Franklin. The font of all wisdom."

He grinned, but the train was slowing as it moved into the station. Electric lights anchored to the tunnel walls rolled past the windows as the brakes kicked in and slowed the train. He gave her a wink. "You survived your first subway ride beneath the Hudson."

She let him help her rise. "You must think I'm so foolish."

"Never. Bossy, prim, obsessed—you can be all those things, but never foolish. Can you ride it on your own tomorrow, or should I come fetch you?" He'd welcome the opportunity to spend more time with her. Tomorrow's conference would be crammed with activity as men learned of his appointment and started clamoring for attention.

"I'll be fine. And congratulations again on your appointment. I'm sure that sort of accomplishment was a real high-wire act. Not many men could pull it off."

Once again she made him feel ten feet tall. She didn't fawn or flatter him, and a compliment from a woman like her was worth twenty from the Gramercy Park heiresses constantly thrown his way.

"I'll see you tomorrow, Dr. Werner, when it will be seventy-five days and counting. They can't go fast enough for me."

Given the dazzled way she smiled up at him, she felt the same. He only hoped she still felt that way after the judge ruled against her.

Rosalind saw little of Nick during the final day of the conference. The announcement of his selection as the next commissioner caused men to swarm around him, already jockeying for influence. Rosalind watched from a distance, impressed by how easily Nick mingled with these scientists and academics.

On Thursday morning, it was time for Nick to make good on his promise to visit her lab for a demonstration of chlorine's ability to treat water. Rosalind paced the narrow aisle between the laboratory tables, her nerves getting the better of her as she awaited his arrival. Dr. Leal was out at the reservoir, overseeing the building of the chlorination system. She was running out of time to dissuade him from his reckless plan to secretly chlorinate the city's water, making it essential that she persuade Nick to their side.

An awful chugging noise came in through the open window. It sounded like one of those dreadful automobiles, but no one ever drove to the laboratory. People either walked from the trolley station three blocks away or arrived by carriage.

She couldn't help smiling when she recognized Nick behind the wheel of a grand automobile with its top folded down. Its carriage was a glossy royal blue, and he sat on a bench covered with tan leather. A grin broke across her face as she dashed outside to meet him.

"Hello, Rosalind," he said in a voice eager with the same excitement she felt. How could she be rendered breathless merely by the way he said her name? Foolish, but she'd been a fool from the moment they'd met.

"I should have known you'd have one of these things," she said with a glance at his pricey automobile.

"My pride and joy," he said as he vaulted out of the vehicle, not even bothering to open the door.

"Let me show you inside," she said, a helpless grin on her face. To her delight, he seemed curious about everything as she gave him a tour of the lab, showing him the workstations and the refrigeration units where they kept testing samples.

"Am I going to meet Dr. Leal?" he asked.

"Dr. Leal is in the field today." She hoped he wouldn't ask for details. She was a horrible liar, but she could hardly tell him that at this very moment, Dr. Leal was up at the reservoir, preparing to chlorinate the water supply of the two hundred thousand people of Jersey City.

"Good," Nick said. "That means I'm entirely in your capable hands. Show me your experiment, Dr. Werner."

She closed her eyes to murmur a fleeting prayer before taking the samples from the refrigerator. So much depended on this demonstration.

"I've selected both typhoid and diphtheria for the experiment," she said as she set the rack of test tubes beside a microscope.

She put on her spectacles and began preparing the slide, using a dropper to put a single bead of blue-tinted water onto the glass. The blue dye made it easier to see the live diphtheria cells once they were under the microscope. She looked through the lens and twisted the dial to bring the organisms into focus.

"Have a look," she said as she moved away from the table.

Nick stepped up to the microscope and fine-tuned the knob. After a moment he straightened.

"Did you see them move?"

"Yes."

She opened the slide and dropped a bead of chlorinated water on top of the blue speck, and covered it again. "We'll wait a while, and you'll see that the treated water has the ability to kill the diphtheria cells."

Instead of flirting with her, he fired off a series of probing questions. What was the percentage of chlorine in the water she just used? How long would the effect last? Could the fact that she covered the slide skew the results?

It was thrilling that he took her seriously. For the next hour, he listened patiently as she explained the various processes for diluting chlorine and infusing it throughout the reservoir. He wandered the laboratory and asked questions about their equipment, the racks of research manuals, even the plumbing for how they hooked up the sinks within the laboratory tables.

Finally, he came to the one piece of personal decoration she allowed to hang over her desk. The old photograph was the only one she had of her parents, taken shortly after their marriage. A gleam twinkled in her father's gaze, while her mother had a calm, solid look, as though she was determined not to move and spoil the photograph.

"Your parents?" Nick asked, and she nodded.

"They died of cholera when I was ten. They're the reason I went into this field." It seemed such a paltry explanation. Their death had torn her world asunder, altering the course of her entire life. It was the same for thousands of people who suffered the ravages of catastrophic illnesses lurking in their water.

"Your mother was a beautiful woman," Nick said. "You've got her eyes. Your dad looks fun, like he's got a world of mischief in him."

"I'm afraid I don't remember him well enough to say." She only remembered the things that mattered to a child. That he had a booming laugh and liked to tease her by hiding candies in the most unexpected places. That he had a nice singing voice as he lulled her to sleep at night, and that she adored him. She never had the chance to know him as an adult.

"It seems so unfair," she continued. "They had such aspirations, but they died before anything came of them. My father was in the middle of writing a book about the birds of North America. My mother wanted to learn how to play the violin, and my father ordered one from New York, but it arrived a week after she died. So many unfulfilled dreams, all because of a glass of water." She traced a finger along the rim of the frame. She could barely even remember what they looked like except for this single photograph. "As the years go by, my parents seem to slip a little further away from me. Gus barely remembers them, and when I die, nobody will be left to remember what wonderful people they were. I don't know why that bothers me, but it does."

Nick said nothing, but his eyes were soft with understanding.

After an hour, it was time to show him the treated slides and the efficacy of her research. She inserted the treated slide beneath the microscope, adjusting the dial to cause the cells to zoom into clarity. She held her breath, examining each rod-shaped cell, looking for a trace of life. There was none. Refusing to let the smile show on her face, she backed away from the microscope and gestured for Nick to take a look.

The microscope dial looked tiny in his big hand as he twisted the knob, his face intent with concentration as he peered through the eyepiece. It seemed to take forever, but she mustn't rush this moment. Every single cell on that slide was dead, and there was no need for her to point out the obvious.

Finally he met her gaze. "They look dead."

"They are."

His handsome face looked troubled. "But is it safe?"

Without a word, she walked to the refrigerator, got out the pitcher of water, and poured herself a glass. She met his eyes as she took the first sip, then continued drinking, lifting the glass higher, not pausing until she had drained it.

She set down the glass.

"That was treated water?" he asked.

"It was. It's the only thing we drink here. I've been drinking it for years."

"And you've never had any ill effects?"

"Never. It's fast and inexpensive. It can purify millions of gallons quickly and efficiently."

He folded his arms across his chest, his face still mistrustful. "It will never replace filtration."

"Of course not," she agreed. "We need both. Instead of doubling filtration units, all we need to do is add a little chlorine. It's time to at least try—"

"Chlorine smells bad. People won't like it in their water."

"Sometimes, but we're getting better at adjusting the levels, and we think most people won't even be able to tell it's there."

"Until you've got it right, we're sticking with filtration." His voice was hard and inflexible. It rubbed her the wrong way. This was exactly how he had sounded in the courtroom, as though he was the world's greatest authority on water, when all he did was endorse an old-fashioned technique that wouldn't keep up with demand as cities grew larger and more congested.

"Filtration works," he insisted. "It's slow, expensive, and the filtration plants are an eyesore to all of humanity, but they work, and they're safe. You say chlorine kills diphtheria, and I can see that it does. But what does it do to a human kidney? To a human liver?"

"I've been drinking it for three years with no ill effects."

"What about in ten years?" he demanded. "Or twenty? Fifty?"

She raised her chin, her anger twisting tighter. "We don't know for certain, but I know what *cholera* can do, and it's horrible. Babies can die within hours, adults within a day. And you're fooling yourself if you think filtration can screen out those microscopic cells you just saw die under that slide. That's antiquated and dangerous thinking."

Instead of getting angry in return, he dropped his head, looked away, and took a heavy breath. It was a fascinating transformation, as though all the fight drained out of him and he became a different man. A kinder man. When he met her gaze again, his eyes were full of appeal.

"Rosalind, we're both fighting for the same thing. Clean and safe drinking water for everyone." He nodded to the microscope. "If what you just showed me can be proven safe, I will dance in the streets and celebrate. Until we're sure, I'm sticking with what we know. Those big, expensive, and ugly filtration plants—no one likes them, and I wish there was a better solution, but for now filtration is the best we have."

He sounded so caring. Conciliatory, even. But she couldn't give up the fight. "Chlorine is better. I know it in the marrow of my bones."

"Oh, Rosalind," he said in an aching voice. "I adore people like you. Dreamers who will someday make the world a better place, even though you have to put up with people like me along the way. We test each other. We goad and poke and strive because we can't afford to be wrong. The stakes are too high."

He kept his gaze trained on her as he closed the distance between them. His normal swagger had vanished, replaced with a hesitancy she found unexpectedly moving.

"I'm sorry," he said gently. "I know you hoped this day would go differently."

All she could do was nod. His tenderness hurt, for if he knew that she was hiding Dr. Leal's chlorination plan, the admiration in his face would turn to outrage.

Nick ducked his head so he could see her better. "Would you ever consider someone like me? As a suitor? I never went to college and I don't know any foreign languages or what fork to use at classy dinners, but I think you are very fine, Dr. Werner. A very fine lady, indeed."

Her heart squeezed. She had enjoyed a few brief courtships in Germany, but nothing like this heady attraction to a man so completely different from herself. His blatant pursuit was flattering, but there was more to it than that. His generosity of spirit and blunt honesty were hopelessly appealing.

She could not return his honesty. To the bottom of her soul, she wished she could be as open and honest, but to do so would ruin Dr. Leal.

"I wish this court case wasn't between us," she said.

"In two and a half months it will all be over. Will I have a chance with you?"

Win, lose, or draw, she wanted Nick Drake. "Yes."

All she said was a single word, but it was as if the world had suddenly shifted. The hesitancy in Nick's face was replaced by a quiet joy that warmed her heart. But his next words stunned her.

"I'll do anything I can to help investigate your chlorine idea," he said. "If you need research funds, I'll pay them. Lab space, I'll buy it. I don't know how medical tests work, but tell me what you need, and I'll get it for you. I'm not a stupid man, and I understand what I just saw beneath those slides. But you've got to prove to me that it's safe before I can support it. I don't know if it will take years or decades, but I'll help you. You can count on me, Rosalind."

His full-throated support was humbling. Within the space of an hour, he had opened his mind and taken the first, crucial step in her direction. There was no trace of pride or stubborn commitment to his original position. All she saw was a genuine desire to find the best way to deliver clean water. She longed to return his honesty, confess everything that was taking place out at the reservoir, and beg for his understanding.

But it was impossible. Nick must never learn of Dr. Leal's plan to release the chlorine early, or that she had played any part in covering it up. As fast as Nick's respect for her had flared to life, it would vanish in a flash if he was betrayed.

Chapter SEVEN

On Friday morning, Nick arrived at his sister's elegant apartment before dawn with a heavy heart. He hoisted his groggy daughter higher in his arms as he strode toward the elevator that would take him to Lucy's sixth-story apartment. This was a message that should be delivered in person, and since she and her husband would be headed to their office soon, he needed to intercept them before they left for the day.

Lucy and her husband worked for rival news agencies. Lucy was a telegraph operator for the Associated Press and handled stories wired into the New York office of America's premier news agency. Her husband, Colin, was the New York manager for Reuters, the British equivalent. Between the two of them, they always knew what was going on in the city.

If Reuters hadn't heard the report Nick was bringing, surely the AP would. This wasn't the sort of news Lucy and Colin should hear from a newswire.

Their uncle was dead. The man they'd battled in a decades-long lawsuit and who had haunted their nightmares was finally dead. The last time Nick had seen Uncle Thomas was in a courtroom five years earlier as his son was sentenced to ten years in prison based on evidence Lucy turned over to the authorities. Uncle Thomas and his wife had been staring daggers at him. They hadn't exchanged a word since. Nick had learned of Uncle Thomas's death last night and been unexpectedly troubled by it.

And ashamed. Family was the most important thing in the world. Inheriting a fortune had taught him that. Dining on fancy plates and wearing tailored clothes were nice but didn't bring the bone-deep security and love that a family provided.

Uncle Thomas had been a snake who could rival any Shakespearean villain, but he and Aunt Margaret had a strong marriage. No matter how much Nick despised Uncle Thomas, this morning his widow was grieving. It was something he had firsthand experience with. He wasn't sure how to deliver the news to Lucy without reopening the Pandora's box of painful memories, but she needed to know, and he didn't want her hearing it from someone else.

"Lady Beckwith's floor," he said to the elevator attendant as the man turned the crank to close the doors. Nick still felt a little foolish calling his baby sister by a title, but she had married a baronet.

He bobbed and rocked a little to keep Sadie awake as the elevator climbed higher and delivered them to his sister's sixth-floor apartment. Colin answered his knock, wearing a burgundy silk dressing robe casually thrown over his broadcloth shirt and suspenders.

"Hello, Nick," Colin said. "And look at this charming little sleepyhead." He gave a gentle tussle to Sadie's dark curls, but his welcoming smile dimmed at Nick's serious expression. "Come inside. We've got strawberry crumpets. Lucy? Your brother is here."

Nick stepped inside the apartment, so different than the shabby place where he and Lucy grew up. Instead of well-worn furniture that had come down through generations of Drakes, the pieces in Lucy's apartment were even older, harkening from Colin's seventeenth-century estate in England. Nick always felt a little uncomfortable sitting on furniture that had probably once hosted kings and dukes.

Lucy strode into the room, dressed in a plain black skirt and canary yellow blouse that offset her jet-black hair. "What's going on?" she asked.

"I'm taking Sadie to stay with Bridget's parents while I head out of town for a few days. Something unexpected has come up."

Lucy must have noticed the tension in his voice, for she lowered herself into a seat, her eyes concerned. "Tell me," she said.

"It's Uncle Thomas. He's dead."

Warmth fled from Colin's face. "Can the devil ever really die?"

Silence descended. Uncle Thomas had caused generations of trouble in their family, and Nick didn't expect Colin to have much sympathy.

"How did you find out?" Lucy asked.

Nick didn't want to tell her. Lucy had made a complete break with the Saratoga branch of their family, and she'd always assumed he had too.

He hadn't. Guilt over the family rift started plaguing him within weeks after the lawsuit had been settled. It had been easy enough to become friendly with one of the footmen at Oakmonte, the grand country estate where his aunt and uncle had lived for the past thirty years. Oakmonte had been purchased with money swindled from his grandfather, and to this day, Nick had never set foot on the property. But footmen had their price, and Nick gladly paid it to be informed of everything that went on behind Oakmonte's grand façade.

He took a seat at the breakfast table, gently bouncing Sadie on his knee. "I got a telephone call from one of the servants at Oakmonte," he admitted.

Lucy's eyes narrowed with bewilderment.

Sadie started to rouse and noticed the strawberry crumpets on the table. Without warning, she lunged for one. He scooped her back into his arms more securely.

"Can I steal one of your fancy rolls?" he asked. "Apparently I haven't been feeding my child properly."

Lucy went about filling a plate for both of them, but he could tell from the stiffness of her movements that she didn't approve of him being in touch with the folks over at Oakmonte. And she still didn't know the half of it.

He shifted Sadie into a chair as Lucy set a plate of muffins topped with generous mounds of syrupy strawberries before her. Sadie picked up a strawberry with her fingers and popped it in her mouth with a grin.

"So what happened?" Lucy asked as she took her own seat.

"Uncle Thomas has been having seizures for the past few months," he said. "None of the doctors they consulted had anything sensible to offer. Last night he had a big one and died a few hours later."

"I can't say I'm shattered at the news," Lucy said. "Thank you for coming all this way to tell us, though. And thank you for bringing Sadie! My goodness, I saw her only last weekend, and it looks like she's grown a whole inch."

Lucy held out a cup of coffee for him, but he couldn't take it. He looked away, embarrassed by this awful surge of emotion that suddenly choked him. He leaned over to kiss the top of Sadie's head so Lucy couldn't see his face. His baby smelled of lemon soap and happiness.

Except she wasn't his baby anymore. She was a child who could walk around and dress herself and chatter up a storm. Bridget would be so proud of this beautiful little bundle of light and energy.

"Nick?" Lucy asked softly. "What's wrong?"

He took a moment to gather his thoughts, for he didn't know

how to express this complicated swirl of grief and regret mingled with a blinding sense of urgency to make things right.

"You don't know, Luce," he finally said. "You don't know what it's like to lose a spouse. One day you've got a friend and a partner, and then the next . . ." He stopped, unable to keep talking on this subject. "Anyway, Aunt Margaret has got to be miserable, and I feel a little sorry for her."

He reached for the cup of coffee, embarrassed that his hand shook as he drank. At least Aunt Margaret had known that her husband was ill and she'd had time to prepare for the wall of grief. It wouldn't be like when Bridget died.

"Your aunt will be fine," Colin said in a cool voice. "She's a born survivor and always has been."

Nick wasn't so sure. Margaret had married into the Drake family and stood in lockstep beside her husband throughout the ongoing family vendetta, but all the truly vile things had been orchestrated by Uncle Thomas and their son. Now Margaret's husband was dead, her son in jail, and her reputation in tatters. And in the last few years, Aunt Margaret had done something he secretly envied.

She had gotten a college degree. With her reputation destroyed and having lost all hope of joining the social elite of New York, she had rolled up her sleeves and made something of herself. The footman who had been passing Nick information said that after Margaret got her college degree, she put it to work teaching immigrant women how to read.

"I'm going to pay my condolences to Aunt Margaret," he said. "It's time to end this ridiculous rift. I'm going to Oakmonte, and if I'm welcome, I will attend Uncle Thomas's funeral as well."

Colin looked uneasy. "I wouldn't get close to that woman. I've heard she set up some kind of school for immigrants, but it's all in hope of cozying up to the charities run by the

Vanderbilts. Margaret is, and always has been, a brazen social climber."

Nick felt his blood heating. Maybe Colin didn't mean to sound like a snob, but Nick was grateful for the reminder. This was the sort of disdain his daughter would someday face. The daughter of a plumber would never be genuinely accepted in the rarefied world of Manhattan high society. Outsiders needed allies. *Sadie* was going to need allies.

"Her motives don't matter," Nick said. Margaret was a human being, and today she was grieving. He would offer what comfort he could.

"I'm not sure you grasp the depth of her hatred," Colin continued. "Two years ago, someone launched a campaign in London to have my title revoked."

Nick blanched. "Can they do that?"

"It takes an act of Parliament to strip a man of his title. It almost never happens, but someone tried, sending anonymous messages to the House of Lords and publishing accounts in low-level newspapers implying I dabbled in underage prostitution. It was complete hogwash with no chance of success. The goal was simply to embarrass me, and that was accomplished. I hired an investigator to ferret out the source of the newspaper stories. He never learned the name, but the payments came from Saratoga, New York. Your aunt and uncle are the only people I know from Saratoga."

A tug of old misgivings stirred back to life. Growing up, Nick had lived in terror of his uncle, but Margaret always hovered in the background. It was her husband who led the charge with the zeal of a jackal.

"So you don't know if it was Thomas or Margaret who initiated the rumors?"

"Thomas and Margaret are a matched pair," Lucy said. "Thomas was the public face throughout the lawsuit, but I always sensed that Margaret was the wind in his sails. I don't think you should have anything to do with her."

Colin and Lucy both stared at him, their faces guarded. Unforgiving. It wasn't who he wanted to be.

"Thank you for breakfast," he said as he abruptly stood. "I have no idea if Margaret will welcome me, or if she'll hurl firebombs at the sight of me, but I know this much. I wasn't perfect during that feud, and neither were you, Luce. I'm willing to forgive Margaret and try to mend the rift. My family isn't big enough that I feel comfortable cutting people out of it. If Margaret is willing to put the past to rest, I will join her in it."

Lucy looked hurt by his words, but Colin was grim. "I hope you don't live to regret it."

Chapter EIGHT

Nick stared at the grand country estate of Oakmonte as the carriage rounded the bend. He'd heard about Oakmonte all his life but had never seen it. Sitting at the end of an emerald green lawn, it looked like someplace a duchess would live, which made sense, as Aunt Margaret had once aspired to grandeur. The daughter of a green grocer, she had adapted to life in the upper class like a duck taking to water. Her wardrobe was imported from Paris, and she hired French chefs and affected a mild English accent.

All that had come crashing down five years earlier when her son was arrested over a plot to assassinate President Roosevelt. Uncle Thomas tried to cover for his son and nearly went to prison himself, thoroughly ruining his reputation and his wife's. The downfall of the family had been Lucy and Colin's doing. Now Tom Jr. was in jail, Uncle Thomas was dead, and only Aunt Margaret remained.

Nick didn't hate Margaret. On the rare occasions he had encountered her when he was growing up, she'd always been decent to him, usually giving him little wrapped chocolates from a tiny case she always carried. Those chocolates had been amazing, melting in his mouth within an instant and tasting so different from the cheap cocoa bars he bought for a penny. More than anything, he remembered the way she smelled. She wore rose-scented perfume that smelled better than anything in Nick's world. To this day, he always associated the scent of roses with fancy rich ladies.

The carriage drew up the circular drive to the front of the house. "Can you wait a few minutes?" Nick asked the driver of the hansom cab. For all he knew, Aunt Margaret would fling him out of Oakmonte before he could cross the threshold.

"Aye, sir."

Nick mounted the wide steps leading to the landing. He'd thought there'd be more activity. Uncle Thomas had died two days ago, and he'd expected there to be at least a few neighbors stopping by to pay their condolences, but all seemed peaceful. It was so quiet that he could hear the leaves rustling in the forest behind the house.

A servant answered the door at his knock.

"Is Mrs. Drake home? I'd like to pay my respects."

He gave her his name, and the girl blinked in confusion a few times. "You're family?" she said in surprise.

At his nod, she led him into the foyer of the house and asked him to wait while she disappeared down a hallway that gleamed with polished wood and smelled like lemon wax. A series of arched windows stretched the length of the front hall, but most impressive was the double staircase descending from the second floor, the flights of steps encircling the room like a pair of welcoming arms. There had probably been a lot of fancy parties in this house back in the day.

Now it was eerily silent. The floorboards creaked a little when he shifted his weight, echoing off the high walls. He could even hear himself swallow.

Finally the clicking of footsteps announced the return of the maid. "Mrs. Drake is in the garden, if you'd care to follow me."

So, it seemed he would be welcomed with no ceremonial hurling from the parapets. It would have been easier to get booted out.

Once outside, he spotted Margaret quickly. In the deep green garden, her black widow's weeds stood out in sharp contrast. They fit her willowy figure perfectly, with a high ruffled neck that kept her chin raised. They were no blood relation, but Aunt Margaret had similar dark hair with icy blue eyes. She stood amidst a rose garden, a basket over one arm and a pair of pruning shears in her hand.

"This is a surprise," she said as he approached. Her voice was cold, her face like stone.

"I came to offer my condolences."

Her eyes narrowed. "Another surprise. I thought I heard the faint echoes of a celebration coming from Manhattan."

He deserved that. He despised Uncle Thomas and felt no grief at his passing, but that didn't mean he couldn't feel sympathy for Margaret.

"It's true there was no love lost between our families, but I am sorry for your loss. I came as soon as I heard."

A hint of softening tinged her eyes, but it didn't spread. "Is your sister with you?"

"No. Lucy had . . . she had obligations in the city."

Aunt Margaret's smile was bitter. "Rejecting her uncle's obituary from the newspapers, I expect." At his confused glance, she continued. "We were prepared for Thomas's death and had his obituary already written. Our man of business wired it immediately to the New York newspapers. I just received word that every one of them has declined to print it. Did Lucy have something to do with that?"

"No, ma'am. Lucy is just a telegraph operator. She doesn't have any say in what gets printed."

"Her husband, then?"

It didn't surprise him that Aunt Margaret wouldn't even say Colin's name. The hatred between those two ran deep.

"Ma'am, I'm not here to fight old battles. I want to make peace. I don't have much of a family left, and neither do you. There's no reason you and I can't . . . I don't know, can't try to get along."

Silence stretched between them. He had extended the olive branch as far as he intended. It was up to Margaret to make the next move. She remained on the opposite side of the rose garden, watching him through guarded eyes. It reminded him of a snake preparing to strike, but perhaps that was just decades of distrust handed down through the generations. No one had said mending this breach was going to be easy.

A few bees droned in the nearby flowers, and he swatted a gnat away from his face. He really hated the outdoors.

"Do you have any influence with the warden of Sing Sing?" she asked.

He blinked at the unexpected question. With enough money, a man could have influence with just about anyone, but that didn't mean Nick was going to use it. "Maybe. Why?"

"I would like my son to attend his father's funeral." She kept her head high, her face expressionless, but for the first time, he saw the vulnerability just beneath Margaret's spun crystal façade. She was on the verge of cracking.

A surge of pity welled within him. "I'll see what I can do."

"Good." Aunt Margaret turned and began pruning a bush. The conversation was over.

Nick took the cab to the nearby town and wired a message to his lawyer. He offered to pay any costs associated with transporting and guarding a prisoner on leave. He spent a few hours in the village, cooling his heels while awaiting a reply. It was going to be a costly negotiation, and a number of palms would need to be greased, but money didn't mean much to Nick. If he could buy a little goodwill from his aunt, he would do so.

In the end, a full day of negotiations came to nothing, and Tom Jr. was refused leave. Aunt Margaret was stoic as she absorbed the news, staring sightlessly at the cooks who were preparing a meal for the funeral luncheon. All of Uncle Thomas's favorite foods would be served. Smoked salmon quiche, baked cheese and pancetta, and maple spice cakes. The kitchen was a flurry of activity, but Margaret stared out the window as though she were a statue, motionless.

Nick hated to bring up another potentially painful topic, but he desperately wanted to know.

"Will Ellie be coming to the funeral?" He hadn't seen his young cousin since she was eight years old and mysteriously disappeared from Oakmonte. Of all the Saratoga Drakes, Ellie was the only one he liked, and he never quite understood why she had been shunted away so completely all those years ago.

The barest flinch crossed Margaret's face at her daughter's name. "No. Ellie is in Rome and won't be able to get here in time."

"I see." He'd heard rumors of Ellie's brilliance at the piano, but all he remembered was the sweetly annoying eight-year-old girl whose arms were barely long enough to reach down the length of the piano keyboard. She'd desperately wanted to play with her older brother and cousins, but she was several years younger, and Tom Jr. had no use for her.

"Why won't anyone ever play with me?" she had sobbed as she trailed after them. Aunt Margaret would tell her to hush up and set the little girl back at the piano bench to continue practicing. The last time Nick had seen Ellie, she had been bawling her eyes out while trying her best to stumble through a sonata.

Well, it seemed Ellie had finally made something of herself and felt no compunction to return to the family that never had time for her.

Aside from Aunt Margaret, only six people came to the funeral. Two lawyers, a business associate, the priest, the local doctor, and Nick. Announcements had been posted at the local church, but no one else from the village came. The cluster of mourners looked pathetically sparse in the sprawling cemetery.

Nick shared a carriage back to Oakmonte with the family's doctor, who was incensed by the poor attendance at the funeral. "The complete shunning by the community haunted Thomas. He adored Margaret and desperately wanted to make up for the damage he'd done to the family's reputation. It was hopeless, and the stress aggravated his condition."

"And my aunt?"

The doctor shook his head. "Margaret locks everything down behind that iron will of hers, and it's hard to tell. I kept a careful watch on her at the grave site. Her face was utterly emotionless, but I saw something in her eyes. I couldn't tell if it was grief or rage, but I fear for her. She and Thomas were completely devoted to one another. I don't know how she will fare now that he's gone."

The funeral luncheon was an additional embarrassment. Tables groaned under the weight of a dozen quiches, maples cakes, and endless trays of diced fruits and vegetables. No one expected the high society of Manhattan to show up at Thomas Drake's funeral, but Margaret had obviously expected members of the local community. She disappeared into her room immediately following the pitiful funeral, leaving Nick to make awkward conversation with the doctor and Bruce Garrett, a quarry owner from upstate New York. Bruce was a handsome man, with hints of silver threading through his coppery red hair.

"Thomas funded my limestone quarry when no one else believed a man like me could make a go of it," Bruce said. "He may not have been an angel, but that sort of loyalty isn't something I forget."

Nick and Bruce had met several times before, and none of the meetings had gone well. Part of Nick's new job was to oversee construction of a huge reservoir in upstate New York. The city was running out of water, and the state was about to break ground on the new reservoir on land not far from Garrett's quarry, which was a problem. The watershed for the coming reservoir needed to be pristine, and the runoff from Garrett's quarry was a constant source of tension between them.

Bruce lowered his head and glowered at the near-empty room. "Thomas was a pariah, but people ought to have shown up to support Margaret. Apparently the vipers wanted to deliver one last sting."

Nick stared at the feast laid out before him. This grand social snubbing was the sort of petty meanness that had wounded Bridget to her core. She had a gentle kindness that could warm the coldest of hearts, but Bridget didn't have a drop of blue blood, old money, or the ability to pretend that she did. The knives had been out for the girl with an Irish accent who had the audacity to join the upper class. Toward the end, Bridget began taking a carriage back to their old neighborhood to socialize with the girls at a millinery shop where she once worked.

All Nick wanted to do was escape this sad house where a grieving widow hid in her bedroom to avoid the blatant signs of her complete and total ostracism. At least the servants were respectful, but each time they came and went from the dining room, he caught them exchanging embarrassed glances with one another.

He wouldn't participate in Aunt Margaret's shame by abandoning her and running back to the city. He would at least make an effort to mend the badly frayed fabric of their shrinking family. More than anyone, he understood how tragically short life could be.

Nick awoke before dawn the following morning, restless to get home. The earliest train to Manhattan would not leave until ten o'clock, so he prowled the first floor of Oakmonte, searching for something to read. This house had been built to impress, with all the trappings of a grand estate, so surely there would be a library somewhere. He wandered down wide hallways with tall ceilings and walls covered with antique tapestries that looked like they'd been imported from a castle in Europe. Even so, his footsteps echoed. The house was cold, empty, and too large for one woman with no family left at home.

At the end of one hallway, he spotted a wall of books through an open doorway and headed toward it. He hadn't read a book since graduating from school, even though he read two daily newspapers and three weekly magazines to keep abreast of the world around him. A house this isolated in the country wouldn't have a current newspaper, but he could find a book to help pass a few hours.

He didn't notice Aunt Margaret until he was all the way inside the room. She perched motionless, watching him from a desk in the corner. How could a woman look so striking and so cold at the same time? She wore the same black gown as the day before, a stark contrast to the warm beige and ivory colors of the room.

"I'm sorry, I didn't realize you were in here," he said.

She stared at him through pale blue eyes, the only color on her chalk-white complexion. It was unnerving.

He gestured toward the wall of books. "Would you mind? It's still a few hours before my train arrives."

She gave a single nod of acknowledgment, and he moved closer to the books, scanning the titles, but it was impossible to concentrate. He sensed her gaze on him, watching, judging.

He looked down and sighed. "I lost my wife three years ago," he said quietly. "I remember how it feels."

He turned and was surprised to see a rim of tears pooling in Margaret's eyes. She lifted her head to stop them from falling. He grabbed a footstool and dragged it across the room to sit near her.

"It gets better. I know it doesn't feel like that now, but it will get better."

She stared out the window. "No one understands," she whispered. "They think that because Thomas fell afoul of the law, he was an irredeemable scoundrel, but he wasn't. I loved him. With every heartbeat, with every breath. I will miss that man every hour for the rest of my life."

Nick said nothing. He would not utter a syllable against Uncle Thomas, even though he hadn't been worthy of her admiration.

"I have nothing left to live for," she said, staring out the window with that oddly serene face. It unnerved him. "When I awoke this morning, I stared at the ceiling and thought that I really wouldn't mind if I died today."

"Don't say that. I expect it's hard to imagine that you'll ever smile again, but you will. And then someday you will laugh. And then will come the evening when you prepare for bed and realize that the whole day passed without grief moving in to darken it."

Her façade momentarily cracked with a flash of anger, but it vanished quickly, and she went back to staring out the window. A clock ticked somewhere, emphasizing the terrible silence. He would go stark raving mad if forced to stay isolated in this vacant house, but perhaps Aunt Margaret didn't have many options. Even though she tried to redeem herself by pouring money into that immigrant school she funded in Manhattan, no one showed up for her husband's funeral. She carried his taint and was still a pariah.

Not if he could help it.

"I was appointed to an important position in New York," he said. "I'll be giving a fancy speech in Central Park in a few weeks. I would be honored if you came." He could hear Lucy shrieking in protest, but Lucy was free to continue shunning Aunt Margaret if she wanted. He no longer felt compelled to twist the knife.

Aunt Margaret seemed touched by his invitation but didn't quite know how to respond. She glanced around the library, as though searching for the words. "That seems remarkably civilized."

He laughed a little. "No one has ever called me civilized before." Lucy called him a force of nature, and most of the bureaucrats staffing the water board thought his appointment had been a howling mistake.

"Please," he coaxed. "Half the city is waiting like vultures for me to fall on my face. It would be nice to have an ally there in case I blow it."

She averted her eyes and looked like she was about to cry again. "You came to Thomas's funeral. The least I can do is come to your speech."

As much as he wanted to flee this desolate place and get back home, it felt wrong to leave her here. When Bridget died, he'd been surrounded by family, friends, and coworkers. During those first few days, he stumbled about in dazed disbelief, unable to believe his young and healthy wife was gone. The fellowship of others had helped, but Aunt Margaret had no one aside from the servants, who seemed intimidated by her.

"Will Ellie be coming home?" he asked. "I know you said she's in Rome and couldn't make it for the funeral, but surely she'll want to make her way back home soon, won't she?"

Aunt Margaret shook her head. "I don't want her interrupting her career. She is a brilliant pianist, the toast of the city. Kings and princes come to hear her play. We are . . . I am very proud of her."

Ellie had always been talented on the piano, but Nick was still surprised she had succeeded with it. First her studies had been interrupted when she was sent away for bad lungs, then she was sent off to some special school that was supposed to help her quit stuttering. Finally, when she was eight, she was sent off somewhere to study piano, and Nick hadn't seen or heard anything about her since.

"When you next see her, will you give her my regards?"

Aunt Margaret gave him that long, uncomfortable stare again. She was impossible to read. He couldn't tell if the expression in her eyes was remorse, hate, or anguish. All he knew was that she did not welcome any discussion of her missing daughter.

"Of course," she finally said.

It was a relief to leave Oakmonte, even though he had no idea if he'd made any progress in mending the family rift. Aunt Margaret's steely veneer was so unlike Rosalind's forthright honesty. The tension he'd been feeling for the past few days eased merely at the prospect of seeing Rosalind again. From the hour they met, he'd been bowled over by her quirky intelligence and prim wholesomeness.

The judge's ninety-day deferment kept them in an uncomfortable limbo, but he was tired of waiting. His next few weeks were dense with work obligations and travel, but whenever possible, he was going to pursue Dr. Rosalind Werner with all the fervor roiling inside him. He wanted a simple, honest woman he could trust down to the marrow of his bones, and with each day, he grew more certain that woman was Rosalind.

Chapter NINE

Rosalind tromped down the wood-chip path leading to the Boonton Reservoir. It was July, and the leaves of the tamarack trees of the forest around her were a deep, vibrant green, reminiscent of the woodsy mountains of Germany. She loved everything about the outdoors—the wet, peaty scent of the soil, the air alive with birdsong, all beneath the immense, sheltering sky.

But not today. Today she had one final chance to convince Dr. Leal to stop his reckless plan to chlorinate the water in the Boonton Reservoir. The lure of Nick's promised research funds might do the trick. After his visit to the lab, it was obvious Nick could be recruited as an ally. He'd vowed to dance in the streets if she could prove chlorine was safe. He'd promised her money for research. With Nick's resources, they could accelerate their research into the safety of chemically treated water. That promise was her best hope to persuade Dr. Leal to delay the release of the chlorine.

The man-made reservoir was twenty-five miles west of Jersey City, surrounded by a fortress-like wall to protect it. Before the water was delivered to Jersey City, it went through a massive filtration system of sand and a layer of aluminum sulfate to strain out debris and algae. The filtration system was barely adequate to clean the water at the best of times, and during stormy weather, it failed.

The small building housing the chlorination system had been built right alongside the reservoir. It looked so ordinary from the outside, and yet inside it housed a revolutionary pump system that might someday change the world. The sharp odor of calcium hypochlorite prickled her nose as she stepped inside.

Both Dr. Leal and Mr. Fuller wore work pants, plain shirts, and had their sleeves rolled up as they connected a pump to the feed lines. One tank held the chloride of lime solution, which would funnel into a larger tank to be diluted with water before being pumped into the reservoir. Mr. Fuller was the engineer overseeing the project, and Dr. Leal had worked alongside him every day.

Both men looked startled as she entered the building. Dr. Leal's face had a guarded look, but he managed a friendly greeting as she stepped inside. Since the hour he revealed his intentions, she had been trying to dissuade him each time they met. She had less than a day to convince him, for the chlorine drip was scheduled to be connected tomorrow morning.

"Dare I hope this is a cordial visit to wish us well on our venture?" Dr. Leal asked.

"You know it's not."

Mr. Fuller's expression turned hard as he went back to hooking up the apparatus, his movements quick and efficient. It reminded her of Nick's effortless competence as he installed that washroom at the Hester Street Orphanage.

"Nicholas Drake has agreed to fund medical tests on the effects of chlorine on humans," she said. She didn't like even speaking Nick's name in this room, for he would be incensed by what was happening only a few yards from where she stood.

"There have been plenty of tests," Dr. Leal said gently. "My own father worked on tests for chemical purification before you were even born."

Rosalind winced and looked away at the mention of Dr. Leal's father. Just as she specialized in waterborne diseases because of what happened to her parents, so did Dr. Leal, whose father had been a physician during the Civil War. Although never wounded on the field of battle, the elder Dr. Leal contracted amoebic dysentery during the war. He survived the initial illness but suffered from debilitating aftereffects for the next seventeen years before finally succumbing to the disease. It had been a long and agonizing way to die, all from drinking tainted water.

"We need to do a better job of communicating with ordinary people," she said. "No one reads our scientific reports, and our work certainly didn't persuade the judge. The judge listened to Nick because he speaks in a way people can understand. We need to take this battle to the newspapers and the churches and public schools."

"And how many years will that take?" Dr. Leal asked.

She had no answer for him. All she knew was that Nick had been violently angry at the possibility that chlorinated water might be "tested" on his daughter without his permission, and his concern was valid. If she couldn't stop Dr. Leal, chlorine was about to be tested on the two hundred thousand people who drew their water from this reservoir.

Mr. Fuller turned toward her, hands on his hips and not nearly as patient as Dr. Leal. His eyes were accusatory. "You *know* we're right," he said fiercely. "You *know* we're acting in the best interest of the people who will drink this water, and yet you stand to the side and plead for more tests that will take decades to complete. Who is the irresponsible one here, Dr. Werner?"

The accusation stung. There were risks associated with long-term exposure to chlorine, but there were greater risks in doing nothing.

Mr. Fuller had not stopped his tirade. "Last year more than a hundred people in Jersey City came down with typhoid because they drank water from that reservoir," he said, pointing furiously out the window. "That was an easily preventable outbreak, and what did the judge do? Order another filtration plant! We know it's impossible to filter bacteria out of the water supply. All it will do is pacify a frightened population. I'm tired of pacifying them. I'd rather protect them by dropping this feed into the reservoir. By the end of the week, every man, woman, and child drinking from that reservoir will be safer than they are today. How many people must die before you will act?"

Trepidation filled her as she eyed the arrangement of tanks, pumps, and tubing. It looked and smelled ominous, but every word Mr. Fuller said was correct. The mixture of chloride of lime would be diluted into microscopic traces once it was dispersed throughout the seven billion gallons of water contained in the reservoir. The chlorine would be undetectable except for the plummeting rates of disease.

"Are you going to keep our secret, Rosalind?" Dr. Leal asked.

Her mouth went dry as she stared at him. This was the moment of truth. Far from the kindly physician she'd always known, Dr. Leal looked like a warrior bracing for battle as he awaited her answer. Mr. Fuller was just as stern, watching her as though she were a bug he would squash if she dared threaten the secrecy of their actions.

She swallowed hard. It wasn't that she was afraid of them; it was that she didn't know what to do. This was breaking all the rules. Secrecy was wrong. People had a right to know, didn't they? Every nerve ending in her body screamed that releasing chlorine into the water supply was unethical and a violation of scientific protocol.

She also knew that every person in the city would be safer the instant their water was purified. Last week she'd read of two more children who'd contracted typhoid. It wouldn't have happened had the chlorine drip been in place.

"We could use your help," Dr. Leal said. "We need samples drawn and analyzed throughout the city. It's going to take a lot of work, and I don't want to trust outsiders. The closer we can monitor the water at various points throughout the city, the better we'll be able to adjust the process. Rosalind . . . will you help us?"

She sagged and looked away. Once she was committed to this project, there could be no turning back. This decision would be the culmination of her most cherished dream, or a disaster that could harm thousands and mark her with shame forever.

Either way, Nick would never forgive her.

Her mind wrestled with the decision, but in her heart, she knew what was best.

"I've heard enough," she whispered. "I'm on board."

Rosalind was unbearably sad as she walked down the tree-lined street toward home. Everything looked precisely as it had when she'd left that morning. The lawns were neatly groomed, and the lane was shaded by sprawling linden trees. A few American flags propped on front porches waved gently in the breeze, and a dog barked in the distance. It all looked so utterly normal. Children played hopscotch in the street, and a woman used a watering can to douse her hydrangeas.

By this time tomorrow, chlorinated water would be reaching into every one of these homes, and no one would know. Her neighbors would go about drinking, cooking, and bathing with that water, never knowing the revolutionary change that had just taken place.

And she would not breathe a word about it. For better or for worse, she was now part of Dr. Leal's plan and would do everything humanly possible to facilitate it.

A crushing weight descended on her chest, making it hard to breathe as she trudged the last few blocks home. She braced her hand against the bark of a gnarled oak tree to catch her breath, the avalanche of doubt sapping her energy. How had it all come to this?

Laughter floated from behind the hedge bordering her house, and she recognized Ingrid's voice. Rarely did she hear her sister-in-law laugh, so Rosalind paused to peer through the shrubbery. Ingrid and Gus sat on the front steps of her house. Gus was on the top step with Ingrid sitting in front of him, encircled by his arms. It was a perfect summer's evening, and the love radiating from her brother's face was obvious even from this distance. Ingrid smiled and murmured something to Gus, and his laughter was warm and full.

The sight made Rosalind ache even more. No woman who kept the kind of secrets she harbored was worthy of unabashed devotion. This time yesterday, she had been savoring a delightful infatuation with Nick Drake. That was gone now. If Nick ever learned what she had agreed to do, he would despise her forever.

She drew a heavy sigh and rounded the hedge, opened the gate, and walked up the path to her house. Both Gus and Ingrid sobered when they saw her, but Gus rose and summoned a smile.

"Hello, Rosalind, how was your day?"

She managed to return his smile. "Fine. Nothing very interesting."

The lies had already begun.

Nick embraced his new job as commissioner for the State Water Board like a hawk launching into flight. It was a powerful and exhilarating feeling, marred only by short fits of blinding panic as the immensity of the task became clear. Two other commissioners had already resigned because of their inability to wield the reins. He was determined not to fail.

Most of it was second nature to him. He knew exactly what the men digging the tunnels needed. He understood the difficulties of laying pipe beneath rivers, through bedrock, and over mountains. The men in the trenches trusted him, and the politicians believed him. Since taking the helm, he had pushed two contracts through, calmed a simmering rebellion at the Avenue D Pump Station, and hired two hundred men for jobs on the reservoir. More progress had been made in the week since he'd been appointed to this position than his predecessor had accomplished in six months. The challenge gave a surge to Nick's days unlike anything he'd ever known.

Except that he was continually distracted by a petite research scientist whose sparkling blue eyes were perfectly offset by her wire-frame spectacles. He loved those spectacles. He loved her prissy maxims and her eager curiosity and forthright honesty.

As he went about his day, thoughts of her constantly intruded. When he went beneath the city streets to inspect a newly installed pump and emerged covered in muck, he heard her prim voice in his head. *No problem can't be remedied by a little soap and hot water*. As he scrubbed up in the washroom, he gave his hands an extra lather of lye soap, wondering if lye was as good as chlorine, and it thrilled him that Rosalind probably knew the answer off the top of her head.

He'd just settled back behind his desk when his secretary intruded. "Your housekeeper telephoned while you were below ground," Miss Gilligan said. "She wants to know how many people will be coming to dinner tonight."

The corners of his mouth turned down. "Three adults, plus Sadie," he said tersely.

Because Rosalind had turned down his invitation to join him for dinner. *Again.* He'd telephoned her twice since returning from Oakmonte, and both times she turned him down, claiming work in the laboratory prevented her from getting away. He was eager to see her again, but more importantly, he wanted her to meet his daughter. So certain had he been that she could join them on Friday night that he'd invited his sister and her husband for dinner so they could all have a chance to meet each other.

Well . . . it couldn't be helped. Part of Rosalind's appeal was her crusader-like devotion to her cause, and he couldn't fault her for working hard. Apparently she was so busy that she hadn't even returned his latest telephone call in person but had her brother leave a message with his housekeeper. Were he the suspicious type, he'd almost think she was avoiding him.

It was six o'clock before he arrived home. It was a rich man's apartment, but the furniture was ordinary and plain. He didn't feel comfortable with gilded decorations or fussy knickknacks. Everything here was masculine, strong, and well-made.

Everything except the nursery. He supposed he needed to start calling it something else now that Sadie was three years old, but her room had the best of everything. A miniature piano, a rocking horse of carved ebony wood, and a dollhouse that looked like Versailles. On the other side of the room was a shelf of books, a map of the world, and a trunk made to look like a treasure chest and filled with the best toys available.

Sadie sat at a miniature table with her nanny, who read to her in French.

"*Bonne soirée*, Monsieur Drake," the nanny chimed.

"Hello, Jeannie," he replied. He had no idea what she'd just said, but it was important for Sadie to know foreign languages, and he'd hired a pricey French nanny to be sure Sadie would someday speak the language like a native. He'd hired another tutor to teach her etiquette, and an overpriced chef to ensure she acquired an appreciation of fine food. Someday Sadie would attend a highfalutin boarding school, and he didn't want her being embarrassed by not knowing the difference between caviar and capers. He couldn't teach her these things, which was why he had a staff to help.

Sadie vaulted across the room the moment she spotted him. "Did you miss me, Daddy?"

He scooped her up and whirled her in a circle. "I always miss my best girl!" he boomed, causing a cascade of delighted squeals. He was still laughing as he set her back down. "Aunt Lucy and Uncle Colin are joining us for dinner. Won't that be nice?"

"Do I have to wear my fancy clothes?" she asked with a little frown.

"How do we dress when we have visitors for dinner?"

"In fancy clothes."

"Right you are," he said. "Let's have Jeannie help you change into one of your new dresses and put your hair up with some of those classy ribbons. You'll be pretty as a picture."

He went to inspect the dining room, nodding in approval at the array of fine china and rows of silverware lined up like sentinels beside each place setting. In the center of the table stood porcelain serving bowls and silver candlesticks. This wasn't how he or Lucy grew up, but his brother-in-law had attended school with Queen Victoria's grandchildren and took this sort of dining for granted. Nick wanted Sadie to, as well.

Lucy and Colin arrived, and she pressed a fancy apple tart into his hands as she and Colin breezed inside. "Where is this woman I've been hearing so much about?" she asked. "The world-famous research scientist?"

"She couldn't make it," Nick said gruffly. "Off performing her world-famous research duties."

Maybe he'd exaggerated the "world-famous" part a bit. Rosalind avoided publicity like a bat fleeing sunshine, but he was proud of her and wanted to show her off. More than that, he wanted to introduce her to his family. Maybe it was a little premature, but he was tired of being alone, and Rosalind seemed as eager as he. That was what he adored about her. She was refreshingly open, without a trace of artifice.

"How was the funeral?" Lucy asked the moment they were all seated. Her voice was cool, but she couldn't mask the curiosity on her face.

"Sad," he said. It was the only word he could think of to describe the half a dozen mourners standing awkwardly before a feast prepared for hundreds.

"And Margaret didn't serve you a poisoned cup?" Colin asked.

The disdain in his voice rubbed Nick the wrong way. Margaret wasn't a perfect woman, but Nick didn't delight in seeing her crushed beneath a wall of grief and complete social ostracism.

"She was hanging in there," he said. Barely. Her husband was dead, her adored son was in jail, and the daughter she'd never seemed to want was nowhere to be seen. It still bothered him that he hadn't seen Ellie in almost twenty years. He twisted the stem of his water goblet, staring at it and wondering how to frame his question. "Do you have any contacts in Rome?" he asked Lucy. As a telegraph operator for the AP, Lucy received transmissions from journalists stationed all over the world. He knew enough about the way telegraph operators gossiped with each other over the wires to suspect she might know someone in Italy.

"The AP has four or five correspondents in Rome, but I don't have any special affiliation. Why?"

"Aunt Margaret says Ellie is living in Rome. That she's a famous pianist. Is it true?"

"I have no idea," Lucy said with a shrug. "I haven't thought of Ellie in years."

"Who is Ellie?" Colin asked.

"She's Aunt Margaret's other child," Lucy replied. "She was a surprise baby and a lot younger than Tom Jr. It was so strange. Margaret doted on Tom as though the sun rose and set on him, but never had any time for Ellie and always shunted her aside. It was hard not to feel sorry for her. She was so eager to play with the rest of us, but Tom was so horrid to her that inevitably she'd start to wail and cry. Then Margaret would swoop in and order Ellie from the room. Usually to go practice on the piano."

Ellie had showed remarkable talent for so young a child, but she didn't seem to enjoy it much. All she'd wanted was a little attention from the older kids. Nick was the only one who ever gave it to her, but he wished he'd been kinder.

"If Ellie has become a well-known pianist in Europe, it would be reported in the newspapers, right?" he asked.

"Possibly," Colin replied. "The news agencies get reports of concerts when a composer debuts a new piece or when royalty are in attendance. So sometimes yes, sometimes no."

That wasn't good enough. Nick's curiosity had been stoked, and he wanted to know more than just where Ellie was. He needed to know what had happened to her. Now that Uncle Thomas was dead, it was time for this family feud to end.

"Don't you think it's strange that she's never returned to New York? Aunt Margaret and Uncle Thomas spoiled Tom Jr., even though he never did anything noteworthy other than plot and scheme. And they've supposedly got a daughter who has kings and princes coming to hear her play, but they never breathe a word of it? I don't buy it."

Lucy picked at the fish on her plate. "This flounder is so tender. I wonder if your chef might share the recipe?"

"Would you please stick to the topic?" Nick asked in exasperation. "Can you ask one of those AP reporters in Rome if they know of a piano player named Ellie Drake?"

"Nick, you're being ridiculous. That's not how it works."

"Then tell me what to do!" he exploded. "I need to find out what happened to her. She's *family*, Luce. Don't you get that?"

Sadie's face screwed up at the sudden tension in the room, and he hauled her onto his lap to bounce her on his knee.

"I get family, Nick, and we've always had a good one," Lucy said, her voice a combination of hurt and exasperation. "I never considered the Saratoga Drakes to be in any way related to me. They were merely snakes who lurked in my nightmares, ready to lash out, steal, and squash us. Through everything, you and I were always united. We walked through fire together and came out stronger on the other side. I wouldn't recognize Ellie Drake if she knocked on my front door. You wouldn't either."

Wrong. Ellie's forest-green eyes welling with tears as her mother dragged her away from family gatherings haunted him to this day. It wasn't possible to forget eyes like that. From the day he was old enough to wear long trousers, he'd always felt protective of the women in his life. Whether it was making sure Lucy's childhood tricycle was in good working order or opening a door for a lady on the street, women were to be protected. Sometimes he could be a little blunt about it, but he didn't know how to stop. Something told him that Ellie was in trouble, and he wanted her to know she wasn't alone in the world.

"Sorry, Lucy," he said with a casual air. "Don't think anything about it."

Colin set down his fork, his face unusually somber. "Don't trust Margaret Drake," he warned. "That woman is a viper and doesn't know how to be anything else."

Wrong. Margaret had gotten a college degree and was helping the poorest immigrant women in the city learn to speak English. There had to be some good in her somewhere.

"I hear you, Colin."

That didn't mean Nick was going to pay any attention to him.

Chapter TEN

Rosalind scrutinized the water sample beneath the microscope. It was the thirtieth sample she'd tested this afternoon, and it was as good as the others Dr. Leal had collected from various points throughout the city. Their test was working.

Soon there would be more testing than the two of them could handle on their own. Dr. Leal had agreed to use students from the nearby college to help. By the end of the week, they would have an additional twelve students to collect and test samples.

As she recorded her findings in her notebook, a chugging noise from outside broke her concentration. Nick was the only person she knew who had an automobile, and she darted to the window to look.

It was him! She was partly thrilled, partly horrified that Nick was here. He'd arrived in his ridiculously glamorous automobile with a little girl beside him. His daughter? Rosalind dropped the notebook and raced down the hallway and out the door. Maybe she could find out what they wanted before he had a chance to get inside the lab.

The rackety engine sputtered to a halt, and Nick met her gaze, stopping her in her tracks with his dazzling white smile.

"Dr. Werner!" he shouted as he vaulted out of the car. "You're back." He gave her a wide smile.

"Pardon?"

He strode to the other side of the automobile and lifted the girl out of the vehicle. "We were here earlier this morning and knocked on the door. We must have missed you."

"Oh."

"This is my daughter, Sadie," Nick said with pride. "Sadie, this is Miss Rosalind."

My goodness, Nick's daughter was a pretty little thing, looking up at Rosalind with curiosity in her wide blue eyes. Her dark hair was pinned to let sausage curls dangle from the crown of her head.

"It's very nice to meet you," Rosalind said, not quite sure how to speak to a child.

Nick's smile was part eager, part nervous. "I thought it would be a good idea for the two of you to meet because . . . well, just because, I guess."

"I'm glad you stopped by," she said, even though she wasn't. If she'd known he was coming, she would have put away the large map of Jersey City that showed the testing locations. The map was clearly labeled "chlorine concentrations."

"We stopped by around ten o'clock this morning, but there was no one here," Nick said. That was because she had gone to meet Dr. Leal out at the reservoir to collect more samples.

"We looked in the window," the little girl said.

"I see." The last thing Rosalind wanted was anyone prowling around the lab, even if it was someone as uninformed as Nick and a little child. If they'd seen that map, he would have questions about it.

"Sadie has never been inside a research laboratory, and I wanted to show her."

He was clearly asking to go inside. It was a warm afternoon, and Nick swatted at a gnat that buzzed around his face. Standing out here was awkward, and refusing to let him into the lab might trigger suspicion.

"Then by all means, let's go inside."

Rosalind would have to take the map down and hide the stack of notebooks that had "chlorine concentrations" printed on the front label. Prickles of sweat broke out over her skin as they walked down the dim hallway toward the lab. She didn't think he'd be able to figure out what she was doing, but his unexpected presence rattled her. She would have to lie, and she hated that.

Nick was several paces behind her, holding Sadie's hand as the girl scurried forward. He was telling her not to touch anything and to be on her best behavior for Miss Rosalind.

Rosalind hurried ahead and yanked the map off the wall, then rolled it up. She was wiggling it into a tube as Nick stepped inside the lab.

The first thing Sadie did was lunge toward a row of glass beakers. Rosalind gasped and lifted them away. "Not a good idea to play with the typhoid," she said. The samples were dead, but still. . . .

Nick scooped the girl up, holding her securely against his chest. "I think this will go better if I carry her," he said with a grin.

"Probably."

He looked around the lab. "I thought I might meet Dr. Leal today."

"No, he's out in the field." She declined to add anything else. The less said about their work, the better.

An uncomfortable silence stretched in the room.

"What a pretty dress you're wearing," she said to Sadie.

A sudden surge of bashfulness caused the girl to bury her face in Nick's neck, but Rosalind's comment about the dress was true. It was surely the most expensive dress Rosalind had ever seen on a child, full of lace, pin tucks, and deeply set gores in the short skirt. A child's purse of matching fabric was tied to her wrist, and glossy patent leather shoes completed the outfit.

"We wanted to look our very best to meet Miss Rosalind, didn't we?" Nick prompted, and the girl nodded against his neck, still unwilling to show her face. "I've been telling her about you," he whispered.

"You have?" Rosalind said.

"I think about you all the time," he said in an even softer voice, making her catch her breath. Then the spell was broken as he jostled the child, prompting the girl to lift her head. "Miss Rosalind is going to show you what she does in her lab. She is a very smart lady," he said as he flashed Rosalind a wink.

That wink sent a bolt of electricity straight through her. Somehow, seeing this bold man being so tender with his daughter made him even more appealing, even as Rosalind wished he wasn't here.

Using the most basic terms, she showed Nick's daughter the beakers of water and how she used special magnifying tools to look at things that were too tiny to see. There was no hope of getting a child that young to focus a microscope, so Rosalind decided to show them to the sitting area and serve some cool lemonade from the refrigerator.

Lemonade that had been made with chlorinated water. She hadn't thought about that until the glass was in Sadie's hands, Nick steadying it as she drank. It was perfectly safe, but guilt crashed down on Rosalind at the thought of what Nick would say if he knew his daughter was drinking chlorinated water. The instant Sadie set the glass down, Rosalind moved it to the other side of the sitting area.

"So does Dr. Leal ever spend any time here, or are you doing all the work?" Nick asked.

"He does plenty of work."

Nick snorted. "I've been here three times and never seen him."

"I told you. That's because he's out in the field."

"You don't need to sound so defensive. I wasn't accusing him of anything."

She looked away, wishing his visit hadn't made her so apprehensive. It wasn't Nick's comment that upset her, it was that what happened in Germany still haunted her. "I'm sorry," she said, all the heat in her voice gone. "It can be a delicate situation. Dr. Leal and I work so closely together, and sometimes it can cause unseemly comments. And then if we aren't seen working together, other people assume that either he's doing all the work or I am. It's a no-win situation."

Nick nodded, but he still seemed ill at ease, staring out the window while he appeared to struggle for words. "I saw him testify in court," he said. "He's still a young man. And a widower. Have you . . . I mean, both of you have been to college and share the same interests. It seems to me that you might—"

"No. We don't. There has never been anything but a professional relationship between us." At last she could speak with complete honesty and candor. Dr. Leal was the soul of kindness and professionalism, but she didn't find him attractive in a romantic way.

Silence stretched between them. Nick's gaze wandered around the lab again, lingering on the soil samples in glass jars. She held her breath, hoping he wouldn't ask about them.

"Would you like to go for a drive with me?" he said.

"Yes!" She'd only ridden in an automobile a few times, and she didn't care for the racket, but she'd gladly accept his invitation if it meant getting him out of the lab.

As she slid onto the automobile's bench covered in rich leather with deeply set squabs, Nick walked to the front of the engine and began manipulating cranks and levers to prime the engine.

When he braced one hand against the fender and bent forward to grab a lever on the base of the engine, Sadie scooted to Rosalind's side, pressing her little body against her.

"This is when it happens," the girl said.

"Ready, Sadie?" Nick shouted.

"Ready!"

He gave a mighty jerk on the lever, and the engine roared to life. Oh my! What a loud chugging noise. It made the whole car vibrate.

Nick hopped into the seat beside Rosalind and flashed a grin. "We need to wait a minute until it starts purring," he said.

"Purring?"

"Shh, just listen."

How could she not listen? Even with both hands clamped over her ears, the noise was awful. Then the clatter slowed . . . smoothed . . . and relaxed into a steady hum. She lowered her hands.

"Hear that?" Nick asked. "Beautiful!"

He moved his feet across a series of pedals on the floor, pulled a lever on his left side, and the automobile began backing up. Oh heavens, this was fun. In the past she'd ridden in cars with the bonnets pulled up, but the carriage of Nick's car was open to the sky.

And he was so competent. He seemed entirely at ease as he manipulated the clutch, cranks, and pedals. Some women might be attracted to a man's looks or flirtatious charm. Not her. All it took was a man who could handle machinery and fix things to turn her head.

The bench was tight for the three of them, and Rosalind sat in the middle with only an inch between her and Nick. It felt like she was part of a family, especially when Sadie unexpectedly slipped her little hand inside Rosalind's. The engine was too loud to carry on a normal conversation, but it felt good to simply enjoy the ride without the pressure of conversation.

Nick drove them down the main avenue, past the public library and the courthouse where the water case had been heard. Mercifully, he didn't bring up the court case as they drove along the newly paved roads, his automobile weaving in and around the lumbering wagons and pedestrians. Jersey City was developing so rapidly that it was starting to look like Manhattan, but Rosalind knew a park where they could get some fresh air. Nick obliged, following her directions until they arrived at a park where a brook attracted local fishermen and grassy areas proved irresistible to boys eager to toss a ball around.

"What now?" Nick asked after he brought the car to a halt and turned off the engine.

"We have a nice afternoon in the park," Rosalind said.

Nick leaned forward to look at Sadie. "What do you think, Sadie? Are you up for a day in the park?"

"I don't know." The child looked a little anxious as she scanned the wide open green space.

Nick walked around the car and lifted her out. "I'm afraid you're going to have to show us how to have a nice afternoon in the park," he said. "I'm not much for the outdoors."

Was he serious? But there was no teasing in his expression as he helped her alight from the car. Rosalind spent every free moment she could get walking through the countryside or boating on a nearby lake. She'd always been something of a country mouse, while Nick was certainly a man of the city.

"Let's begin by having a stroll toward the river," she said. "You don't enjoy being outside?"

He shrugged. "I'm city-born and bred. I'm just not used to it, I suppose."

"Oh, there's nothing I love more than walking beneath a

green canopy of leaves," she said, and he seemed amused by her enthusiasm. "My parents had a summer home in the country, so I've always enjoyed the outdoors."

"I've got a question for you," he said as they drew closer to the river. "You've said enough for me to figure out your family probably came from money, am I right?"

Both her parents came from upper-crust families, the kind who had summer homes in the country and townhouses in the city. Their wealth went back generations and came with boating, horseback lessons, and travel abroad. Still, speaking about money went against her sober German heritage.

"We never lacked for anything," she acknowledged.

"Where did you go to school?" he asked.

"Heidelberg University."

"Not that. I mean when you were little. Did you have a governess or go to a boarding school? Private tutors?"

"Oh heavens, no. My brother and I went to the local school along with everyone else." Her parents had been wealthy, but no one would know it by looking at them. She and Gus wore well-made but plain clothes, her mother wore no jewelry aside from her wedding band, and all the men in the family were expected to be gainfully employed. "Why do you ask?"

Nick took a seat at a picnic table while Sadie went to pick dandelions. Rosalind winced as the girl stepped into a muddy patch, but neither Sadie nor her father seemed to mind the smears of muck on her shiny patent leather shoes.

Rosalind joined Nick at the table, sorry to see that his good humor had fled. He seemed unusually subdued as he watched his daughter yank at the dandelions.

"I want the best for her," he said. "I heard that most rich people send their children away to be educated. It doesn't seem right to me, but I want her to have the best of everything. I don't want people looking down their nose at her if she doesn't speak French or play the harp or whatever it is rich girls are supposed to know how to do. So I want to know how you were raised."

"I don't play the harp or speak French," she admitted. "The only reason I speak German is because I had to move there after my parents and grandfather died. Your daughter will be fine. She's only three, and there's plenty of time before you need to worry about this."

But she couldn't help noticing how oddly the girl was dressed, as though she was about to sit for a formal portrait. Did she always dress like this?

Rosalind phrased her question carefully. "Sadie is very nicely dressed today. Are you going someplace special?"

"Nope," he said casually. "I brought my car across because I need a new distributor on the engine. There's a shop in Jersey City where I buy that sort of thing. I also figured it would be a good excuse to come visit you."

"Is the car in need of repair?" she asked, embarrassed at the hint of panic in her voice. She was entirely ignorant about automobile motors except that they broke down all the time.

His grin was reckless. "Not after this morning. I got it switched out in short order."

"You did it yourself?"

"I wouldn't trust anyone else. When I bought this car, the first thing I did was take the engine entirely apart and rebuild it from the ground up. I'll show you how, if you like."

She was spared a reply when Sadie gleefully jumped into a puddle with both feet.

Nick vaulted from the table and scooped her up. "Look at how you've soaked your pretty shoes," he said, but he didn't seem angry.

Sadie reached down to rub the mud away with her hands, which caused another problem.

"Oh dear, do you have a towel somewhere in your car?" Rosalind asked.

"No need," Nick said, using his handkerchief to wipe the child's hands, then casually tucking the cloth back in his pocket. He hoisted Sadie onto his lap to watch boys playing stickball in the nearby field.

"She really ought to wash her hands," Rosalind said. "With soap. And those shoes will be ruined if they aren't treated properly."

Nick shrugged. "She's got a dozen more just like them."

"So is this how she dresses every day?"

"Most days. As I said, I want her to have the very best."

Rosalind thought the best for a girl that age would be comfortable play clothes, but Nick hadn't stopped speaking.

"Whatever it takes, Sadie will have it. Private tutors, dance lessons, languages. From the day Sadie was born, I made sure she had the best. I hired the most expensive doctor in Manhattan to attend Bridget at her delivery, and had private nurses on hand to tend the baby, especially since Bridget . . . well, someone needed to look after the baby since Bridget got sick pretty quickly."

"You had a home birth?"

He nodded. "I wasn't going to send my wife to a public hospital. I wanted her to have the comfort of her own home, with the full attention of the best doctors and nurses. That never happens in a hospital where the doctors are tending dozens of other people at the same time."

Rosalind closed her mouth and looked away. Hospitals had a far better track record for safely delivering babies than mothers who gave birth at home, mostly because hospitals practiced routine sanitary measures that were impossible to replicate in a home setting. A good hospital had tile floors and metal tables that were regularly scrubbed with disinfectant, and the bedding was bleached after each use. Such measures were impossible to replicate at home, where sanitary concerns were usually limited to having a doctor wash his hands before examining a patient.

"How did your wife die?" she asked softly.

"Childbed fever," he said brusquely.

It was a catchall term for any bacterial infection following the delivery of a child. It could happen in a hospital, but the rates of childbed fever shot up during home deliveries. In securing the best for his wife, Nick may well have contributed to her death.

Sadie started chewing on her fingers, and Rosalind instinctively tugged them down. Nick sent her a disapproving look.

"Her hands are filthy," she said defensively. "Perhaps we can head back to the lab. We have a washroom she can use."

"A little dirt never killed a child," he said in a mild tone. "When I was a boy, we played handball in the back alley with rubbish pulled out of trash cans."

She stood, refusing to comment on his childhood standards. "But you want the best for Sadie, and I think that means washing the germs from her hands. I know it doesn't sound logical, but a microscopic germ can shut down an entire immune system. It can infect the digestive tract, cause the respiratory system to fail. It can kill a healthy woman who just gave birth; it happened to your wife!"

Nick's mouth compressed into a hard line as he scooped Sadie up and stalked over to the public fountain, leaning over so the girl could dunk her hands in the splash pool.

"Happy?" The censure in his tone hurt, but he had a right to be angry over her implication that Bridget could have died due to careless hygiene.

"Nick, I'm sorry. Of course I have no way of knowing for sure. . . ."

"That's right, you don't," he snapped as he carried Sadie back toward the car.

Their day in the park was obviously over. He didn't say a

word as he cranked the engine back to noisy life, sparing Rosalind the need to make conversation on the ride back to the lab. Guilt raced through her. She shouldn't have mentioned his wife.

The ride was bumpy as the car jostled over potholes that he didn't bother to avoid. Rosalind eyed his knuckles, white as he clenched the steering wheel. The automobile sputtered to a stop outside the lab, and he turned to her, his eyes unexpectedly somber and full of regret.

"I've never considered that Bridget might have been put in danger by not going to a hospital. I only wanted the best for her, but I'm sorry I lashed out at you. Sometimes the truth is hard. So hard I wish I could run away from it and never look back, because it makes me sick inside." He sighed and looked away as if drained of energy. "I shouldn't have groused at you for telling me the truth, even if I didn't want to hear it. Don't ever be afraid of telling me the truth."

This pain-filled confession was the last thing she expected, and his honesty was humbling. Would he still be so conciliatory if he knew about the chlorine that was even now being mixed into the water supply?

He had just handed her the perfect opportunity to tell him about their plan. She swallowed hard, trying to find the right words. He wouldn't be happy. He'd probably storm and rage and want to confront Dr. Leal immediately, but Nick might be able to help them. He was more open-minded than she'd originally assumed.

But when she opened her mouth, she took the easy way out.

"I should get back to work," she said before shuffling out of the car and slinking back to the laboratory like a coward.

The money Rosalind had inherited from her parents was not nearly as abundant as it once had been. When she arrived in

America three years ago, Dr. Leal was in desperate need of a qualified research assistant but had no funding to pay for one. She needed an opportunity to prove her scientific credentials in America, and in Dr. Leal she found an open-minded man whose research interests perfectly dovetailed her own. It was a mutually beneficial relationship, but it did not pay the bills.

Fortunately Rosalind had stumbled into a unique opportunity shortly after arriving in New Jersey. Elmore Kleneman, better known as Doctor Clean, was a soap manufacturer whose home-brew cleaning solution proved remarkably successful. Marketed as "Doctor Clean," the solution was inexpensive and easy to use, making it wildly popular across the United States. Unlike most disinfectants, Doctor Clean had a pleasing pine scent, and housewives liked it so much that they started using it in their laundry and dishes in addition to scrubbing their floors.

Elmore Kleneman was on the verge of selling public shares in his company when his New York investors had insisted he prove his claim with scientific tests. Elmore had no medical training, but the name of his product implied a medical stamp of approval, and that was where Rosalind came in. She ran tests with the cleaning solution, verifying that it did indeed kill germs as well as the more toxic disinfectants did.

Strapped for cash after investing in a huge manufacturing facility, Elmore had offered to pay Rosalind for her work in stock instead of cash. It had been a blessing in disguise. One half of one percent didn't sound like much, but it provided a welcome cushion for her strained finances.

This morning, Elmore was hosting a picnic at his new house to celebrate the three-year anniversary of Doctor Clean. All of his employees and their families had been invited, which was why Gus had accompanied Rosalind to the Kleneman estate.

She was desperately glad for his company, for last week she'd had a strange letter from Doctor Clean's accountant, offering to buy her shares back now that the company was so successful. Peter Schmidt's letter had been politely worded, suggesting that perhaps Rosalind would welcome a cash buyout rather than the modest quarterly revenue payments she had been receiving. The letter worried her. She'd been so stunned at the prospect of her only income drying up that she had yet to respond. She wanted Gus by her side as she talked to Peter face-to-face.

"I'll introduce you to Peter," Rosalind told Gus as they walked up the curving path toward the cottage-style mansion nestled amidst a rolling natural landscape. "He's the accountant who did the paperwork for my stock and handles the quarterly payments."

"So long as he keeps signing those checks, I'm a happy man," Gus said as they drew closer. They rarely discussed it, but money had been tight ever since he and Ingrid moved in with her. Her grocery bill had tripled, and the law school classes necessary to get Gus back on his feet were shockingly expensive, which made Rosalind's determination to secure her position in the company all the stronger.

A servant directed them around the side of the house, where the picnic was already well under way. Elmore Kleneman was a family man, which was why he always held his annual gatherings at a time when spouses and children could be part of the festivities.

"Dr. Werner!" Elmore boomed as he saw her heading toward the gazebo. He looked like Santa Claus, with white hair, a neatly groomed white beard, and smiling eyes. He had married late in life but was making up for lost time by producing a large family in short order. He had a toddler riding on his shoulders and a young child carried over one arm. "I hope you're hungry. We have enough roasted ham to choke an army."

The food was laid out on a picnic table weighed down with huge bowls of sweet potato salad, baked beans, and corn on the cob. A servant carved slices of roasted ham onto a platter, while guests used freshly baked rolls to make their own sandwiches. Rosalind loved that even though Elmore was wealthy beyond imagination, he refused to adopt the stuffy airs of the elite. His annual picnics were relaxed affairs where guests loaded their plates with mounds of food and ate with their hands, and children were welcome to play and shriek with laughter.

She had just finished filling her plate at the buffet table when Peter Schmidt appeared at her side.

"Hello, Rosalind." Peter smiled as he reached for a slice of watermelon and added it to his plate. "Did you get my letter last week?"

This was it. She loathed conflict and feared this discussion had the potential to become quarrelsome. "I did. Yes, I did, and I was hoping to speak with you about it."

"Of course." He looked momentarily befuddled, but he gestured to a spot near the corner of the yard where picnic tables had been set up.

She waited until Gus joined them before speaking. "The offer to buy me out was generous, but I must take the long-term needs of my family into consideration."

Peter peered at her over the wedge of watermelon, confusion on his face as he finished chewing. "That's what I was thinking as well. I know your brother is in law school, and those bills can clobber a person flat. I thought you might welcome the chance to cash out and get a big infusion of money to help."

"Did Mr. Kleneman suggest this?" Gus asked, his tone casual, but Rosalind recognized the carefully worded probing beneath the question. Elmore Kleneman maintained a controlling interest over the company, and Peter Schmidt was only the hired accountant. It was important to know where the impetus for this offer originated.

Peter shook his head. "No need to trouble Elmore about

this," he said. "It was entirely my idea. I remember from when I was putting my son through college how tight finances can be."

"I'd prefer to keep the stock as a long-term investment," she said. "If it's not too much trouble, that is."

Peter laughed. "No trouble at all! In fact, it saves me the bother of preparing buyout papers. Why do you look so concerned?"

Relief loosened the stiffness in her spine, and she managed a genuine smile. "I'm sorry, you've been very kind. I simply hate discussing money."

"Not me!" Peter said. "I love everything about money. Counting it, investing it, figuring out how to balance a financial portfolio. I even collect rare coins for the sheer joy of watching how foreign cultures express themselves through the artwork they engrave on their money."

"You're a coin collector?" Gus asked.

Peter snorted. "My wife would say I'm a coin hoarder. Last year I stumbled across a stash of uncirculated coins minted by the Confederates. They aren't very valuable, but I can't bear to part with a single one."

Gus's eyes lit up. "I've got a collection of thaler coins from Bavaria. We should get together and compare collections."

The conversation drifted to the men's shared interest in coin collecting, something Rosalind found as engrossing as old shoe leather, but it was nice to see Gus enjoying himself, and her relief that no one was trying to push her out of the company was palpable. She was lucky to have stumbled into this opportunity, even though she and Elmore Kleneman could not be more different. While she came from an old and established family, Elmore's wealth was entirely new.

Like Nick's. What a difference in the way Elmore and Nick were raising their family. Elmore's passel of six children were dressed in normal play clothes and ate the kind of food typical of any working-class household. It was much like her own upbringing, rich in experiences rather than material goods. Her parents provided music lessons and hikes through the forest for bird-watching. Their house contained musical instruments and books on every topic under the sun.

As soon as Peter left, she turned to Gus. "Do you ever wonder what our parents would think of how we turned out?" To the bottom of her soul, she hoped they would be proud.

"Not really," Gus said gently. "They seem so far away to me."

"I suppose so." But she couldn't help looking up at the sky—a beautiful, cloudless sky—and praying they were out there, still looking down on them and proud of what she and Gus had managed to become.

I still remember you, she thought as she scanned the brilliant, sheltering sky. *And I thank God for the wonderful foundation you gave us. A thousand times, thank you.*

It was nice to imagine the gentle breeze was perhaps a message from Mama and Papa, that they were there, and that they heard her.

Chapter ELEVEN

Nick's new position as commissioner of the State Water Board came with a top-floor office and a commanding view of the East River. As Nick stared out his office window, he figured most people would see the monumental Brooklyn Bridge or the majestic buildings that climbed higher into the sky each year.

He didn't. When he looked at the city, he saw every manhole cover and sewer drain, instantly remembering the labyrinth of tunnels beneath the city streets. The most impressive monuments in New York weren't the skyscrapers, the bridges, or the park system that was the envy of the world. No, the most impressive engineering feat of this city was the underground system of tunnels and pumps that brought millions of gallons of water in and out of the island each day. That infrastructure was invisible to most people; never to him.

As hard as he'd fought for this appointment, the reality of the job was daunting. New York City was running out of water, and a mammoth new reservoir was about to break ground upstate. On its face, his job involved coordinating the politicians, engineers, and labor union officials to complete the next stage of the water tunnels.

In actuality, it involved uprooting thousands of people, destroying their livelihoods, and forcing them off their land in order to quench New York's thirst for water. Five towns were going to be wiped off the map in order to create the reservoir, and Nick was the man responsible for the wiping. He'd be a naïve idiot if he didn't realize his reputation for bare-knuckle toughness had been the primary consideration for his appointment. The coming year was going to be a rough ride as he laid the groundwork for the reservoir. People liked him in Manhattan; they hated him in upstate New York.

Nevertheless, someone had to do the job, and he had the backbone to see it through. Three times a week, he met with his two fellow commissioners. The governor insisted that the water board be headed by a team of three commissioners to avoid any hint of corruption. Fortunately, Nick liked and respected his colleagues. General Mike O'Donnell, who had earned his renown as a sanitary engineer during the Spanish-American War, was the commissioner for engineering, and Fletcher Jones was the commissioner of finance responsible for the mind-boggling task of figuring out how to pay for a project that was going to be second only to the Panama Canal in terms of size and scope.

On the weekends, Nick tried to fit in a golf game with his fellow commissioners or other men involved in the water project. Golf was a stupid sport he loathed and would never play again if he didn't love it so much. He'd taken private lessons a couple of years ago when he realized how much business was conducted on a golf course.

On Saturday morning, he headed out to enjoy a game with some colleagues in the water business. Given the looming expiration of Dr. Leal's ninety-day extension, conversation eventually worked its way to the court case.

"The city's budget is in limbo until the judge issues his final ruling over their new water system," Jake Paulson said. Jake was in charge of sanitation for Jersey City and had worked closely with Nick during the court case. "Even if we win a complete victory, I expect the water company to declare bankruptcy before they build another filtration plant. They can't afford it."

Nick did his best to ignore the chatter as he aligned himself over the ball. The driver made a satisfying slice through the air as the ball shot heavenward, tracing a graceful arc and bouncing onto the green. He'd shot wide. Probably because his concentration had been ruined by the discussion about that court case. Anything involving Rosalind could completely shatter his concentration, but in a good way.

"I would never underestimate Dr. Leal," General O'Donnell said. "If anyone can figure out a way to turn in a coherent argument, it's Leal."

The trio began walking down the fairway for their next shot, but the conversation soured quickly.

"I admire Dr. Leal, but what do you think about that woman who works in his lab?" Jake's voice was light as he answered his own question. "She's pretty, I'll grant you that . . . but who would want to make love to an iceberg?"

"Apparently she's no iceberg," General O'Donnell said. "Rumor has it they have a spot in the Florida Keys where they spend two weeks every spring. Seaside fishing, frolicking in the sun, or whatever else a man does on a tropical island with his research assistant."

"That's a lie," Nick said. The words lashed out before he could stop them, but he couldn't stand here and listen to Rosalind be smeared like this.

General O'Donnell chuckled as he lined up for his next stroke. "Everyone says Dr. Leal is as sober as a monk, but come on, man. He's been a widower for almost a decade. A man doesn't hire an assistant who looks like *that* if he isn't sneaking a little on the side."

It went against everything Nick knew about Rosalind. Her prim demeanor, her forthright honesty. The idea of her sneaking off for trysts with her employer seemed too seedy for someone as straitlaced as Rosalind. Then again, maybe he was only seeing what he wanted to believe.

He stepped forward to take his shot. With two prominent men in the water industry and three caddies standing nearby, he had to handle this carefully. Rosalind's reputation hung in the balance.

"Slander is an ugly salvo," he said. "Dr. Werner is an attractive woman, and Dr. Leal is a man with eyes in his head, but it's ridiculous to use those facts to spin a vulgar story about two honorable people."

Silence settled over the fairway as he hit the ball with a gentle *snick*. For the rest of the game, there was no more scandalous gossip about Rosalind.

But he thought about it the entire afternoon.

Nick headed straight for the subway the instant the game was over. What he'd heard this afternoon could be only malicious gossip, but maybe not. Rosalind swore there was nothing between her and Dr. Leal, but it did seem unusual for a man and a woman to work so closely in a wholly platonic fashion. What red-blooded man could work alongside a woman like Rosalind and not let it affect him? Nick had been attracted to her within three seconds, and Dr. Leal had been working with her for three years.

Rosalind was free to dally with whomever she chose; she'd made no promises to him. But what he'd heard on the golf course infuriated him. Either Rosalind was catting around with her business partner, or two men he respected were smearing the reputation of an innocent woman. Both were galling. He wouldn't be able to rest until he gave Rosalind a chance to defend herself. And he knew exactly where she'd be. With the clock ticking on their ninety-day extension, Rosalind had been working seven days a week to expedite their research.

He'd worked himself into a twist by the time he approached the squat building housing her lab, so he stood for a few moments outside her door, forcing himself to breathe at a normal rate. If there was any truth to the rumor, he'd accept it. He had no right to probe into her private life, but from their first few minutes together in Sal's Diner, he'd jumped to all sorts of conclusions about her. That she was smart and brimming with integrity and, well . . . pure. Pretty as a moonbeam.

He knocked on the door of the lab and entered without waiting for an answer. Rosalind sat at a table, her back ramrod straight as she made notes on a pad. Mercifully, she was alone. This conversation would have been much more awkward with Dr. Leal in the room.

She was wearing her spectacles but took them off when she spotted him. "Nick," she said as she rose. "I hadn't expected to see you again so soon. I've been worrying that I offended you."

He bit off a cynical laugh and looked away. Their tiff in the park seemed so frivolous now.

"Because offending you was the last thing in the world I intended," she continued. "It's obvious you dote on your daughter, but cleanliness is important—"

"I'm not here about Sadie."

"Oh."

Her gaze darted over the open notebooks spread across the laboratory table. He had no idea what her daily work involved, but it seemed as if a pile of paperwork had exploded across the work surface, the pages dense with charts, maps, and equations. Stacks of index cards littered a table in front of racks filled with test tubes. Some had clear liquid inside, others looked like they held dirt.

"Let me put a few things away," she said hastily, closing the notebooks and then reaching for a cloth to drape over the test tubes. She'd done the same the last time he paid an unexpected visit. Perhaps it was some sort of laboratory procedure to close everything down when stepping away from an experiment.

He rubbed the back of his neck, scrambling for a delicate way to start this conversation. "I played golf this morning," he said awkwardly.

"Yes?" She sounded startled. Golf was a snooty game only country club people played, and she was probably surprised he knew how to swing a club.

"Yeah. I mostly hate it, but I kind of love it too. Anyway, it's good business. I get a chance to talk to people in the government and industry I should know." He moved a few steps farther into the lab. He hadn't changed clothes from this morning and felt a little grubby and clumsy, especially since he was about to dig into her private life, but he had to know. "Anyway, I was playing with one of the other commissioners. He used to be a sanitary engineer in the army—"

"General O'Donnell?"

"Yes. Do you know him?"

"Dr. Leal does. I've never formally met him, but I've read his reports and am familiar with his work. His development of sanitary procedures for mobile army encampments is extraordinary."

He wondered if she would be so complimentary if she knew the filth O'Donnell spread about her behind her back.

"They were talking about Dr. Leal. And you."

The color dropped from her face, and she went very still. It looked like she suspected what he was getting at, and it made his chest tighten. He didn't want it to be true.

"What were they saying?" she asked stiffly.

"That Dr. Leal has a hideaway in the Florida Keys. That you go with him."

"That's a lie," she snapped. "He takes his son to Florida every summer, but I have never accompanied him. I've never socialized with Dr. Leal outside of work. Ever. I don't even call him by his first name, and we've been working together for three solid years." Her words came rapidly. "I don't know how to fend off this sort of talk. I make sure to dress conservatively. I don't flirt or discuss personal issues, I confine myself to discussions about science." Her voice was high and fast, shaking in agitation.

"If you deny it, I believe you."

But it seemed she hadn't heard. She paced the aisle between the tables, both hands clenched. "People talk and gossip, and I don't know how to stop it. I didn't do *anything* to cause this, and still the wagging tongues stir up poison."

"I'll tell them it's hogwash. If they don't stop spreading rumors, I'll sue them for slander." He had no idea if he could sue on someone else's behalf, but he had plenty of money and would do anything to soothe her agitation. He wished he'd never raised this subject, because he'd rather plunge his own hand into a fire than cause her a moment of pain.

She stopped and looked at him, her face cynical. "And do you think suing them will repair my reputation?"

"It couldn't hurt."

"Wrong. It will pour gasoline on the fire and ruin my professional standing, just like it did in Germany."

His brows lowered. "What happened in Germany?"

Her shoulders sagged, and it looked like she aged ten years. "I don't want to talk about this," she said softly, reaching for a shawl. "I need to get out. Go for a walk. Thank you for telling me, but I need to be alone right now."

She headed for the door, and he followed.

"I'll walk with you." He wasn't going to leave her in this mood. Guilt washed through him for bringing the gossip to her attention.

"Please don't."

He dragged a hand through his hair. "Look, I shouldn't have said anything. I can't just walk away when you're miserable and it's all my doing."

A set of keys jangled as she locked the door to the laboratory. He followed her down the hall and stepped out into the sunshine, after which she locked that door too. Her hand remained on the handle even after she locked it, and she kept her back to him.

"I'm asking you to please go away," she said. "I'll be perfectly fine, but I need a little fresh air, and walking always helps." She looked up at him, her pale blue eyes clear but full of anguish. "Please."

He was helpless to deny her anything. Letting her go off alone went against every instinct in his body, but he'd done enough damage for the day. He nodded, loitering by the closed doorway.

He'd give her space, but she was fooling herself if she thought he'd abandon her.

Rosalind walked the quarter mile to the candy factory. It smelled like maple fudge this afternoon. Normally she liked it, but it seemed cloyingly sweet today. Or maybe she'd feel nauseated no matter what the factory made. She braced her hands on the top of the picket fence and struggled to control her breathing.

Did the rumors spring up on their own, or had gossip from Germany finally arrived on American shores? She swallowed hard and leaned her elbows on the waist-high fence, watching men from the factory wheel crates out of the warehouse. The rumors were the least of her concerns. More worrisome was whether she had made the right decision in secretly chlorinating the water without the population's knowledge or consent.

This was the second time Nick had surprised her while she was calculating the effect of chlorine on local soil samples. Now that the feed system had been in place for two weeks, some of that water was being used to irrigate local farms. Dr. Leal had been diligently gathering samples, and she tested them for residual traces of chlorine in the soil. It was drastically different work than what she'd been doing a month ago, and a trained researcher would be able to spot it. Had Nick?

It took ten minutes for the men to load the wagon, and she didn't move a muscle as she watched. The factory's lot was a grassy, tree-shaded patch of land amidst the urban environment. When she closed her eyes, the rustling of leaves and green scent in the air reminded her of happier times in Germany. Back before her world fell apart.

Well. Standing here wasn't going to repair the damage, and she had more soil samples to analyze. She pushed away from the fence and straightened her blouse.

And saw Nick Drake, leaning against a fence post ten yards away.

"How long have you been standing there?" she asked.

He closed the distance between them. "A while. You okay?" He settled in beside her along the fence.

"Yes." She turned to face the candy factory again, unexpectedly moved by the protective kindness on his face. "Sometimes you work so hard toward a goal, and it can all come collapsing down so quickly."

"Are you talking about what happened in Germany?"

"Yes." And maybe it would happen here too. At least Dr. Leal wasn't married.

"You can tell me about it, if you want. I won't judge." His offer was plainly spoken, his eyes soft.

Still she hesitated. A vibrant sense of kinship hummed between them, but that didn't mean she could trust him.

"Rosalind, whatever it is, just tell me. The good Lord knows I'm nowhere close to being perfect."

Nick was so straightforward, but beneath his plainspoken and rough demeanor, he was endlessly kind and supportive. And she wanted to tell him. She had so many secrets and regrets bottled up inside, but this was one she could release.

"I went to college in Heidelberg," she said, her mind traveling back to those enchanted years in the deeply forested valleys and steep fields of grapes. She was eleven when she and Gus were sent to the Bavarian countryside after their grandfather died. Her father's brother lived in an old half-timbered farmhouse, and he and his family raised cows. Soon she and Gus were milking cows and making cheese alongside her cousins, and before long they spoke German well enough to fit in. Her German relatives lived simply but were rich in both land and investments.

While the family worked the farm, her uncle taught chemistry at Heidelberg University. Rosalind had been enchanted by the medieval university, with its gothic architecture and red-tiled roofs. Whenever she imagined what paradise looked like, she saw Heidelberg University.

Her uncle had warned her that the college did not accept women, but she couldn't stop hoping, and Uncle Wilhelm encouraged her dreams. When she was seventeen, she submitted her school marks, letters of recommendation from her uncle and the village schoolteachers, and most importantly, her essay about why she wanted to study.

She wanted to find a cure for cholera. She had always been captivated by the world of medicine, and after watching how fast cholera could rip through a community, she wanted to join the quest to find a cure.

The college never formally admitted her, but out of respect for her uncle and curiosity about the girl who wrote with such passion, they allowed her to attend classes and hire a private tutor. Over the years, she worked with a series of professors, and her interest veered away from medicine and into biochemistry.

It became apparent that it would be easier to eradicate cholera from the environment rather than cure a patient who had already contracted it. Uncle Wilhelm had breathed a sigh of relief when she informed him of her intentions, for he feared that in conservative Germany, no one would consent to be treated by a woman physician.

When she was twenty-one years old, she graduated with a degree despite never having been formally admitted. Then she earned a doctorate through private study, researching how chemicals could affect bacteria in water.

As part of her studies, she'd moved to the college's remote research station high in the mountains above the city. There she lived with other scientists studying forestry, hydrology, geology, and all manner of flora and fauna. The lodge had laboratories, a library, a dormitory, and a large room for communal dining and conversation. As the only female scientist, Rosalind shared a bedroom with the housekeeper and the two maids. Her aunt Fredericka worried that there was no official chaperone, but Uncle Wilhelm had been dismissive. Frau Bergmann had been the housekeeper at the research station for thirty years and was a respected woman who would tolerate no nonsense among the boarders.

"After college I moved to the Berghütte Research Station, ready to conquer the impossible by ridding the world of cholera," she told Nick. How naïve she had been to think it would be so easy. It was a monumental task, but with the boundless optimism of youth, she was bold enough to try.

"One of the scientists at the station studied pollen spores, another the distribution of chlorophyll in tree leaves. Professor Fischer had lived at the lodge for thirty-five years to study the behavior of honeybees. In the evenings, we would dine on a fine meal prepared by Frau Bergmann, and we would talk long into the night. It was a wonderful place." She couldn't block the note of wistfulness in her voice, for no matter how long she lived, those years would surely be the happiest of her life.

"The station's biologist was a man named Stefan Dittmar. He came from the great wine-growing regions of the Rhenish Palatinate. His family was very old and very rich. His brother was a count, but as a younger son, Stefan was responsible for the family's vineyards. He came to the Berghütte every summer to study the effects of heat on mold spores, as that had been a problem on their vines. We met and became instant friends. When I wandered the hillsides to collect samples, he came along, and we shared what we knew."

Beside her, she could sense Nick's muscles tightening, as did her own. She had been so gullible. She could see that now, but at the time, Stefan had seemed like all the other scientists who were there for research.

"One afternoon when we were collecting water samples, he put his hand on the small of my back while we were climbing up a ledge. It wasn't necessary, for we'd climbed that pass many times. I didn't say anything about it when we reached the summit. I just pulled away a few feet."

Strange—even as she spoke, she could feel the imprint of Stefan's hand on her back. That was the only time he'd laid a finger on her, and yet that afternoon almost destroyed them both.

"That was when he confessed he had powerful feelings for me and hoped I would consider him as a suitor. I was appalled. He was married, and I never once considered him in such a light."

She had been so stunned that she couldn't even move her mouth to speak. When she'd finally found her tongue, all she could do was stammer, "But you're married!"

Stefan had actually smiled. "I can get a divorce. Helga married me for money, and she can still have it after the divorce.

You and I need not concern ourselves with such petty things. We can live at Berghütte forever, make our lives up here, just like Professor Fischer. We will live simply and perform research and love one another."

"Stop! I don't want to hear any more. I'm going back to the lodge, and I don't ever want to speak of this again."

He'd appeared shocked by her rejection, disbelief stamped across his handsome features. "But you must return my affection," he said. "I can feel it. Every day as we explore the woods; when we dine in the evenings."

She behaved exactly the same way with over a dozen scientists, and never had there been a hint of impropriety before this moment. She turned to head back down the steep ridge. He had tried to assist, but she shrugged him away. The thought of letting him touch her was sickening.

The next day, she was studying a chemistry text in the lodge's reading room. Stefan approached and asked to go walking with her. They were alone in the room, so she didn't bother to lower her voice.

"No," she said firmly. "And don't ask again."

He continued to pester for the next week, and finally she spoke to Professor Fischer about the unwanted attentions. With his kindly old eyes and graying beard, Professor Fischer was a father figure to most of the young scientists who spent time at the Berghütte.

"Stefan will not leave me alone," she had told him. "I feel him staring at me all day long. I've tried to avoid him, but he watches me constantly, even when I go to the bathing hut."

"I will speak with him," Professor Fischer had said, his eyes grim.

She turned back to Nick, who watched her with a somber gaze. "Stefan packed his bags and left the following day. I never asked the professor what had been said, but he assured me I would have no more trouble from Herr Dittmar. For a week all was calm, but then the letters began arriving."

They came almost every day. They rambled on obsessively, painting a picture of what their life would be like as soon as his divorce was final. Far from being discouraged by her rejection, Stefan vowed to obtain a divorce as quickly as possible, so "his true life could begin."

"I quit reading the letters, and Professor Fischer wrote to Stefan on my behalf, saying the letters were unwelcome and to stop sending them. He also returned all nine letters that had been written to me. It seemed to work. For a while the letters stopped and life went on as normal. Life was wonderful again."

For about a month. Then a man from the post office arrived with a letter addressed to her from a court in Heidelberg. Remembering that morning made her feel sick all over again.

"I was required to sign for the letter, and that was when I learned I was being sued by Helga Dittmar for alienation of her husband's affections."

Nick looked appalled. "Can they do that?"

"They did."

Rosalind had no knowledge of the law or divorce proceedings, but she'd gotten a hard and fast introduction to it. Stefan had filed for divorce immediately after returning home, stunning his bewildered wife. When the packet of love letters Stefan wrote to Rosalind fell into his wife's hands, she was enraged, lashing out at both her husband and the woman she accused of stealing him away.

"Lawyers arrived at the research station to interview everyone. It was mortifying, even though Professor Fischer verified that he'd reprimanded Stefan for his unwelcome attentions. I tried to go on as before, but nothing was the same. The laughter at the dinner table was not as easy, and when I entered a room, the conversation became stilted. The worst part was sharing a bedroom with the housekeeper and the two maids. Frau Bergmann was mostly polite, but the maids were younger than me, and their attitude turned very disrespectful."

Rosalind had not been able to continue at the Berghütte Research Station after the scandal broke. The preliminary hearings for the court case were held in Heidelberg, and it seemed that wherever she went, she heard people whispering behind her back.

"I know you aren't supposed to care what people think, but I do. The hearings were public, and members of the press filled the galleries of the courtroom."

Gus had been by her side through it all, drawing him into the mess as well. He'd just gotten married to Ingrid and moved into a modest set of rooms in Heidelberg when the scandal hit. Rumors had circulated that he helped facilitate clandestine meetings between her and Stefan, all in hope of linking his family to an aristocratic one in the event that Stefan obtained his divorce and was free to pursue Rosalind. Gus had just begun work at a law firm handling wills and estates, but they let him go in the wake of the scandal.

"The two maids arrived to testify. They claimed I often left our bedroom after dark, and the lawyers painted that in the worst light. In truth, I only left to use the privy, or sometimes I awoke at night with a research idea I felt compelled to write down immediately. That was all, but it was enough for the maids to draw unseemly conclusions. The hearings were covered every day in the newspapers. Men at the beer halls placed bets on what had gone on between me and Stefan. Lurid cartoons showing me chasing after Stefan were published. The judge eventually dismissed the case, but the damage was done."

Staying in Germany had been impossible after that. Her uncle knew Dr. Leal and had written a letter of recommendation. Dr.

Leal was in need of an assistant but couldn't afford to pay for one. She had enough money of her own that she didn't require a salary. All she needed was a chance to prove herself.

"I wanted to disappear, but I couldn't abandon my research. So here I am. These rumors about Dr. Leal and I have grown from nothing but the fact that I am an unmarried woman who has the audacity to work alongside a man."

Nick said nothing as he gazed at another wagon pulling into the factory, this time weighed down with barrels of late summer apples. He had a faint smile on his face.

"Next week I'm delivering a speech in Central Park," he said, still staring at the men as they prepared to unload the apples. "It will be my first speech as commissioner, and a lot of important people will be there. I want you there too."

She perked up. It was flattering that he thought enough of her to issue the invitation, but she didn't understand his abrupt change of topic. "Of course I'll be there, if you want me to."

He turned to look at her. "As a woman I have intentions toward. I want to step out proudly with you on my arm and introduce you to the world as someone I care about. It might help squelch the rumors."

As thrilling as his words were, the prospect of accompanying him made her nervous. If it was an important speech, it meant reporters would be there. "Nick, I try to maintain a low profile."

"If any rumors surface, either about Germany or you and Dr. Leal, I'll shoot them down," he said confidently. "I can have my pick of women in New York, and I pick you. I'll go after anyone who slanders your name. I care about you, Rosalind. We may be different on the outside, but beneath all the manners and accents and background, you and I are like a house on fire. The speech next week is a big step for me, and I could use a friend at my side."

It would be a turning point. She could go through the rest of her life hiding behind her initials and fearing the exposure of a faraway scandal, or she could confront it head on. Nick was willing to stand alongside her. He knew everything about her past yet still looked at her with a combination of hope, determination, and raw strength. It shot a bolt of confidence straight into her soul. There was only one thing to say.

"I would be proud to go with you."

He leaned closer and touched his forehead to hers. With their hands clasped and touching nowhere else but their foreheads, it was the most intimate moment of her life. They were together. They were united. They would venture forth into this uncertain and frightening future side by side, and face whatever challenges came their way together.

She felt buoyant as they walked back to the laboratory. Even as Nick got into his automobile and she waved him off, her heart still soared. The smile lingered on her face until the moment she returned to the lab and saw the white sheet draped over her chlorine research.

That cloth was a blunt reminder of everything she was hiding from Nick. In exchange for his heartfelt honesty, she kept a veil over the most important piece of her world.

Suddenly drained of energy, she lowered herself onto a laboratory stool and fingered the edge of the fabric draped over the testing samples, too heartsick to peel it back and get down to work again. Nick would hate what was beneath this sheet, but he wouldn't hate *her*, would he?

They needed more data, and Nick would try to shut them down if he knew about this. Once they proved chlorine was effective in a real-world experiment, Nick would be more likely to understand why she had to keep it a secret, and he would forgive her. Maybe it was her hopeless optimism again, but Nick was smart and wanted a solution for delivering clean water to the masses. He would come around in the end, and when he did, she would be waiting for him. He might hate what she did, but she couldn't believe he would ever hate *her*, and that gave her the motivation to remove the sheet and resume her work.

Chapter TWELVE

Nick walked proudly beside Rosalind as they headed into Central Park. Tonight's extravaganza was in celebration of breaking ground on the mammoth Catskill Aqueduct. There would be plenty of important men making speeches tonight, but it was Nick's first foray into public speaking, and he hated to admit it, but he was nervous. Hundreds of people had already flooded the park for the free food and music that would be offered after the speeches.

The stage for the speakers had been erected alongside the Central Park reservoir. Most people who saw the pristine body of water surrounded by miles of parkland assumed it was a natural lake. It wasn't. It was a man-made reservoir completed in 1862 and fed by the Croton Aqueduct with water funneled from miles away. The reservoir had been supplying the city with drinking water for decades, but it could no longer keep up with demand. Tonight, Nick's job was to sell people on the need for a monumental new aqueduct, covering 163 miles and costing over a hundred million dollars.

He wore a custom-tailored suit and had arrived in the finest of carriages, for he wanted Rosalind to be proud of him. As they walked toward the lake, he filled her in on what to expect.

"My sister and her husband are meeting us, so you won't be alone during the speeches. Colin and Lucy have been married for five years, no kids. Don't ask. Colin is from England and a bit of a prig, but he's okay beneath all the starch. He wrote most of my speech tonight."

"I could have helped with the speech," Rosalind said as they walked beneath trees strung with miniature electric lights. "After all, I know a thing or two about water."

Nick hid a smile. He'd finally gotten around to reading some of Rosalind's research papers, and they were so lethally dull that he'd be accused of abusing the public if he let her write his speech. The idea was appalling, but she looked wounded that he hadn't asked. She genuinely wanted to help, and it moved him.

"I'm not speaking to your college professors tonight, I'm speaking to the masses. And Colin knows how to write a speech that rouses the populace. I think it's something they breed into the aristocracy over there."

"Aristocracy?" Rosalind asked.

He'd forgotten that salient point. "Yeah. Who'd have thought my little sister would marry into blue blood?"

He took her arm and guided her toward the pavilion erected on the north end of the reservoir. A podium rested atop a raised dais, and workers scrambled to hang patriotic bunting across the front. A few hundred chairs had been set out for the invited spectators. The chairs were roped off, lest any of the riffraff try to sit in them. For all its democratic ideals, America was still a highly stratified society.

"Colin is a baronet, whatever that means. Technically, Lucy could call herself Lady Beckwith, but she never does. Here they come."

The pair wended their way through the gathering crowd. Lucy looked smashing, with her glossy dark hair piled atop her head and wearing a peacock-blue gown swathed with layers of chiffon. Colin looked rich and smug, every strand of golden-blond hair slicked back into unnatural perfection. Nick would cut his hands off before he ever put pomade in his hair.

Nick was never much for fancy introductions, so he just spoke naturally. "Colin, Lucy, this is Rosalind Werner, the lady I've been telling you about. Did I lie?"

Colin tipped his head in one of those well-bred nods. "She is indeed pretty as a moonbeam."

"We're so pleased to meet you," Lucy effused, reaching out to clasp both of Rosalind's hands. This was a first. Lucy had foisted plenty of women Nick's way, but she was always cautious of them, scrutinizing them as though gauging the readiness of a soufflé. As badly as she wanted him to find another wife, she worried he'd fall for a fortune hunter. She didn't seem so concerned about Rosalind. Maybe because Nick couldn't stop talking about how smart, how pretty, how perfectly prissy in a charming way she was. Any idiot with a functioning brain could see he was infatuated with her.

He was about to start bragging over Rosalind's work in water research when he noticed Colin's face had gone white, his eyes fixed on a point in the distance. Nick turned to follow his stare.

Aunt Margaret was heading their way, her chin raised at a proud angle as she closed in on them. Her ivory skin stood out in startling contrast to her stark widow's weeds.

"Tell me you didn't invite her," Lucy said.

"I did," he said tightly. "Please be polite."

He'd completely forgotten issuing the invitation, or he would have warned them in advance. Of course, they might have boycotted the event had they known Margaret would be here. But this feud had gone on too long and claimed victims on both sides. It was time their family made peace.

"Aunt Margaret," he said politely as she joined them. "It was good of you to come tonight."

His aunt was an imposing sight. Amidst the gaily dressed people gathered for a late summer's festivities, she was like a gothic heroine proudly wearing black silk, the ruff of her gown framing her face.

"I wouldn't miss it for the world," she said in a honeyed voice. Her face hardened as she turned her attention to Lucy and Colin. "I have not yet had a chance to read all the condolence letters I received after my husband's death, or I'm sure I would have read yours, Lucy."

Nick wished Aunt Margaret hadn't come out swinging, but a part of him admired her gumption. She had plenty of cause to resent Colin and Lucy, and her appearance here this evening was a clear sign she had no intention of cowering away at Oakmonte.

"You aren't welcome here," Colin said coldly.

Nick was about to intervene, but Margaret needed no defending. "In a public park? You forget yourself. In America, the parks are open to everyone, not just aristocrats with an inherited sense of entitlement."

Nick shot Colin an annoyed glance. "Can we hold off on the fireworks until after the speeches? Aunt Margaret is here at my invitation." He stepped to Rosalind's side. "Aunt Margaret, this is Dr. Rosalind Werner. She and I met while working on the water project in Jersey City. She was kind enough to accompany me here tonight." He held his breath, praying Aunt Margaret's frosty demeanor would thaw.

It did. "Dr. Werner," she said in an approving tone. "There are so few female physicians. I'm fascinated to finally meet one."

"I'm not that kind of doctor," Rosalind said with a kind smile, and he had a hunch she had to make that clarification a lot.

As she went on to explain her work in water purification, Nick studied his family. There had been no softening from Colin or Lucy, who both glared at Aunt Margaret as though a snake had just slid into the Garden of Eden. At least Margaret was polite to Rosalind, nodding and asking questions and doing everything possible to make Rosalind feel at home. He couldn't ask for more.

Except possibly a little cooperation from Lucy and her husband. The master of ceremonies was on the stage, checking the height of the podium. Nick was about to deliver the biggest speech of his life, and he didn't want to leave Rosalind in the middle of a civil war.

He took the notes from his jacket and confirmed the pages were all in order. He set a hand on the small of Rosalind's back, and she flashed him a nervous smile. "I need to go soon. Will you be all right? You look anxious."

"I'm only nervous on your behalf, but I know you'll be brilliant."

He brightened. "No worries, Dr. Werner. I'm fearless." Except when it came to his volatile family dynamics. He stepped closer to Colin and Lucy, sending them both a pointed look. "Please . . ." he entreated in a low voice.

There was no time for more words. The master of ceremonies gestured Nick up to stand behind the podium, along with the mayor and other elected officials.

"I'll be fine," Rosalind assured him.

He couldn't resist. On one of the most important days of his career, she was here to share it with him, and she was kind and pretty, and it felt like she belonged beside him for the rest of their lives. He planted a quick kiss directly on her mouth. "I adore you," he whispered, then bounded up onto the stage.

"I don't think I've ever seen him so nervous," Lucy said.

Rosalind didn't know Nick well enough to judge, but she was proud of him as he mingled with the other dignitaries on the stage. She tore her eyes away from him only long enough to head toward the bank of seats. She sat with Colin and Lucy on one side, and Margaret on the other. There were still a few more minutes before the ceremony began.

"Nick tells me you are a baronet," Rosalind said to Colin. "Does that make you Sir Beckwith?"

"Yes, but please call me Colin," he said.

"Or you can call him a backstabber," Aunt Margaret said, calmly staring straight ahead. "Turncoat, traitor, snitch, or maybe just Sir Beckwith. They all mean the same thing."

"It's nice that I can always count on you to be so well-mannered, Margaret," Colin said smoothly.

On another occasion, Rosalind might find it awkward to be seated between such warring parties, but she was too nervous on Nick's behalf to pay them any mind. How could a plumber possibly command the attention of the thousands of people crowded into the park? The seats were filled with dignitaries who'd been invited, but thousands of ordinary citizens stood in the field behind them, waiting for the carts of free food and drink to be wheeled out.

The master of ceremonies spoke, and then the mayor said a few words, thanking some local companies for donating the food. Some hoots of expectation echoed up from the crowd, and Rosalind wished they had held this gathering in an enclosed auditorium. How could Nick be heard over this rowdy crowd?

"And now it is my pleasure to introduce Nicholas Drake, the newly appointed commissioner of the State Water Board, whose job it will be to make sure the city continues to have a bountiful supply of water into the next century. Mr. Drake?"

To her surprise, Nick put on a pair of eyeglasses before stepping up to the podium, the pages of his speech held before him. The other men had spoken extemporaneously, and she worried that reading from the page was a mistake. Public speaking was an art form, and reading a prepared speech was rarely persuasive.

"Sixty-five years ago, the Croton Aqueduct began supplying our city with water," he said in a confident voice, echoing over the park. "It was an accomplishment beyond most people's imagination. Instead of dipping their buckets into a local well for brackish water, people suddenly had a bountiful supply of freshwater pumped down from the pristine Hudson River Valley. The day the water began flowing was declared a public holiday in New York City. People gathered in this very park to witness the reservoir fill with crystal-clear water that had travelled through forty-one miles of pipeline."

Rosalind's tense muscles began to relax. He was doing well. Very well! His voice was strong and natural, even though he read from a prepared script.

"In the decades that followed, our city grew from three hundred thousand people to over four million. We began taking water for granted, because the Croton Aqueduct never let us down. Most of you passed the park's reservoir on your way here tonight, and you can see how low the water level is. That's why we are building a new aqueduct. The Croton Aqueduct brings us thirty-five million gallons of water per day. The Catskill Aqueduct will pump five hundred million gallons a day."

A spontaneous burst of applause started deep in the crowd, and a couple of voices shouted through the din.

"Yo, Nick!" a voice bellowed.

Rosalind followed the voice and saw a group of tough-looking men standing atop a picnic table. They wore the clothes of ordinary laborers, but their grins were wide. Nick flashed a smile and gave them a thumbs-up. It wouldn't surprise her if these were men he once worked with in those underground tunnels.

Nick took off his glasses and set down the pages. Suddenly he was speaking from the heart. "Back when the original aqueduct opened, all people needed was a little water for cooking, drinking, and an occasional wash from a bucket. But now? You people are taking long, hot baths—some of you every day! And those toilets we've all gotten so used to? They take a lot of water, ten times a day." He looked at the men standing on the picnic table. "Twenty times a day for you, Wallenstein!"

The men howled with laughter, and it rippled through the crowd as well. Nick put on his glasses and went back to the speech.

"Our standards are getting higher. Our population larger. The new aqueduct will require a hundred miles of pipeline and a dozen bridges. We're going to tunnel beneath mountains, rivers, and farmland to get it here. We'll drill through bedrock and build bridges to carry it over ravines. It's going to take a decade to build, but we have the vision and technology to accomplish it. And once this marvel of engineering is complete, the pipes will be covered over, and most of us will never think of them again. People will build houses and businesses on top of them. They'll raise crops, play with their children, and never realize the miracle flowing beneath their feet."

Rosalind was awestruck, for Nick's performance was mesmerizing. He spoke with a combination of confidence, charisma, and raw strength. As he continued speaking, she could tell exactly when he veered from Colin's prepared speech. Colin wrote with grandiose imagery while Nick spoke with common sense immediately understood by anyone with a pulse. Both qualities were essential for a great speech, and Nick was hitting it out of the park.

"How long have you known my nephew?" Margaret whispered to her.

Rosalind didn't want to tear her attention from Nick, but he desperately wanted to mend fences with his aunt, and she mustn't be rude.

"Not long," she whispered back, her attention still fastened on Nick's speech.

"And yet you look at him as though he is God's gift to womankind."

Was she that obvious? She didn't care. "He isn't?" she whispered back with a hint of laughter.

Nick's speech came to an end, and the crowd stood to applaud. Rosalind shot to her feet, clapping so hard the palms of her hands hurt, but she was hopelessly proud of him. No wonder he'd earned the governor's appointment to this position. He didn't need to be an engineer or chemist, he needed to be able to sell the most expensive building project in the state's history to a population that hadn't yet experienced a problem in their water supply.

"It was nice meeting you, Dr. Werner," Margaret said as they rose. "I had best get back to my hotel, but I wanted to be here in support of my nephew's speech. He's worth ten of them." She gave a disparaging glance at Colin and Lucy.

"Isn't she a delight?" Colin said after Margaret disappeared into the crowd.

"I'm afraid I don't know enough about her to comment one way or the other." Rosalind did know that when push came to shove, family could be depended on. Gus had stood by her side through a torrent of abuse, and Rosalind had an instinctive sympathy for a widow who seemed to have no family left aside from a few overtures from Nick.

The moment Margaret vanished into the crowd, Colin and Lucy eased. "It was a brilliant speech, my love," Lucy said, beaming up into her husband's face.

"Except when he strayed from the script," Colin said. "Leave it to your brother to bring up toilets in the middle of my scintillating prose."

The weight of two warm hands settled on Rosalind's shoulders.

"Toilets use more water than anything else in a household," Nick said. "Everyone was thinking it. I had to bring it up."

"No, actually, you didn't," Colin said. "In my thirty-nine years on the planet, I've never once felt compelled to discuss toilets in public."

While they talked, a number of men stopped to clap Nick on the back or shake his hand. There was the leader of the plumber's union, then a congressman from upstate New York whose district would be bisected by the aqueduct. Nick spoke to both men with ease, but should Rosalind have been surprised? Since the morning she'd met him for breakfast, Nick had an easy way of communicating with people from the café waitress to the professors at the Water Association meeting. Throughout the entire evening, Nick held her arm and introduced her to each man. His declaration that they were a pair could not have been more obvious if he had held a placard above their heads.

After a while, the stream of men introducing themselves to Nick slowed. The sun sank, the moon rose, and the Chinese lanterns were lit, casting a warm glow throughout the park. Music played in the distance, and tables were laden with platters of sandwiches, pickles, and sliced fruit. Rosalind and Nick served themselves, then headed over to join his family at a picnic table beneath the boughs of a spreading oak tree.

"Tell me you are *not* eating a pastrami sandwich with a knife and fork," Nick said as he sat.

Colin dabbed the corner of his mouth with a cloth. "Forks have been a welcome tool of enlightened society for hundreds of years. I shall buy you some. Tell me, Dr. Werner, how have you enjoyed your first official coming out alongside our new Commissioner?"

"Please call me Rosalind. And I loved it."

Nick brushed away a leaf that had dropped on his shoulder. "I really hate being out in the wilderness like this."

Colin snorted. "It's Central Park, hardly the untouched wilds. Everything here was carefully designed by landscape architects, including the lake, the hills, and the cluster of trees under which we are sitting."

"I don't care," Nick grumbled as he flicked at a ladybug crawling across the table. "Look, there are bugs. They're nasty."

It was surprising that a man as physically imposing as Nicholas Drake should be out of sorts from a bit of nature. Rosalind did her best to hide her smile, but his sister hooted with amusement.

"You spent twelve years working in water tunnels and sewage lines, and you think *ladybugs* are nasty?" Lucy challenged, but Nick gave as good as he got.

"Modern plumbing is a miracle of civilization. Nothing about it is nasty," he said with a grin.

It was in that moment that Rosalind knew she loved him. She met his gaze across the picnic table, and he flashed her a wink. Laughter bubbled up inside her, for this was quite possibly the most perfect evening of her life. She was with a man of strength, intelligence, and character. He was as attracted to her as she was to him, and it was exhilarating.

But at the back of her mind loomed the anxiety of what would happen when he learned about the chlorine. She had to believe Nick would forgive her. He'd forgiven his aunt for some awful family drama, hadn't he? He'd lost his temper a couple of times with her and always quickly simmered down. Once he saw how beautifully chlorine worked, he would be angry, but he'd forgive her. Everything between them was too perfect to imagine otherwise.

But in her heart, she still worried.

As they stepped off the subway on the Jersey side of the river, Nick reached for Rosalind's hand and tugged her a little closer.

"Thank you for riding the subway with me," she said. "You don't have to walk me all the way home."

"Of course I do."

Rosalind was a grown woman who'd travelled the world and was surely capable of finding her way to her house, but he didn't want this evening to end. Excitement still charged through his veins at the triumph of his speech, but even better were the hours afterward. He'd suspected Rosalind would fit in well with his family, and it couldn't have gone better. He wanted nothing so much as to have a day like today happen again tomorrow. And the next day. He wanted the chance to put his skills to use building the Catskill Aqueduct during the day, then to court Rosalind in the evenings.

Instead, he needed to head to upstate on business. "I'm travelling up to the Catskills tomorrow morning," he said. "The location of the new reservoir has been approved, but we may run into some troubles with the watershed."

"What sort of troubles?"

He loved that Rosalind knew exactly what he meant by a "watershed" without having to explain the basics. He would be able to share this part of his life and not worry he was boring her or that she was feigning interest to lure him in.

"The owner of a limestone quarry is causing a lot of runoff from his operation. It might be polluting the watershed. Dealing with Bruce Garrett is going to be tough enough, but I've also got to start scoping out the land for the new reservoir. It's going to force a lot of people off their property."

"They'll be compensated, won't they?"

He wished it was as easy as writing a few bank checks, for the situation upstate was already getting ugly, but he blocked his misgivings from his voice. "Of course. It doesn't mean they won't kick up a fuss. I need to head up there and figure out what sort of work crews will be necessary for clearing the land." And demolishing homes, rerouting railroads, destroying people's livelihoods. The situation had been giving him an ulcer for months, but it had to be done.

He'd rather stay here and spend more long, lingering evenings squiring Rosalind around town. He folded her arm tighter alongside him, wondering if he could steal another kiss tonight.

"I live at the end of this street," she said as she turned down a leafy, tree-lined avenue. The houses were new, with tidy front porches, clapboard siding, and gabled roofs. It was nearing midnight, and it felt like they were the only two people still awake. With grassy lawns and crickets chirping in the underbrush, it was so different than his seventh-story apartment in the middle of a city that never slept.

"It's a nice place," he said, leaning down to pick up a child's bicycle that lay across the sidewalk. He propped it against the fence and took her arm again. "A lot of children live on this street?" It was important to learn if she wanted children. He already had Sadie and would be content with that, but he'd also welcome more.

"Oh yes, plenty of children." She pointed to one of the larger houses on the opposite side of the street. "Judge McLaughlin lives in that Dutch colonial, and he has five children."

Nick lowered his brow. The last thing he wanted to do was discuss Judge McLaughlin or anything to do with the chlorine case, but how interesting that she lived so close to the judge in the lawsuit.

"You know Judge McLaughlin well?"

"Not really. His wife sometimes visits with my sister-in-law, but that's all." She stopped walking and turned to face him on the narrow sidewalk. "I'm sorry," she said in a rush. "I shouldn't have brought his name into this conversation. I've been trying to avoid thinking about the ninety days or chlorine or anything that would—"

"Shh," he said. "I feel the same way."

Rosalind's close proximity to the judge surely meant nothing. There had been over a hundred witnesses called during the two-year trial, and for the most part, the judge ruled in favor of the city.

"Forget I said anything," she rushed to say. "This has been one of the best days I can remember. Perfect, really."

She was perfect. Funny and smart and so perfectly prim it made him want to squeeze her. He lowered his head a little, still gazing at the way the moonlight illuminated her flawless skin with a silvery sheen.

"Thank you for walking me all the way home."

"Of course. Thank you for coming to my speech."

"Of course," she echoed, gazing up at him like she felt the same moonlit enchantment that had dumbfounded him from the moment he met her. He never wanted to look away, but he had five days of slogging around rural New York ahead of him.

"I won't be back in town until Saturday," he said. "Can I come see you then?"

She nodded. "What will we do?"

He knew exactly what he wanted. "How about you, me, and Sadie go to Coney Island? We can ride the carousels, walk along the boardwalk, eat cotton candy."

"That sounds really good." Then a tiny line wrinkled her brow. "Except, I'm afraid you must know . . . I cannot approve of cotton candy."

"Muesli, then?"

"It would be healthier."

He grinned and foresaw years of healthy food, prissy maxims, and undiluted delight heading his way. And on the weekends, perhaps he could steal a little cotton candy for him and Sadie.

"Rosalind!" a voice in the distance shouted.

Rosalind pulled away as a man vaulted over a fence and strode toward them with purpose. Nick instinctively stepped in front of her, fists clenched.

"Don't hurt him," Rosalind said in a rush. "It's only my brother, Gus."

Gus had a slender build, sandy blond hair, and a neatly groomed mustache. He didn't look like much of a threat, but Nick still didn't like the look of disapproval on his face.

"Where have you been?" Gus demanded. "Ingrid and I have been worrying ourselves sick."

Rosalind started to explain that she had stayed for a bite to eat, but Nick interrupted her, extending his hand. "I'm Nicholas Drake. Rosalind was good enough to stay after the speeches to support me as I met with some business associates. Her delay is entirely my fault."

Gus still didn't look happy. "Loitering on a public street in full view of the neighbors is unbecoming. It's the kind of thing that starts rumors, Rosalind."

Nick settled his hands on Rosalind's shoulders. "I don't mind hearing my name linked with hers. It's an honor. And I'll go after any man who implies otherwise."

Rosalind's brother rolled his eyes. "It's all very well for you, but it's Rosalind's reputation that will take a beating."

"It won't," Nick replied. "I'll never let it get that far, because I care for her. My intentions toward your sister are honorable. I wish we were two people who had scads of time and no other responsibilities so we could do everything in a way that would make the fussy matrons of the city beam with approval. But we aren't, so we snatch what fleeting moments we can."

"Then make them really fleeting," Gus said. "Mrs. Henthorn across the street is watching."

Rosalind startled, and Nick fought the temptation to roll his eyes over what the neighborhood busybody thought of his actions. Instead, he took a step back. Rosalind was ridiculously straitlaced, and he would honor that if it would keep her from worrying about what Mrs. Henthorn thought.

"I will see you soon, Dr. Werner," he said with a respectable nod of his head before setting off toward the subway.

Chapter THIRTEEN

Rosalind watched the rain create rivulets on the laboratory window. It had been raining for two solid days, a gully wash that overwhelmed the sewers as water backed up into the street. Her boots and the bottom three inches of her gown were soaked from slogging through puddles to get to the lab this morning. The wet shoe leather was uncomfortable, but Rosalind welcomed the discomfort, for the rain gave them the test they'd been waiting for.

This was it. These were the conditions under which traditional filtration systems could fail. As rain soaked the farmlands, it washed waste and contamination into the streams and eventually into the reservoir, making it hard for filtration systems to keep up. It was in rain-saturated conditions like these that waterborne disease was most likely to crop up in cities.

Unless the chlorine worked. This was the two-pronged attack she and Dr. Leal had envisioned all along. Filtration could handle the worst of the debris, but chlorination could treat the surge in bacterial contamination. Within the week, they would know if their plan had worked.

Dr. Leal paced before twelve newly hired lab assistants from the local college who would help with the increase in testing. They all specialized in chemistry and were eager to embark on their first venture into real science in action. The young men sat at the lab tables, hanging on Dr. Leal's every word.

"I will send you samples collected from each distribution point in the city," Dr. Leal said, walking to an oversized map tacked to the wall. "I will be taking water samples at the city's public buildings here, here, and here." He made marks with his pencil at points throughout the city. "Dr. Werner will be gathering samples from the area surrounding the reservoir. The chlorination feed has been working for the past three weeks, but it hasn't been put under pressure yet."

Excitement gathered in Dr. Leal's voice. His enthusiasm was contagious. Rosalind had never been prouder to work alongside this daring and innovative man, and the students looked just as excited.

"For decades I have worked, and planned, and prayed," Dr. Leal continued. "Our analyses must be flawless, for this is the first experiment of its kind, and we cannot afford a mistake. If it works, this model will be emulated across the nation, and someday, all over the world. You are part of the team that is going to make it happen."

Most of the students looked spellbound, but the youngest man, so slender he couldn't even fill the collar of his shirt, raised a timid hand. "Dr. Leal? If you're so confident this will work, why didn't you just wait for permission from the judge?"

The other students blanched at the blunt question, but Dr. Leal was not offended. The barest hint of a smile twitched his mustache. "Why? Because if I waited the ninety days, the judge might rule against us, and this opportunity would be closed forever. I acted because it was physically impossible for me to sit back and do nothing. Because I am in the fight of my life, a fight against microscopic enemies that can wreak unimaginable devastation. And in such a case, I cannot stand down. That is why."

His words were spoken quietly, but they echoed in the room with the force of a trumpet blast. The next few days were going to be a grueling, wet, and messy slog, but Rosalind sensed they were on the verge of a precipice. History was in the making. She was in the room where it was being written, and she had never been so proud.

Rosalind struggled to hold an umbrella over her head as she gathered soil samples, but her skirts were quickly waterlogged, and it was hard to work while bracing an umbrella against her shoulder. She discarded the umbrella, rolled up her cuffs, and tackled the assignment with both hands.

She was sopping wet by the end of the day. Rivulets of water dribbled from her hair, and her clothes were filthy as she walked home, but it couldn't dampen her spirits. Preliminary results from the lab already showed that the chlorine was working. The real test would emerge in the coming days as the rainstorm continued to batter the county, but she was optimistic and couldn't keep a smile from breaking across her face as she turned down her street toward home.

Her good mood came crashing to a halt as she stepped through her front door to see a mess, papers and books scattered everywhere. Gus sat on the sofa, his arm around Ingrid, who was gently weeping.

"What's wrong?" Rosalind asked.

Gus sent her a grim look. "Ingrid interrupted a burglary this afternoon. Someone broke into the house. We're still not quite sure what was taken."

"Are you all right?" she asked Ingrid. "And the baby?"

"No, I am not all right," Ingrid declared, her voice full of fire.

"I woke up from a nap to find a prowler in the house. Making a mess. Making accusations."

Rosalind wasn't sure she'd heard correctly. "Accusations?"

"I'm sure it doesn't mean anything," Gus said. "I think the burglar was as frightened as Ingrid when she came down the stairs. He claimed to be a friend of yours."

"A *special* friend," Ingrid added. "He said you gave him permission to be here, then he broke a window and ran out the back door."

It only took a couple of steps to peer around the corner at the broken glass and overturned chairs in the kitchen. Some plates had been knocked off the shelf as well. Rosalind hadn't given anyone permission to wander into the house. And she certainly didn't consort with the type of person who would break windows and cause needless damage.

After her pounding heart slowed to a normal pace, she joined Gus and Ingrid at the kitchen table to get the complete story. The man had been creeping through the parlor when Ingrid awakened from a nap and heard movement in the house. Gus had gone to the library to study for an exam, and Ingrid assumed he'd returned early and went downstairs to greet him. When she saw a heavyset man poking through Rosalind's desk, she started screaming. The stranger tried to calm her, claiming to be a friend of Rosalind's and only here looking for something. When Ingrid wouldn't stop screaming, he darted to the kitchen, broke some things, then fled out the back. Ingrid telephoned the police, who had already come and gone. They seemed to think it was a simple burglary that had been interrupted before any real damage could occur, but they suggested Rosalind call if she later discovered something of value missing.

Rosalind made a thorough evaluation of her belongings. The only thing of actual value she had was the Fabergé music box from Nick, and it still sat on the mantel alongside the plain oak music boxes she had made with her own two hands. She was ridiculously glad they had not been stolen. Aside from Nick's, none of them had much monetary value, but the sentimental value was huge. What little cash Rosalind kept in the house was still safely hidden in the tea tin behind a row of books.

Her teeth chattered and a chill raced through her, made worse by her sodden clothing. She felt violated. This home was the sanctuary she'd created after fleeing Germany. She faithfully paid the bank note each month from money she earned from her Doctor Clean stock. It was maddening that a shiftless thief should try to help himself to her hard-earned belongings, then cause needless destruction on his escape. That had been pure meanness.

"Go run a hot bath," Gus said. "I'll borrow some supplies from a neighbor to board up the window until it can be repaired."

An involuntary shiver raced through Rosalind at the thought of Gus abandoning the house while she stripped down and took a bath. Ingrid must have noticed her hesitancy.

"I will stand guard outside the bathroom door," she said. "If anyone dares invade this house, they will see what a strong German girl can do."

Rosalind met Ingrid's gaze. A flash of comradery hummed between them for the first time. As horrible as this incident had been, at least it brought a temporary thaw to the arctic blast that characterized their relationship.

True to her word, Ingrid stood guard outside the bathroom as Rosalind soaked her numb body in a hot, soapy tub of water. Even as the hot water warmed her, the shock of having her house invaded made the chill impossible to shake.

She didn't sleep much that night.

Nick got off the train at Kingston, New York, a town ninety miles north of New York City, bracing himself for his first major test as commissioner of the State Water Board. He would soon be sending three thousand people into this valley to build the reservoir. Construction workers, mechanics, pipe fitters, diggers, dredgers, and linemen. Lumberjacks were already clearing forest land, and soon carpenters would arrive to build dormitories for the work crews.

He also needed to see Bruce Garrett, whose limestone quarry was polluting the watershed, and Nick would have to handle him carefully. They'd established a cordial relationship at Oakmonte during Uncle Thomas's funeral, but when a man's business was on the line, things could change. Bruce Garrett was rich, powerful, and not going to welcome interference in his quarry. Even so, it seemed Garrett was willing to cooperate, as he'd offered to let Nick stay at his home during the visit.

Nick hired a hansom cab in Kingston to take him the ten miles to Garrett's mansion. Rumor had it that the wealth Garrett earned from quarrying limestone had bought him a castle in the hills. As the carriage rounded a bend through the deeply forested land, Nick got his first view of Bruce Garrett's home.

It wasn't a castle; it was a fortress.

Built of pale rock, it perched on the side of the hill that had been cleared of trees. A serpentine path cut up the side of the hill, passing through a series of walls and gates as it led to a three-story house with windows that sparkled in the sun and wide terraces overlooking the valley. Nick had never been to Europe, but he'd seen pictures, and this looked like something a medieval crusader might have built to defend Christendom.

Bruce Garrett was already standing on the terrace in front of his house as the carriage drew near. Nick raised his hand in greeting, and Bruce returned it.

"Welcome!" he said the moment Nick's feet touched the ground. "How's your aunt doing?"

The last time Nick saw Aunt Margaret, she had been slinging poisoned barbs at Colin, but it was going to take time and patience to mend the family rift. "She's doing okay."

"Well, give her my best the next time you see her." There was genuine concern in Bruce's face, and Nick appreciated the gesture.

It was hard not to be impressed with Bruce Garrett's house. Nick had been inside some of the wealthiest homes in Manhattan and had seen plenty of gilded splendor, but Bruce's home was different. It had a roughhewn quality Nick found appealing, built from locally carved stone. Inside, the house had hand-carved furniture and a simplicity of design that was a refreshing change from the obnoxious display of wealth so common in the city.

Nick barely had a chance to set down his traveling bag before Bruce wanted to get to business.

"Come, let me show you the quarry," he said, and twenty minutes later, Nick got his first close-up view of an open-pit limestone quarry.

Cut into the hillside that had once been blanketed with pine trees was an immense scar of exposed rock. Even from a distance, Nick's nose prickled at the scent of chalk.

"That's where we're blasting," Bruce said. "I've got experts in explosives to drill and set off the charges, which shears off the rock. Manual laborers use sledgehammers to break it up into pieces small enough to load aboard the wagons." He went on to explain how the rock was superheated in coal-fired kilns and then broken down into cement mix.

Nick looked down at the ground. They stood half a mile from the kilns, and yet the grass was coated with a layer of pale white dust. It was fly ash from the kilns. When it rained, it would sink into the groundwater.

Bruce pointed to a village in the valley below the quarry.

"That's Duval Springs," he said. "It has around two thousand people, half of whom are employed by my quarry."

Nick stared at the village nestled in the valley alongside a swift-moving river. Most of the structures were houses, but it was easy to see the town square lined with shops, cafés, and a few churches. From this vantage point, it looked like the picture of small-town prosperity. A year from now, it would be obliterated. Duval Springs had the bad luck to be planted precisely where the state wanted to build their new reservoir.

He glanced back at the limestone scar Garrett's quarry cut into the forested hillside. There was no easy way to broach this conversation. "You know why I'm here."

The cordial expression remained on Bruce's face, but his eyes went on alert. "I do. You were still in short pants when I started this quarry, and I've never had any complaints from the government in all those years."

Nick crouched down to run his fingers over the grass. He stood and showed the chalky dust to Bruce. "This is going to be a problem. Your operation is on top of groundwater that will someday be piped into Manhattan."

"Then find another source for your water," Bruce snapped. "We've been minding our own business up here for decades. We were here long before anyone ever dreamed of a new reservoir to keep New York City happy."

Nick held up his hands. "I agree with you, but there's an ugly term called *eminent domain*. It's some fancy Latin phrase that means that what the government wants, it's going to get. They'll have to pay for it, but you'll have to cooperate with them. The quarry is polluting the groundwater with dust and ash."

"And how does one make cement without a mill?" Garrett's voice seethed with contempt, and Nick did his best to put him at ease.

"Look, we've built the Brooklyn Bridge, and now men are

flying in airplanes. If we can figure out how to make men fly, we'll figure out how to keep your quarry in business. Right?"

"Don't think you can pacify me with your pretty speeches," Bruce bit out. "Where is the flow line going to be? Don't pretend you don't know what I'm talking about. I have a right to know."

The flow line was the most controversial decision in the entire project. It was the geographic boundary defining where the new reservoir would be built. Everything above the flow line was safe. Anything below it would be submerged under billions of gallons of water.

"Duval Springs is below the flow line," Nick admitted. "Those people will have to move. Your quarry and home are safe. Figure out a way to clean up the runoff, and you'll be fine."

It was humbling to see a strong man almost weep with relief. Bruce let out a mighty sigh, closing his eyes as the magnitude of what he'd just heard penetrated. The entire tone of the visit shifted once Bruce had been assured that most of his operation would be unaffected by the coming reservoir.

Bruce clapped him on the back. "Come! Let's head into town for a beer and a celebration."

Nick stiffened. The only nearby town was Duval Springs, and he was thoroughly hated in Duval Springs.

"Let's stay up here," he suggested.

Bruce pulled a frown at him. "You sure? The Duval Tavern is famous. George Washington once stayed there."

Which was why Nick wanted to keep far away. Every time he contemplated driving those people off their land, it made the ulcer in his stomach worse. He didn't see any point in subjecting himself to a celebratory evening in a tavern he would soon order demolished.

Over the next two days, he rode throughout the valley, surveying everything beneath the flow line that would require demolition. It added up to thirty-five farms, a dozen apple orchards, ten churches, two railroad depots, a lumber mill, two cemeteries, forty shops, and six hundred homes. All of them were going to be laid to waste, and thousands of people would be kicked off their land. It was his job to supervise the army of demolition experts and work crews that would make it happen. All he wanted was to escape this valley of doomed villages and despairing people.

He missed Rosalind. This job was hard enough without the constant longing to get home to a woman he hadn't been able to court properly because of endless work commitments. The ache became so bad that he wrapped up the final inspections quickly so he could get home a day early. Rosalind wasn't expecting him until Saturday, when he'd promised her a day at Coney Island with Sadie, but it was hard to court a woman with a three-year-old in tow. He arrived back in the city on Friday, early enough to have lunch with Sadie and lavish praise on her newfound mastery of using a hook to button her own shoes.

Then he put on a fresh suit, bought a bouquet of roses, and set off for Rosalind's lab to surprise her.

Did she like surprises? He was about to find out.

Chapter FOURTEEN

When Nick arrived at Rosalind's lab, he was taken aback by a group of men he'd never seen before, bent over microscopes. Rosalind wasn't there.

"Is Dr. Werner available?" he asked, feeling a little foolish with a dozen roses clutched in one hand and a bunch of strange men staring at him. He had to step aside as another man hustled into the room, carrying a rack of water samples in little glass jars. Where had all these people come from?

"She's out at the reservoir taking soil samples," one of the men said. "She'll be back in a few hours."

"Oh."

Disappointment trickled through him, but he wasn't going to wait for her here where there'd be no privacy. Ten minutes later, he had fired up his automobile and replenished the gasoline for a drive to the Boonton Reservoir. Maybe this wouldn't be so bad. The forest surrounding the reservoir offered plenty of privacy, and maybe he could persuade Rosalind to neglect her duties for a stroll with a man who'd missed her desperately for the past five days.

The car rocked and bumped along the gravel path as he rounded a bend of trees and spotted the reservoir in the distance. Surrounded by a twenty-foot wall of granite block, it was an impressive system, nearly bankrupting the private investors who'd spent millions on it along with twenty-one miles of tunnels, conduits, and steel pipe.

He slowed his car, studying the reservoir. Something looked different than the last time he was here. A small building had been erected at the base of the reservoir wall. It wasn't large enough to hold a new filtration plant, but it didn't look like housing for the staff either.

There was no sign of Rosalind. He picked up the bouquet of roses, headed to the squat new building, and peeked inside the window. A grin spread across his face as he recognized her slender frame leaning over a table of little glass bottles. He tapped on the window to get her attention.

She looked startled at first, then afraid.

"Don't worry, it's just me," he called as he headed toward the door.

He opened it and stepped inside. It looked like she had another laboratory set up here, with complicated tubing and giant tanks, all bubbling and gurgling. It smelled bad.

"I couldn't wait until tomorrow to see you again," he admitted. He ought to be embarrassed, showing up like a lovestruck idiot with a bunch of roses, but he couldn't stop smiling so widely that his face hurt.

"Oh," she said. "Welcome back. Your trip was profitable?" She still had a hand to her throat, her face a combination of startled confusion and something else he couldn't quite name.

"Nothing about dealing with Bruce Garrett is going to be profitable for the state. I was trying to figure out how much it's going to cost us to pay him off."

"And?" she asked as she slid around to the front of the table, blocking his view of her experiments. Which was fine. He wanted to talk about her, not test tubes or court cases.

"And I still don't know. But I saw a vendor selling roses at the railway station, and suddenly it became vitally important for me to bring some to you right away."

He held them toward her, but she didn't move a muscle. Why was she acting so oddly? He pulled the roses back and shifted on his feet.

"What are you doing out here?" he asked. "The lab back in the city is crammed with a bunch of men I've never seen before."

"Yes. We've brought on a few students from the college to help us with some tests."

"What kind of tests?" He glanced at the oversized tank in the corner. He'd never seen anything like it. His smile froze as he scrutinized the odd tank. He glanced back at Rosalind, who still hadn't answered him. "What kind of tests?" he asked again, rubbing his nose. It stank in here. Like chemicals.

The oversized tank had a rope of steel tubing coming from the top, the kind used for acidic chemicals. A shorter, squat tank had similar tubes and a flow switch attached to the larger tank. Which meant they were doing something with the reservoir water. Treating it, somehow.

He dropped the roses on the floor and looked at her in stunned disbelief. No. No, *she wouldn't dare*.

"What kind of tests?" he demanded, his voice lashing out to echo in the bare brick chamber.

The guilt on her face was all the answer he needed. It was chlorine. He reached out to grab the dial beside the tank, ready to twist it shut.

"Don't touch that!"

He whirled to face her. "What is it?"

"You know what it is," she said faintly.

He looked at the system, the dials and switches hooked up

to a complicated series of tubes, all of it carefully calibrated. It was hooked into the reservoir only yards away, chlorinating the water. Every cell in his body wanted to yank the steel tubing out of the wall, but he didn't know what he was doing. He couldn't risk somehow dumping an overload of chemicals into the water supply.

"Who knows about this?" he bit out.

Her face had gone chalk white, and she seemed too petrified to answer. He stepped closer, and she backed up until she bumped against the wall. He needed to know if this had been authorized by the judge, but given the guilty look on her face, he doubted it.

"Who else knows about this?"

"Just the people working in our lab," she stammered.

The betrayal seared. The audacity and arrogance it took to build this operation was appalling, and to think, she had been a part of it all along. He couldn't even bear to look at her.

On the worktable was a collection of bottles, sample plates filled with soil, and a stack of notebooks. One of the notebooks was open, the pages filled with charts and dates. This test had been going on for weeks!

He lunged for the notebooks and scooped them up before she could stop him.

"Give those back!" she shouted, but he paid her no mind as he headed for the door.

She tried to grab the notebooks from his arms, but he brushed her aside and strode to his car. Rosalind kept trying to pry the notebooks from him as he leaned into his car to unlock the glove compartment. The moment the compartment was open, he deposited the books, slammed the hatch, and locked them inside.

"Give those back," she demanded. "I need those notes. They prove everything."

"What about Judge McLaughlin? He lives right across the street from you. Does he know what you've been doing?"

"No. He doesn't know anything."

"He will soon." Nick raised the hood and began priming the engine.

Rosalind had climbed inside the carriage of the car, trying to pry the glove box open with a hairpin. It wouldn't do her any good. The engine roared to life, and he hauled her out of the car, dumping her a few yards away.

He lunged into the driver's seat. Rosalind was shouting at him, but he couldn't hear over the racket of the engine. Not that he'd care to listen. He would never listen to anything she said again. Never hang on her words like the besotted idiot he'd been all because she was pretty and smart enough to pull the wool over his eyes.

She stood behind the car, blocking his ability to back up, and he couldn't go forward because he was too close to the building to turn around. He twisted in his seat to glare at her. "Get out of the way," he ordered.

"No." She didn't budge.

"Back away!"

"No. Not unless you give me those notebooks back."

"Forget it."

"You're not leaving with those notes." She smacked the back fender with the palm of her hand.

He rose up in the seat. "If you lay one more finger on my car, I'll throw you in the reservoir."

"You wouldn't dare."

He roared with anger. "I didn't think you would dare dump chlorine in the water supply, but I was wrong about that, wasn't I?"

She held up her hands in appeal. "Don't let your temper make you do something stupid," she said, struggling to control her breath. "If you would let me show you the results of our test, you would change your mind. Nick, *it's working*. Don't destroy those notebooks."

"Do you think I'm a barbarian? That I would destroy something because I'm afraid of it?"

Indecision warred on her face, and she paused. Her next words made him even angrier. "Would you?"

Everything was collapsing beneath him. All his wild hopes for a future with her, a woman who seemed so smart and pure and who accepted him even though he didn't come from a fancy background like hers.

He tried to block the bitterness from his voice, but it leaked in anyway. "No. I'm not a mindless savage who destroys information that leads to the truth. But you aren't who I thought you were, and I don't think I can ever forgive you for that. *Now back away*."

She did. He backed his car out and sped toward the city without a backward glance. He had evidence of a crime that needed to be turned over to a judge.

Rosalind stood dazed and appalled as Nick's car roared away, her notebooks in tow. He had the results of her research. He had *stolen* them! She had to get them back, but she also had to get to Judge McLaughlin's house. She had no idea how fast Nick's car could drive, but it was over twenty miles to get back home, and the roads were bad. A horse and wagon might be faster than his car.

She hiked up her skirts and ran to the opposite side of the reservoir where one of the filtration plant workers kept a horse and wagon for transporting equipment back to town. It took a full five minutes to get there, and she was breathless as she staggered into the clearing where the plant workers manned the filtration machinery.

"Jack! Can you give me a ride back to town?" she shouted.

"No problem, Dr. Werner," he said as he hauled a sack of

charcoal pebbles toward the storage barn. "Just let me finish unloading this—"

"Now," she said. "I'm sorry, but it's an emergency, and I need to get back to Jersey City right away."

Jack dropped the sack with a thump. "Let's go."

The horses were already hitched to the wagon, and they were on their way within moments. She clenched her teeth as they bumped and jostled along the dirt path toward the main road. There was no sign of Nick's car other than its wheel marks in the dust. She silently urged the horses to move faster, wondering if even now Nick was laying his case before the judge. Or destroying her notebooks. Those notes documented one of the most important scientific experiments anywhere in the world.

She couldn't blot out the memory of how happy Nick looked when he arrived, holding those roses and his face flushed with anticipation. It had all drained away when he realized what she was doing.

Traffic clogged the roads as they got closer to Jersey City. The main street was crowded with horse-drawn wagons, bicycle riders, and pedestrians. She sucked in a breath when she spotted Nick's car navigating traffic, jerking and stopping as he maneuvered through the masses. His sleek automobile could move through the crowd faster than their lumbering wagon.

"I'll get out here," she said to Jack.

"You sure? I don't mind taking you the rest of the way."

"I'll be fine," she said as she clambered off the driver's bench and onto the street.

She could cut through backyards and get to the judge's house faster than Nick could navigate through the traffic on the streets. There was no room for pride as she gathered up her skirts and ran. If she had a prayer of beating Nick to the judge's house, she had to move fast.

Running behind the hardware store let her cut quickly through to her neighborhood. She cut across more backyards and scrambled over fences until she finally arrived at her street. She ran down the center of the street, trying to power through the stitch in her side that made it hard to breathe. She jammed a fist against the ache as she rounded a bend and finally spotted the judge's house. There was no sign of Nick's car.

She cut across the judge's front lawn, staggered up the steps, and pounded on his door. From the end of the street came the rumbling of a car engine, probably Nick, but the curve of the road made it impossible to see.

She swallowed hard, waiting. She pounded on the door again. The judge's wife answered. With fading auburn hair and a toddler propped on one hip, she looked like the epitome of domesticity.

"My heavens, whatever is the matter, dear?"

"Is the judge home? I need to see him at once."

Mrs. McLaughlin's eyes widened, and Rosalind felt the woman's disapproving gaze travel from her disheveled hair all the way down to her muddy shoes. The older woman planted herself in the middle of the doorway, mild censure on her face.

"We're just sitting down to dinner." And it didn't look like Rosalind was going to be invited inside. The chugging of an automobile drew closer and slowed down. Nick had arrived.

Rosalind pushed her way into the house. "This won't take long," she said, hurrying down the front hallway toward the sounds of children. Nick's footsteps thudded on the front porch behind her.

The judge sat at the head of the dining table with children lined up on either side, a large roast and bowls of steaming vegetables already in place.

"Judge McLaughlin," Rosalind panted. "I need to speak with you right away."

Nick barged in front of her. "Not before you talk to me."

"What's all this, then?" Judge McLaughlin demanded. "I recognize you," he said to Nick. "You testified in the water case."

"Nicholas Drake," Nick bit out. "I testified on behalf of the city, and this is Rosalind Werner. She's a scientist for the other side and has been acting in bad faith. She and Dr. Leal have been ignoring your ruling."

"We have not!" she said.

Mrs. McLaughlin stepped forward and snapped her fingers. "Come along, children. It looks as if your father has business that simply cannot wait," she said with a pointed glare.

Rosalind kept her eyes fastened on the judge as the children shuffled out of the dining room. He was a cool one. With steel-gray hair and the build of an athlete, he hadn't moved from his seat as he calmly stirred a spoonful of sugar into his coffee. He took a long sip before turning his eyes to them.

"Well?" he asked as soon as the others had cleared out.

Nick pounced. "I just came from the Boonton Reservoir, and they have a chlorination system in place. It looks like it's been in operation for weeks, maybe longer."

The judge turned his attention to her. "Is this true?"

"Yes," she said simply, for there was no point in soft-pedaling this.

"Everything is already in operation," Nick said. "They've got dissolving tanks feeding chlorine into the city water system even as we speak. That coffee you're drinking is full of it."

The judge was in the middle of another sip when he pulled the cup away from his face, eyeing it as if it had suddenly sprouted fangs. "Really?" He sniffed it and took another tiny sip. "I can't taste it at all."

"That's because it's full of coffee and sugar," Nick said. "Try drinking something straight out of the tap."

The judge stood and headed through an arched hallway into a white-tiled kitchen flooded with sunlight from a window over the sink. Rosalind and Nick followed. The judge took a clear drinking glass from the shelf and lowered it beneath the faucet. Water gurgled in the pipe as he filled the glass. He held it aloft, scrutinizing it carefully. He wiggled it, sniffed it, and then tasted it. Rosalind held her breath as he kept the water in his mouth for a moment, swallowed, and smacked his lips. He took another sip, this time swishing it around in his mouth before swallowing again.

"Ha! I can't taste a thing. Are you sure it's chlorinated?" he asked her.

"I'm sure," she admitted.

"Well, I'll be darned," he said, sounding almost amused.

Nick's eyes flashed. "They've been chlorinating it for weeks. They didn't ask anyone's permission. They just went ahead and started their experiment, using the entire city as their test subjects."

"And it's been working," she said. "That glass of water is safer than the water from any other city in the United States."

"That's your *theory*," Nick bit out. "We don't know for sure, and you had no right to barge in and start that illegal test without permission."

The judge set down the glass and folded his arms as he gazed out the window, a quizzical expression on his face. He didn't seem troubled so much as intrigued. "Actually, there's no law against it."

"There darn well ought to be!" Nick exploded. From a distant room, the toddler started crying at the outburst.

Judge McLaughlin looked annoyed. "Then I suggest you return to New York and pass that law. But don't expect New Jersey to kowtow to it."

Nick stood with a look of stunned disbelief on his face, his jaw hanging open as he stared at the judge. "You're not going to do anything? They ignored your ruling! They barged ahead without permission—"

"My ruling gave them ninety days to make their case. I confess, I didn't expect them to proceed in such an unconventional manner, but there's no law against it."

Rosalind stared in amazement, so overwhelmingly relieved that she felt dizzy, but Nick was snapping mad.

"This won't end here," he bit out. "I'll go to the press. I'll make sure everyone in the country knows what's going on here. I'll find some way to shut this down. They're not going to get away with this."

"He stole my notebooks," she said. It was a harsh word to use, but the results of their experiment were locked in the glove box of Nick's car. The judge could get them back.

"I'm turning them over to the press," Nick said. "They're evidence of a crime."

"Not if that 'crime' took place within New Jersey state lines," the judge said. "You have no authority here, Mr. Drake. I am ordering those notebooks returned."

Rosalind could scarcely believe her luck. Judge McLaughlin had been in the courtroom for two years of testimony and government reports. He had a firm grasp of both sides of the issue and obviously had been at least partially swayed by Dr. Leal's testimony about chlorine. He never would have authorized the ninety-day extension otherwise. And he'd just thrown them another lifeline. She kept any hint of triumph from showing, for Nick had a right to be enraged.

He was silent and motionless, but a muscle bunched in his jaw, and his eyes were fierce as he worked through the problem. His clenched fist held the automobile's key to the glove box, and it would be impossible to get it without his consent. He looked mad enough to explode, but he managed to hold on to the fraying ends of his temper.

"I don't accept your claim that no law was broken," Nick finally said. "I am a commissioner of the State Water Board in

New York. What you do in New Jersey affects us too. If you put poison in your water, sooner or later it leaks over to us. And groundwater doesn't respect state lines."

The judge gave a quick snort of laughter. "Ha! Good point. I will take custody of the notebooks until the matter can be decided."

Nick agreed. Rosalind and the judge followed him to his automobile. His steps bristled with anger as he strode across the lawn. She stood a few feet away as he leaned into the open carriage and unlocked the compartment beneath the driver's bench.

She swallowed hard as he emerged with the notebooks. The temptation to snatch them away made her hands tingle, but she clasped them together, still feeling mildly sick as her notebooks, each page a priceless trove of information, were handed to Judge McLaughlin.

"These will be secured in a locked storage room at the courthouse," the judge said. "Once tempers have cooled, the possession of these notebooks will be handled in a lawful and orderly manner. And now, I would like to return to a very fine roast prepared by my loving wife. Good evening to you both." He headed up the path to his house, her five notebooks tucked into the crook of his arm.

She waited until the door closed behind the judge. "Nick—"

"Don't say a word," he growled.

"Nick, I'm sorry."

"How can you live with yourself?" he demanded, and the contempt in his eyes made her flinch. At first she'd suffered plenty of doubt over the decision she made, but as the weeks unfolded, her sense of certainty had grown.

"I can live with what I've done, and my family will live. Everyone on this street will live. I know that because we've figured it out. Nick, it's working—"

"Shut up," he said. "You've lied and hidden and evaded. Everyone on this street has been your lab rat, and you've got the nerve to justify your actions." He slammed the glove box closed, then turned around to face her again. "And you know what the worst thing is?"

She swallowed hard, bracing herself for another searing assault.

"The worst thing is that for the past two months, I imagined myself in love with you. I thought because you were pretty and smart and feminine that it somehow meant you were perfect. I let myself imagine getting married, welcoming you into my family."

"I was thinking the same thing—"

"Well, quit thinking it. It's over."

He stalked to the front of the car to turn the crank. The sudden roar of the engine made her jump, but she didn't back away. He ignored her as he rounded the car and got inside. "Nick, please . . ."

"Not another word, Rosalind. I don't ever want to hear from you again."

She stood motionless as he drove away, knowing she had just lost something very precious.

Chapter FIFTEEN

Rosalind went straight to her bedroom after returning from Judge McLaughlin's house. When Gus tapped on her door at dinnertime, she apologized and begged to be left alone, for it would be impossible to talk with Gus or Ingrid without cracking. She lay awake most of the night, knowing that she needed to confess the theft of her notebooks to Dr. Leal.

By morning, she was calm enough to tell Gus what had happened, and he helped her put the problem in perspective. Ingrid prepared breakfast only a few yards away and listened to every word.

"Dr. Leal is the one who brought Nick into your business in the first place," Gus said. "He can hardly blame you for what happened."

"I still feel responsible. A third of our data has been seized and might never be returned. I would pull out my own eyeteeth if I could avoid having to tell him."

"Why are you so afraid to stand up for yourself?" Gus said. "You've done nothing to be ashamed of."

Ingrid huffed as she sliced apples atop a bowl of muesli.

Rosalind pretended not to hear, but there was no point in delaying the inevitable. She drew a sobering breath, murmured a prayer for strength, and set off for the lab.

Rather than reveal the terrible news in front of a dozen students, she asked Dr. Leal to step outside, where they spoke beneath the spreading branches of a linden tree. As much as she'd feared a terrible fit from Dr. Leal, he was the epitome of logic and reason.

"We will proceed at full speed with our experiment despite the gap in the data. The judge may rule in our favor, in which case we can quickly plug the gap."

"But what if he doesn't?" she asked in a trembling voice.

Dr. Leal's smile was grim. "That's something over which we have no control, so we'll do our best with what we have. It's all God asks of us."

It was as though a weight had been lifted from her. She would continue working toward their goal with all engines running at full steam, refusing to let external threats slow her steps or discourage her commitment. It was all that God asked of her.

Nick intended to blow the lid off the illegal experiment. Maybe it wasn't any of his business, since his authority ended at the boundaries of New York, but his conscience didn't know how to turn itself off when crossing a state line. He'd lain awake all night wrestling with his options. Most frustrating was the fact that his thoughts kept straying back to how he could protect Rosalind from the firestorm he intended to create. She'd hidden from the limelight ever since what happened in Germany, but he didn't know how to insulate her from this. Or why he should even care. She'd knowingly embarked on this reckless and unethical experiment and deserved any public retaliation she got.

Nothing rivaled the power of the press for stoking public anger, and luckily he knew two people highly placed in the newspaper industry.

It was only eight o'clock in the morning, a little early to be calling on his sister on the weekend, but he was glad he hadn't left it any later. As he was about to board the elevator, the doors slid open to reveal Colin and Lucy on their way out of the building.

"We're heading off to Central Park for some bird-watching," Lucy said. "Want to come?"

He could think of nothing as mind-numbing as being stuck outdoors watching birds. "No," he said abruptly. "Can I pick your brains for ten or twenty minutes first? It's important."

Lucy looked a little taken aback. It was Saturday morning, after all, but she nodded and guided him to the secluded courtyard behind their building. Enclosed by ivy-covered brick walls, they took a seat at the wrought iron table.

"What's going on?" she asked.

The quiet setting contrasted with the turmoil roiling inside him. Colin and Lucy both knew about his work on the Jersey City court case, so he was able to get to the point quickly. He told them how Dr. Leal had abused the judge's trust by proceeding with chlorinating the water supply.

"I want every newspaper in the country to report on this story," he said. "The judge will be forced to act if picketers and protesters make his life miserable."

Colin shifted in his chair. "We can point a few reporters in your direction, but we can't force the newspapers to print anything. That's not how news agencies work."

"I know how news agencies work," Nick snapped. "I also know that you could bang on a few doors to help me out, Colin. I need to sound the alarm."

Then Lucy asked the question Nick had been dreading. "Where

is Rosalind in all of this? Didn't you say she was involved in the Jersey City case? Maybe she could help."

"Rosalind can't help," he said bluntly. "I need to know how to get as many newspapers on the case as fast as possible."

"What do you mean Rosalind can't help?" Colin asked. "I should think she is perfectly placed to contact all sorts of people who live in Jersey City who are concerned with water purity."

"Could you please forget that woman's name?" Nick tried to mask the tension in his voice, but given the way Colin and Lucy both stilled, he hadn't done a good job of it.

"Oh dear," Lucy said. "Was Rosalind part of . . . part of the—"

"Yes. She's up to her eyeballs in it, so please forget she and I ever shared any kind of association." Or that he'd fallen hard for her within five minutes. Or that he'd imagined she was the perfect woman for him.

"Look, I don't think the press is the best way to go," Colin said. "Once you turn the story over to a journalist, you have no control over how it plays out. They may share your outrage, but it's just as likely they will give Dr. Leal a platform to make his case. Jersey City has spent a fortune on lawyers and litigation. *They* are your natural ally, not the press."

Colin had a point. Over the next few minutes, they outlined the various lawyers and municipal officials Nick could marshal in the case against Dr. Leal.

He stood to leave, and Lucy put her hand on his arm. "Nick, I'm sorry about Rosalind. I know you had—"

"Lucy, would you please just drop it?" he snapped, then felt worse for grousing at her when it was Rosalind he was mad at. He pressed a quick kiss to her forehead. "Sorry, Luce. I'm in a mood, but I shouldn't have taken it out on you."

Too many lives hung in the balance for him to ignore what Rosalind had done, and Colin's recommendation was sound.

If Nick played his cards right, he could be in Jersey City within the hour and have the lawyers and municipal officials gearing up for battle first thing on Monday morning.

Monday morning dawned like any other. Rosalind rose early and played with the baby to give her sister-in-law a few moments to herself. For most of the past six months, Rosalind had taken over minding the baby while Ingrid bathed, dressed, and sometimes read the morning newspaper, all in hope of winning a little warmth from her sister-in-law.

It hadn't worked so far, and the temporary thaw that happened after the burglary had been just that: temporary. Ingrid seemed to take it for granted that Rosalind would mind the baby for an hour each morning. Normally that wasn't a problem, but since her notebooks had been seized, she and Dr. Leal needed to come up with another way to compile their data. She didn't have time to finish feeding the baby today. Gus had gone to the library to study in peace, but Ingrid still lingered in the washroom.

Rosalind tapped on the washroom door. "Ingrid? I am late for work. Can you finish feeding Jonah?"

"I'm in the bath," came the shout from behind the closed door.

"Yes . . . can you hurry? I'm late." She had less than ten minutes to get to the streetcar stop. It would be another twenty minutes if she missed it.

Three minutes later, Ingrid emerged to take Jonah, not bothering to hide her frustration at having her bath disturbed. Rosalind ran the five blocks to the streetcar stop and had to wave her hand madly to get the driver to wait for her to sprint the final block and spring aboard.

She still felt a little disheveled as she arrived at the laboratory.

She finger-combed her hair as she drew closer, because good heavens, who were all those people outside the lab? Had Dr. Leal failed to arrive early to open the building? It would be a disaster if the entire team was late getting started because they'd been locked out.

But these people weren't her lab assistants. There were women in the mix, plus a lot of older people she'd never seen before. One of them held a camera, and two others had notepads. They hovered in small groups and showed no interest in stepping aside as she approached the front door.

"Pardon me," she said as she angled through a cluster of people blocking the door.

One of the men with a notebook perked up. "Are you Rosalind Werner?"

"I am," she said. Had she missed a meeting?

All of a sudden the mood grew chillier.

"I'm a reporter for the *Evening Star*. Would you care to comment—"

"Dr. Werner, I need to speak with you immediately," a bald man interrupted. He wore a fine suit with a pricey gold watch chain. She recognized him. He was one of the lawyers for Jersey City during the trial. He grasped her elbow and tried to tug her off the path.

She jerked her arm back. "I need to get to work."

"We need your testimony regarding the flaunting of Judge McLaughlin's orders. Failure to speak with us could be considered an obstruction of justice."

"Are you threatening me?"

"I am reminding you of your responsibility to the citizens of this city," the lawyer pointed out.

"The ones you've been trying to poison," a red-faced woman accused. "How much poison have my three children drunk because of you?"

"When were you planning on telling us?" someone from the back of the crowd shouted. A bright flash momentarily blinded her as the photographer took a picture.

She whirled away, reaching for the front door, but it was locked. Panic clouded the edges of her vision as people bumped into her from behind. She had a key in her reticule, but her hands shook, and she dropped it on the pavement. As she reached down for it, the hailstorm of questions continued. *How much chlorine is in our water? Were you ever going to tell us? Are you really a doctor?* She tried to insert the key in the lock, but she was being jostled so much by the people behind her that she missed.

As if an answer to her prayers, the door suddenly opened and Dr. Leal pulled her inside. A howl of protest rose from the crowd, and the lawyer tried to push in after her, but two of the college students shoved him back out the door.

The instant they were all inside, a student leaned against the door to slam it shut.

"What's happening?" she asked in a shaky voice.

Dr. Leal was astonishingly calm. "What's happening is that we're going to return to the lab and finish compiling the city water report. Outside we have a handful of reporters who have already been provided with a written statement outlining our activities and the success of the plan. We have no obligation to speak to them further."

"What about the lawyer?"

"We *especially* have no need to speak to the lawyer. Don't let him bully you into thinking otherwise."

She followed Dr. Leal and the others down the hallway to the laboratory, where students filled every station and dutifully conducted tests. It was a wonderfully reassuring sight. The structure and logic of science would continue to be played out in this room. Science was a rational discipline, not like the whirlwind of angry emotions whipping up outside their door.

"Let's go into my office to discuss the state of affairs," Dr. Leal said.

Far from being upset by the commotion outside, Dr. Leal was almost levitating with excitement. "I don't know how the reporters were alerted to the issue, but I suspect it was Nicholas Drake, as he is the only man from the opposition team who knows what is going on. Given the publicity, the judge can't wait until the ninety-day deferment ends to address what we have done. A hearing has been ordered for next week. I am the principal witness."

She sucked in a breath. "Are we going to be punished?"

"Doubtful. Based on what you told me about Judge McLaughlin's reaction, he is curious but not insulted. In any event, the city's lawyers are in a twist over it and are going to try to shut us down. I doubt they'll succeed."

It had been bad enough when Nick attacked her for what she'd done. Now the newspapers and lawyers would be piling on as well. She wasn't cut out for this. All she wanted was the safe, rational world of laboratory testing. She'd never wanted to be on the front lines of controversy.

"I don't know how you can be so calm about this," she whispered.

"My dear, I am beyond calm. I am ecstatic. The results of our tests are exactly what we'd hoped. In one week, we will have the opportunity to present our findings to a court of law. It isn't us who are on trial, it is science itself. And I am confident we will win."

Rosalind wished she shared Dr. Leal's confidence, but the role of public crusader didn't come easily to her. She wasn't a rule-breaker or a scofflaw. She was the girl who paid her bills early, walked to the corner to avoid jaywalking, and never missed a deadline.

Now she was at the forefront of a risky venture to change the way this country handled water. Life would be so much easier if she wasn't compelled to join this crusade. Each morning as she left home, she braced for a barrage of hostility, but after the initial upheaval, things took an unexpected turn. Although the articles in the newspapers stirred the concerns of a suspicious public, the stories also dazzled sanitary engineers and water authorities throughout the nation.

A stream of telegrams bombarded Dr. Leal, seeking more insight than could be gleaned from the snatches of information in the press. Almost every day, they had visits from scientists and engineers, asking to see the chlorination system in action. Water specialists from as far away as Chicago and Washington came to witness the revolutionary system. Rosalind let Dr. Leal take the lead in explaining the engineering components while she summarized the work being done in the laboratory. She felt an immediate kinship with these men. They spoke the same language. Their mutual appreciation for science made it easy for her to find common ground with them.

That all changed on Friday, when a man unlike the others came riding up to the Boonton Reservoir with the vigor of an elite athlete. He casually tied his stallion to the hitching post, giving Rosalind plenty of time to admire his tanned, weather-beaten skin, blond hair, and steel-blue eyes. He had the ramrod-straight bearing of a general.

Because he was one.

"General Mike O'Donnell," he introduced himself as he strode across the lawn to shake Dr. Leal's hand.

Rosalind recoiled. This was the man who had participated in the unseemly gossip about her and Dr. Leal while on the golf course with Nick. It was a struggle to remain composed as his gaze trailed to her and he sent her a generous smile.

"You must be Dr. Werner," he said, closing the distance between them. She offered her hand, but instead of a handshake, General O'Donnell bowed and pressed a fleeting kiss to knuckles.

She withdrew as quickly as courtesy permitted. During these final few days before the court hearing, they needed to show their system to as many sanitary engineers as possible. The fight to win chlorination of water was going to be fought city by city, and if they could move New York into their column, it would be a huge coup.

She swallowed back her distaste and followed Dr. Leal and the general inside the chlorination facility. General O'Donnell scrutinized the setup in fascination. He asked no questions but listened intently as Dr. Leal explained the system.

"Impressive," he finally murmured. "I gather Nick Drake is kicking up a fuss over it?"

Rosalind bit her lip. Even thinking about Nick summoned a surge of regrets, and she let Dr. Leal answer the question.

"We haven't given up hope of convincing him of the merits of the system. We will do anything we can to assist New York, should you wish to adapt the technique for the larger reservoirs. New York would be a powerful ally in publicizing the advantages of chlorination."

Rosalind stood to the side, grateful to be left out of this conversation, for it was in this very room where she had watched Nick's admiration for her morph into cold disillusionment. He still might come around to seeing their side. He was an intelligent man and desperately wanted to do the right thing.

But no matter what the fate of their chlorination experiment in the years to come, she knew Nick would never look at her with the same openhearted admiration he once had. She'd been a fool to ever think he could.

Chapter SIXTEEN

Nick's fingers beat a nervous rhythm atop the canister of documents resting across his lap, keeping time with the rackety chugging of the train as it carried him farther north. Nothing about this business trip to Duval Springs was going to be pleasant, but delivering these charts to the town's mayor counted as the worst thing he'd ever been asked to do. It was why his predecessor at the water board had cracked under the pressure and been forced to resign.

Nick wouldn't crack. The governor had appointed him to this position because Nick had the muscle to push this initiative across the finish line. That meant clearing thousands of people out of Duval Springs and arranging to have their homes and businesses pulled down and demolished. No one said it was going to be a cakewalk, and Nick had been bracing himself for the confrontation during the entire two-hour train ride.

The only bright spot was reading the morning newspaper covering the ongoing outrage over the chlorination of the Boonton Reservoir. The mayor of Jersey City had sent a request to Judge McLaughlin for an immediate cease and desist, but the paper had no comment from the judge. All Nick could hope was that the mayor had more success with the judge than he had. The memory of being forced to turn Rosalind's notebooks in to the court's custody still chafed.

His gaze trailed out the window, and he wished his chest didn't still ache each time he thought of Rosalind. Why couldn't she have waited until the expiration of the ninety-day order? If the judge ruled in her favor, he would have accepted it like a man, put on a good face, and then joyfully continued courting her. He wouldn't have let a legal case come between them.

But dishonesty did, and that meant Rosalind would be forever in his past.

The train slowed as it approached the town, chugging slowly past the general store, a couple of churches, and the red brick schoolhouse. This was the kind of village so perfect it ought to be painted on a postcard. It was Nick's job to tell the mayor that the location of the coming reservoir had been finalized, and Duval Springs was about to be destroyed.

Bruce Garrett had warned him what to expect. "The Duval brothers run that town like it's their own private fiefdom. Alex Duval is the mayor, and the town hangs on his every word. Especially the women. Don't let your wives or daughters anywhere near him. The brother also has a lot of power in town, and the two of them are troublemakers."

The muscles in Nick's legs ached as he stood and waited for the dozen other passengers in the car to disembark. He could have paid for a private compartment, but he never felt comfortable splurging on such luxuries when he was alone. He was still a man of the people, no matter how large his bank account had grown.

Not like the mayor he was about to meet. The Duval family had been in control of this village for two hundred years. It had been named after a French fur trapper who settled the area in the seventeenth century, and his descendants controlled the village to this day.

Nick tucked the tube of maps under his arm while scanning the fresh paint on the train station and pristine flower boxes lining the main street. He couldn't deny the Duvals did well by the town, but they were still a pair of entitled men who had inherited everything they owned and refused to see reality.

A woman setting out bread in front of the general store nodded and smiled at him. She obviously didn't know who he was. Not so with the group of men already knocking back beer on the patio of the tavern. A man with a face as gnarled as an old apple shot a stream of tobacco juice at Nick as he walked passed. Nick shifted just in time, but a few droplets still hit his boot. He clenched his teeth. He had bigger battles to fight than a tiff over tobacco juice. Besides, the man had a right to be angry.

"You're not welcome in this town," another man hollered from the patio.

Nick ignored him and kept walking toward the town hall. It wouldn't take long to deliver these maps, and then he could get out of this doomed village on the next train heading back home.

The town hall was a red brick building with white columns and an American flag in the front. It was one of the town's newer buildings, probably only twenty years old, but already the wooden steps had been worn smooth by countless footsteps over the years. The mayor's office was housed in a single room to the left of the front lobby. A young woman staffed the desk.

"I have an appointment with Mayor Duval," Nick said. He couldn't meet her eyes. She was young and fresh-faced, and her welcoming smile was a giveaway that she had no idea why he was here.

Not so with Alex Duval, whose eyes were as hard as flint as he rose from his desk. He was a young man, barely over thirty, but with an air of command from having spent most of his adult life in the army. Nick had dealt with him before, but always from opposite sides of a courtroom as Duval Springs launched a series of injunctions to stop the coming reservoir.

"Hello, Alex," Nick said tersely.

"Let's go to the tavern," the mayor said.

Nick shook his head. Men were already drinking at the tavern even though it was only one o'clock in the afternoon. Tempers were going to get hot, and he didn't want alcohol in the mix.

"We can meet here," Nick said. "Your desk is big enough to spread out the maps."

"But not big enough to have other people at the table. My brother will want in on this conversation, as will the local mill owners. Everyone is already gathering at the tavern."

Nick's jaw tightened. So the men of the town had been waiting for him, and given the fresh tobacco juice on his shoe, things were already getting heated.

Alex headed toward the door, but Nick walked in the opposite direction, setting the tube on the mayor's desk and wriggling out the curled up maps. He wasn't going to be bullied into walking into the lion's den over at the tavern. He used a pencil cup and a coffee mug to weigh down the curling ends of the map.

Alex's curiosity got the better of him, and he wandered back to the desk to scrutinize the map that had been years in the making. In the center of the six-foot map was a stark red line that encircled forty-three miles of rural New York. It was the flow line where the future reservoir would be created, and smack in the middle of the circle was the idyllic village of Duval Springs. In the coming year, thousands of workers would move into the valley to dismantle every house, shop, school, and church in the town. The remnants would be mounded up, set on fire, and the ashes swept away, as though the town had never existed.

Nick watched as Alex studied the map. The young mayor

didn't move a muscle, but the color drained from his face, and his eyes widened. It was impossible not to feel sympathy.

"You can see that Duval Springs is within the flow line," Nick said as gently as he could. "I've brought a court order giving the residents of the village nine months to settle their affairs and leave. I'm sorry, Alex."

Without a word, the mayor pushed the mug aside to curl the map back up. He didn't bother to insert it into the tube, just strode out the door and toward the tavern.

Nick followed, but at a distance. The men at the tavern were about to learn that their entire lives were going to be upended through no fault of their own. The Duval brothers had put up a valiant battle over the past few years, showing up at court hearings and hiring lawyers to argue their case in Manhattan. They had been allowed to have their say. The city's authorities listened respectfully, but everyone could guess the outcome.

Everyone except the people of Duval Springs, who had refused to accept the inevitable.

Ahead of him, Alex spread the map out on one of the outdoor tables of the tavern, and half a dozen men gathered around to scrutinize it. Hercules Duval, the owner of historic Duval Tavern, could not be more different than his younger brother. Well over six feet tall and built with a wall of muscle, he looked like a Viking. If a glare carried heat, Nick would have burst into flame.

Nick kept a respectful distance from the table, but minutes passed, and none of the men spoke as they stared at the map showing the destruction of their world. It was a cool day, but perspiration beaded up and rolled down Nick's back. He'd come to town to deliver the map and the court papers. Decency demanded that he stay to answer questions, but all he wanted to do was sprint to the train station and get out of this condemned village.

"I'll answer any questions you have," he said quietly, bracing himself for the onslaught that was sure to happen. It didn't take long.

The man whose face was like a shriveled apple stepped forward. "I built an extension on my boardinghouse two years ago," he said. "I took out a loan for five thousand dollars, and now you tell me the state is going to pull it down? Is the state going to pay off that bank note?"

It was a fair question, and Nick didn't know the answer. "The state is going to compensate you for all property that can't be moved. I don't know about paying off loans."

"I've got twenty acres of apple trees," another man said. "Fifteen acres are in the flow line, and five aren't. Is the state paying for those five acres too? Because there's not much use in maintaining an orchard of five acres."

Hercules Duval folded his beefy arms across his chest. "Richard, why are you even talking about leaving your orchard? This isn't over yet."

"It's over," Nick said. "You can bury your head in the sand and pretend that the world will stop turning if you keep praying, or you can roll up your sleeves and figure out the next chapter in your lives. It won't be here."

Hercules snorted. "The people of this valley survived the Dutch invasion, the French and Indian War, and the British. We can survive New York City trying to steal our water."

Nick hated this. He hated every second of knocking the foundations out from beneath these men, of grinding their thin sliver of hope into the dust, but it had to be done.

"Government appraisers will be coming into town to take an inventory of the village. I suggest you cooperate and allow them onto your land. They can't get an accurate—"

"My mother died last April," the mayor said. "We buried her

in the family plot alongside eight generations of Duvals. What do you propose we do about that cemetery?"

Nick shifted his weight. Cemeteries were a thorny problem likely to rub salt into the wounds of these people, but all graves would have to be moved. It would be a public health disaster to build a reservoir atop human remains, and government surveyors estimated the valley contained over four thousand graves that would need to be unearthed and reburied elsewhere.

"The government will pay six dollars per body that needs to be disinterred. You're free to move your mother to any cemetery above the flow line."

Hercules lunged forward and shoved Nick back a few feet. "No one is touching my mother's grave," he growled. "Take your six dollars back to New York and shove it where the sun doesn't shine."

A couple of other men banged their fists on the table, grumbling in approval. One man drained his beer and hurled the empty mug at Nick's head. He ducked in time, the glass shattering in the dusty street behind him. He kept his hands at his side. He wouldn't meet anger with anger, but it was getting hard.

"You will have the opportunity to relocate any family graves you choose. If you refuse to move your mother's body, I will make arrangements to have it done for you."

"You and what army?" Hercules roared, then punched Nick in the face.

The force smacked him against the side of the tavern. Everything was spinning as someone put him in a headlock, using a knee to deliver a swift series of blows to his gut. Nick dropped to the ground, tugging his attacker down and rolling over him, firing back with his fists. Someone else kicked him in the ribs. A surge of energy mixed with anger fueled his muscles, powering him to ignore the pain as he got up on his feet just in time to block a punch from a thick-set man.

"That's enough, Jack," the mayor said, hauling the thick-set man away, but a kick from behind sent Nick sprawling back into the dust. More blows fell.

"Nice town you've got here," Nick managed to gasp. It was four against one. Blood filled his mouth, and one eye swelled so badly he couldn't see through it. Someone jerked him upright and punched him in the face so hard that he hit the ground again. Dirt went up his nose and down his throat. He coughed, struggling to get a breath.

"Break it up!" the mayor shouted in a commanding voice, and the beating immediately stopped.

Nick lay curled in the dusty street, holding his breath because it hurt too much to breathe. Slow footsteps approached, and he braced himself as a pair of dusty boots came into his blurry line of vision. There wouldn't be much he could do if another round of kicks were heading his way.

It was the mayor. Alex squatted down beside him, his voice emotionless.

"I can call someone from the Garrett place to come get you," he said. "Or we can put you on the train back to Manhattan. What's your pleasure?"

He chose Garrett's mountainside fortress, as it would be physically impossible to make a two-hour train ride home in his current condition. One of Bruce's bodyguards arrived half an hour later with a wagon. Nick had once thought it idiotic for a real man to need a bodyguard, but maybe he should reconsider it the next time he came to Duval Springs.

And there *would* be a next time. The construction of the reservoir was going to take years, and the Duval brothers couldn't intimidate him into backing down.

It was embarrassing how much help he needed getting into

the back of a wagon. He lay prone in the wagon bed, gritting his teeth each time the wheels bumped over a rut in the road. He'd been in plenty of back-alley brawls in his younger days, but never anything like this. His shoulder, probably dislocated, hurt the worst. He could tell the instant the wagon left the jarring dirt path and rolled onto Bruce Garrett's smoothly paved expanse before the mansion.

Nick leaned on the bodyguard as he staggered toward the house. A flight of six slate stairs loomed before the massive front door, and he clenched his teeth and concentrated on lifting one foot, shifting his weight, and making it to the next step. It was slowgoing and would have been impossible without the bodyguard bearing most of his weight. Each movement hurt, leaving him light-headed and breathless.

The front door flew open before he reached it.

"Oh, Nick!" A pretty woman with red hair and green eyes winced with sympathy as he painfully struggled up the final step. "We heard you had a mishap in town, but I see that was an understatement." She reached out to shake the bodyguard's hand. "Thank you for making the trip. I'm afraid the housekeeper has already closed the kitchen, but she'll make you lunch. If she gives you any trouble, tell her Eloise sent you."

He prepared to follow Eloise into the house, but to his surprise, she slid to his side and wrapped a gentle arm around his waist.

"You can lean on me," she said. "I've got a bedroom prepared, and the doctor has already been called. Should I call Lucy too?"

"No. Don't call Luce," he managed to choke out. The last thing he wanted was his baby sister to see him like this, all weak and staggering around like a whipped dog.

"I heard Lucy got married," Eloise said. "And to an aristocrat! Who would have guessed it?"

Nick shot a curious glance at her through his one good eye.

Did they know each other? He had a memory for faces, but she was a stranger. He'd remember a knockout like her, but she acted like she knew him, so maybe the pounding on his head had scrambled his brains some.

A servant emerged from a back room with a snifter of brandy. Nick reached for it and downed it in one swallow, welcoming the burn as it trailed down his throat. How long was it going to take the doctor to get here?

The bedroom was thankfully on the first floor, since there was no way he'd be able to get up that staircase in the front hall. He was filthy with blood, sweat, and dirt, but couldn't worry about it as he lowered himself to the mattress. Everything hurt. He'd have to buy Garrett a new bedspread, because this one would be ruined. He let out a stream of curses as he lay back on the bed, his ribs howling in pain.

"Sorry, ma'am," he said between gritted teeth. "I'm not usually such a bounder."

"Don't worry about it, Nick. You were always my hero. Here, let me help you out of your shoes."

He was too miserable to protest as she tugged his boots off, but what had she just said? He cocked his head to see her better.

"Do I know you?" he asked through swollen lips.

Her hands stilled, and now she was looking at him with a wounded expression. "You don't remember me?"

Something about that wounded expression in her eyes triggered a memory . . . like a lost little girl. His eyes widened. "Ellie?"

She sat down on the mattress beside him. "Of course."

"I thought you were in Rome!" he choked out. "Guess you got back."

"Rome? I've never been to Rome in my life."

That was odd. "Your mother said you were in Rome. At least, I think she did." The brandy was beginning to cloud the edges of his memory. "Piano. She said you were a great pianist."

The color drained from Eloise's face. "Oh, I see. I should probably touch base with her so I know what the story is. These little slipups can be so embarrassing."

She dropped one boot and went to work on the other. "Enough about Mother. Tell me what I can do to make you more comfortable before the doctor gets here. More brandy? An ice pack? Just tell me what you need, and I'll go to the ends of the earth for it."

The doctor arrived with a large bottle of pain-killing morphine, after which everything was a blur. Nick roused with a roar when his arm was manipulated back into his shoulder socket, but after that there was only pain and mind-numbing thirst. Every time he felt himself clawing up through the fog of sleep, the pain made him want to sink back into oblivion.

And every time he awoke, Eloise was right there, waiting with a cool glass of water, leaning over him, smelling like vanilla and sunshine. He tried to thank her, but he was too weak or drugged to make his mouth work. She always stopped him when he tried to thank her.

"Shh. When I was growing up, you were the only person who was ever nice to me. I'd do anything in the world for you."

Her voice was soothing, like warm velvet. He struggled to maintain his focus, but the drugs were making it hard to see, and one eye was completely closed up. He couldn't make out her features, just the brilliant reddish-auburn hair worn in a braid and impossibly green eyes in a pale face.

Another figure stood behind her, his hands on her shoulders. Bruce Garrett. Nick ought to rise and say something, thank him for the welcome after being beaten half to death.

"Don't try to talk, my friend," Bruce said gently. "Eloise will look after you."

Nick closed his eyes, too tired to respond.

Nick awoke, his head throbbing and entire body stiff, but most of all he was ferociously hungry. For the first time, there was no sign of Ellie—or Eloise, as she now seemed to be calling herself. Every time he emerged from the fog of sleep, he'd seen her here, often with Bruce right alongside her. He remembered them reading together. There, in the corner by the window, Eloise had been at one side of the table, reading, and Bruce had been pacing the room. They seemed very comfortable with each other.

A little bell was on his bedside table. He felt pretentious using it, but he needed help and doubted he'd get very far if he went in search of it. The drugs had worn off, and the simple act of sitting up made it hard to breathe. Tight bandages bound his ribs, his right arm was in a sling, and his lower lip was crusted with blood. At least he was able to open his left eye, which had been swollen shut for what seemed like days.

Shortly after he rang the bell, a portly woman with frizzy brown hair hustled into the room, carrying a platter loaded with a pitcher of water and, mercifully, a bowl of something that smelled delicious.

"How is our patient feeling this morning?" she asked in a bright voice.

"Fine." A lie. Everything hurt and throbbed, but all he cared about was whatever smelled so good. "Hungry."

"I expect so. Sit up, and I'll prepare a tray for you." She introduced herself as Mrs. Hofstede, the housekeeper who also did a bit of work in the kitchen. "I hope you like tomato soup. The doctor said he didn't think you should be eating anything too hefty, but I grated up a big wedge of cheese into it, because otherwise I didn't see much point in plain tomato soup."

When he tried to smile his entire face hurt, but that bowl of soup was moving closer, and he'd never smelled anything so good. And it tasted divine. Warm, tangy, and oh, that cheese. How long had it been since he'd eaten?

He polished off the last of the soup and was still famished. "Is there any more? I hate to clean out Garrett's pantry, but I'm starving."

"I expect you are," the housekeeper said as she took the bowl from him. "You've been out of commission for three days."

Three days! He'd been wallowing here for three entire days? He pivoted on the bed to put his feet on the floor.

"Now don't you worry," Mrs. Hofstede soothed. "Mr. Garrett called your house and let them know about the mishap, so there's no need to panic. Your sister even sent up a box of your favorite lemon cookies."

"Is Mr. Garrett here? I'd like to speak with him."

"He's out at the quarry, but I'll send a message that you're awake and would like to see him. He usually comes in for lunch. Is there anything you need? Just say the word, and we'll take care of it."

He shifted his weight. Beneath the nightshirt he was wearing, he was naked. "Are there some clothes I can borrow? Mine were a mess, but I expect most of it will come out in the wash."

She shook her head. "I'm afraid your shirt was a goner, and the doctor had to cut your trousers off. We had one of the servants go into town to buy a fresh change of clothes. I'll send him in."

It annoyed Nick to spend a dime in Duval Springs, but he could hardly return to New York in a nightshirt, and he was too big to fit in Garrett's clothes. A stable man came in to help him change, and then Nick carefully picked his way across the room to step through the bedroom's double doors onto a flagstone patio stretching along the back of the house. From here he could see all the way down into the valley, the sloping mountainside covered with forest except for where Garrett's quarry cut into the land like a bright ivory scar.

As badly as his body ached, it felt good to be out in the fresh air with a view of the sprawling valley. The housekeeper brought another bowl of soup, a platter of warm rolls, and some grapes. He was just about to tuck into the soup when he spotted Bruce Garrett striding up the path leading to the patio, taking the steps two at a time.

"Back among the living, I see!" Bruce called.

Even watching Garrett's vigorous climb made Nick's body ache, but he nodded with a grateful smile. "I'm indebted to you for your hospitality. I think the folks in Duval Springs would have just as soon poisoned me."

Bruce flung himself into the chair opposite him, his face a study in grim acceptance. "The reservoir is dividing the valley. Some are eager for the influx of jobs, but people below the proposed flow line are fighting like rabid dogs."

The reservoir's flow line wasn't "proposed" anymore. It was a done deal, but Nick didn't want to quibble about wording. The people of Duval Springs could pack up and leave, or they would be forcibly evicted. Beating him to a pulp hadn't frightened him, it just hardened his resolve.

"Where is Ellie?" he asked. "I haven't seen her in years and was surprised to see her here."

Bruce reached for a handful of grapes and tossed a few in his mouth, chewing slowly as he surveyed the mountainside. "Who?" he finally asked.

This was ridiculous. Each time Nick had emerged from the fog of drug-induced sleep, he'd seen the two of them together, quite cozy.

"Ellie Drake," he said tightly. "She's my cousin and Margaret Drake's daughter. She was here when I was brought in and seemed to have the run of the place as she got me settled. Where is she?"

"Ah, you mean Eloise," Bruce said, although Nick had a hunch that Bruce knew exactly who he'd been referring to. "She's my accountant. She was up here to reconcile the end-of-month statements."

"She works for you?"

He shook his head. "She works for Millhouse Jones in Manhattan. They've handled my books for decades, but she was assigned to the quarry a few years back. That girl is an absolute genius with numbers."

"She called you 'Bruce.'"

Garrett's mouth stiffened as he tightened his fist. "What are you implying?"

"She seems like more than an employee. The two of you seem very close." When Nick staggered in the front door, she'd been ordering the servants around as though she was the lady of the manor.

"Drag your mind out of the gutter," Garrett warned, his voice as sharp as the glare in his eye.

"Ellie Drake is my cousin," Nick said. "Her parents never gave a fig about her, and if she's alone in the world, I'm not going to stand aside and let some rich older man take advantage of her."

Bruce stood up. "I'll have a carriage brought around, and then you can get out of my house."

He didn't see Bruce Garrett or Eloise again. Within five minutes, a carriage arrived at the front of the mansion. The housekeeper informed Nick that the next train to Manhattan would leave in less than an hour, so they had to hurry.

As if catching the train was the reason for his banishment from the Garrett mansion. It was more like Nick had come dangerously close to revealing something about Eloise Drake that Garrett wanted hidden.

It was going to be a painful journey back to Manhattan. At

least he had a newspaper to divert his attention from the gnawing pain. He rarely went this long without reading the papers and eagerly devoured stories about the mayor's new budget and a proposed subway line beneath the East River. He turned to the last page of the newspaper, where they covered news from the tri-state area.

And he saw it.

The judge in the chlorine case was holding a hearing *today* on whether Dr. Leal should be allowed to continue his unauthorized chemical testing. Today! The matter of the notebooks would be decided too. All this had been happening while he was napping in bed like an infant.

Suddenly he was grateful for having been unceremoniously thrown out of Garrett's mansion. He had no idea how fast he could get to Jersey City, but one thing was certain. He was going to be in that courtroom when the judge ruled.

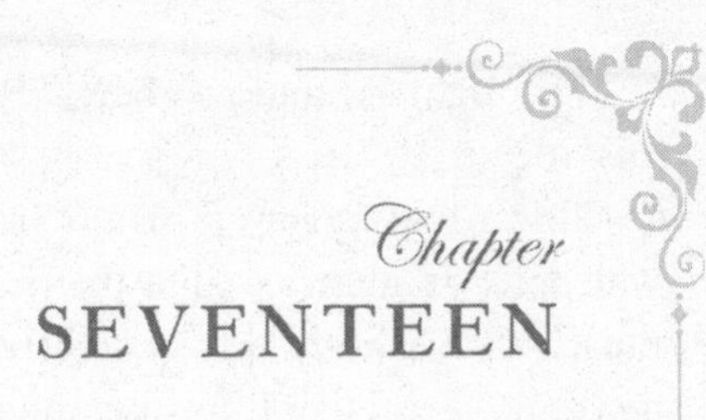

Chapter SEVENTEEN

Rosalind sat in the back row of the packed courtroom, waving a fan in the overheated room. The hearing to determine the fate of her notebooks and Dr. Leal's ability to continue the chlorine tests was about to begin, and she'd never been so nervous in her life. They were on the cusp of something great, but it could all come crashing down if the judge ordered a halt to their research.

Dr. Leal was the only witness, which was a blessing, for she dreaded speaking in public. She got tongue-tied, nervous, and unable to speak with the ease that came effortlessly to Dr. Leal. She admired his poise as he calmly placed his hand on the Bible and took an oath to tell the truth, then began fielding a barrage of angry questions from the city's attorney.

There were no impartial observers in the courtroom. Across the aisle, the benches were crammed with city officials, angry lawyers, and journalists who scribbled furiously to keep up with the rapid-fire interrogation of Dr. Leal. Her side of the courtroom was filled with scientists and the laboratory assistants who had been helping with the analysis. To Rosalind's surprise, General Mike O'Donnell slid onto the bench beside her only a few minutes after the hearing began.

"I thought I'd find you here," he said quietly. "What have I missed?"

"Just a few warm-up insults from the city's attorney," she whispered, embarrassed at the tremor in her voice, but every muscle in her body was so tightly wound that it was hard to be calm. "I feel like I'm watching a puppy being savaged by a wolverine. Dr. Leal is a very brave man."

The general reached over to squeeze her hand. "He's got the best ally any man can have. He's got the truth on his side."

Modesty prompted her to pull her hand away. Surely General O'Donnell hadn't meant anything by the gesture. It was simple kindness, and his presence today gave her a shot of badly needed confidence. Other sanitary engineers from the tri-state area were on their side of the courtroom, but as a man in charge of New York City's water supply, General O'Donnell was the most prominent of their supporters. The fact that he had come to their side of the courtroom was a powerful declaration of support.

She just hoped his presence would not cause problems for Nick. If there was a falling-out among the three-member board of commissioners, the public would instinctively side with General O'Donnell, a war hero with decades of public service to his credit. Nick's appointment was still controversial. It was anyone's guess how Fletcher Jones, the third member of the commission, would vote.

As the morning progressed, Dr. Leal calmly touted the success of the experiment, seeming to anger the city's lawyers, which was odd. A rational person ought to be thrilled that the city now had an efficient and low-cost means of providing pure water to their citizens, but the lawyers had been circling like sharks all morning.

"Would you give chlorinated water to your own wife?" a lawyer for the city demanded. "Your own child?"

"I would, and have done so," Dr. Leal said calmly.

Sitting behind his elevated desk, Judge McLaughlin listened to every word, rarely intervening but taking copious notes. After a short break for lunch, Dr. Leal was back on the stand, continuing to take abuse from the city's attorneys, who questioned everything from his academic credentials to his decision to hire students for processing the test results.

Rosalind fanned herself, anxious on Dr. Leal's behalf and wondering how much longer this line of questioning would drag on. A commotion near the doorway caught her attention. The man hobbling into the courtroom reminded her of Nick, except that his face was covered in bruises.

She stood for a better look, because good heavens, it *was* Nick, and he looked horrible. One side of his face was swollen with purple bruises, and he had a cut on his lip and an arm in a sling.

The glare he shot her made her freeze. It had been more than a week since she'd seen him, and it appeared his fury had not cooled. He limped past her to take a seat on the city's side of the courtroom, lowering himself gingerly onto a bench.

She couldn't move, couldn't think. People stared at her as she remained standing, but she was too dumbfounded by Nick's terrible appearance to move.

The judge tapped his gavel. "Dr. Werner? Have you something to say?"

"No sir," she said, quickly dropping back into her seat.

Dr. Leal continued his testimony, but she couldn't tear her eyes away from Nick.

"Do you know what happened to him?" she asked General O'Donnell.

"He got into a tussle upstate with some folks who are angry about the new reservoir. Don't worry. Nick's a tough son of a gun."

The firestorm of abuse hurled at Dr. Leal continued. "And how are we to have faith that the poison you are dumping in the water supply is effective?"

"We have six weeks of data proving it. I am confident any qualified scientist in the country can examine the reservoir water and confirm its purity. The notebooks in Judge McLaughlin's custody are proof of it."

"We have only your word for that," the lawyer said, contempt dripping from his voice.

"Dr. Werner and twelve doctoral students in chemistry can attest to what is in those notebooks. I am prepared to submit them to any qualified expert in the country for interpretation."

Judge McLaughlin raised his chin. "Dr. Werner is in the courtroom. I'd like to ask her to the stand for her assessment."

The bottom dropped out of Rosalind's stomach, and she felt light-headed. Oh, this was awful.

General O'Donnell nudged her, and she stood on knees that felt like water and made her way to the front of the courtroom. Dr. Leal had already vacated the witness box, and she headed straight toward it, not daring to look to her left or right, lest she catch sight of all the angry people glaring at her.

The amusement on the judge's face was her first sign that she'd done something wrong. "Would you please return to the registrar to be sworn in?" he asked.

Only an idiot would have walked straight past the man who stood with a Bible already held forth. Heat flushed her face as she walked back to him, laid her hand on the grainy leather, and took her oath.

After taking a seat behind the witness box, she kept her gaze riveted to the table before her, but even so, she sensed Nick's smoldering presence in the back of the courtroom. She would not let him frighten her. She had truth on her side.

"Please characterize the nature of the information you were

collecting in the notebooks currently in the court's custody," the judge asked.

Her tongue was glued to the roof of her mouth, and she wished she had a glass of water. "It is mostly an analysis of how chloride of lime affects oxygenation in the water," she stammered. "It triggers a form of combustion as the organic matter is oxidized . . . which, of course, bacteria is organic matter, so the effects are dramatic—"

The judge cut her off. "Just characterize the conclusion," he prompted.

"After chlorination, the water is rendered sterile. Our conclusion is that chlorine works," she said simply.

The judge banged his gavel. "I am prepared to rule," he said abruptly. "Dr. Leal may continue with his experiment until the expiration of the ninety-day deferment. After his report is submitted, the court will render its final verdict. For now, Dr. Werner's notebooks will be returned, and the experiment may proceed."

Her breath left her in a rush. Thank heavens!

The courtroom erupted into a mix of applause and angry grumbles. Reporters dashed down the aisle, racing for the few public telephone booths to call in their stories. Townspeople clustered together, looking stunned at the abrupt decision. Dr. Leal beamed at her from the front row, but all she could see was Nick painfully navigating his way through the packed courtroom toward the door.

"Nick!" she shouted, but if he heard her, he did not turn around. She angled around the people crammed in the aisles, twisting between them to make her way toward Nick. He was still moving slowly, and she caught him in the lobby, laying a hand on his good arm.

"Nick, can we talk about this?" she pleaded, but if anything, her soft tone seemed to set him off.

"Don't pretend you're sorry," he growled. "Don't try to sweet-talk me into believing anything you have to say. I saw you cozying up to O'Donnell. Trying your charm on him now?"

She gasped, but before she could defend herself, General O'Donnell was right there at her side.

"Don't be an idiot, Drake. I've had a chance to review Dr. Leal's work, and it's sound."

"Who told you that?" Nick demanded. "Did she smile and tell you how wonderful you were at the same time she was twisting the dial on that chlorine drip behind your back?"

She flinched at the scorn in his voice. "Nick, this isn't the place—"

"Then where is the place? We had plenty of time over the past few weeks, and yet somehow you never got around to it. Congratulations on getting your notebooks back so you can continue with that underhanded test. You must be—"

The general cut him off. "Their methods were unconventional, but their science is sound."

"He's right, Nick," she said, wishing he would at least look at her.

Bystanders bumped into Rosalind, angling around her to get to the front door, but some loitered nearby, listening in. At least one reporter had his notepad open and was scribbling down every word. The last thing she wanted was the personal details of this argument spilled out before the press, but Nick was on a roll and didn't seem to care.

"So the two of you are on the same side now," Nick said, his voice dripping with contempt. "You *know* what he said about you behind your back on that golf course, and still you're cozying up to him. What a convenient arrangement you have. First Dr. Leal sends you to soften me up, and now you're going after another admirer."

She recoiled at the insult. It was Heidelberg all over again.

Even knowing she was vulnerable to matters of reputation, he stood in a public courthouse and threw mud on her anyway.

She scrambled to defend herself. "All I did was consult with General O'Donnell on a scientific experiment. To suggest anything else is just vulgar."

"Well, I'm obviously a vulgar man," Nick shouted. "I've never been to college or sailed down the Danube, so that makes me a real peasant in your eyes, right?"

"Let's continue this conversation in the judge's chamber," Dr. Leal suggested. Rosalind wasn't sure when he'd arrived, but she was grateful for it. "Both sides have legitimate—"

A reporter interrupted them. "General O'Donnell! Are you going to chlorinate the water in New York City?"

"Over my dead body," Nick growled.

"What does the third commissioner have to say about chlorine?" the reporter pressed.

"Keep Fletcher Jones out of this," the general said. "While you're at it, keep Drake out of it too. I am in charge of sanitary engineering in New York, and I'll be calling the shots. I'll gather a team of the best consultants—"

"And the prettiest, I'm sure," Nick said. "I wonder if she'll let you kiss her too."

"Now that is beyond enough!" she snapped. Normally she ran from this sort of confrontation, but he'd pushed her too far. "If you think I will be a doormat while you trample over me and Dr. Leal, you are gravely mistaken. You can follow us into the judge's chambers to discuss this in a civilized manner, or you can stand out here and try to shout us down, but you can't put a lid on our research. The truth is going to come out, and your tantrum won't stop it."

Her words took him aback, and his wounded expression made him appear suddenly vulnerable. "I don't have a problem with the truth," he said quietly. "I value the truth so highly that

I insist upon it. I once thought you were as pure and pretty as a moonbeam, but you didn't trust me enough to be honest. You lied and schemed and evaded."

"I didn't!" But she had. The truth clobbered her, and she wanted to melt into the floor. It hurt to meet his gaze. "I'm so sorry," she whispered.

"I am too." He turned and stalked away.

Rosalind could still hear the clicking of cameras and the excited murmurings of the journalists as she returned to the laboratory with Dr. Leal and the research assistants. She couldn't afford to retreat home to nurse her wounds in private. They had work to do.

Already the students were entering the data from her notebooks into the overall report. George Fuller was there to help strategize the next steps.

"I saw General O'Donnell speaking with you in the courtroom this morning," Dr. Leal said. "What were you talking about?"

"He said I shouldn't be nervous about the outcome. That we have the truth on our side."

Mr. Fuller was unusually somber. "I'm glad O'Donnell sees the truth, but we need to start thinking bigger than winning in Jersey City."

"What do you mean?" she asked.

"Jersey City is small potatoes," Mr. Fuller said. "The real prize is New York City. And Philadelphia. Chicago, Boston, Atlanta. We need to make the case for chlorination to the rest of the nation."

"But we need to win this battle first," Dr. Leal said in a cautious tone.

Mr. Fuller shook his head. "Judge McLaughlin is only one man. Don't put too much credence in his decision one way or the other. With luck, Jersey City will be a symbolic victory, but we need to prepare for a war on the national level. I want to roll this technology out to the rest of the country, and the battle will be fought city by city." He turned his gaze to her. "You say General O'Donnell is supportive of chlorine?"

"He seemed to be," she agreed.

"Then we start with him. Come. We need to plan this carefully."

Rosalind tried to concentrate on the conversation at hand. After all, what could be more important than ensuring a pure water supply in cities all across the nation? Millions of lives depended on it.

But trying to focus on the conversation wasn't working. Behind her cool expression, it felt like her dreams were crumbling. A piece of her had hoped that Nick might forgive her once the court case was over, but that hope was gone. The scorn in his eyes, the awful words he'd hurled at her in full view of the press and half the town were impossible to forget. She'd seen an angry, vengeful side of Nick she didn't know existed. It had been aimed directly at her. Even if Nick could forgive her, she would never be able to wholeheartedly trust him again.

"Rosalind?" Dr. Leal's voice interrupted her wayward thoughts.

"I'm sorry. What did you say?"

"Can you get General O'Donnell to provide a written endorsement of the chlorination technique?"

She barely knew the general, but he had singled her out for attention in the courtroom this morning. Yes, he'd said some unseemly things about her on a golf course, but this crusade was more important than her personal pride. Since she was ten years old, she'd known exactly what she wanted to do with her life, and General O'Donnell could be a powerful ally.

"I'll get it," she said.

Mourning Nick's loss was a waste of her time, but winning General O'Donnell to their side could be a triumph.

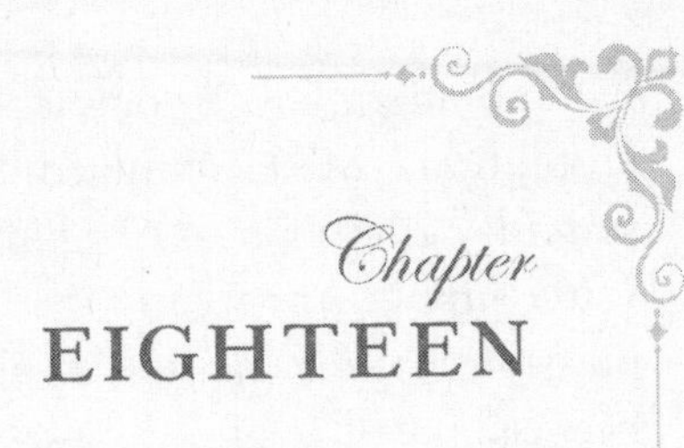

Chapter EIGHTEEN

Nick headed to the office early the following morning. General Mike O'Donnell occupied a suite of offices on the opposite side of the building, and Nick had an apology to deliver.

As it happened, he didn't even have to wait until he got to the ninth floor. General O'Donnell was waiting for the elevator when Nick entered the lobby of their office building.

"I'm sorry I acted like an angry boar in court yesterday," he said gruffly as he drew up alongside Mike to wait for the elevator.

The general shot him a skeptical look. "Do you really think I'm susceptible to a pretty face?"

Nick had been. "Not really. I was just in a mood. I'm sorry you were in the line of fire."

The elevator doors opened, and the attendant inside gestured them both aboard.

"Don't worry about it," Mike said with a hearty clap on Nick's bad shoulder, the one still in a sling.

Nick grunted at the jolt of pain but didn't complain. Mike knew exactly what he'd been doing with that carefully controlled smack, and Nick deserved it.

"You might have a tougher time earning Fletcher Jones's absolution," Mike continued. "Reporters swarmed his office yesterday afternoon, asking him about chlorine in New York's water supply. Apparently they were under the mistaken impression that the decision would be made by a majority vote between the three of us."

The elevator attendant chimed in. "We had six reporters in the space of three hours," he said. "Then protesters got word of chemicals being dumped in the water, so they started rushing the building. I had to spend an extra hour last night just getting dirt out of the carpets."

"Sorry about that," Nick said to the attendant, digging into his pocket for a few coins. "Please accept a belated tip."

His public spewing of anger seemed to have caused a rumpus all around, even for the staff in his building. Fletcher was a master of finance, but the mild-mannered bean counter had probably been appalled at the rush of reporters.

"I'll swing by Fletcher's office and apologize in person," Nick said, regretting his outburst in the courtroom more with each passing minute. He'd wanted to hurt Rosalind, and he had. He just wasn't proud of it, nor how others had been swept into the maelstrom.

The elevator doors slid open, and they both stepped out. "Come to my office first," Mike said.

Nick followed, curious about the general's enigmatic expression as they passed through a set of double doors into the suite of offices occupied by the engineers and draftsmen already planning the new aqueduct. They crossed the large workroom filled with blackboards, blueprints, and drafting tables toward the private offices.

The general's office was a reflection of the man, with well-made but plain furniture, a sparsity of decoration, and an entire wall of bookshelves weighed down with engineering manuals.

He gestured to the work table, and Nick sat. In short order, Mike grabbed three heavy binders of paperwork and set them on the table with a heavy thump.

"This is the research the army has been doing into chlorine," he said, taking a seat on the opposite side of the table and paging through the binders. "The Americans lost more men in the Philippines to waterborne disease than combat. For months I lived in a sweltering tent and watched my men drop like flies around me. I set up latrines well away from sources of water, but even so, the mobile filtering devices we used couldn't keep up with demand. In frustration, I finally ordered the cooks to put a few drops of chlorine into the cooking water and any water used for public drinking. Cases of typhoid and dysentery evaporated."

He pushed the binder, open to a page filled with tables and statistics, in front of Nick, but Nick didn't want to look at it. "That's it? Just added a few drops?"

"A few drops of chlorine, stir, and wait an hour. It didn't taste great, but it protected my men."

It sounded very different than the complicated system at the Boonton Reservoir, with dilution tanks and calibrated drip lines. When he pointed this out, Mike nodded.

"The setup for Jersey City is impressive, but I was under battlefield conditions in the Philippines. Disease was mowing down our troops faster than the enemy, and I needed to put a stop to it. In the years that followed, I kept in touch with the men in my unit. As far as I can tell, there has been no lingering aftereffects from the chlorine."

Nick looked away. A battlefield decision was very different than what was going on in Jersey City. Even if Nick had been stationed in the Philippines, he didn't know if he'd have had the nerve to foist an experimental solution on unknowing men. He said as much to the general.

"Make no mistake, we are still in a war here at home," Mike said. "The enemies are microscopic invaders, and it takes constant vigilance to hold them at bay. Most of the time filtration can do the job, except when summer rains overwhelm the system. So we need to decide if we accept a few hundred deaths each year as the normal cost of living in a city, or do we roll the dice and stop disease in its tracks. I rolled the dice in the Philippines, and I've never regretted it."

"And there were no long-term effects?"

"Chlorine poisoning shows up quickly. Burning in the nose or esophagus. Maybe some blood in the stool or vomiting. Once it is flushed out of the system, a person's health returns to normal. With the miniscule amounts we used, we never had an issue."

Nick glanced at the tables of statistics before him, years of carefully observing men in a controlled environment. This was the kind of long-term data he'd been searching for, and it backed up Rosalind's theories.

He remembered the day in her laboratory when she'd showed him how quickly chlorine killed germs under the microscope. He'd told her that if she could prove chlorination did no long-term damage, he'd be the first man to dance in the streets in celebration. She hadn't known about General O'Donnell's medical studies, or she would have told him.

"Why didn't you tell Dr. Leal about this?"

"I didn't know what he was doing until you blew the whistle. Had I known, I would have backed him up. Scientific research shouldn't be done in isolation. Usually we publish our research in journals or at conferences . . . except when the topic is too hot. I wasn't particularly eager to let it be known that I used an experimental technique on enlisted soldiers, and Dr. Leal had his own reasons for wanting to avoid the glare of publicity."

Well . . . this was good news. Extraordinary news. Chlorine could never replace filtration, but if the chemical could safely obliterate the threat of microscopic disease, it was a miracle beyond anything he'd expected to see in his lifetime.

Rosalind had been right. They now had the answer to delivering clean water safely and inexpensively.

Instead of elation, a heartbreaking sense of loss weighed on him. Things should have gone differently for him and Rosalind. If she could have trusted him enough to be honest, their lives could have been so much better. The crush of shame darkened his spirit, for his temper had done a fair share of the damage that ruined any hope of a future for them. They had both burned their bridges with each other, and his sadness was overwhelming.

In an effort to get Rosalind from his mind, Nick turned his attention to the mystery that had haunted him ever since the world-class beating he'd taken in Duval Springs. A future with Rosalind was a lost cause, but not so with Aunt Margaret and Eloise.

He needed to see Aunt Margaret to dig out the truth about Eloise. He took a carriage to the Lower East Side, trying to hold rigid to keep the pain bearable as the carriage jolted over potholes and broken pavement. He finally arrived at the school for adult immigrants shortly before the dinner hour. The school was in a modest storefront nestled between a meat monger and a cigar shop. A large sign over the door read *Classes in Writing and Speaking English*. Beneath the large text, the phrase was repeated in Italian, German, Russian, and Yiddish.

Rumor had it that Margaret came to the school every Tuesday and Thursday to oversee the accounts and ensure the teachers were on task. He had no warm feelings for his aunt, but he still admired what she had created here. There was dignity to be had in a hard and thankless task like this.

The door squeaked as he entered. It smelled musty inside,

and to his right was a large room of women reciting phrases from a McGuffey Reader. On the other side of the hall was a small office. He stepped inside to speak to the secretary manning the front desk.

He startled when the secretary looked up, for it was Aunt Margaret. He'd never seen her dressed in anything but the finest silks, but today she wore a plain black dress with a cameo at her throat.

She burst into laughter when she saw him. Apparently realizing how rude it was, she clamped a hand over her mouth, but her eyes still danced with amusement.

"What happened to you?" she asked with a pointed look at his sling. He tried to give her a good-natured smile, but it made his face hurt, and he didn't much feel like it anyway.

"I ran into a spot of trouble upstate."

Her eyes took on a strange gleam. "It looks like more than a spot of trouble. It looks like a pair of strong fists."

More like four pairs of fists, but he didn't want to relive the event. He wanted answers about his cousin.

"Fine, whatever you like," he said. "I came to ask a few questions. Is there someplace we can speak privately?" Accusing his aunt of lying about her only daughter wasn't something he wanted to do within earshot of her employees, but Aunt Margaret's shrug was nonchalant.

"Privacy is something that is never in abundance in this neighborhood. This is the best we can do."

The office had no door and only a large desk in the center. The walls were covered with mismatched filing cabinets and bookshelves loaded down with spelling manuals and basic readers. Despite her callous welcome, he had to remember that Aunt Margaret was doing good work here. He owed her respect.

"I was up at Bruce Garrett's house last week," he said, noticing the stiffening around Margaret's lips but no other change in her expression. She was going to be a tough nut to crack, and he decided to confront the situation head on. "I saw Ellie while I was there."

Margaret didn't seem surprised by his statement. She just kept looking at him with that oddly unnerving stare, her face as still as the cameo at her throat.

"She said she's never been to Rome in her life. She's working as an accountant, not a pianist."

The sound of heavily accented women reciting rote verses filled the empty air, and Margaret seemed as composed as a long-stemmed rose.

"What would you like me to say?" she finally asked.

"I just want to find out what happened to my cousin. I don't know what she's doing these days or where she lives, but maybe I can help her. I've got a lot of connections in the city."

Margaret's smile was bitter. "Eloise will land on her feet. You can always count on her for that, if nothing else."

Obviously there was no love lost between Margaret and her only daughter, but Eloise and Bruce seemed to have some kind of connection. On the few occasions Nick emerged from the fog of a drug-induced slumber, the two of them had seemed quite cozy as they sat at the corner table. They had been laughing together. She had called him Bruce. Perhaps Margaret's contempt had something to do with an unwholesome relationship. Bruce was an attractive man, still fit and vigorous despite his age, with only a hint of silver threads in his coppery-red hair.

The same color as Ellie's hair. Both Margaret and her husband had inky black hair, as did their son. Only Ellie had that distinctive russet shade.

Suddenly, a possible reason for Ellie's shunning became clear. "Is Bruce Garrett her father?"

It was a wild guess, but it didn't seem to surprise Margaret as she rose and fixed him with an icy stare.

"Let me make something clear," she said as she rounded the desk. "Thomas Drake was the love of my life. That man pulled me out of obscurity and gave me a glorious existence. And if there was a time when his interest faded and I did something rash to get his attention . . . well, he stood by me in the end. He took me back, and I loved him with every cell in my body. I will do everything possible to burnish his memory, no matter how long it takes or who it hurts along the way."

Apparently that meant banishing a daughter who had an uncanny resemblance to one of Thomas's business associates, but he sensed there was more beneath Margaret's statement. There was a veiled threat in there, even though he'd done nothing but extend the hand of friendship to her since Thomas's passing.

"I'm not your enemy, Margaret."

"No?" she asked with a curious smile. "It didn't feel that way when you were on the opposite side of the courtroom during my son's trial. You looked triumphant; like it was the best day of your life."

Tom Jr. deserved everything the judge had thrown at him, but mending fences was going to require both of them to quit looking at the sins of the past and simply move forward. He hadn't been perfect during those years either.

"I'm ready to let bygones be bygones," he said.

"That must be easy for a man in your position," she countered. "Perhaps I'll be willing to declare a cease-fire when the scales are balanced. I lost my husband and my son. Who will you lose, Nick?"

It was a threat. He heard it as clearly as a warning shot fired across the bow of a ship. He took a step forward so that he bumped into her, knocking her back a few steps.

"What are you implying?" he demanded. He had an innocent daughter and a sister. It was a pitifully short list of people he cherished, but he wouldn't let Margaret hurt either one. He wouldn't even let her threaten them.

"I'm pointing out the obvious. You aren't so pure. You invited yourself to Oakmonte and acted like a high-minded hero, but it was *you* who ruined my husband. I will hate you until my dying day." Malice exuded from her voice, matching the glittering anger in her face.

He was poleaxed. Never had he seen such undiluted hate aimed squarely at him, and he hadn't expected it. The most chilling thing about her statement was that she seemed to enjoy her hatred. She savored it.

Lucy and Colin had been right about Margaret, and he'd been a gullible fool to get anywhere close to her. Even standing in her presence tainted the air and made it hard to breathe. There was something fundamentally flawed in Margaret. She had rejected her daughter. Stabbed him in the back when he tried to offer her friendship. He simply needed to walk away from her.

"I guess we have nothing left to say to each other," he said without heat.

He felt her gaze trailing him the entire way out the door. All he wanted to do was get home and hold his daughter close. Not that he feared Margaret would really try to harm Sadie, but today had once again reminded him how pitifully small his family had become. After meeting Rosalind, he'd deluded himself into believing that was about to change. He thought he'd soon have a wife and perhaps more children, but Rosalind had let him down too.

When he walked into his apartment, Sadie was sprawled on the floor of the parlor, playing with her dolls. A beautiful smile broke across her face when she saw him. She pushed to her feet, carrying a doll in one hand and trotting as quickly as she could toward him. He ignored the pain in his side as he sank to his knees to hug her.

"Do you want to play with this?" she asked, offering him the doll.

"Oh, sweetheart, I've been waiting for this all day."

And it was true. Sadie offered pure love with every beat of her heart. No matter what, he would love and support Sadie for the rest of her life, even if she disappointed him. Even if her choices veered from his own. He couldn't imagine how Margaret could reject Eloise, but he would give Sadie whatever she needed to spread her wings and soar.

Rosalind awoke slowly, rolling over on her mattress and squinting against the sunlight streaming through her filmy white curtains. She rarely slept late enough to be awakened by the glare of morning sunlight, but it felt good. For the first time in months, she'd gone to bed filled with the belief that her endeavors were on the cusp of fruition. She and Dr. Leal had been strategizing for the past two days on how best to present their results at the end of their ninety-day deferment, and she was confident of their work.

She fumbled on the bedside table for her spectacles. Ten o'clock! It was a Saturday, but even so, how embarrassing to waste so much time buried beneath a mound of bedding. She flung back the covers and reached for her gown. She had work to do.

In short order she had dressed, finger-combed her hair, and was ready to face the day. The plan was to finish entering the data from the soil, groundwater, and test sites into a final report, then deliver it all to the printer. They would print two thousand copies, enough to send to every water department and chemistry professor in the nation. They needed additional allies, and by broadcasting their research, surely other scientists would join the crusade. Today was the first day of the rest of her life.

She scampered down the steps, a helpless grin on her face.

Ingrid flung a folded newspaper squarely at her chest.

"It looks like we must move to Mexico or to Russia to escape your scandals!" she screeched.

Rosalind managed to clutch the newspaper before it dropped to the floor. "What are you talking about?"

But heaven help her, she feared she knew. There had been reporters in court the other day to hear the shouting match between her and Nick. She clasped the newspaper to her chest, afraid to look at it.

Gus sat at the dining table, bouncing little Jonah over his shoulder. His face was pale. "It's pretty bad, Rosalind," he said. "It's on pages four and five."

She sank onto the bottom stair and took a deep breath. Whatever was in this paper, she would handle it. She had beat cholera when she was ten years old and had been waging battles ever since. Whatever was in these pages was just another hurdle she would cope with. It was only on pages four and five, so how bad could it be?

She opened the newspaper and was confronted with a photograph of her and Nick in the alley behind the orphanage. The caption was damning. *Nick Drake and the infamous Rosalind Werner in happier times.*

Her mouth went dry as she glanced through the headlines on the two-page spread. There were three separate stories. One covered Thursday's hearing about the chlorination test, and a separate story covered the shouting match between Nick and General O'Donnell. The third story was the worst. *Rosalind Werner Is No Stranger to Scandal.*

She blanched, too appalled to even read the story. All she could see was damning words in the first paragraph. *Heidelberg. Divorce. Alienation of affections.*

Mortification kept her frozen on the steps. She didn't know

what to do. When her world collapsed in Heidelberg, she had fled to America. Where could she run this time?

"I'm so sorry," she said on a shattered breath. Gus was training to be a lawyer. Would this ruin his chance to be accepted into the bar? It had ruined his ability to find work in Heidelberg. He and Ingrid had to uproot their entire lives once before because of her, and now it was happening again.

"Rosalind, we'll get through this." Gus sounded tired, and she couldn't even bear to look at him.

It was the same thing he'd said in Heidelberg, all because he was still grateful to her for saving him from cholera. He hadn't complained when she went to college and stirred up a hornet's nest of disapproval in their rural village because she dared to enter a man's field. Gus never complained because even after all these years, he felt indebted to her for saving his life.

No more. This wasn't his fault, and Ingrid had a right to be furious. Rosalind was going to solve this mess on her own.

It took effort to push to her feet and meet his eyes. "I'm sorry to be an embarrassment to you yet again."

"Rosalind, you aren't an embarrassment to—"

"Yes, I am." In the corner of her vision, she saw Ingrid vigorously nodding, but this wasn't about her hostile sister-in-law. This was about salvaging her own reputation so that Gus wouldn't take another blow to his career by standing alongside her. It was time to free Gus of his debt to her.

She went back upstairs for her walking boots. Instead of going to the lab, she was headed to Manhattan today. The subway was the quickest way to get there, and she tried not to think about how terrified she'd been the first time she rode it. Nick had sat alongside her, holding her hand, teasing her, coaxing her to breathe each time she inadvertently started holding her breath. She'd been so in love with him that night.

Well, that was obviously in her past.

After arriving in Manhattan, she took a cable car to Nick's building, then rode the elevator to his sixth-floor apartment.

A plump housekeeper answered her knock. "Can I help you, ma'am?" she asked in a heavy Irish accent.

"I'm here to see Nick Drake," Rosalind replied firmly.

"Is he expecting you?"

"He ought to be."

Rosalind stepped around the housekeeper and pushed her way into the spacious main room that had surprisingly tall ceilings topped with walnut crown molding. The bones of the room were a rich man's apartment, but the furnishings were on the ordinary side. From somewhere in the rear of the apartment, she could hear Nick reading a nursery rhyme, his fine baritone struggling to emulate the exaggerated voice of a fairy godmother. She followed the voice until she came to a room fitted out like a schoolroom, with miniature tables, chests of toys, and a blackboard. Nick sat on a child-sized bench, his knees practically drawn up to his chest as he read to Sadie.

He looked up in surprise, setting the book down before scrambling to his feet. "Rosalind?"

She hit him in the chest with the newspaper. "You caused this. You fix it," she commanded.

Nick caught the newspaper. He hadn't yet looked at either of the papers delivered to his house each morning. It was Saturday, the only day of the week he had free of obligations, and Sadie knew it. She savored the chance to come running into his bedroom on Saturday mornings and pounce on the mattress, waking him up and demanding his complete attention. It was his favorite morning of the week.

"What does it say?" he asked Rosalind, dreading the answer. He'd never seen white-hot anger on her face, but there it was, blazing out of her porcelain-blue eyes like she was about to combust.

"I'll wait until we can speak in private," she bit out after a quick glance at Sadie. "I have more self-control than to hurl dirt in front of people best left out of it."

The arrow found its mark. Whatever this was, it must be bad. He called the housekeeper and asked for Sadie's bath, and then he led Rosalind into the dining room, where he could spread the newspaper out before the wide bay window.

Nick skimmed the three stories, his anger turning hotter with each paragraph, for this was much worse than a rehash of the courthouse spat. It was a treasure trove of salacious gossip from Germany, a blow-by-blow account of Frau Dittmar's accusations against Rosalind. It recounted gossip from the maids at the remote mountain research station, where Rosalind supposedly met her married lover for trysts in the woods.

This story had been in the works for a while. The necessity of sending to Germany for details of the court case had probably taken weeks, but it was Wednesday's explosion at the courthouse that made it newsworthy. Until Wednesday, Rosalind had been just another of dozens of people involved in the Boonton Reservoir case. After Nick's rotten behavior at the courthouse, he had linked her name with two powerful men in New York City. Now the newspaper had an excuse to run a story they'd obviously been sitting on for a while.

"Aw, Rosalind, I'm so sorry about this."

"Not as sorry as I am."

That was surely true. He and General O'Donnell would endure a few days of ribbing, but then life would go on. Not so with Rosalind. She was forever damaged because he came storming into her life.

"What would you like me to say? I'm sorry. A thousand times, I'm sorry."

Her smile was bitter. "I don't remember much about my parents, but one of the things my father always said was to ignore what men say and pay attention to what they *do*. I want you to *do* something, Nick. Fix this."

He stared helplessly at the damning newspaper, noting the bylines on the stories. The two covering the courthouse confrontation were signed, but the one about Germany was an anonymous article.

But Nick knew who had taken the photograph. It was Frank McLean from the *New York World*, and Nick had promised him an exclusive story about his work with the orphanage in exchange for not publishing the photograph.

He didn't know how he could fix this, but he owed it to Rosalind to try, and he knew where to start.

Frank McLean was nonchalant about his sale of the photograph. "Some lady offered me two hundred dollars for it. That was worth a lot more than the exclusive interview about the orphanage you offered."

"What lady?"

"She didn't give me her name. She came to our office right after we printed that story about you in the orphanage. She wanted to know all sorts of details. When she learned about the photograph, she offered to buy it."

Nick had a good suspicion of who it was. "Middle-aged woman? Dark hair, blue eyes? Cold as ice?"

"That's her."

Fury clouded Nick's vision. If Margaret had been in the room, he'd be tempted to strangle her. But wasn't that the sort of senseless revenge that had gotten them all into this mess? Their family feud began almost fifty years ago, but for Margaret, it was alive and simmering.

"I hope the two hundred dollars serves you well, for you've just lost my trust, and plenty of contacts are about to dry up for you."

Frank sent him an exasperated look. "Take it easy, Nick. It's just a photograph, nothing you can't—"

"It's a photograph that has been used to smear a good woman's name. Enjoy your two hundred dollars."

As he walked home that evening, one of Rosalind's starchy proverbs intruded. *Glass, china, and reputations are easily cracked and never well-mended.* She had been laughing when she said it. How little attention he had paid at the time, but the statement was painfully true. Anything he did to offset this disaster would be no more than a crude bandage plastered over a delicate and luminous work of art.

But he still needed to do what he could for Rosalind. It would be impossible to stuff the Heidelberg gossip back into the genie's bottle, but perhaps there was something else he could do to prove how sorry he was. He could give her something she didn't even realize that she wanted.

To do that, he needed the help of Dr. Leal and George Fuller, but he knew where he could find them and was determined to make it happen.

Chapter NINETEEN

Rosalind used to enjoy the walk to her house from the streetcar stop. It was only a five-block walk, but she loved these compact, well-maintained houses with tidy lawns and brimming flower boxes. They signified a degree of professional success, and she felt a sense of accomplishment each time she strolled toward home.

Not anymore. Now women peeked out the window as she passed, their faces a mix of curiosity and derision. The Germans had a word for it. *Schadenfreude*: the niggling burst of delight taken in another person's misfortune. Rosalind had witnessed the subtle gloating from her neighbors each time she walked down the street or stepped outside to retrieve the morning newspaper. Even the children knew about her shame. As she walked past a pair of boys, one leaned over to whisper in the other's ear. They let out a rude noise, pointed, then ran off amidst gales of laughter.

It was best to ignore them. She still had the respect of Dr. Leal, and if any of the college students helping at the lab thought she was a fallen woman, they did not show it to her face. They were all too busy racing to complete their analysis and print the report ahead of the judge's ninety-day deadline, which was less than a week away.

Something was going on in the front of her house. Neighbors stood in a line along the modest picket fence, but a big black automobile blocked her view of the house. Her palms started sweating as she saw the emblem for the local police department stenciled on the side of the car. She picked up her skirts and ran. Had there been another robbery? Or something wrong with the baby? He could have fallen down the stairs or burned himself in the kitchen.

"Get out of my way," she ordered as she cut through the crowd of onlookers.

Relief surged through her as she spotted Gus and Ingrid on the front porch, the baby happily sucking his thumb as Ingrid bounced him on her knee.

"What's happening?" she asked Gus, panting from the sprint home.

"The police are inside," he said in a low voice. "They're looking for something."

She blinked in confusion. "What? Why?" If they needed something, all they had to do was ask, and she would produce it. Could this be related to the chlorine tests?

"They wouldn't say, but they have a warrant."

"A *warrant?*" she asked, unable to keep the appalled tone from her voice. Weren't warrants something used in criminal investigations? A lot of people were angry over the chlorine tests, but Judge McLaughlin said they hadn't broken any laws. Maybe the city was trying some low trick to cast aspersions on her character.

"They've been here for almost an hour and don't appear to have found anything," Gus said, "but they're still looking."

"This is ridiculous. I'm going inside."

The police refused to let her pass. "All members of the household must remain outside until our investigation is complete," the brusque sergeant said.

"But what are you investigating? I haven't done anything wrong!" She wrapped her arms around her middle and hoped her nervous trembling couldn't be seen by her curious neighbors. How mortifying to have this on top of everything else. There would come a time when Dr. Leal wouldn't be able to continue standing behind her. Maybe even Doctor Clean would be forced to distance himself and his company from their association, and she needed that quarterly infusion of cash from her stock.

In all likelihood, this was some tactic by the city to embarrass her and cast doubt on the validity of the chlorine study. Soon this would all be over, and she could go inside and strategize with Gus about how to diffuse the pointless attack on her reputation.

Ten minutes later, she learned otherwise.

"Please come inside, ma'am," the sergeant said tersely.

She shot to her feet and crossed the threshold, glancing in dismay at the stacks of books mounded on the floor and the drawers pulled open. Her house was a mess! It was going to take hours to put this all to rights.

When Gus and Ingrid tried to follow, the sergeant stopped them. "Just the homeowner. Everyone else needs to remain outside."

"He's my lawyer," Rosalind said. "I have a right to an attorney, and I want Gus with me."

Neither police officer looked happy about it, but the sergeant nodded gruffly, then directed her back to the kitchen, where papers had been stacked on the table. Gus was right beside her as they stared at the assortment of papers and a few bound ledgers.

"We have a warrant to seize these materials. Acting on a confidential tip, we came looking for evidence of a scheme to embezzle funds from the Doctor Clean company. It looks like we found it."

She gaped at the paperwork, speechless. Why would she need to embezzle from Doctor Clean? She already earned a comfortable income every quarter.

"I've never seen those papers in my life," she choked out. "They aren't mine!"

"And yet they were in your possession. They corroborate our tip that you are funneling money to a bank account in Germany."

She tried to formulate a sentence, but all she could do was stammer. She wouldn't know how to perpetrate an embezzlement scheme if her life depended on it. A chill raced through her so strongly that her teeth started chattering.

"Those papers don't belong to me," she managed to get out.

The sergeant held up a piece of paper. "This letter is addressed to you from Mr. Peter Schmidt. You know him?"

Peter was the accountant for Doctor Clean and sent her the quarterly revenue from her stock. He'd offered to buy her out earlier in the summer.

"Yes, I know him, but I've never seen that letter—"

"Rosalind, you don't have to talk to them," Gus interrupted. "In fact, you shouldn't."

"But I haven't done anything wrong, and I'm willing to answer any questions. I want this cleared up right away."

Gus grabbed her arms and turned her to face him, his voice stern. "Get used to the idea that we aren't going to clear this up tonight. I need you to listen to me and follow my advice. Someone is trying to frame you, and they are ten steps ahead of us. Anything you do on the spur of the moment will probably play into their trap."

She swallowed hard. Everything Gus said was surely correct, for the odd assortment of financial papers and bank statements weren't hers and had to have been planted, probably by the man who broke into her home a few weeks ago for no apparent reason.

"We have a court order to take you into custody, ma'am," the sergeant said. "You'll have to come with us. Now."

"Are you arresting me?" This couldn't be happening. Any moment she was going to snap awake from this nightmare and find herself safe in bed and planning her day at the laboratory.

"Yes, ma'am. If you come along quietly, there will be no need for handcuffs. If you want to be difficult, we can cuff and frog-march you out past all your neighbors. Your choice."

Her mouth went dry, and she glanced at Gus, who looked as helpless as she felt. Finally, he found his voice. "What about bail?" he asked. "Can we both go down to the courthouse and pay that now to avoid this whole farce?"

The sergeant shook his head. "A bail hearing will be held at a later date. It's up to a judge to determine how serious the offense is."

In the end she decided to go quietly. Only a handful of on-lookers still loitered outside her house, but they watched as she stepped up into the back of the glossy black police wagon. Gus wasn't allowed to go with her. She'd never felt so alone as when the door of the wagon slammed shut, enclosing her in a dim compartment that smelled like sweat and had only two hard benches along each side.

She was on her own.

In her wildest nightmares, Rosalind had never wondered what the inside of a women's jail looked like, but she certainly hadn't expected *this*. Jersey City wasn't large enough to have a female jail, so women were held in a separate section in the men's jail. That "section" was in the converted attic, a long, narrow room beneath the steeply pitched roof. The wall of heat as Rosalind walked inside almost knocked her flat.

Ten bunk beds filled most of the floor space, but there were only eight women in the attic. Four were pickpockets, two were here for public drunkenness, and the teenaged girl had lit a schoolyard trash can on fire. The only truly alarming inmate was Melinda, a massive woman with beefy arms who worked as a cook at the local train depot and had been accused of poisoning her employers.

"Did you?" Rosalind asked in trepidation, expecting a quick denial. Didn't everyone in jail deny the accusations?

Melinda's triumphant expression took her aback. "Some people just need poisoning," she said ominously.

Rosalind quickly retreated to a vacant bed as far away from Melinda as possible, fanning herself in the motionless heat of the attic. Attics were always warm, but this one seemed unusually oppressive.

"It's because we're over the kitchen," one of the women explained. "You'll want to strip out of that getup, or you'll die of heat up here."

Rosalind wore a high-collared cotton blouse with a woolen vest made by her aunt in Germany. Never in her life had she shown her bare arms in public, but all the women in this attic wore nothing but bloomers and a chemise. They draped their clothing over the iron bedsteads, and the entire room smelled like dirty laundry.

"I'll be okay," Rosalind said, clutching her hand to her throat, which the other women thought hysterical. The girl who'd set the trash can on fire hooted and called her a fussy prude.

A woman named Gabriella, who looked far too skinny to be sporting such an obviously pregnant belly, sprawled on the bunk next to her, fanning herself with vigor. "We won't tease you when you change your mind. It's only going to get hotter as the ovens downstairs cool off."

"Can't we open the window?" Rosalind asked. There was a large one at the end of the room, but it was closed.

"The warden says it's an escape risk, and it's been nailed shut," Gabriella said. "We can keep the door open, so that helps a little."

Another surprise. The women weren't even locked into the attic. At Rosalind's look of astonishment, one of the inmates explained that the prison kept two vicious dogs at the base of the stairs, and if any woman tried to leave, the whole jail would know it.

Everyone was here only until their trial could be held or a family member was able to post bail. None of these women had been able to come up with the bail money, and they were stuck here until their trial. It was outrageous that these women should be incarcerated in this sweltering attic for want of fifty dollars. Rosalind had hoped to be released by tomorrow morning, but she'd been told by the warden that it would be a few days, since the judge only heard bail hearings twice a week.

It was another embarrassment. Would Judge McLaughlin be responsible for setting her bail? He was the only judge she knew, and it would compound her mortification if the man who lived down the street from her learned of this humiliating event.

The women had been right about her inability to remain fully clothed for long. It was impossible to sleep while drenched in sweat, and Rosalind gave up, stripping down to her chemise like the others. Even so, the air was stagnant and oppressive, and she lay awake most of the night, staring at the starlit sky out the window.

It was a casement window, with two large sections that ought to be able to swing out but had been nailed shut in the interest of security. At the top were two narrower windows, no more than a foot high, but they were simple pieces of glass mounted to the window jamb.

Rosalind eyed the smaller windows. If she had her music box tools, she could attach a hinge to the top of each of those two narrow windows and prop them both open. Just thinking about how much those few inches could cool the room made the heat feel even more oppressive.

With luck, Gus would be able to get her out soon, so thinking about how she could modify this space was pointless. She finally drifted into a feverish doze in the hours before sunrise when the heat faded a few degrees.

The jail insisted all the female inmates perform chores during the day, and Rosalind welcomed the reprieve from the hot attic. Most of the women were assigned to kitchen duty, but the poisonous Melinda was obviously precluded from kitchen work. That meant she was assigned to show Rosalind how to assist in the laundry.

It wasn't a complicated task. Melinda did the scrubbing while Rosalind performed the wringing. As the hours passed, Rosalind held her breath each time a person walked past the open door, certain she was about to be called to the visiting room to talk with Gus. Her fingers grew waterlogged as she lifted socks from the rinse tub, then fed them through the wringer of the clothes press and turned the crank. At first the job seemed easy, but a blister soon formed at the base of her thumb, and residue from the soap made her skin tighten and itch.

It was late in the afternoon before a guard came to tell her Gus was in the visiting room. Her clothing was spattered with water and sweat stains, but she must have looked even worse than she felt, as Gus blanched in horror when he saw her.

"I don't look that bad, do I?" she said, trying to summon a bit of humor. Soon this would all be over, and she'd have a story to tell her grandchildren after the mortification wore off.

Gus merely shrugged as he took a seat opposite her in a small room with four tables and a warden's desk at the front. Two of the other tables had tough-looking male inmates at them. She didn't relish discussing private business with so many strangers in the room, but she didn't have much choice. She looked at Gus with expectation.

"I don't have any good news," he said. "The judge has set your bail at five thousand dollars."

"Five thousand!" she gasped. "The other women need only pay fifty dollars. The largest bail I've heard was a hundred dollars. *Five thousand?* Are you sure?"

"They said you're a flight risk because you have family in Germany, where you've spent most of your adult life. They think you also have plenty of money stashed away in some German bank account, all swindled from Doctor Clean."

Her mind reeled at the news. She didn't think she could endure another night like last night, but even worse, how could she prove herself innocent while locked up here doing other people's laundry?

"I'll never be able to raise five thousand dollars," she whispered. Unless she could borrow it from someone. Nick was ridiculously rich, but they weren't even on speaking terms. She swallowed hard and met Gus's gaze. "Doctor Clean?" she asked.

The expression of pained sympathy on Gus's face did not bode well. "I wish to heaven I didn't have to tell you this, but after Doctor Clean was informed of the charges, he cut all ties with you. There is a moral turpitude clause in your original contract, so he's got the right to cut you loose without a penny. He did so."

She curled over. She had no other income aside from Doctor Clean. The quarterly bank note on her house came due at the end of next month. Most of the money from her parents had been going toward her living expenses, and Dr. Leal couldn't afford to pay her.

She also needed to hire a real lawyer. Gus hadn't passed the necessary tests to practice law in New Jersey and wouldn't be permitted to defend her in court. It was becoming apparent there was no quick escape for her. Whoever was framing her had put a lot of work into forging those documents and persuading the judge she was a flight risk.

"What about Peter Schmidt?" she asked. "Have they arrested him too?"

"They tried. He was able to post bail right away, but Doctor Clean has fired him as well."

She thought quickly. "Could you seek him out? My hunch is that he's also innocent and is being targeted as a way to get to me."

"Maybe," Gus said. "Or it could be that Schmidt really has been siphoning funds from the company and used you as some kind of decoy. I'll know more in a few days."

Her muscles ached as she climbed the stairs back up to the attic, weary, water-stained, and depressed. She felt like weeping as the wall of heat clobbered her.

Well, she wasn't going to weep. She was going to find a way to rig those top windows open. Two sets of hinges rimmed both of the large lower windows that were nailed shut. All she had to do was transfer the hinges to the upper windows and cut a seam into the jamb. Over the years, she had attached the lids to dozens of music boxes, and the principles of rigging something to swing open and closed were the same.

She couldn't do it without tools. If she had a screwdriver and a jigsaw, she could have the smaller windows open before nightfall.

The warden was instantly suspicious when she asked for the tools.

"Those are weapons, and you are criminals!" he said.

She drew herself to her full height, grateful for the high-necked collar that gave her an air of dignity even in this humiliating situation. "I am a biochemist, and these women are pickpockets. The tools are more likely to be stolen than used as a weapon."

Unless Melinda got her hands on them, but given the way all the women in the attic were silently cheering her on, she didn't think Melinda would interfere.

The warden seemed a decent man, and within an hour, the tools were provided. Rosalind was grateful for Melinda's muscular build as the older woman used the jigsaw to cut the upper windows from the frame. Rosalind detached the hinges from the lower windows, and it didn't take long to get them installed on the upper casement. By nightfall, the attic had two narrow windows that created a healthy cross-breeze with the open door on the other end.

She had the gratitude of everyone in the attic, especially Gabriella. The pregnant inmate planted herself beneath the open casement, sagging against the wall to enjoy the breeze.

"When are you due?" Rosalind asked.

"Two more months," she said. "I should get out in a couple of weeks when my husband's ship gets back. My bail is only fifty dollars, but I won't have it until Benjamin sails back into town."

The way Gabriella's face softened when she said *Benjamin* made Rosalind ache. She remembered feeling that way. Gabriella must have noticed, for she perked up from leaning against the side of the wall.

"Have you got a man?"

The question touched a nerve. For a while, Nick had seemed so perfect, he made her heart soar. It had been the most exhilarating feeling . . . like she had spread her wings and taken flight. She didn't think she'd ever be able to let her guard down like that again.

"No," she admitted. "I don't have a man."

It hadn't taken Nick long to get what he needed from George Fuller, which was why he found himself wandering the streets of Washington, D.C. the following day. He was as dazzled as any sightseer as he gaped at the massive government buildings that looked like ancient Greek temples. In the early morning sunlight, the white granite was almost blinding. Everything here was so different than in New York, where the narrow streets were dwarfed by towering skyscrapers that blotted out much of the sky. Here the view was expansive, letting him see the massive Capitol building, the Library of Congress, and the Washington Monument.

The stark differences made him realize how limited his view of the world had been, for he'd never traveled farther than a couple hundred miles from New York City. He'd never *wanted* to go anywhere else. Washington was a surprise and a place he'd like to explore, but he wasn't here as a sightseer. He had business to conduct.

He'd carried the oversized canister filled with blueprints all the way down from New York, complete with a dozen pages of notes and an affidavit from both Dr. Leal and George Fuller. In a perfect world, they would have accompanied him on this mission, but both were monopolized by the final stages of the chlorine test.

"Everything you need is on those blueprints," Mr. Fuller advised.

Nick would have to take it on faith. He'd never applied for a patent, but he understood enough about how bureaucracies worked to navigate the process. He had dropped the paperwork off first thing this morning at the Patent Office, and had been cooling his heels walking down the National Mall like a tourist.

At three o'clock, he returned to the Patent Office, wondering if he would be successful or if this entire trip had been a waste of time. Money could buy expedited patent service, and Nick wanted to be on hand to explain the unusual details he wanted for this particular patent.

He was directed to the third floor office of Neville Bernhard, the patent examiner who would decide the fate of the chlorinator. The patent examiner's office was as odd-looking as the man. Nick had to duck to avoid the model of a hot air balloon dangling from the ceiling. Charts and mathematical equations covered the walls, and the surface of his desk was cluttered with miniature models of mechanical contraptions. Atop it all was the blueprint for Mr. Fuller's water chlorinator.

"I am in love with this invention!" the patent examiner roared the instant Nick entered his office. Neville Bernhard was the tallest and skinniest man Nick had ever seen, and he constantly twitched with a tick in the side of his face, but his eyes were sharp and intelligent. "So many of the applications I review are a waste of human time and energy," the patent examiner said. "Yesterday I lost an hour of my life processing the patent for a head-mounted umbrella. I was reading a patent for a cat exercise machine when your request crossed my desk. A method for safely chlorinating water . . . well! You've made my day. My month, my year."

Neville rummaged around his desk for a pair of spectacles, then scanned the paperwork sent by Mr. Fuller.

"You are an agent sent on behalf of the inventor?" Neville asked.

"I am. Mr. Fuller asked me to deliver it in person. I will be underwriting all the expenses associated with the patent." Of course, the biggest expense was going to be putting it into commercial operation. Nick was going to underwrite some of the start-up costs as well, but in exchange, he had a single request.

It was a departure from bureaucratic red tape, and it was a favor that was going to require the cooperation of the twitchy, eccentric man sitting before him. The Patent Office had a three-page document with rules for the naming of patents, and any deviation from the norm required jumping through some hurdles. Nick had come all the way from New York to do the jumping.

The patent examiner took off his glasses and looked at Nick. "The contents of the patent are in order, so I'm ready to sign off on the notice of allowance. The only oddity is the name. It's too long, and frankly . . . confusing. Sometimes inventors want their names on the patent, but I have no idea who Frieda and Augustus Werner are."

They were Rosalind's parents. They were the reason she had entered this field and had inspired her to work toward making the world a safer place. They were the people Rosalind feared would be forgotten. He was here to make sure that didn't happen.

"They were two people who would have benefitted from this patent," Nick said quietly. "Their daughter worked very hard on their behalf. Mr. Fuller's letter has endorsed naming the invention in their honor."

The patent examiner took a moment to skim the letter, the corners of his mouth turning down. He didn't look pleased, and Nick clenched his fists, marshalling his arguments should the request be denied. Rosalind had never asked him for a single thing, and he'd given her precious little aside from the short end of his temper. He instinctively knew she would value the naming of this patent in her parents' names more than any diamond or treasure he could buy her.

"Here's the thing," Neville said. "Patent Guideline 15.7 under the naming conventions discourages the use of personal names or brands in a patent title. So unless you can give me a good reason . . ."

"What is the definition of a guideline?" Nick asked.

"A guideline is a principle used to determine a future course of action, policy, or conduct," the patent examiner recited from memory. Nick was glad he didn't work in the legal profession and wasn't required to spout off chapter and verse of bland government manuals. Still, he caught a note of humor in the older man's face and suspected there was still a chance.

"So a guideline has room for maneuvering." Nick was no lawyer, but he had a good head on his shoulders and was willing to use it in order to slam this unconventional request across the finish line.

"Usually. Provided there's a good story involved. And since you came all the way from New York, I suspect there's a good story here."

Nick pulled out the desk chair, prepared to tell Rosalind's story in exchange for a one-day turnaround on the patent.

He got it.

At six o'clock he headed out the door with the paperwork for the chlorinator, named in honor of Frieda and Augustus Werner. He wished he could present it in person to Rosalind, just to see the expression on her face when she knew her parents would live forever through this piece of technology that would make the world a better and safer place. A piece of him wanted to rush home to New York, wipe out the last month from his memory, and try to start again with her.

Then again, maybe he ought to stay another day or two in Washington for the simple joy of being an ordinary tourist. He was thirty-six years old and had never visited a city of any size other than his own. Rosalind wouldn't be waiting for him. A physical ache squeezed his chest, and it had nothing to do with his injured ribs. He just missed her. He missed what he thought they could have together, but he would never trust a woman who could look him in the face and lie as she had.

Could he? She'd been painted into a tight corner and acted in the best interest of science.

He'd made his position brutally clear, and only an idiot would go spilling scientific secrets in front of him when she knew he would blow the whistle on her. Within seconds of learning it, he'd scooped up her notebooks and risked his neck speeding over lousy roads to take them straight to the judge.

A heavy sigh escaped him. No matter how disappointed he was, he wished he hadn't publicly attacked her. She hadn't deserved that. Hopefully his gift of securing the patent in her parents' name would help ease the sting of what he'd done.

By the time he returned to his hotel overlooking the Potomac River, an avalanche of exhaustion overcame him. The bedsprings squeaked as he eased down onto the mattress, the aches in his body starting to catch up. It was easy to kick off his shoes, but harder to lean down and pull off each sock. His damaged ribs screamed in protest, and for once in his life, he wished for a valet like other rich people.

He'd just gotten the last sock off when a knock sounded on his door. He wasn't about to get up to open it. "Who is it?" he yelled.

"The front desk clerk has received a telephone call from New York for you. The gentleman is waiting on the line."

It could be important. It wasn't about Sadie, for it would have been his housekeeper calling if something was wrong with his daughter. That meant it was probably water department business, and he was going to have to go downstairs and answer it.

He sighed and pushed himself off the mattress, walked to the door, and opened it. "Do you know who is calling?"

The porter looked at a note in his hand. "Dr. John Leal."

That was a surprise. Nick had no idea why Dr. Leal would be calling him, but he'd better take the call.

"I'm coming," he grumbled, but he wasn't going to torture himself by pulling on his shoes and socks again. If the people of Washington fainted at the sight of a man's bare feet, they didn't have enough problems in their life. He padded down the hallway, down a flight of stairs, and across the hotel lobby to the front counter. The hotel clerk handed over a telephone receiver.

"This is Nick Drake," he said.

"Rosalind has been arrested."

Nick couldn't believe he'd heard correctly, but he asked Dr. Leal to repeat it twice then tell him the charges. It had nothing to do with the scandal in Germany, but some bizarre embezzlement scheme he couldn't begin to understand. Never in a thousand years would he have thought Rosalind would have embezzled money, but he didn't think she would have lied to him about turning on a chlorine drip either.

"Did she do it?" he asked.

"Of course not! I don't know who is behind this, but she needs five thousand dollars for bail. I don't have that sort of money, and neither does her family."

Rosalind had deceived him once before, so she wasn't quite as pure as the driven snow. She might bend the rules for a cause, but he didn't think she'd lie or cheat for personal gain. There was a big difference between the two.

Silence stretched across the telephone line, and it was obvious Dr. Leal was calling Nick for help with bail. He was used to people asking him for money, but if he opened his wallet every time a charity or needy associate came knocking, he would have been drained dry years ago. He'd never expected the request to come from Rosalind, but that didn't really matter.

"Where do I send the money?"

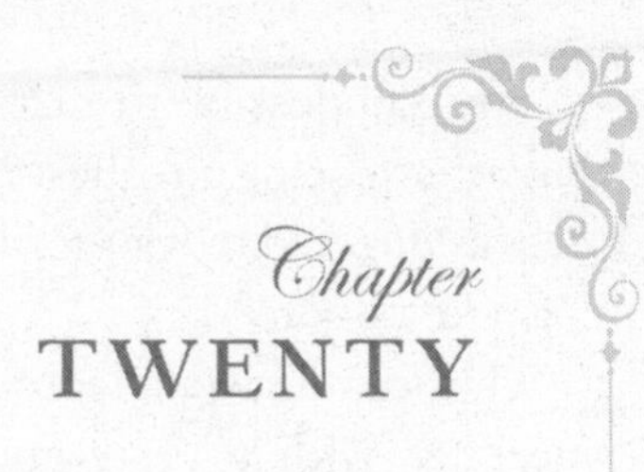

Chapter TWENTY

Nick grew convinced that Aunt Margaret was behind Rosalind's troubles during the long and uncomfortable train ride back to New York. Dr. Leal had told him the details of the evidence against Rosalind, and it was possible that Margaret had arranged it all. He remembered the cunning glare in her eyes when she had taunted him on their last meeting. *I have lost my husband and my son. Who will you lose, Nick?*

He'd assumed her threat meant she would go after someone in his family. Now he suspected she was going after Rosalind, and the gears had been in the works for a long time. Margaret had first met Rosalind at his speech in Central Park, and according to Frank McLean, she bought the photograph of Nick and Rosalind a few days later.

The first thing Nick did on returning to the city was pay a visit to Margaret herself. He'd never been to her Manhattan apartment, and its grandeur took him by surprise. When he'd been trying to extend the olive branch, he had assumed her newly found social conscience would have prompted her to start living more modestly. She hadn't. She lived in one of the most prestigious apartment buildings in New York City, complete with a view of Central Park.

It was impossible to guess if she would be willing to see him, but after placing a request through the apartment's doorman, he was directed to wait for her at an elegant café on the building's first floor.

The Scandinavian Tearoom was the last place he wanted to meet her. With its pastel colors, delicate china, and little vases of flowers, it was the sort of fussy gentility that always made Nick feel out of place. It wasn't the spot for the knock-down, drag-out fight he wanted, but Margaret had picked the place, and she held all the cards right now. He would grit his teeth and play along until he got what he needed.

He was the only man in the tearoom. Clusters of women sat at various tables, their ramrod-straight spines coming nowhere close to the back of their seats, their faces showing only the serene composure he'd seen on department store mannequins. He took a seat at the only unoccupied table. It was too short for him to get his knees beneath it and too small for the amount of china and silver covering its surface. He glanced at the menu engraved on fine linen paper, rolling his eyes at the prices before tossing it aside.

"Just a pot of tea," he said to the waiter. He'd eat nails before paying five dollars for a few pastries. He wished he'd brought a newspaper, as it was obvious Margaret intended to make him wait. He drummed his fingers on the table, growing hotter and more impatient with each passing minute. The tea was delivered in a porcelain teapot with hand-painted figurines of nymphs frolicking in some sort of garden, but he didn't touch it.

Margaret finally made her appearance after a full twenty minutes. He narrowed his gaze on her whip-thin figure as she wended her way through the tables toward him. He did not stand as she approached.

"Don't you look dainty," she said in a mocking voice as she lowered herself onto the seat opposite him.

"I didn't know you had any interest in photography," he said bluntly. "Even for you, paying two hundred dollars for a grainy picture of me in an alley seems a little much."

"I consider it money well spent. I'd like to find more pictures of Dr. Werner, as the public seem fascinated with her. Oh, wait," she said, pulling her face into an exaggerated look of dismay. "She's in jail, so I suppose no new pictures for now. Such a pity."

Anger simmered inside him as Margaret poured herself a cup of tea from a porcelain teapot that cost more than most people earned in a month. A sapphire the size of a walnut glittered on her hand, and she beamed with smugness.

"Why do you need all this?" he demanded with a glance at the gilded surroundings. "A hundred-dollar teapot to serve a dime's worth of tea? A five-dollar lemon scone that's no better than the five-cent pastries served on Orchard Street? It's revolting, and you sold your soul for it."

"Have you learned nothing?" Her voice was as cool as a duchess's. "We are no blood relation, but as my husband's nephew, I expected a little more cleverness. We aren't even twenty seconds into a negotiation, and already you've lost your temper."

She was right. The goal was to get Rosalind out of jail, not shame his aunt's nonexistent sense of decency.

He swallowed back his anger and spoke calmly. "What will it take to call off your dogs?"

She set the teapot back on the tray without a hint of a *clink*. "Perhaps this is the time for you to surprise me with a tempting offer."

"Money? An appointment on some fancy board? Just name your price."

"My husband always said I'm priceless," she said in a cloying voice that made his toes curl. She leaned forward and lowered her voice. "Frankly, I'm enjoying your misery far too much to be interested in 'calling off my dogs.' Besides, you ought to be thanking me. I was curious about the young woman you held in such high regard. Imagine my dismay when the investigator I hired found such distasteful revelations about her. And she looks so prim too! Such a pity that when one peeks behind her façade, she's no better than a common trollop hankering after some minor German aristocrat. A married one, at that."

Nick and Rosalind had their differences, but she was still one of the finest people he knew. Aunt Margaret was surely among the most despicable.

"It's easy to throw mud from a distance," he said. "On any given day, you can dig up something nasty to score a point against a decent woman, but over the course of a year? Or a lifetime? You can't throw enough mud to ruin a woman as fine as Rosalind Werner. Your family lied, cheated, and swindled to amass a fortune. Rosalind never got rich from the work she does. She lives in a house plainer than your gatehouse at Oakmonte. When your honor and dignity are measured against Rosalind's, you can't hold a candle to her."

As he spoke, his shame over his falling-out with Rosalind grew deeper. Rosalind wasn't perfect, and he'd done her a disservice in expecting her to be.

"Once again, your temper is getting the better of you," Margaret said, and he cursed himself for falling into her trap. She had always thought the sun, the moon, and the stars revolved around her son, and his imprisonment was a thorn in her side she couldn't forget. She had engineered a similar punishment for Rosalind. The key to getting Rosalind released was probably the same one that would open the door for Tom Jr.

"What if I can get Tom out of prison?" Nick asked.

The question surprised her, but only for a moment. Her smile was grim as she shook her head. "Tom knew the risks when he earned that prison sentence. I'm not willing to bargain with that."

"Are you *that* consumed with revenge? Even when your son's freedom hangs in the balance?"

"Even so." Her voice radiated warmth and pleasure. "I ought to thank you. I was so despondent after my husband died that I wanted to follow him into the grave. Your visit gave me a reason to keep on living. I'm having fun balancing the scales, so thank you, Nick."

He wanted to take his fist to the fussy china dishes and smash them to pieces just to shake that unearthly composure, if only for a second.

"I suppose I shouldn't be surprised you won't bargain with Tom's freedom," he said. "You found it easy enough to turn your back on Ellie. A girl who only wanted to please, who longed for a fraction of the attention you showered on your bratty son. What a shining example of motherhood you are."

"You're so pathetically naïve," Margaret said. "You think I've done wrong by poor, neglected Eloise? That she is an innocent pawn in all this?" She leaned in even closer, lowering her voice to a nasty whisper. "Who do you think manufactured all those accounting ledgers to frame your adored Rosalind?"

He reared back in his chair. Ellie wouldn't . . . would she? He didn't really know her anymore. He hadn't even recognized her at Bruce Garrett's house.

"Did you put her up to it? Blackmail her somehow?" he asked.

Margaret leaned back and topped off her cup of tea. "It wasn't very difficult. As you say, Eloise has always been so eager to please, and she was more than happy to help once I explained the situation to her."

"You've got a lot of nerve. I'll turn this back on you and see you both in prison."

"Careful, Nick," she purred. "You have a lot more to lose than me. Such a charming little daughter. And a sister who managed to marry into blue blood. They always say the higher one climbs, the mightier the fall. Do you really want to risk all that?"

He shoved to his feet, towering over her. "You touch my family, and I will see you dead," he lashed out. "I swear it."

She dabbed the corner of her mouth with a napkin, then glanced at the other ladies in the tearoom. "I've noted your threats," she said calmly. "As did everyone else in this room. Have a lovely day, Nick."

He stood motionless as she stepped around him to leave the tearoom. His anger smoldered, and he had never felt so helpless. Rosalind's reputation and freedom had been stolen, all because her life had crossed paths with his. He had to figure out a way to save her, but this wasn't something money could buy.

Aunt Margaret had tried to play it cool, but she had made one mistake. By revealing Eloise's role in creating that set of fraudulent books, he now had an avenue to prove Rosalind's innocence. He couldn't believe Eloise would do such a thing, but the evidence manufactured against Rosalind had been done by a professional, so there might be some truth in it.

It was time for him to discover who his young cousin really was.

Rosalind sat at the only table in the attic, trying to filter out the three women bickering over a card game and concentrate on Dr. Leal's final report. She ignored the ache in her back from bending over the washing tub, her waterlogged fingers, and the hunger from skipping dinner this evening. Lining up, submitting to inspection, and heading to the dining hall took over an hour, and she couldn't spare the time for it. She only had a few hours to review Dr. Leal's final report before the jail declared lights-out at nine o'clock.

Their ninety-day deferment was over, and the report would be submitted to Judge McLaughlin tomorrow. All it needed was for her to proofread it a final time and affix her signature to the cover page. No matter what happened during the rest of her career, this was her landmark accomplishment. Even if Judge McLaughlin ruled against them, this report would be read by scientists all over the world. It was a powerful stepping-stone into the future.

As she read deeper into the report, Rosalind's confidence grew, and she was filled with such overwhelming pride that it was getting hard not to weep. They had done it. They had crossed the finish line with a convincing report that had taken courage, ingenuity, and a few strokes of luck to create. Despite the awful calamity that had befallen her, no one could take this accomplishment away from her. She might spend the next months or years in prison, but this report would forever gleam as her proudest achievement.

She turned to the last page and was gratified to see the long list of scientists and engineers who had signed their name in support of their findings. Men in charge of water systems from Cleveland and Atlanta and Chicago had all endorsed it. And New York! General O'Donnell had endorsed—

She gasped, her eyes widening in disbelief at Nicholas Drake's name.

Her heart nearly stopped, but she stared at his name, reading it over and over just to be certain she wasn't seeing things. It hurt to see, but she was happy. Thrilled. Somehow she'd always known Nick would come around in the end. It was impossible to know who had persuaded him or how it had happened, but all three commissioners from the State Water Board of New York had endorsed this report, and that was going to count for a lot.

She added her signature to the cover page with a flourish. Never had she been prouder to sign her name than at this very moment. Ten minutes later, the warden declared lights-out, and she lay atop the mattress, a foolish grin on her face, too excited to sleep. Even with the newly open windows, it was still swelteringly hot, but she didn't care. Sometimes it was important to focus on the good things in life rather than worry over the bad.

She was still elated when Gus arrived first thing in the morning to meet her in the visitor's room.

"It's perfect!" she declared as she handed him the signed report. "Tell Dr. Leal I have no corrections or suggestions, and nothing in my life has given me more satisfaction than signing my name to that report."

"Good! Rosalind, I think I'll be able to get your bail soon. I can't be certain, but—"

"Gus, we don't have time to worry about bail. You need to get this report to Dr. Leal so he can turn it over to the judge. Our ninety days expire today."

"But I wanted to tell you, it looks like your bail money may come through. An anonymous donor—"

"Really? Good." She nudged Gus toward the door. "Hurry!" she urged. "We can talk about bail later, but for now, nothing else matters until that report is in the judge's hands."

Because in the grand scheme of things, what happened to her didn't matter nearly as much as protecting people from the fate that had befallen her parents. A piece of her had never imagined that she would actually play a part in this amazing scientific adventure, but it was real, and it was happening right now, and never had she hoped so desperately for Judge McLaughlin to see the wisdom of their case.

It didn't take long for Nick to find his cousin Eloise. Bruce had said she worked for the accounting firm of Millhouse Jones, which meant she was likely to be found somewhere in the imposing building on Pine Street in the heart of the financial district. Based in London but with offices throughout Europe and America, Millhouse Jones was the most prestigious accounting firm in the world. Eloise must be smart to have landed a position here.

The lobby of the firm was designed to impress, with a high ceiling, potted palms, and mahogany desks topped with shaded green lamps. Nick's footsteps were muffled by thick imported carpets as he approached the balding clerk at the front desk.

"I'd like to speak with Eloise Drake, please."

The clerk peered up at him over the top of his spectacles. "Does Miss Drake handle one of your accounts?"

"No, I'm here on a personal matter. It's urgent."

The clerk's mouth turned down. Nick probably wasn't doing Eloise's reputation any good by calling her out this early in the morning, and he amended his request.

"She's my cousin. It's a family emergency."

The clerk pushed away from his desk and disappeared down a hallway. Nick used the time to survey the office. Two wings of private offices branched off from the main lobby. They were tightly spaced, like a rabbit warren of hundreds of accountants and bookkeepers plugging away at the business that made New York hum.

His first sight of Eloise took him aback. Her reddish-brown hair was styled like a Gibson girl, and her clothing was smartly tailored, with a nipped-in vest, necktie, and slim skirt of indigo blue. She looked spectacular and so unlike the insecure little girl he once knew, but the hint of a smile betrayed her.

"Hello, Nick," she said. "You're looking better than you did the last time I saw you."

"At least I'm able to stand on my own two feet," he said, squeezing her hands in welcome.

"What can I do for you? I know our firm audits the accounts for the water board, but they're handled by an entirely different department."

"I'm here on a personal matter," he said.

Her smile stiffened as she glanced at the clerk, whose peering gaze saw too much. This was going to be a difficult conversation, for Nick was about to accuse her of collusion in a crime, and it was best done away from the prying eyes of the front desk clerk. Nick wanted a witness, but not this one.

"My office is this way," Eloise said.

Nick shook his head. "This place makes me feel claustrophobic. There's a park across the street. Let's go there."

She cast a nervous glance at the disapproving clerk. "I'll only be a few minutes," she said.

"I'll note it on your time card," he replied sourly.

Eloise pressed Nick for details as they boarded the elevator, but he shook his head and nodded to the attendant. "Let's wait until we are alone," he said as the elevator doors slid closed.

They rode the rest of the way down in silence, and then Nick led her across the street to the yard of Trinity Church, a green oasis amidst the towering buildings. Pathways curved throughout the churchyard. He walked in silence until he reached an old sycamore tree, its trunk gnarled and twisted with age.

"I had an interesting conversation with your mother," he began.

The welcoming expression on Eloise's face cooled, but she still looked calm as she took a seat on one of the marble benches. "Oh?"

"She said you produced a set of fake accounting ledgers for her." He remained standing and watched her expression carefully. It didn't waver, but her chin lifted a tiny fraction.

"I'm not comfortable with the word 'fake.' I did some accounting work for my mother to correct a discrepancy in my father's financial ledgers."

Uncle Thomas still owned Drake Industries, a corporation worth several million dollars, but Nick would have thought they had their own accountant.

"And you believed that?"

A stab of hurt flashed across her eyes, so like when she was a little girl and no one wanted to play with her. Then it vanished. The coldness in her face reminded him uncomfortably of Margaret.

"If you're accusing me of something, just spell it out." She stood and took a few steps toward him. He wasn't good at judging people. He tended to believe whatever they said and couldn't spot subterfuge, but she certainly seemed convinced of her position.

"I'd rather hear what you have to say about it."

"My mother runs a charitable school for immigrants," Eloise said, an edge having slipped into her cool voice. "For a while, my father funded it with money taken from Drake Industries. It was perfectly legal, but he never accounted for those withdrawals in the financial records. Now that he's died, my mother wants to sell the company, and she needed the books amended to reflect those withdrawals. All I did was some free accounting work for the family business."

Things became clear. Doctor Clean was a publicly traded company, meaning their financial records were available to any interested investor. It would have been easy for Margaret to get a copy of those records, which she passed off to Eloise as the financial statements for Drake Industries.

"You created a fraudulent set of books for a publicly traded company," he said. "Two people are on the hook for it, and one of them is sitting in jail right now."

The color drained from her face, and she looked ready to faint, but he kept up the pressure.

"Two innocent people are being framed for embezzling from a fifteen million dollar company. There's going to be a criminal investigation, and the records you created are the linchpin. You need to testify to what you've done."

"She wouldn't do this to me," Eloise whispered.

"She did."

Eloise turned to stagger toward the bench, but her knees gave out before she got there. She sank to the ground and curled over. She didn't make a single sound as she rocked in the grass. It was impossible to doubt her. Margaret had used her own daughter in a criminal enterprise in a twisted game of revenge.

He knelt beside her. "You'll be okay," he said gruffly. "I'll provide a lawyer for you. You won't be punished for this. All you have to do is tell the truth."

"And send my mother to jail?"

Nick grunted. Why Eloise should care what happened to Margaret was a mystery. "Maybe. That would be for a judge to decide."

He helped Eloise up from the ground and onto the marble bench. Grass clippings clung to her skirt, and he swiped them away.

"She's my mother," Eloise whispered. "We never got along very well, but I've always wanted . . ." Her voice choked off, but she didn't need to finish the sentence for Nick to understand. As a child, Eloise was so desperate for approval she would do anything for attention. When Margaret came asking for a favor, he didn't doubt Eloise would have moved mountains to comply.

"She doesn't deserve your loyalty," he said. "A cat can give birth, but that doesn't mean it will love its children."

Eloise sagged even further, and when she spoke, her voice was so soft that he could barely hear it. "If I come forward, I'll lose my job."

"I'll get you another one."

She shook her head. "No firm in the world would hire an accountant who has confessed to falsifying records. Being an accountant is more than a job to me. It's . . ." She gazed off into the distance, and this time her face took on a wistful softness of great beauty. "I grew up in a storm-tossed world. My family ignored me. I was shuttled from schools to distant relatives to a convent. And then one day I discovered mathematics, and suddenly the world made sense to me. Math is order and reason and logic. I understand the rules, and I am good at them. And it turned out the world needed people who can grind through endless pages of numbers. I love being needed. I love everything about this work." Her voice trailed off, and it looked like she was going to be sick.

He put a hand on her shoulder. "I'll find you another job. I have a lot of influence in this city."

"Nick, there are only six female Certified Public Accountants in the state, and I'm one of them. We had to fight hard to be taken seriously, because most men doubt a woman can balance their own grocery bill. And you want me to confess to being duped into carrying out a fraud? What will it do to those other women who have managed to become CPAs? I have to be perfect. *We* have to be perfect."

She rose, and it looked like it took every ounce of her strength to stand upright. She drew a deep breath and raised her chin. "I'm sorry, Nick. I need to think about this for a while."

She didn't look back as she trudged across the lawn, heading toward the imposing building and a job she apparently loved more than common decency.

His eyes darkened. He didn't really know Eloise. She'd been born into the lap of luxury but surrounded only with vipers. Maybe he couldn't blame her for lacking a moral compass.

Two men stepped from behind the sycamore tree.

"Did you hear what she said?" Nick asked.

"We've got everything we need," the police officer replied.

Was he any better than Eloise? He hadn't known what he was going to hear this morning, but the odds were good that it would be damning, and he needed impartial witnesses to hear it. The police were the best shot he had, and he'd brought Eloise to this churchyard bench like a shepherd leading a lamb to slaughter.

"Are you going to arrest her?" It hurt even to ask the question, but he needed to know. If Eloise's story was true, she might plead ignorance to what she'd done, but ignorance was no excuse in the eyes of the law.

"That will be for the district attorney to decide."

Nick took everything he'd learned straight to his attorney, Vincent Ruskin. Although it ought to have been a simple matter to get Rosalind out of jail, the case straddled both New York and New Jersey lines, which complicated things, as did his desire to protect Eloise. She was a victim too, and he didn't want to throw her to the wolves in the process of freeing Rosalind.

Which didn't endear him to Rosalind's brother. Gus had been attending every strategy meeting Nick held in his office, complete with a New Jersey lawyer and private investigator.

"Why can't the police formally question Eloise?" Gus asked as he paced before the desk in Nick's office. "Demand she answer their questions, and if she doesn't, place her under arrest? They did as much to Rosalind."

"Because they can't *find* Eloise," Nick ground out, doing his best to hold on to the ends of his fraying temper. The district attorney had ordered a search of Eloise's office for corroborating paperwork. She was asked to leave the office during the search, but instead of waiting in the lobby, she headed straight to the train station and fled town.

Nick's private investigator had reported that a woman matching her description bought a ticket to Kingston the day after their confrontation in the churchyard, which meant she was hiding out at Bruce Garrett's mansion in upstate New York.

The place was a literal fortress, and there would be no getting through to her unless Bruce wanted him there. So far, all Nick's telephone calls had been refused.

"You know where she is," Gus said.

"What makes you think that?"

Gus clenched his fists and leaned forward. "You claim to have hired the best private investigator in the city, and his report is right there in that file, and you won't let me look at it."

Nick thrummed his fingers atop the closed file, racked by indecision.

His lawyer's voice was sympathetic, but that couldn't soften the sting of his message. "You need to pick, my friend. Loyalty to Dr. Werner or to your cousin, a girl who doesn't seem to mind that an innocent woman is rotting in jail."

A girl who'd only sought the approval of her mother, who had been fighting for it since childhood, and in return for her devotion had been stabbed in the back by Margaret. And now Nick was doing the same.

He stood and wandered to the window, hands fisted as he glared outside, as if the answer to his dilemma was somewhere in the crowded streets below. Behind him, Gus and Vinni discussed strategy, throwing around legal terms Nick didn't understand. Affidavits, indictable offenses, constructive fraud and extrinsic fraud. All of it ratcheted his headache higher.

Gus suddenly had the bright idea to file civil charges on top of the criminal ones as a way to put pressure on Eloise. The excitement in his voice made Nick's temper snap.

"Listen to yourselves! You're talking about how to ruin an innocent girl who's just barely finding a foothold in this city!"

"And what did that 'girl' do to my sister?" Gus demanded.

Nick looked away, stalking back and forth in an office that suddenly felt too small. He was being painted into a corner, and he hated it. No matter what step he took, someone was going to be hurt. That day in the churchyard still haunted him. He'd chosen Rosalind over Ellie, and he hated himself for it. It was the right thing to do, and he would do it again, but he still felt sick over it.

Sometimes there were no easy answers. Rosalind had been painted into a corner over that chlorine case, and he hadn't shown her an ounce of sympathy over the decision she made. When both sides are right, how did one choose? He'd ripped Rosalind to shreds over her decision, and now he was in the same situation.

A quick knock broke into his thoughts as General O'Donnell opened the door and met Nick's gaze across the office.

"The judge in Jersey City has his final ruling on the chlorine case. It's going to be announced in an hour."

All bickering stopped as everyone ran for the elevators.

Rosalind lay on her cot, her blouse damp and sweat-stained from another day at the laundry. The scent of lye saturated her hair, and even now she could smell it. When she got out of here, she'd never use lye again.

And according to Gus, she would be released on bail soon. Someone had come through with the money, although Gus insisted the person wished to remain anonymous. It was the sort of thing Nick might do. He had been willing to attach his name to their final report, which meant he had finally seen reason, and perhaps was willing to forgive her.

She rolled into a more comfortable position and tried to ignore the ongoing spat between Gabriella and Melinda over an extra muffin left over from dinner. Most people wanted Gabriella to have it because of the baby, but Melinda insisted that as the person who performed the hardest manual labor, she was entitled to it. Finally someone suggested Rosalind be called in to render the decision. As the calmest-thinking person among them, Rosalind had already been asked to settle disputes on three separate occasions.

She sighed. She'd rather get up and play mediator than listen to them caterwauling for the next hour.

"Can't you just split the muffin down the middle?" she asked.

Gabriella's voice was exasperated. "I suggested that, but Melinda won't compromise. And the doctor said that I should be eating more than prison rations."

"Then get your no-good husband to bring you something," Melinda demanded.

"How can he do that when he is at sea?" Gabriella shrieked.

Rosalind slid the muffin toward Gabriella. "Eat it quickly," she said. "I'm sure that next time Melinda will be willing to split it with you."

A noise from outside caught her attention. It sounded like someone shouting her name. As she turned to look at the window, a clatter of pebbles sprayed against the plate glass.

She scurried to the window. If someone broke the glass, the jail might replace it with something that couldn't be rigged to open.

More than a dozen people were congregated on the lawn outside the prison. Dr. Leal was there and Gus—good heavens, even Nick was there, all of them grinning and craning their necks to see her. They were surrounded by the students who had been assisting them in the lab.

"Rosalind!" Dr. Leal shouted up at her through cupped hands. "We won! The judge just handed down the final ruling, and we won!"

The others on the ground bellowed in mighty roars of approval, cheering and applauding. She couldn't help shrieking too. She jumped up and down, screeching like a crazy woman, but they had won! She placed her hands on the glass, barely able to see through the sheen blurring her vision. Thank God! *Thank you, God, for letting the judge be brave enough to rule this way.*

"Congratulations, Rosalind!" Gus hollered. "I never doubted you could do it!"

She glanced at Nick, whose expression radiated with joy and pride. She looked away as though she'd been burned. It hurt too much to look at the man who'd brought her such pain during the happiest moment of her life.

She had a million questions, but the crack in the window was so high. She grabbed a chair to stand on so she could get her face close to the crack.

"What happens now?" she called down, looking only at Dr. Leal.

"We move forward as planned," he shouted back. "One step at a time. We won the first battle—a huge one—but there are more on the horizon. Cincinnati has telegrammed. They want our help replicating the process."

It was happening! Their research was already starting to make the country a safer place, and she was torn between laughter and tears. The students cheered and took swigs from a bottle, and Dr. Leal grinned like an idiot.

And Nick . . . well, Nick was climbing the maple tree right beside the jailhouse. Fist over fist, he climbed higher. The attic was on the third floor, and this was dangerous. Given his abhorrence for the outdoors, this was probably the first time he'd ever tried to climb a tree in his life.

"Nick, you're going to kill yourself," she called out the window.

He'd grown up in Manhattan; he didn't know how to climb trees. Besides, she didn't want him up here. It was wonderful that he'd changed his mind about the chlorine, but that couldn't obliterate the chasm still between them.

He reached the second story but still didn't look at her. He was too busy scanning the spindly branches for a way to get even higher, but there were no other branches to latch onto. He was still ten feet below her and wobbling at a dangerous angle when he swiveled his head to meet her gaze.

He shouted in a confident voice. "Two months ago I said I wanted to be the first man to dance in the streets if chlorine worked. I'm sorry I was such a dolt along the way, but I want to keep my promise and dance in the streets with you. As soon as you're out of jail, we'll dance and celebrate and set the city on fire."

Her eyes softened. How easy it would be to get swept up into his enthusiasm, but it would be wrong. She'd been reckless and impulsive once before and couldn't afford to risk her heart again. It was impossible to stop a wistful smile, and she had to talk around the lump in her throat.

"Go out and dance, Nick," she managed to choke out. "Today is a magical day, a once-in-a-lifetime kind of day, and it shouldn't be squandered." This was going to be hard. She drew in a ragged breath and forced herself to meet his eyes. "Don't wait for me. I'm not the right person for you."

It hurt to say the words. It hurt even worse as the elation on Nick's face faded into pained resignation.

"Oh, Rosalind . . . don't say I've ruined everything. Tell me how to make things right, and I'll do it. I know I've hurt you. I was wrong and I'm sorry. I hit you where I knew it would hurt the most, but if anyone in this city doubts that you are a bright, shining woman of honor, I'll change their minds. Let me try. Every hour of every day, I'll set you up on a pedestal so high the whole world will see it. I've been a jerk and an idiot, but I can't shake this insane idea that we can be perfect together. I adore you."

What could she say to that? That all was forgiven? It wasn't. She loved him but couldn't trust him. He'd hurt her too badly.

She touched her fingers to the glass, then turned to look at the students and Dr. Leal below. They couldn't hear what she and Nick were saying, and the celebration continued unabated. They hooted and hollered, waving a piece of paper she assumed was the judge's ruling.

"Go down and join them," she said through the crack in the window. "Give them my very best, but I need to say good-bye to you, Nick."

He swallowed hard, and she wondered at the howling ache that opened in her chest as he lowered himself hand over hand back down to the ground, turned, and walked away.

Chapter TWENTY-ONE

Nick couldn't blame Rosalind for turning her back on him. He'd taken a pure, shining gift and trampled it in a fit of bad temper. That didn't mean he would obediently go away. They had both hurt each other, but he wasn't giving up. She would be released on bail soon, and he needed a permanent solution to protect her from further attacks orchestrated by Aunt Margaret.

He invited himself to dinner at Colin and Lucy's apartment, desperate to make progress unraveling the plot woven by their aunt. Lucy was appalled when she learned what Margaret had done to Rosalind.

"But why aren't they letting her out of prison?" she demanded. "If the police officers overheard Eloise admit to forging those ledgers, why didn't they let her out of jail that very day?"

Nick smiled tightly. "They think I may have bribed Eloise into making up a story that would set Rosalind free. Margaret denied everything to the police when they confronted her with Eloise's story, so they're still investigating."

A part of him couldn't blame his cousin for not wanting to testify against her mother, but he was still incensed that she had disappeared. Rosalind was sweltering in a cramped, stifling jail cell right now because of Eloise.

"I don't suppose there is need for a new accountant at the AP, is there?" he asked.

Lucy shrugged. "I have no idea."

"Colin? What about Reuters?" As the managing director of Reuters, Colin held a lot of power over that sort of thing.

"We have a separate accounting agency," he said. "Millhouse Jones."

Great. The firm that had fired Eloise when they learned about the investigation.

Colin rose from the table and went to the sideboard, pouring himself a cup of tea. "I'm reluctant to raise the topic, but do you believe Margaret is done? Or does she have more victims lined up?"

Margaret had implied as much at the Scandinavian Tearoom, gloating as she taunted him with how much he had to lose.

"I think she may be on a roll," he said. "It was probably just a lot of blather, but she mentioned the pair of you. And Sadie. We need to be on the lookout."

Colin shot him a glare. "What is that supposed to mean?"

"It means that I've hired a little muscle to be on hand when I can't be at home," he said. "It means I've told my people not to let any strangers into the apartment. I suggest you do the same."

Colin wadded up his napkin and threw it down. "Brilliant," he muttered. "Now we must barricade our own home against that woman's poison?"

Lucy had gone white, her hand clutched over her midsection. Her surprisingly *large* midsection. Instead of the wasp-waisted gowns she usually favored, Lucy wore a loose tea gown. Come to think of it, she'd been favoring such gowns for months.

His gaze flew to hers. "Are you pregnant?"

"Seven months," she said.

"Seven months! Why didn't you tell me?"

Her eyes looked a little watery, and her voice was soft. "I've lost three babies so far. They all happened after only a few months, so the doctor thinks this one will stick, but I didn't want to announce anything until . . ."

Her voice trailed off, and his chest split wide open, knowing his little sister had been enduring these calamities and hadn't breathed a word of it. And now he had just dumped a heap of stress into her world, all because he'd had the harebrained idea to be nice to Aunt Margaret.

"Ah, Luce . . ." he said in an aching voice. "It's the best thing in the world. I don't want you worrying about a thing. I'll pay for bodyguards, doctors, the works."

"Thank you, Nick," Colin said dryly. "I have been practicing my telephone skills for years, and I think I'm up for the challenge of summoning help."

Nick stood, reluctant to bring up the topic, but he didn't want Lucy repeating the mistakes he'd made. As much as he wanted to deny the facts, he owed it to his sister to share what he knew.

"When the time comes, it would be best to go to a hospital," he said. He explained what Rosalind had told him about the dangers of infection during home births. Although he'd been incensed when she first suggested it, Nick had asked General O'Donnell's opinion, and the general confirmed that hospitals had a better track record for keeping infection at bay. There could be no more denying it, and Nick would wonder until his dying day if Bridget's death was his fault.

A part of him accepted that God worked in mysterious ways, and that Nick couldn't expect his puny human brain to understand the infinities of the universe. He didn't know why Bridget had to die so young or why Lucy had lost so many babies. He didn't know why he'd inherited a fortune or why Rosalind was orphaned at such a tender age. Maybe it was all part of some grand plan to use his talents and money to help pave the way for a new era of science.

All he knew for sure was that he needed to become a better man than he'd been over the past few weeks. Helping Eloise get another job would be a start. She had been fired because of him, and at least this was one area where he could repair the damage he'd caused.

Unfortunately, that meant appealing to Fletcher Jones, the commissioner of finance for the water board. Fletcher was a world-class stickler for rules, regulations, and decorum. He was also the kind of man Nick always secretly envied. A Yale education, travel abroad, appointments to powerful positions dropped into his lap.

But there was nothing easy about his conversation with Fletcher the next morning.

"My cousin has several years of experience handling private accounts," he said, pacing the space before Fletcher's glossy walnut desk. "Rumor has it she's a genius with numbers."

"And precisely what are her qualifications, aside from being your cousin and accused of fraud?"

"She's a CPA. That's some kind of fancy accounting certification."

"Thank you," Fletcher said archly. "I know what a CPA is. I still don't hire people accused of fraud."

Nick tried to make light of it. "I don't think the district attorney is going to file charges against her. She was tricked into creating those fraudulent records."

Fletcher shifted in his chair, his fingers thrumming against his immaculate desk. "I'm already fully staffed."

"Make room." Nick had been bending over backward to meet every request the finance department sent his way, and this was the first time he'd ever come to Fletcher asking a favor. He intended to get it.

"I run a tight ship," Fletcher said. "I don't have any openings until the Catskills project opens up, and those people will be working upstate."

"At Duval Springs?" Nick asked. An assignment in that town meant she would have to work with the Duval brothers, and Nick's shoulder still ached from the beating he'd taken last time he was up there. He didn't want her within a stone's throw of that simmering hostility as thousands of people were evicted from their homes.

"Yes, Duval Springs," Fletcher affirmed. "I can't imagine any city woman would want to be sent into the middle of nowhere for a basic accounting position."

But Fletcher hadn't seen the longing in his cousin's face when she spoke about her love of mathematics. She'd probably take a position on the moon if it meant she could keep working in her chosen career. Nick was almost certain Bruce Garrett was her father, so she wouldn't be without a protector in the face of the Duval brothers.

"Eloise has family in the area. I think she would take it."

Fletcher still looked skeptical, but if Eloise was willing to fall on her sword and confess to what she had done, Nick was going to get that position for her.

After six days in jail, Rosalind stepped into the August afternoon and savored the cloudless expanse of blue sky overhead and the fresh, green-scented air.

"Don't get too close to me," she warned as Gus helped her into the rented cab. "I reek to high heaven and can't wait for a bath."

Gus had been a hero. He had come twice a day to visit her, negotiated with the prison warden for buckets of ice to be sent up to the attic, and brought baskets of home-baked treats, always with plenty to share. Most importantly, he'd teamed up with a high-priced lawyer who had managed to get all the charges against her dropped.

"Who paid the bail?" was her first question as the carriage set off toward home.

"Nobody. The charges were dropped, so there was no need for bail."

"Then who paid the bill for that attorney?" she pressed.

"He wants to remain anonymous," Gus said as he pretended to look out the carriage window.

"Nick?" He had both the money and the guilty conscience. She bet it was Nick.

"Like I said . . . he wants to be anonymous."

"I think it's Nick. The only other person I know with that kind of money is Doctor Clean, and he thinks I belong in jail."

"It wasn't Doctor Clean. Let's drop the subject, shall we? You're free. Enjoy every moment. The laboratory students are planning a celebration in Central Park this evening. There's a Shakespeare play, and then a picnic under the stars. Dr. Leal and all the others will be there. Do you want to go?"

She drew a deep breath, savoring the taste of clean, fresh air. "Yes." The prospect of an evening under the stars with good friends was energizing. "Yes, I'd like to go. But who paid for the lawyer?"

"Rosalind, why does it matter?"

"It matters because I don't like being indebted to anyone." Especially Nick. She needed to put their brief, glorious fling behind her and move forward without any lingering obligations.

A sense of well-being flooded her the instant she stepped back inside her cottage. How she had missed this! The scent of lemon polish and cedar planking. Her cozy mantelpiece filled with handmade music boxes and windowsills lined with potted herbs. She would not cry. She was a strong woman with newfound resolve, and she wouldn't become a blubbering watering pot, but oh, this was wonderful.

Ingrid proved typically chilly as she descended the staircase to greet Rosalind, but the baby sent her a huge, drooly smile and a shriek of joy.

"Hello, Jonah," Rosalind said, working once again to control her surge of weepy joy as she kissed the baby's soft hair and breathed his powdery smell. "Thank you for all the baking you did," she said to Ingrid. "The women and I deeply appreciated all your homemade cookies."

"Of course," Ingrid said with a regal nod. It was hard to read her, and Rosalind didn't have the energy to try.

"Well. I think everyone would appreciate it if I went for a quick bath."

She needed to escape, partly because she was filthy, but just as much because she didn't want to ruin the afternoon by blubbering in front of anyone. Wasn't it strange how this surge of emotion seemed to keep coming in waves? Just when she'd found her footing, the littlest thing, like the scent of Jonah's baby powder caught her by surprise and made her weepy again.

Twenty minutes later, she was freshly bathed, powdered, and changed into a clean dress. She spritzed herself with a generous splash of her favorite lemon verbena cologne. Most importantly, she was composed. It had taken a while to collect her senses and calm her tumult of emotions, but she was safe and would handle the future with well-prepared rationality.

Dinner preparations were under way when she emerged downstairs.

"That smells delicious," she said to Ingrid's back as her sister-in-law whisked flour into gravy. "Is there anything I can do to help?"

Ingrid looked over her shoulder. "You can lay the table."

Gus cleared his study materials off the table, and Rosalind

reached for a tablecloth, but something looked different in the tiny area. The furniture was the same, as were the gingham curtains on the window.

There was a new picture above the sideboard. Some sort of framed legal document, almost like a stock certificate, except plainer. She stepped closer, but without her spectacles, it was impossible to read the small print.

"What's this?" she asked as she reached for her spectacles. A patent? Fancy, boldly embossed letters proclaimed it was from the United States Patent Office, but smaller print below looked like it had been banged out on a typewriter:

The Frieda and Augustus Werner
Freshwater Chlorinator

The breath froze in her throat. She glanced at the name of the patent holder: George Warren Fuller. She barely knew him. Mr. Fuller certainly didn't know what had happened to her parents or even their given names.

She clamped a hand over her chest to still the pounding of her heart. "Why would Mr. Fuller name the patent after Mama and Papa?"

Gus stood directly behind her, a reluctant smile on his face. "I guess he already has so many patents that he didn't mind sharing the stage."

"But why? And why Mama and Papa?"

"Someone asked him."

"You?"

He shook his head. "Not me."

It had to have been Nick. He was the only one who knew she feared her parents would be forgotten. *Oh, Mama . . .*

They would forever burn brightly in her memory, but now her parents' sacrifice would be remembered. She'd worked for years to ensure they had not died in vain. Never had she imagined they would be memorialized in such a fashion, and it got to her.

The first snivels caught her unaware. She clamped a hand over her mouth to block the tremors of weeping. She turned away and shut her eyes, causing two fat tears to roll down her face. Despite her effort, gulping sobs slipped out anyway. She was helpless against the weeping that began deep inside and welled up, causing her to shake with repressed tears.

Gus's hands were heavy on her shoulders. "Don't cry, Rosalind. . . ."

She couldn't help it. She didn't know if she was happy or grateful or mourning the loss of her parents afresh . . . all of it, probably. The weeping turned heavier, engulfing her whole body and making it impossible to stand upright. She curled over. Weeping turned into sobs, and then sobs turned into bawling. Gus guided her to a chair, even as huge, wrenching sobs made it hard to walk. Fat tears splatted onto her skirt. She cried so hard she could barely breathe.

"Please stop," Gus said. "You're scaring me. You're scaring the baby. Heck, you're even scaring *Ingrid*."

A gulp of laughter mingled with her tears, for Ingrid stood motionless in the kitchen, watching her as if waiting for a bomb to explode.

"I'll be okay," she said, wiping the tears from her face. This had just taken her by surprise, and it was all too much. Nick wasn't a perfect man, but it hurt to remember how generous and thoughtful he could be.

"Do you still want to go to the park?" Gus asked. "I'm sure the others will understand if you'd rather stay home."

The crying jag had sapped her energy, but it would be good to go out with the students. She owed them so much, as they had carried out her duties during the final days while she'd been incarcerated. It was time to resume her normal life.

And she needed to get her mind off Nick. Her gaze trailed to the patent, the most thoughtful gift she'd ever been given. Her debts to him were growing, and the prospect of getting sucked back into the vortex surrounding him was terrifying.

Yes, a night of Shakespeare in the park was exactly what she needed.

Nick's conversation with Colin and Lucy confirmed his determination to win Rosalind back. When Lucy and Colin talked about the coming baby, they had the cautious gratitude of soldiers emerging from a hard-won battle. It was not undiluted happiness, but a quiet kind of confidence that came from surviving life's challenges alongside a partner. He hadn't realized the private struggles they'd been fighting, but they had persevered and were the stronger for it.

He wanted that sort of life with Rosalind. Life was short, and neither of them were perfect. He hadn't been fair to her in assuming she was.

According to the warden at the jail, she had been released shortly after lunchtime. The first thing he did upon arriving home after work was place a telephone call to her house.

A male voice answered on the other end. "Hello?"

"I'd like to speak with Rosalind, please."

Even across the telephone wires, Nick could hear the reluctance in Gus's voice. "I don't think she wants to speak with you."

It would serve him right if Rosalind refused to ever speak to him again, but they owed it to one another to clear the air. He would never stop hoping they could work toward a reconciliation, and that meant not letting her brother bully him into giving up too easily.

"I don't have time for this. Just get her on the phone."

"Why should I?"

"Because it is *her* house, *her* telephone, and *her* service that she is paying for. Now get her on the phone," he barked.

"She isn't here."

Nick rocked back on his heels. "It's seven o'clock in the evening. Where is she?" If Rosalind had another suitor, it would only be natural for her to want to spend her first night of freedom with him, but the thought scorched.

"She wouldn't want me to say. And besides, she would kill me if she learned that I told you she went to see the Shakespeare play tonight in the park. And that she's with the entire crew of lab assistants, who plan to have a picnic under the stars near Summit Rock. She would really hate that."

Nick smiled and bowed his head in gratitude. "Thanks, Gus."

Chapter TWENTY-TWO

Rosalind hoped the play would be one of Shakespeare's comedies, but no such luck. It was the eternally moody Hamlet with his complicated family.

She sat on a blanket in the park and gave up concentrating on the play. On her first night of freedom, she wondered what Melinda, Gabriella, and all the other women in the jail were doing right now. She wondered if her reputation would ever be restored. But most of all she wondered about Nick.

According to Gus, this entire fraud had been cooked up by Nick's vengeful aunt, so it would make sense for him to help her get out of jail. But getting the chlorinator patent named after her parents? That went beyond the call of duty. She couldn't stop thinking of the way he'd looked, clinging to that tree outside her jail window. *"I wanted to be the first man to dance in the streets if chlorine worked."*

She had gone dancing with the lab students instead, who led her in an impromptu jig when a pair of buskers played the fiddle before the performance started. It had been a nice sentiment. Everything about her and Nick's early days had been fabulous, a wild and glorious free fall with no limits and no caution. It couldn't have lasted, but she would always regret the way it ended.

A student hunkered down on the blanket beside her. "Hello, Dr. Werner."

She gasped and whirled, for it was Nick alongside her, his face brimming with tenderness. She instinctively pulled back a few inches.

"Did Gus tell you I was here?"

The corners of his eyes crinkled in pained amusement. "Will there be a death in the family if I say he did?"

Maybe it was just as well. She and Nick had too much unfinished business for her to keep avoiding him. And the play was depressing.

"Thank you for the patent," she said.

If there was any doubt that he was behind the patent, it vanished as his eyes warmed and he leaned in. "You liked that, did you?"

"Shh!" someone said behind them.

"Let's go for a walk," he suggested, holding out his hand. It would be so easy to take it and slip back into his world.

"Let's watch the end of the play," she whispered. "Ophelia just drowned herself in the castle pond, but Hamlet doesn't know yet."

"I'll bet that's going to ruin their water supply for weeks," Nick said.

She stifled a snort of laughter, causing the lady in front of her to turn and shoot her a glare.

"Come on, let's go," Nick prodded. "*Hamlet* is awful. Everyone dies in the end."

"Shh!" This time the person behind them gave Nick a shove to the shoulder.

"Please, Rosalind . . . we have business to discuss."

It was true. She took his hand and let him pull her upright.

They picked their way through the crowd to the grassy lawn in the distance. After they reached the wood-chip path, she took care to keep an arm's distance from him. Chemistry thrummed between them, just as it always did when they were together, and she had to handle this cautiously. Not like before, when she rushed headlong into his arms, heedless of the consequences or even knowing who he really was before she fell under his spell.

They headed toward a pond surrounded by a line of maple trees. With fewer lampposts, it was darker here, but she still sensed every square inch of Nick's presence as he walked beside her. The air was alive with sound. The squawking of a mockingbird was surprisingly loud, and the drone of crickets mingled with rustling leaves.

"You ought to love this," Nick said. "All this outdoors and your beloved green canopy."

She caught her breath. "You remember that?"

"I remember everything." His voice sounded profoundly sad. "I remember being so dazzled by you that I could barely string a sentence together. I remember marveling at how a lady could be so delicate and dainty while also being so smart and committed to a cause. I wondered how a working-class guy like me could have a chance with a woman like you, but by some miracle, I did. And then everything fell apart so quickly."

"It's probably just as well," she said. After the day at the courthouse, she swore she'd never forgive him . . . but did she really want to carry that grudge for the rest of her life? Nick's temper often got the better of him, but it always blew over eventually. And she wasn't a shrinking violet anymore. If she could stand up to Melinda, she could stand up to anyone.

"It's *not* just as well," Nick pressed. "And besides, I think we can work together. If not on a personal level, then a professional one. General O'Donnell wants to consider chlorination in New York. You could help us with that."

"So could Dr. Leal."

"I want you, and I'm the man who signs the contracts."

She halted. He was moving too fast again, and even talking about contracting with New York was ridiculous at this hour of night. "Who paid for my lawyer?"

He slanted her a look, as though she were an idiot.

"Thank you. I'll figure out some way to pay you back."

"Come do a little consulting on the New York water project, and I'll consider it paid off."

"Don't be ridiculous. You're just doing this because you feel guilty. Or you're hoping to start things up again, and that's not going to happen."

"I've already got the contracts prepared and ready to sign. Dr. Leal told me he's going to spend most of the next few years traveling, and a lot of cities will be skeptical of you because you're a woman. If you're the lead consultant in New York City, no one will doubt you. Come by my office Monday morning, and you can sign the contract."

Her mind worked quickly, a niggling sense of pride stirring to life. She'd never been hungry for fame, but working on the largest water system in the nation would be an important step. Everything he said about some cities refusing to work with a woman was true.

"What about the other commissioners? Will they object to having me as a consultant?" She didn't need to mention her tattered reputation. Given the grim set of Nick's mouth, he was already thinking about it.

"Maybe, maybe not," he finally said. "Fletcher can be a real stick in the mud."

"Then I want to sign the contract tonight." He looked stunned at her agreement, and she followed up with her reasoning. "If the contract is signed, there won't be much Fletcher Jones can do, right?"

Nick smiled widely, looking deliciously masculine, pleased, and roguish. "I like the way you think."

The magnetic spell was weaving itself around them again, and she took a cautious step back. "If I sign the contract, you know it doesn't mean anything beyond water. H_20 and chlorine, right?"

"If that's all I can get." He spoke with the forthright confidence she'd always admired. "I knew within five minutes of meeting you that we both wanted the same thing. Clean water. Then the personal stuff got in the way. I still want that personal stuff, I can't lie about that . . . but if a straightforward business relationship is all you can offer . . . well, I'm a patient man."

They took a streetcar to Nick's office building. There was nobody on the top floor, and their footsteps echoed in the long, tiled hallways as they headed toward the suite of offices where Nick worked. His keys jangled as he unlocked the first door, then led her through the reception area and toward another set of closed doors leading to the private offices. Only a little light leaked in through the windows, and the desks and filing cabinets loomed like dark shadows in the silent office.

"This is where I work," Nick said as he unlocked the door to a private office. There was a hint of hesitancy in his voice as he led her inside. With a metallic click, he pulled the lever on the brass electrical plate, then switched on a lamp sitting on his desk. "This is my office," he said unnecessarily. Normally he was so confident, but not now. He looked at her with caution on his face and shifted his feet. He was nervous, anxious for her approval.

"Very nice," she said simply. "Where's the contract?"

"Oh, um . . . let me find the papers. I wasn't expecting to do this until next week."

While he sorted through stacks of files on his desk, she

scanned the office. There was the desk on one side and a huge conference table on the other. Bookshelves had been built into the wall, most of them weighed down with pedestrian-looking manuals. A few of the shelves had elegant wooden accordion doors that could be rolled back to reveal a hidden cubby. Each accordion door had a tiny brass lock on it, but the keys were in the locks, so there probably weren't state secrets inside. She grasped one of the keys to lift the door, impressed by its smooth glide. She wasn't sure what to expect inside the cubby, but a miniature dollhouse certainly wasn't it. There was also a rag doll and a tin of chocolates.

She swiveled to look at Nick, who was still riffling through files, but he grinned when he saw where she was looking.

"Sometimes Sadie visits me in the office, and I can't have her getting too bored."

The cubby door glided silently closed as she lowered it back into place. Higher up was another accordion door, and this time she saw the typical male forbidden fruit. A box of imported cigars and a half-full bottle with a familiar label.

"I thought you didn't drink liquor," she said.

"I don't," Nick said. "Just a beer now and then."

Rosalind picked up the bottle of brandy, holding it up for his view. His brows lowered.

"That's not mine," he said, a note of concern in his voice. The bottle was half-empty, so it seemed a little strange to deny drinking it.

"It's all right, Nick. My family in Germany often has brandy with their meals. They even cook with—"

"But that's not mine," Nick insisted. His hands were planted on his hips as he scrutinized the bottle, his face drawn in unease. "I was in that cabinet not two days ago for a cigar, and that bottle *was not there*. Someone planted it."

Suddenly, even holding the bottle made her nervous. She set it back on the shelf with a gentle *click*. "Is it possible the cleaning staff has been tippling in your office?"

"Possible. Not likely." Nick tossed a file folder at her as he went to inspect the rest of the items on the hidden shelf. He grabbed a small slip of paper resting alongside the cigar box, and as he studied it, his face went white.

"What's that?" she asked.

"It's a hat-check ticket from the Scandinavian Tearoom. It's on the ground floor of my aunt's apartment building."

"And?"

"And I never checked a hat there or anything else. I've only set foot in the place one time in my life, and none of the cleaning crew would have gone there. Someone planted this ticket. The brandy too."

"Your aunt?"

He looked baffled as he unscrewed the bottle's cap and sniffed it. "It smells like brandy," he confirmed. "I don't know what she could be planning, because it's not illegal to drink."

"It could be wood alcohol," she said quietly. "At the Berghütte Research Station, some of the men brewed their own. It's stupid and dangerous, because moonshine can make a man go blind."

If there was too much methanol in the mix, it triggered chemical reactions in the body that produced formaldehyde and formic acid. The combination was deadly, first destroying the optic nerve, then causing seizures and convulsions. In the worst cases, it could kill a man. Of course, the scientists at the research station thought they were too clever to brew bad liquor, but they had a makeshift way of testing it. A heated copper rod dunked in liquor triggered the production of formaldehyde if the liquor was bad. The characteristic stink of formaldehyde was a sure warning the liquor was dangerous.

"Have you got a penny?" Rosalind asked. She had no idea if the makeshift solution would work, but it couldn't hurt to try.

Nick produced a penny, and he had a box of matches alongside the cigars. She poured a little liquor into a glass, averting her face as she did so. As a scientist, she knew that breathing the fumes was harmless, but everything about Margaret Drake gave her the jitters.

There were no tongs in the office, but a pair of scissors would work. She held the penny clamped between the scissor blades while Nick struck a match, then held it beneath the penny. The flame traveled down the length of the match, drawing ever closer to his pinched fingers, until he shook the match dead, then struck another. Then another. The penny turned black, but after the fifth match, the penny's rim took on the characteristic glow of heated metal. First yellow, then, by the seventh match, an orangey-red. It took nine matches before the penny looked hot enough for the experiment.

She carefully shifted the penny over the glass of brandy. "Here we go," she said as the penny dropped.

It hissed, sizzled, and then the nose-stinging reek of formaldehyde hit her.

She reared back. "It's wood alcohol," she said.

Nick cursed under his breath and raced to the telephone. His hand was shaking. "Connect me to Lucy Drake," he said in an urgent voice, then provided the exchange. She'd never seen Nick look so shaken, but if Margaret would plant poison in his office, she might do so at Lucy's house too.

After a dozen rings, the operator broke in. "There appears to be no one home, sir."

"Keep trying," he ordered.

"It's ten o'clock at night," the operator said in a semi-scolding tone. "Most people don't answer their telephones this late."

"Keep trying!" Nick shouted.

After another dozen rings, an irritated Colin picked up the receiver.

"Don't eat or drink anything in your house," Nick ordered. "Not a drop, even if it looks like water. Margaret planted poisoned brandy in my office."

Colin didn't need any further urging, for it looked like Margaret was out to bring them all down.

Nick had never been so rattled in his life. After talking to Colin, he called his housekeeper with the same warning. They couldn't trust anything in the house. It was only because the brandy was so out of place in his office that they'd bothered to investigate, but Margaret could have just as easily poisoned the milk, the jam, *anything*.

He instructed Rosalind to call her brother, not only to tell him not to eat or drink anything in their house, but to tell him not to expect her home that night. The subways and ferries had stopped running an hour ago, and she had no way of getting across the Hudson.

He had no doubt Margaret was behind this. If anyone came to harm . . . if Lucy lost her baby or if Rosalind's little nephew was hurt . . .

But he couldn't lose his head now. Rosalind's face was white with fear, and he needed to figure out a way to diffuse this situation immediately.

On their way to his apartment, he stopped at Sal's Diner. Even at midnight, the counter was occupied with plenty of late-night customers seeking a decent meal, some hot coffee, or perhaps simple human companionship. Nick didn't want a meal, he wanted a couple loaves of bread, a jar of jam, a bottle of milk, and a round of cheese. It was an unusual request, but they knew him well and gladly supplied his needs. It would suffice until his housekeeper could restock their pantry tomorrow.

As they waited at the counter for their food, Nick noticed

Rosalind gazing around the diner with a faint smile. In this tense, wretched night, he needed to know what had lightened her spirit. "What?" he prompted.

"This is where we first met," she said, then glanced back to the last booth in the diner. "Right at that table. I felt like I had met my best friend and Prince Charming all at once."

The compliment hurt, for he still wanted to be those things for her.

As they left the diner, he carried the sack of food in one arm and offered his hand, palm up, to Rosalind. He held his breath, waiting. She didn't move a muscle, and he lowered his hand, but he wasn't giving up.

"Rosalind, life is short," he said. "If one of us had taken a swig of that brandy . . . or gotten hit by a streetcar on the way to the park . . . well, it would be a real shame if things ended for us like this. You don't have to accept my apology if you aren't ready, but maybe you could hold my hand?"

He offered it again. This time, she hesitated only a moment before slipping her hand into his.

It felt right to walk along the city streets with her beside him. They were a matched pair, different in so many ways, but she was the right person to share this dreadful night with. He wanted to share all his nights with her, the good and the bad.

At his apartment building, they had to shake the doorman awake to get the elevator working. The only time Rosalind had been to his home was that awful morning when she threw the newspaper at him after he dragged her name through the mud. He had a long way to go to make up for that, but he would begin tonight. He would light a fire in the fireplace and prepare a late-night snack of sliced bread and cheese from the diner. Maybe not the most romantic of evenings, but somehow he sensed she would be game for a cozy, quiet night.

No such luck. He realized that the moment he stepped through his front door. Every light in the apartment was ablaze as his housekeeper and Jeannie piled food in the middle of the parlor, almost like they were preparing a bonfire. They both wore gloves. He'd never realized how much food his apartment housed until he saw the bags of flour, rice, apples, and dried beans. Jugs of milk and cider were propped alongside a smoked ham, loaves of bread, and a side of bacon. They summoned Pete the elevator operator to carry it all down to the dumpster, warning him not to touch or give away anything.

After an hour, the apartment was finally cleared of everything edible, and Nick sent the two servants to bed, leaving him and Rosalind in the parlor. Though it was August, he lit a fire. Rosalind perched on the edge of the sofa, warming her hands.

"I think I'm too wound up to sleep," she said. "Do you have anything I can read? A fat novel, perhaps?"

He shook his head. "Only some kiddie books for Sadie, but I've got subscriptions to all the city newspapers, if you'd like."

She winced when he said *newspaper*. He frowned, then turned back to continue stoking the fire, jostling the logs until they crackled with a satisfying snap and flare of warm light. They had to talk about this. He'd dump his entire fortune in her lap if it would help alleviate the tarnish he'd flung at this insanely good-hearted woman.

"I'll issue a retraction," he said, still staring at the fire.

"It won't help."

"Maybe if we got married, it would calm the wagging tongues." He set the poker back in the stand and risked a glance at her.

She stared at him as though he'd gone insane. "You would marry me to save me from a scandal?"

"No, I would marry you because I love you. And, um . . . that's what I was really trying to say. I love you, and I think you're wonderful, and I would be over the moon if you would be my wife."

His mouth went too dry to keep speaking. Her eyes were still big with surprise, but it was different. She had a watery look as though she was fighting back tears.

He sat beside her and reached for her hands. She pulled away to the far end of the sofa, clasping her hands modestly on her lap. He obligingly slid to the opposite side of the sofa and did the same, trying not to laugh. It was Rosalind's straitlaced modesty that had attracted him in the first place. As much as he wanted to lunge across the space between them, he mirrored her prim posture.

"Um, I think it's your turn to talk," he said.

"Oh, Nick . . . we rushed into things once before, and it was all a little too fast for me."

He absorbed her words, parsing them carefully. "But you're not saying no . . ."

"No! I mean . . . yes, I'm not saying no. So yes." She flushed as laughter got the better of her. "What I mean is that I think the world of you, and it would be nice if we could try to court just like normal people. And maybe someday . . ."

It wasn't exactly the ringing endorsement he'd hoped to hear. He'd hoped she would fling herself across the sofa and into his arms, along with all sorts of unwholesome, un-Rosalind kinds of behavior, but he was a patient man. He would have to up his game.

"Okay," he said, still sitting on the far side of the sofa like a good Puritan. "I'm not the kind of man who is good with words or who can spout fancy poetry. I'll never be a big fan of Shakespeare or the opera, but I'll take you whenever you want to go. I can't compete with your college professors, but I can make you laugh. I'll be a good father to any children we have. I'm loyal. I'll guard your back and come through for you in a storm. I can fix a leaky faucet, and I've got a good shoulder to cry on. And I'll wait for you until the stars fall from the sky.

So don't feel like you need to rush into anything. When you're ready, I'll be waiting."

She hadn't moved a muscle, not even to breathe. When she finally got around to talking, she sounded a little shaky. "Actually, I think you're pretty good with words, Nick."

He didn't answer, just stared at her and grinned like an idiot. He could sit here and smile at Rosalind until the sun rose.

They talked for hours that night. The only time he budged from his spot on the far side of the sofa was to stoke the fire. Sometime in the early hours, they both drifted off to sleep, propped up in their respective corners of the sofa.

Sadie woke them up as she drifted into the main room, dragging her blanket and looking at him through bleary eyes.

"How come you're sleeping in your clothes?" she asked, not even questioning Rosalind's presence.

For her part, Rosalind jerked awake, finger-combing her hair and looking as flustered as though she'd been caught with her hand in the cookie jar.

Nick rapped on Jeannie's closed door, for as much as he welcomed the chance to let Sadie get to know Rosalind a little better, it couldn't happen this morning. He needed to walk Rosalind to her subway stop, then head down to the police station to file a report against Margaret for planting poisoned liquor in his office.

A few minutes later, he rode the elevator down to the ground floor with Rosalind. Pete the elevator operator was still on duty. "Anything else for me to carry down, sir?" he asked in an eager voice. Given the size of the tip Nick had given him last night, it was little wonder that Pete would be anxious for more business.

"Not today, Pete." He fiddled with Rosalind's fingers as the elevator lowered. Maybe he shouldn't have been so hasty, discarding everything from the apartment last night. If Margaret had managed to plant something toxic in his home, it would have been more evidence against her.

The elevator stopped, and he released Rosalind's fingers. "Ready to face the day?"

She gave him a confident nod. "Ready."

Their eyes met, and the zing of chemistry flared to life. He was still suppressing a grin as he strode into the lobby, Rosalind beside him matching his stride in perfect harmony.

A man wearing a New York City police uniform blocked his path. "Mr. Nicholas Drake?" he asked. Additional police officers stood nearby. Had they already gotten word about what happened in his office last night?

"That's me," Nick acknowledged.

"We need you to come down to the precinct to answer some questions about the murder of Margaret Drake. You need to come immediately."

Chapter TWENTY-THREE

Nick refused to leave the lobby of his apartment building until the police told him what was going on. It didn't take long.

In an uncharacteristic move, Margaret had given her housekeeper the day off yesterday, insisting Mrs. Loomis visit her family in Brooklyn. When the housekeeper let herself into the apartment last night, she'd heard terrible noises from the bedroom and found Margaret writhing in pain, barely able to breathe, and completely blind. All were classic symptoms of wood alcohol poisoning. As Margaret lay twisting in agony, she named Nick as the man who'd brought her a bottle of brandy as a peace offering. She drank some of the brandy in her afternoon tea and accused him of poisoning her as she was carried to the hospital. The doctors said Margaret would be dead before lunchtime.

Once again, Nick had underestimated his aunt. Margaret hadn't been trying to poison him. She was planting evidence in his office so she could make her suicide look like a murder and frame him for it as her final act on earth.

Nick used the telephone booth in the lobby to call his attorney and private investigator, arranging for them to meet him at the police station. Then there was nothing for him to do but follow the officers.

"I'll go with you," Rosalind said.

"No. Absolutely not."

She looked stunned at his refusal, but he didn't want her there. This was degrading enough without having Rosalind witness his humiliation.

He followed the officers out the door. The police had a carriage waiting, and Rosalind kept pestering him to go along. There was only room for four people in the carriage, and he wanted Pete, the elevator operator, to come with them. Pete could testify that Nick feared poison had been planted in his apartment. Pete was mostly an unbiased witness, but it would have been better if Nick hadn't tipped him so lavishly last night. It could be interpreted as a bribe.

"I can squeeze in," Rosalind said, already trying to nudge her way into the carriage.

With firm hands, Nick grasped her shoulders and turned her in the other direction. "I'm sure the work at the laboratory is piling up and waiting for your attention," he said.

He did his best to ignore her wounded look as he put five dollars in her hand and pointed her to the nearest subway station. This was his mess to solve, not hers.

When he got to the police precinct, he learned that Margaret's diary had been left on her nightstand, conveniently opened to the page recounting her meeting with him at the Scandinavian Tearoom, when he had threatened to kill her. In her diary, Margaret noted her mortification that so many of her neighbors heard the alarming threat. She listed the names of the ladies who witnessed his outburst, and as Nick sat in the hard chair of the police detectives' office, he saw two of the well-dressed ladies coming in to make their statement. Margaret had planned well.

"I want to see that diary," Nick's lawyer groused. "It's obvious Mrs. Drake planned to frame him, just as she tried to frame Rosalind Werner."

"The diary has already been turned over to the district attorney," the detective said.

"Then make a copy," Vinni replied.

"We can do that," the detective said, "but it might be more productive to get a transcript of what she's been telling folks at the hospital. The doctor claims she is incessantly rambling about your gift of the brandy."

"I thought they said she'd be dead by lunch," Nick said. "Is she still alive?"

A glance darted between the two detectives. "The last we heard, she is holding steady."

Aunt Margaret was supposedly suffering convulsions, breathing difficulties, and blindness. All of those conditions could be faked. Nick wouldn't put anything past Margaret Drake.

"I want to see her."

The detective almost sputtered his mouthful of coffee onto his desk. "That is not likely to happen. It would be considered a security risk."

"What hospital is she at?"

"Again, that is not something I am at liberty to disclose. Mrs. Drake's safety is of the utmost importance."

Vinni stood. "Fine. Then the questioning of my client is over. Margaret Drake is known by the court system to have orchestrated a systematic campaign to frame my client and his family. Aside from her manufactured evidence, you have no probable cause to detain my client. We're leaving."

Nick stood and followed his attorney out the precinct door, down the front steps, and onto the bustling street.

And straight into Rosalind, who loitered at the lamppost at the bottom of the stairs.

"I thought I told you to go home."

Her chin lifted. "I'm loyal too. Loyal enough to stand on this street corner for the past two hours and note every message delivered here from St. Agatha's Hospital."

"St. Agatha's?" He glanced at his attorney, already heading toward the nearest livery station. "Let's go."

"I'm coming with you!" Rosalind said, scurrying after him.

He didn't even break stride, just extended his hand to her, which she clasped, grinning up at him. They were a team, and he'd been an idiot trying to pretend otherwise.

The scent of carbolic acid permeated the air as he stepped inside St. Agatha's. The police had obviously telephoned to warn the hospital of their likely arrival, for the moment they inquired about a patient named Margaret Drake, the young lady staffing the front desk summoned a security guard.

"Mrs. Drake is not receiving visitors," the guard said. He was a skinny man with a wiry build. Nick wouldn't have any difficulty plowing past him, but he needed to play this smart. This wasn't the place for brute force.

"I'm not a visitor. I'm family," Nick said.

"Then she's especially not seeing you."

"Rumor has it she's not 'seeing' anything. Is that true?"

The security guard folded his arms across his chest, trying to look tough and refusing to say another word. Vinni tried some fancy lawyer-speak, but it didn't make much of an impression either, and within two minutes, a pair of burly hospital orderlies showed up to add to the muscle. And these two looked like they could carry out business.

The standoff continued, but a faint melody cut through the haze of Nick's anger. Piano music.

It was no ordinary music. It was haunting and profound—

layers of music cascading down and then building up again, unlike anything he'd ever heard before. He turned his head, trying to determine where it was coming from, because music like that could reach straight to the human soul, and he wanted more.

"Do you hear that?" he asked Rosalind.

"It's beautiful."

That was an understatement. Even the burly hospital orderlies seemed to be holding their breath to listen.

"It's coming from the chapel at the end of the east wing," the lady staffing the desk said. "The daughter of one of the patients has been playing on and off all morning. I've never been so tempted to abandon my desk and go listen."

It had to be Eloise. Nick clasped Rosalind's hand and headed down the east hall, following the music as though the Pied Piper were leading him straight to the chapel. He stood in the open doorway, spellbound as he watched.

The chapel was empty save for Eloise at the piano and a single man in the front pew. The man was doubled over, face buried in his hands. Eloise's eyes were closed, the music flowing effortlessly from her fingers as they glided over the keyboard.

The music scudded to a stop when she noticed Nick. She didn't rise or acknowledge him in any way. She just stared at him from the piano bench, her spine straight and stiff as a bayonet.

The man in the front row straightened and whirled around. It took a moment for Nick to place him, because in the past Bruce Garrett had been a big bear of a man, but today he looked gaunt and hollow.

"Why are you here?" Eloise finally asked.

"Rumor has it your mother is ill," Nick said.

Eloise raised a brow. "She's dying. She went into a coma about an hour ago."

"You certain about that? From what I hear, it sounds like she might be faking it."

Eloise bowed her head, her voice exhausted. "She's not faking. We got here last night, and she was vomiting blood and her lips were blue. You can't fake that."

Against Nick's will, a wave of pity took root. In the past hour, he'd convinced himself that this was just another of Margaret's schemes, but no. She really did hate him enough to embark on this self-destructive path. He reached out for the end of a pew, his hand shaking as he lowered himself onto the bench.

"If you're here to convince me to speak to the police, you needn't bother," Eloise said. "Once mother has passed, I'll provide a complete confession, but I will be loyal to her until the end."

Unbelievable. Sweet, sad Ellie, always so desperate to please. Even now, as Margaret lay unconscious on her deathbed, Eloise was doing her best to please her coldhearted mother. And then she would fall on her sword by confessing to participating in a fraud.

"There's no need," he said. "The testimony of the police was enough to get the judge to drop the charges."

Eloise covered her face with her hands and sagged so abruptly that Bruce rushed to her side. He sat beside her on the piano bench, propping her up. As Nick watched the two of them, he was stunned he hadn't recognized their physical similarity immediately. They had the exact same shade of hair and eyes. They were father and daughter.

When Eloise straightened, she was once again composed. "I'm very sorry for all the trouble I've caused you," she said quietly to Rosalind, then looked at Nick with all the grief in the world in her bewildered eyes. "I know Mother is making more wild accusations against you. Once she's gone, I'll do whatever I can to help." She managed a weak smile as she looked at her father. "I'd like to go back to Mother now. We can stay with her until she passes."

Bruce nodded and helped Eloise up from the bench. Her chin was high as she walked away.

For the life of him, Nick could not figure out the mystery of Eloise Drake. She was as poised as a duchess and had musical talent to rival any virtuoso. She had no cause to love a mother who had rejected her from the hour of her birth, but even after this monumental stab in the back, Eloise was still loyal to Margaret.

Two hours later, it was announced that Margaret Drake had died.

Chapter TWENTY-FOUR

One week after Margaret died, the medical examiner declared her death a suicide, and the police dropped the investigation into Nick. The women from the Scandinavian Tearoom had proved to be powerful witnesses in his favor. The moment Nick had made his unusual appearance at the ultra-feminine tearoom, they had cocked their ears to eavesdrop on the entire conversation and heard Margaret blackmail, goad, and threaten Nick all in the space of five minutes. In addition, a doorman at the building where Nick worked admitted to accepting twenty dollars for allowing Margaret Drake into Nick's office after hours. She claimed to be planting a birthday surprise, and the doorman was too interested in the tip to investigate that Nick's birthday was in February.

With their legal worries behind them, Rosalind let Nick begin courting her. She resolved to go slowly this time and do everything so properly that her conservative aunts in Germany would beam with pride. On Sunday mornings, Nick came to Jersey City to escort her to church, and each Saturday, she, Gus, and Ingrid went to Manhattan to take Nick sailing on the bay.

The first time they went sailing, Nick arrived with Sadie

dressed in a precious little silk outfit with a matching cap and purse. Ingrid was horrified, muttering in German about the waste of fine silk getting ruined on a boat. Nick didn't understand German, but he could hear disapproval, and as the day wore on, it was obvious that silk dresses had no place on a twenty-foot sloop. That didn't stop him from having a marvelous time as Rosalind and Gus handled the sails. The wind buffeted them with a clean breeze, and their laughter bounced over the water.

It was the first of many Saturdays sailing on the bay. In the afternoon, they would pull into a cove to share a basket of good bread, salami, and cheese. After the first Saturday, Nick dressed Sadie in a plain cotton smock short enough to allow her to scramble around on the boat as Gus showed her how the rigging worked.

Those Saturdays were golden, their memories sustaining Rosalind through the work week when she couldn't see Nick, but she took his telephone call each evening, and she could tell him how work progressed in the lab. Ever since the court ruling, Dr. Leal had been flooded by requests from cities across the nation to consult on their water systems. He could now afford to pay her a salary, and two lab assistants were formally hired once the students returned to class in September.

In the following weeks, she answered correspondence from all over the country about the details of their project. It was exhilarating. By the end of the year, their chlorination system was going to be rolled out in two dozen cities. Could she ask for anything better?

As she sealed an envelope to the Atlanta water authorities, one of the lab assistants interrupted her.

"There's a visitor for you, Dr. Werner."

She looked up to see Elmore Kleneman standing awkwardly in the door of the laboratory. He looked as uncomfortable as a sinner in church. Accusing her of theft and having her incarcerated for six days might have been the cause of his discomfort.

She did her best to summon a welcoming smile. If Dr. Clean had stood beside her from the outset, she might never have been arrested, but maybe she couldn't blame him. The evidence had looked pretty bad.

"Come in," she said, gesturing toward a chair at their lunch table.

"I'd like to speak to you privately, if you don't mind." His voice was conciliatory, and this overdue conversation was probably best handled outside.

"It's a lovely day for a walk," she suggested and led him down the hallway.

Elmore didn't even wait until they reached the door before he began apologizing. "I hope you know how sorry I am about that whole ugly incident."

"It was a difficult time for all of us," she said. Her most of all. Peter Schmidt had his reputation dragged through the mud as well, but at least he hadn't been forced into a sweltering attic jail cell.

"I've brought a peace offering," Elmore said once they were outside and under the shade of a maple tree. "It's the world's best fruitcake, homemade by my wife. The recipe has been in her family for generations."

The tin of cake was surprisingly heavy, and Rosalind accepted it with a gentle smile. An envelope taped to the lid was probably some sort of formal apology, but she would wait to read it later.

Elmore hesitated, looking more uncomfortable than ever. "I've gone ahead and included a check for the value of your shares in the company," he said with a nod to the envelope. "You must understand, the public image of my company is squeaky clean and wholesome. Of course I know that the criminal charges against you were hogwash, but those other stories in the newspaper, the ones about Germany . . . well, it just isn't the sort of thing I'd like associated with my company. I'm sorry, Rosalind. We're buying you out."

It was a kick in the teeth. Maybe it was silly, but she hadn't expected this, and it hurt. What was she supposed to say? She tried to smile politely. She was always polite.

"I understand," she said. "Of course I do. And thank you for the fruitcake. It was so thoughtful of you." She wanted to throw it on the ground and kick it into the next county, but she gamely held out her hand and wished Elmore and his company the best.

He smiled but seemed eager to disengage and be on his way. She'd never seen him march so quickly as he headed back to the main road and the streetcar stop.

This wouldn't hurt so badly if she hadn't thought so highly of Elmore Kleneman. Was this scarlet letter going to follow her for the rest of her life? It shouldn't matter what other people thought of her, but it did, and it hurt. She'd already started consulting on the New York City water project, where everyone treated her with the utmost respect, but perhaps there would always be people who harbored disapproving thoughts behind her back.

She wished Nick was here. He could always make her laugh and put things in perspective.

She returned to her desk, struggling to lift her sagging spirits. She drew a calming breath and raised her chin. After all the trials and tribulations she'd been through, this was such a tiny thing, but it was still difficult to concentrate on her recommendations for chlorine concentrations in the Baltimore water facility. She calculated the mathematical equation three times and came up with three different results. She threw her pencil down in frustration. This sort of analysis required her full attention, and she couldn't focus.

"I'm going home for lunch," she told the assistants. "I should be back by one o'clock."

She almost always had lunch at the office, but she abandoned her cheese sandwich in the icebox and headed home. Perhaps the walk would do her good.

Coming home for lunch was a bad idea. Gus had his law books spread out on the kitchen table, and Ingrid was in full swing in the kitchen. A kettle of soup simmered on the stove, and Ingrid whisked cream into a pan of gravy. The tiny counter space was filled with chopped mushrooms and bowls of bread crumbs. Ingrid sent her an unwelcoming glare as Rosalind nudged inside. The soup certainly looked more appealing than her cheese sandwich.

"That smells good," Rosalind said. If she hoped the compliment would soften Ingrid's attitude, she failed miserably.

"What do you need?" Ingrid asked. "As you can see, I am very busy."

"I thought I'd come home for lunch. Perhaps grab some of the dumplings from last night's dinner."

She angled around the stove and accidentally bumped the handle of the pan. Ingrid lunged for it before it tipped over, but the whisk fell on the floor. Rosalind reached for it to clean it off, but Ingrid was not appeased.

"How can you be so clumsy? You're ruining the *Jägerschnitzel*!"

Rosalind said nothing as she rinsed the whisk, but sure enough, the sauce for the Jägerschnitzel was beginning to burn. She returned the whisk quickly and retreated from the kitchen.

A piece of her wanted to throw Ingrid out of the house and tell her to go live on the Lower East Side with all the other new immigrants to this country. What kind of Jägerschnitzel could Ingrid make in a tenement without running water or a proper kitchen or a pretty garden with fresh herbs? Would she still be so crabby?

Rosalind sighed as she drifted to the window. This didn't feel like her house anymore. Diapers and baby bottles were scattered everywhere, and Ingrid reigned supreme in the kitchen. Once this had been the perfect house for Rosalind. She'd bought it right before the new subway line was announced, and since then, its value had soared. She could never afford a house like this were she to buy it today. With the subway only a few blocks away, people were clawing to live on this street.

The subway Nick taught her to ride. Even though she was a country mouse and he was a city boy, she and Nick were a pair. She felt more at home with Nick than in this too-small house.

Without a word she marched upstairs, rummaged through her bureau, and removed a stack of papers. Bank notes, legal records, a list of addresses of her family in Germany. She finally found the document she was looking for—the title to the house. It was the single most valuable thing she would ever own, but she no longer wanted it. She didn't need it. She knew where she belonged, and it wasn't here anymore.

Her footsteps were loud as she clattered down the stairs, nudged Gus's law books to the side, and laid the title flat on the table. She signed the back with a flourish.

"Here!" she said, thrusting the title at Ingrid. "It's now your kitchen. Your herb garden. Your house. Take it."

Ingrid looked horrified, holding up her hands and backing away.

Gus stood. "Rosalind, what are you doing? I'm sure Ingrid didn't mean—"

"I didn't!" Ingrid stammered, looking appalled. "It's your kitchen! Of course I know that—"

Rosalind set the paper on the table. "It's your house now."

Ingrid was a difficult woman, but Rosalind had to acknowledge that she paid a higher price than any of them for what happened in Heidelberg. Ingrid had to leave her family, venture to a new country where she barely spoke the language, and live off the charity of relatives. All because of Rosalind's naïveté. Money or the gift of a house could never erase the damages, but at least the gesture was an acknowledgement that Rosalind understood her role in the sacrifice Ingrid had been forced to make.

Rosalind gazed around the interior of the house, a cozy space she had worked to make her own, but her heart wasn't here anymore. It was with a brash, bold plumber who lived in the center of Manhattan. A smile tugged at her mouth. She was ready to leave. Ready to step into a new life with a man she loved to the marrow of his bones.

"I want you and Gus to have the house," she said without a hint of bitterness, only gladness. "I'll move out by the end of the year. Keep everything, for I won't need it where I'm going. There's only one thing I want." She nodded to the framed patent for the water chlorinator.

Nick wasn't in his office when she arrived in Manhattan. His secretary said he was underground inspecting a pumping station and didn't know if he would return to the office at all that day.

"And how do I get to him there?" Rosalind asked.

The secretary looked appalled. "You can't go below, ma'am. There are rules about things like that."

In the last few months, Rosalind had learned a lot about bending the rules. She had never seen the vast underground waterworks, and given her job, it seemed about time that she did.

She traveled to a structure erected on a street corner known as a hog house, where underground workers came above ground for their meals and for meetings.

Rosalind presented her best smile to the man at the counter. "I'd like to go below to see Nicholas Drake," she said.

He looked at her like she'd grown a second head. "They don't let women go down in the tunnels, ma'am."

She brightened. "I'm a biochemist and will be doing water consultation for the city. I'm sure Mr. Drake would authorize my visit."

He matched her smile. "And I'm sure he won't, ma'am. You'll have to wait over there."

"Oh. All right," she said as she shuffled off to wait at a picnic table.

So much for her newfound assertiveness. She repressed a smile, for she had learned which battles were worth fighting and which were not. Nick might not like her interrupting him in the middle of his work, and this conversation was too important to botch.

She loved him and was ready to make a life with him. She didn't want to live on the other side of the river when her heart was here. She sat at the picnic table, tearing at a little splinter and watching the minute hand of the clock crawl at a snail's pace.

It was ten minutes after six o'clock when Nick emerged from below ground. The elevator doors opened, and a cluster of men poured out, some in business suits, others in coveralls. All of them blinked in the sudden sunlight.

Nick had his shirtsleeves rolled to his elbows, and his hands were stained with grease. She watched as he studied a timetable posted to the bulletin board and talked about installation schedules with the man beside him.

She stood and finally caught his eye. His teeth flashed white against his tanned face.

"Dr. Werner," he said with warm approval, then turned back to the pair of businessmen. "Sorry, Jackson, important business with Jersey City's water supply awaits." He closed the distance between them.

"I'm not here on water business," she admitted.

"Even better," he said with a wink before heading over to a washstand and scrubbing up, the scent of pine and pumice tickling her nose. After a moment, he dried his hands and joined her at the opposite side of the picnic table, casually linking his fingers with hers. "Well?"

This was it. She cleared her throat and glanced around the hog house. The elevator continued to off-load workmen every few minutes, and a handful of men lingered at the tables, helping themselves to hot coffee or a sandwich. It wasn't exactly where she'd ever thought she would become engaged, but then again, she'd never imagined a man like Nick Drake would come storming into her life.

"Doctor Clean let me go today," she began.

"He didn't!" Nick shot to his feet, outrage stamped on every one of his features.

She tugged on his hands to pull him back down. "It's okay," she said. "I felt a little guilty collecting dividends when I wasn't even doing testing for him anymore. He paid me for my shares and cut me loose. He said the company's image was squeaky clean, and, well . . ."

It was easy to see the heat gathering behind Nick's dark eyes. "I'm never using that slop again," he growled as he sat back down.

"There's nothing else like it on the market. It really is a remarkable cleaning solution." She wouldn't have endorsed it if she thought otherwise.

"I don't care. He never gets another penny from me."

She squeezed his hands. The big, strong, workingman's hands she loved so well. "Fortunately, I know the recipe and can mix it up in the kitchen."

"Cheaper than he can sell it?"

"One-tenth the price."

Nick flashed her a grin. "Good! I may be rich, but I still love to save a dime."

She drew their clasped hands toward her and kissed his

knuckles. "Do you remember that night in your apartment when you said you didn't want to rush me into anything, but that when I was ready, you'd be waiting?"

"I pretty much think about that night all the time." His face was cautious, guarded concern mingled with hope.

She wanted to lunge across the table and leap into his lap, but she'd been on this earth long enough to know that delayed gratification was one of the most oddly delicious sensations on earth. And she loved that Nick was willing to wait for her.

"I'm ready, Nick. I'm ready to dance in the streets with you and climb mountains and dream about what dragons we're going to slay next. I've always been a little timid where dragons are concerned, but I feel braver with you beside me. I'd be honored to be your wife."

Nick's eyes gleamed. He never broke his steady gaze, but he kissed the back of her left hand, and then her right. "It's a deal, Dr. Werner."

He stood and scooped her up into his arms. It was terribly inappropriate to kiss a man in front of a dozen laborers and a public inspector, but she didn't care. This was her man. He was her future. From this day forward, they were a team.

And instead of scorn, the men in the hog house cheered.

Epilogue

Six months later

Nick wanted a small wedding, but after inviting his old friends from his plumbing days plus the people from his current job, they were already at a hundred people. Rosalind wanted her laboratory assistants, Dr. Leal, and all the people from the Jersey City water company, so over two hundred people filled the clubhouse.

Rosalind looked spectacular in a satin wedding gown, but after the ceremony, he'd seen precious little of her. They were practically mobbed the moment they stepped inside the reception hall, with people stepping forward to pound him on the back and push champagne into his hand. Rosalind was tugged away by a passel of women wanting to admire her dress.

Nick spotted Lucy on the far side of the room and made his way to her table, where she sat with four-month-old Amanda on her lap. Colin hovered in the neighboring chair, lavishing attention on his daughter.

Nick joined them. "If you don't quit gawking at that baby,

she'll get scorch marks on her skin. Too much doting will do that to a child."

"What poppycock," Colin said. "If that were true, she would have burned to a crisp months ago."

Nick grinned. "I may not always have my facts straight, but at least I've never used a word like *poppycock*."

It was almost four o'clock in the afternoon, and he was famished. He helped himself to some chicken appetizers wrapped in fancy imported cheese. "This sure beats a plate of baked beans, eh, Luce?" he joked, remembering the years they had lived together and eaten canned food because neither of them could cook.

"I love canned beans," she said.

It looked like he wasn't going to get a chance to eat much, for as soon as the orchestra started, General O'Donnell flagged him down. "No one else can dance until you and Rosalind have the first dance."

Sure enough, most of the crowd had parted, and Rosalind was making her way toward him. By heaven, she was lovely! He shot to his feet and escorted her to the dance floor.

"Pretty as a moonbeam," he whispered in her ear as he stepped out into a waltz, grateful for the dancing classes he'd taken a few years ago. He might be a plumber, but he knew how to lead a lady around a dance floor and did so with confidence. Never had he felt so proud as he did cradling Rosalind in the shelter of his arms as he waltzed her across the floor. He smiled down at her, doing his best to ease her nerves. Rosalind never liked being the center of attention, but he was loving every moment.

After their dance, others joined them on the dance floor. The music was good, the champagne plentiful, and everyone seemed to be enjoying themselves.

"It looks as if your cousin has found a suitor," Rosalind said with a nod to the far side of the dance floor.

Eloise's red hair made it easy to spot her, but Nick scowled when he noticed she was dancing with Fletcher Jones, who had hired her to work as an accountant upstate. It was a challenging assignment, and Eloise had returned to town a few weeks earlier. She and Fletcher had been inseparable ever since, and it annoyed Nick down to his toenails.

"I've been trying to ignore it," he grumbled. "Apparently they play games with their adding machines, seeing who can solve mathematical equations first."

Rosalind looked like she couldn't decide if she was charmed or appalled. "Truly?"

"Yeah. Truly."

"Well then!" she said brightly. "It sounds like they're a good match for each other."

"I'd like it better if he wasn't signing her paycheck," Nick grumbled.

He actually didn't like anything about the situation at all. Maybe he was overprotective, but there was something odd about Eloise's abrupt return from the valley. She'd been miserable, and Fletcher had wasted no time swooping in to the rescue. When Nick said as much to Rosalind, she laughed his concerns away.

"If you're this protective over your cousin, I dread the day when a suitor comes calling on Sadie."

"That won't happen until she's thirty, so we don't need to worry about it yet." He grinned and pulled Rosalind closer as they danced, smiling down into her eyes. "You married a protective man, Dr. Werner."

"Dr. Drake," she corrected.

A huge smile split his face. "I like the sound of that."

He pulled her closer as they danced. How thankful he was that she had forgiven him, and that he'd stepped down from his lofty, judgmental stance before he ruined everything. Neither he nor Rosalind were perfect, but together they clicked and hummed and sparkled, and he loved every minute of it.

Dr. Leal tapped Nick on the shoulder. “May I cut in?” he asked in a gentlemanly tone.

Nick didn’t particularly want to surrender his bride, but Rosalind didn’t belong to him alone. He admired her dedication to research, and Dr. Leal was a huge part of her success. He stepped back and watched the two laboratory partners, both so modest and self-effacing, and yet already they’d taken extraordinary strides toward making the world a safer place.

They lived in the biggest, boldest city in the nation. In the years to come, they would face steep challenges as they carved out a daring future, but he had the right woman at his side. Together, they would be unstoppable.

Historical Note

Although most of the characters in this novel are fictional, Dr. John Leal and George Fuller are the real-life heroes who implemented the first chlorine feed system in the world.

The lawsuit at the center of this novel, *The Aldermen of Jersey City vs. the Jersey City Water Supply Company*, originally ordered the defendants to build a massive new system of infrastructure to ensure clean water. Dr. Leal's startling choice to secretly implement his chlorine feed during a ninety-day appeal was a controversial decision, resulting in public outcry and threats of legal action. The efficacy of chlorine for safely disinfecting water was soon apparent, and the court ruled in his favor. The city immediately appealed the decision, resulting in another two years of litigation. The lawsuit was finally concluded in May of 1910, when the court once again ruled in Dr. Leal's favor.

Dr. Leal and Mr. Fuller spent the next several years helping cities adopt the technique. Deaths from cholera, typhoid, and other waterborne diseases immediately plummeted wherever chlorine was implemented. By 1914, more than half the population of the

United States was receiving chlorinated water. Chlorination of municipal water systems is now standard practice in the United States.

Dr. Leal never sought fame or enrichment for his work. He died in relative obscurity when he was only fifty-five due to complications from diabetes. In 2013, the city of Paterson, New Jersey, erected a monument at his grave, memorializing him as a "Hero of Public Health." He has been credited with saving millions of lives around the world.

Questions for Discussion

1. Rosalind hid the chlorine experiment from Nick because she believed she had right on her side. Are there ever instances when covering something up for the greater good can be justified?

2. Rosalind is inspired to research clean water due to a tragedy in her life. Have you ever had a powerful experience, either good or bad, that inspired you toward a cause?

3. Nick and Rosalind fell for each other fast, but how well did they really know each other? Is it possible to fall in love with someone after only a few meetings?

4. Rather than lavishing material goods on their children, Rosalind's parents ensured she had a modest upbringing that was rich only in a variety of books and experiences. Nick is the opposite in how he is raising Sadie. How was the household where you grew up? How should one balance material luxuries with practical and scholarly experiences?

5. Nick is able to forgive Rosalind's lie because she did it on behalf of a scientific cause rather than personal gain. How do you feel about this? Was she justified in lying? Are all lies equally damning?

6. When the court case turned against Dr. Leal, he responded: "That's something over which we have no control, so we'll do the best with what we have. It's all God asks of us." Rosalind takes comfort in this. Are there times when you let things beyond your control discourage you? How might you reframe the problem with a wider perspective?

7. Rosalind's guilt over what happened in Germany causes her to become highly deferential to Ingrid. Is this sort of capitulation ever effective? Was there a better way Rosalind could have handled the situation?

8. Aside from their common interest in water, Rosalind and Nick are complete opposites. What are the problems with choosing a partner from a starkly different background and temperament? Advantages?

9. Nick's rise into the upper class makes him self-conscious and defensive about his humble roots. Do you have any qualities that make you feel less than worthy? How might you lean on that quality to make you a more compassionate person?

10. Rosalind's reputation can never be fully restored after the damaging gossip from Germany arrives in America. Most people have incidents in their past they regret. What is the most productive way to handle those regrets? And does it matter what others think?

In 2019,

LOOK FOR ELOISE DRAKE'S STORY IN

Eloise Drake's prim demeanor hides a turbulent past. After overcoming exile, abandonment, and heartbreak, Eloise has finally built a world of perfect stability and put a disastrous love affair behind her. A mathematical genius, she is now a successful accountant for the largest engineering project in New York. Unfortunately, the assignment puts her squarely back in the path of the man who once broke her heart.

Alex Duval is the mayor of a town on the brink of destruction. The state has seized control of his village and is about to wipe it off the map in order to flood the valley and build a new reservoir. Alex is stunned when he learns the woman he once loved is part of the team charged with clearing the land. As his world begins to crumble around him, Alex devises one last, risky plan to save his town, but he needs Eloise and her unique skills to make it happen. The long-shot quest will require courage, stamina, and every ounce of their combined ingenuity to overcome the odds against them.

Different in nearly every way, can these star-crossed lovers come the chasm between them to save the town?

Elizabeth Camden is the author of eleven historical novels and has been honored with both the RITA Award and the Christy Award. With a master's in history and a master's in library science, she is a research librarian by day and scribbles away on her next novel by night. She lives with her husband in Florida. Learn more at www.elizabethcamden.com.

Sign Up for Elizabeth's Newsletter!

Keep up to date with Elizabeth's news on book releases and events by signing up for her email list at elizabethcamden.com.

More from Elizabeth Camden!

In this prequel to *A Daring Venture*, news telegraph operator Lucy Drake's livelihood is in jeopardy because of Sir Colin Beckwith. But when Colin's reputation is jeopardized, Lucy agrees to help him in exchange for his assistance in recovering her family's stolen fortune. However, the web of treachery they're diving into is more dangerous than they know.

A Dangerous Legacy

You May Also Enjoy . . .

Seeking justice against the man who destroyed his family, Logan Fowler arrives in Pecan Gap, Texas, to confront the person responsible. But his quest is derailed when, instead of a hardened criminal, he finds an ordinary man with a sister named Evangeline—an unusual beauty with mismatched eyes and a sweet spirit that he finds utterly captivating.

More Than Meets the Eye by Karen Witemeyer
karenwitemeyer.com

In the aftermath of tragedy, Grace hopes to reclaim her nephew from the relatives who rejected her sister because of her class. Under an alias, she becomes her nephew's nanny to observe the formidable family up close. Unexpectedly, she begins to fall for the boy's guardian, who is promised to another. Can Grace protect her nephew . . . and her heart?

The Best of Intentions by Susan Anne Mason
CANADIAN CROSSINGS #1
susanannemason.com

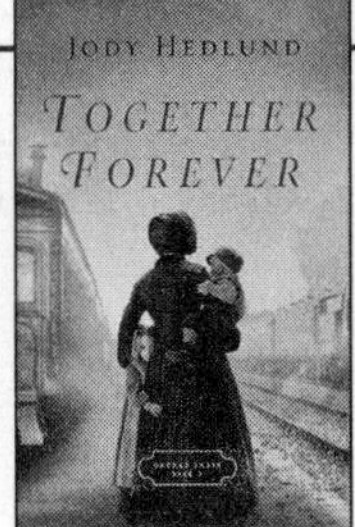

Marianne Neumann became a placing agent with the Children's Aid Society with one goal: to find her lost sister. Her fellow agent, Andrew Brady, is a former schoolteacher with a way with children and a hidden past. As they team up placing orphans in homes in Illinois, they grow ever closer . . . until a shocking tragedy changes one of their lives forever.

Together Forever by Jody Hedlund
ORPHAN TRAIN #2
jodyhedlund.com